RAUNCHY 2

MAD'S LOVE

T. STYLES

NATIONAL BEST SELLING AUTHOR OF *RAUNCHY*

CARTEL PUBLICATIONS
PRESENTS

PUBLISHER'S NOTE:
This book is a work of fiction. Names, characters, businesses,
Organizations, places, events and incidents are the product of the
Author's imagination or are used fictionally. Any resemblance of
Actual persons, living or dead, events, or locales are entirely coinci-
dental.

Library of Congress Control Number: 2011910657
ISBN 10: 0984303065
ISBN 13: 9780984303069
Cover Design: Davida Baldwin www.oddballdsgn.com
Editor: Advanced Editorial Services
Graphics: Davida Baldwin
www.thecartelpublications.com
First Edition

Printed in the United States of America

What's Poppin' Fam!!

The Cartel Publications loves and appreciates your business and support, ALWAYS!
Getting right down to it, "Raunchy 2: Mad's Love"...MANNNNNN, this joint right here is absolute FIRE!! I know I told ya'll that "Raunchy" was T. Styles' best work, but I stand corrected. T. Styles' best work is in the palm of your hands! This joint goes! It will make you laugh, get mad and feel some kinda way all at the same time. I read this in one sitting! I could not move until I finished it and I was in awe and shock when I did! Damn T!!! Maybe I should just say this book is T. Styles' best work TO DATE cuz I know she will continue to keep 'em coming!

Aight ya'll in keeping with tradition, with every novel we shine a spotlight on an author who is either a vet or a new comer makin' their way in this literary world. In this novel, we recognize:

"James Frey"

James Frey has penned novels such as, "My Friend Leonard" and his most famous novel, "A Million Little Pieces". That novel was an excellent cautionary tale whether fiction or not and we at The Cartel Publications appreciate his literary journey.

On that note Fam, I'ma let ya'll do what it do! Go 'head, call out sick from work, go grab your favorite snack and get ready to read one of the best novels of the year!

Be easy!

Charisse "C. Wash" Washington
VP, The Cartel Publications

www.thecartelpublications.com
www.twitter.com/cartelbooks
www.facebook.com/publishercharissewashington
www.myspace.com/thecartelpublications
www.facebook.com/cartelcafeandbooksstore

DEDICATION

I dedicate this to Charisse Washington. Your support and inspiration throughout my career is invaluable. I would not be the writer I am had it not been for your belief in me. You give me wings.

Foreward

To all of the skeptics, or naysayers who said "Raunchy" was too nasty, I'd like to personally give you my ass to kiss.

Raunchy is defined in the Webster's Dictionary as being **earthly**, **vulgar**, and **sexually explicit**. So if you had a problem with any of these things, why pick up *and* finish reading a book with this title? There are plenty other titles with less risky names. Some are even in my own bibliography.

I chose the title Raunchy because it is an incendiary title designed to stir emotions and cause conflict. Although Raunchy is the primary characteristic of the main character, Harmony Phillips, she is a product of a fucked up environment and, as you'll read in "Raunchy 2", was unable to stop the destructive cycle from reaching her kids.

Still, the Raunchy series has a method to its madness and I appreciate all of those who received the message. So, without further adieu, I bring to you the second edition to the series, and I pray you are taken on an exciting heart wrenching journey.

T. Styles

"My life couldn't be more fucked up then what it is right now, and I got all intentions on making the world around me feel me on this shit too."

- Mad Phillips

PART ONE

PROLOGUE
Spring of 1994
Galveston, Texas

Six year old Madjesty and Jayden Phillips, non identical twins, slammed down their glass jars repeatedly trying to catch more roaches on the filthy wooden floor. Since the boys didn't have any unbroken toys, they resorted to old school methods to stay busy and keep their hearts occupied. They'd stop ever so often to scratch their skin which was riddled with insect and rodent bites. The room smelled of piss and unwashed clothes and it was so hot that the odor permeated throughout the small house.

The spring heat in Texas covered the state like a heavy quilt under the blazing sun. And even though nighttime had fallen on Galveston, it was still sweltering. No one expected this year to be so uncomfortable and those without air conditioning suffered the most. Already six heat related deaths were reported and the weatherman advised everyone to stay inside to remain cool or consequences would continue to be fatal. But just like anything in life, some folks just don't fucking listen.

"Hold up," Madjesty said, "spray me with some more water first."

Jayden picked up the water bottle filled with dirty water and sprayed him as requested. This was how they kept cool but the results were always short lived. In seconds, the heat would fry their skin and they'd be sweating all over.

Focusing back on the game Madjesty looked at his brother's jar.

"You cheatin', Jay! I got more than you!" Madjesty said pointing at his upside down glass jar that was once used for honey. Five roaches crawled haphazardly around the glass looking for a way out. Madjesty was wearing a white t-shirt so soiled it looked brown and he wasn't wearing underwear. "You ain't got but like three."

"Ahn, ahn! I got like six roaches!" Jayden said pointing at his jar with four ghetto crawlers inside. Just like his brother he didn't have any clean clothing and wore nothing but a pair of filthy boy's underwear to cover his body. The heat attacking him so unmercifully now, that his brown skin was dripping in sweat.

"Count 'em again! And I bet I'm right." Madjesty persisted.

Both boys were incorrect, but because they weren't doing well in school, neither could count properly. Luckily Ramsey, although drunk, spoke perfect English and demanded that the boys use correct language around the house, at least while he was home. Had it not been for him, things would have been way worse for them in school.

"How come you like Tisa?" Jayden asked tapping his jar.

" 'Cause she like me I guess." Madjesty shrugged.

"Well I think girls are dumb. And I don't like 'em."

"Well you like, mama." Madjesty frowned. *"And sometimes I don't like her."*

"Because she's mama. We gotta like her."

"Says who? I hate her the most sometimes."

"That's mean, Madjesty." Jayden frowned.

"No it ain't!" He shook his head. *"Anyway, I'm not thinking about mama. Because Tisa gonna have my baby. Watch."*

"That mean you have to have sex. You know how to do that?" Jayden asked with wide eyes.

"Naw. But I'ma learn." Madjesty said hopefully. *"I'ma learn and have like six kids, a dog and a wife. And a big house with lots of food and stuff."* He paused, taking his dream in fully. *"Watch, you'll see."*

"Not me. I just want enough money to eat what I want and do what I want. And I want mama to love me a whole bunch." He opened his little arms widely. *"Like this much right here."*

Madjesty frowned. *"That dream dumb!"*

"Your dream dumb!"

They were about to catch more bugs when they heard their mother come home. Cutting the lights off in the room, they rushed to their beds to hide. Throwing the covers over their heads they waited for Harmony's wrath.

The blue cotton dress Harmony wore was drenched with sweat and vomit, as she wobbled into the house she shared with Ramsey. Thrown out yet another bar for not being able to hold her liquor, she was disoriented and all over the place. The moment the door was open, she fell down at the threshold before picking herself up to lean on the wall for support. Making her way to the kitchen, she was on a hunt to find the bottle of liquor she believed she hid from herself during one of her many attempts to quit.

Opening and slamming cabinet drawer after cabinet drawer, she didn't care about the noise she was making or the fact that her twins were due in school the next day.

"Whereeeeeeeeee is my vodka?!" Her words slurred and she wiped the sweat off of her scarred face. *"You dirty, niggas betta...you betta...give me my shit!"* During her drunken stupors, she always believed they stole from her.

If Ramsey, Harmony's on again off again boyfriend wasn't away in DC visiting his grandmother with his son Dooway, as he did two months out of every year, she would've never gone this far.

"Do...I said...do," she fell on the floor, *"do ya'll, niggas hear me?!"*

"Madjesty," Jayden whispered from the top bunk in their room. *"Don't make a sound."*

"Okay." Madjesty replied shaking. The sheet on top of his body was so stiff due to being dirty, that it felt like paper against his skin.

"You gotta pretend you sleep. Don't go help mama if she ask 'cause she'll hurt you again."

"But she's gonna be mad."

"MADJESTYYYYYYY!" Harmony yelled scaring the living shit out of her boys. *"COME HERE!"*

Jayden was frightened for his brother. He remembered the time Harmony bashed his head into the wall just because he didn't come to her quick enough. But Jayden hoped if they ignored her, that she'd be sleep within the hour.

Not knowing what to do, Madjesty started weeping. For whatever reason, Harmony loved calling on him when she was at her worst. Partially because although he was timid, he did have bouts of anger and she liked to antagonize him the most. In her mind, he gave her a reason to be abusive. No one would question why she'd have to beat a child who was unruly.

"She gonna be mad if I don't go. She gonna be mad at me."

"IF I GOTTA...YOU DIRTY NIGGAS DON'T LOVE ME," she started mixing her thoughts together. *"I'M THE MOTHER OF THIS HOUSE! THESE...THESE BITCHES AIN'T GOT SHIT ON ME! I HAD MONEY! MY DADDY GAVE ME MONEY! THEY JUST STOLE IT FROM ME!"* She continued on a mental rant, spewing anything that came into her mind at the moment. *"IF I CALL YOU AGAIN, MADJESTY I'MA KILL YOU! DO YOU HEAR ME?! I'MA...I'MA...KILL YOU!"* She pulled herself up off the floor again for the moment. *"I'M NOT FUCKING WITH YOU!"*

Madjesty hopped out of bed wearing the white-soiled t-shirt and no underwear. Creeping out of the room, he bypassed the dirty clothes in the hallway. The moment he approached the kitchen, he smelled the alcohol fuming from his mother's body.

"Mama," Madjesty said approaching her. Harmony lie on the floor with her dress rose and her vagina exposed. "Are you okay?"

"Wherrrrreeee the fuck is my liquor, nigga? Huh?"

"I don't know, mama." Tears fell down his dirty face. "I don't have it."

Harmony lifted her head to look into her son's eyes. Madjesty was a cute kid who had the weight of the world on his shoulders. "You look too much like a bitch. That's what I hate about you. You think you're prettier than me don't you?"

"No, mama." Madjesty said shaking his head repeatedly. The idea of being pretty period, disgusted him. He certainly didn't want to be prettier than his own mother.

"Yes you do you dirty, nigga! Showin' your split tale and shit around this house! What I tell you 'bout showing your split tale?"

Madjesty was always confused on what a split tale was but he was too afraid to ask. He didn't understand it was a vagina because he wasn't supposed to have one. I mean, why hadn't she used the word pussy or coody cat like he'd heard her say many times when referring to herself?

"I don't remember, mama." He shivered.

"You wear pants in this house, nigga! Always!"

"Okay, mama, I'm sorry."

"Shut the fuck up and bring your crusty ass over here to help me up."

Madjesty rushed over to her and tried to lend his body to help her stand. Harmony uncaringly bared all of her weight onto his small body. Using the table for support also, it toppled over knocking her and all of the dirty dishes upon it to the floor. Angry at the world for her own pathetic behavior, Harmony picked up a coffee cup, threw it at Madjesty and it gashed his head, crashing at his feet.

"Ahhhhhh," He cried out holding his face. Backing away from the broken cup on the floor, his tiny feet bled from small cuts. "It hurts!"

"Get the fuck out of here, you stupid nigga! Always wanting somebody to feel sorry for you. GOOOOOOO!"

Madjesty ran out of the kitchen, holding his head. Blood poured down his face making it difficult to see. He was so frightened, that he didn't feel the true pain until he was out of her sight. Once in his bed, the pain hit him like thunder and it was excruciating.

"YOU DIRTY NIGGAS BETTA STAY IN YOUR ROOM! I DON'T WANNA SEE EITHER OF YOU NO MORE TONIGHT!" She hollered, as if someone wanted to be around her demonic ass.

Sobbing uncontrollably because of his discomfort, he tried to shield the sound of his cries by covering his mouth with both hands. Harmony *hated tears. She said they made you weak and she was having none of it from her boys.*

Jayden hopped off the top bunk and locked the door. Feeling safe, he eased into his brother's bunk to console him. His underwear was soiled with dried feces from not knowing how to properly wash himself.

"Don't cry," Jayden said holding his brother in his tiny arms. "Please don't cry. Mama doesn't like when you cry. And I don't like to hear you cry either, Madjesty."

"But it hurts," Madjesty, sobbed blood oozing out of his head. "It hurts real bad too."

"I told you not to go, Madjesty. I told you not to go."

Mother monster continued to roam around the house trying to find the next thing to do. The next thing to hate about her life.

"YOU BETTA STAY IN THAT ROOM!" Harmony continued not feeling any remorse. "I'M NOT FUCKING AROUND!" As minutes went by, what she'd done faded in her memory as if twenty years passed since the horrible event.

"I gotta go to the bathroom," Madjesty said. Blood trickled down his face and he had to urinate. "I gotta go bad."

"No, she's gonna do worse." He whispered. "You gotta hold it." Jayden continued rocking his brother in his arms. "You gotta hold it."

"But I can't. I gotta go now."

Silence.

"Then do it in the bed. It's okay." Jayden said.

"I don't want to."

"It's okay. I won't tell. I promise."

Feeling nothing left to do, Madjesty allowed urine to exit his body, which dampened the bed and soaked his brother's underwear. It didn't stop Jayden from maintaining the hold on his brother. Their bond was unbreakable and unshakable.

"It's okay. You had to do it. I don't care if I get wet."

Madjesty continued to cry. The embarrassment and shame was over-powering. "I'm sorry."

This was the reason the room stunk so badly. Harmony frightened her children so terribly, that they were afraid to do anything outside of it, including go to the bathroom.

At the end of the day, Harmony wasn't armed with what it took to be a mother, nor did she care. Life dealt her a fucked up hand and she took it out on all who chose to love her, including her children. All that was left was a hollow shell of the woman who might have been anything other than a monster, whore and a drunk.

"One day she gonna pay for everything," Madjesty promised. "One day she's gonna pay real bad too."

"It's okay." Jayden said holding his brother tighter. "At least we got each other."

LITTLE SCHOOL OF HORRORS
THE NEXT DAY

It was unbearably hot in the twins' room and the house was covered in suffering silence. As always when Harmony came home from a night of drunken escapades, if they were lucky, she would be sleep until three the next afternoon.

Nudging Madjesty softly, Jayden tried to wake him up for school, which was only a few blocks from the house, before they were late. He knew waking him up abruptly could cause him to be frightened and wake up swinging, possibly hitting him in the face like he did many times before.

"Madjesty, its time to get up." He said nudging him and then jumping out the way.

Madjesty rose and looked at his brother. "She not up is she?"

"I don't know."

Madjesty climbed out of bed. "I'm hungry. You?"

"Yeah." They hadn't eaten anything since the molded bread they consumed yesterday morning. "But we gotta hurry up to school before we get in trouble."

They fished around the dirty clothes on the floor trying to find the best of the worst. Already on the fifth wear of most of their outfits, they settled on some jeans and shirts so funky they needed to be burned instead of worn. Once dressed, they tiptoed past Harmony who was asleep in the bathroom.

When they made it outside, they looked for Pimp Fast Tony, who ran three young prostitutes that sold their pussies all hours of the day or night. If they found him, he would give them pocket change to buy snacks at the corner store provided they promised to tell Harmony to come talk to him about business. What business he wanted with Harmony was beyond them, but the boys never said a word to her, afraid she'd find out that they'd been bumming for food and money in the neighborhood.

Pimp Fast had a daughter by his youngest whore Crissa and her name was Tisa Adams. Madjesty loved Tisa the moment he saw her face. Her smooth brown skin and wide eyes lifted Madjesty to the highest point whenever she came into a room. Tisa's long brown pigtails always smelled of Ultra Sheen hair grease and her skin of Dove soap. Days would go by and Madjesty could never seem to understand why she liked him so much. But there was one thing he loved about Tisa above all...her smile and how it always seemed to make his problems go away.

Tisa always had money to spend on things she wanted like Boston Baked Beans and Lemonheads while Madjesty barely ate on a regular basis. Tisa's father and mother although dysfunctional loved her with all they could give while Harmony despised the ground her children walked on. No matter what their differences, Tisa never seemed to care about what people said about Madjesty. She liked him and that was the bottom line.

"He's not out here." Madjesty said sadly, not seeing his shiny black Cadillac.

"Guess we gotta go to school without eating." Jay responded.

"Again."

The moment the twins entered the doors at school, students tormented them. First grade was brutal and they prayed for the day it would all be over. They couldn't make it to their seats before their classmates pinched their noses and backed away from them because of the foul odor rising from their skin.

"Damn, they funky!" One boy yelled.

"Pewww!" The most popular girl in school added. "How come ya'll never wash up?"

Instead of starting a fight by demanding that they leave them alone, the twins ignored the insults. They were passive and scared of confrontation so in their minds if they didn't say anything back to the rude children, they would eventually leave them alone.

Madjesty looked at the teacher's desk and noticed he wasn't there. The twins hated when the teacher arrived late because it meant the children would have more time to taunt them.

"I'ma go sit in my seat," Jayden said softly. "Love you."

"Love you, too." Madjesty said.

Jayden walked to his seat that was in the back of the room and Madjesty took his seat in the front. It fucked him up that so many people didn't like him. All he wanted was to belong and to be loved, instead he was humiliated almost everyday of his life.

When everyone settled down, Madjesty prepared for the worst part of the day. His stomach was filled with anxiety because of what he endured daily in class. Knowing what was coming, he stiffened his neck as best he could and sat up straight. The gash on his forehead inflicted by his mother was crusted. Until a few sweat drops poured down his face and dampened the wound.

Sensing a presence behind him, Majesty waited until, "WHACK" He was hit in the back of his head with an encyclopedia, forcing his face violently into the wooden desk. The class erupted in laughter as Antwan Bolden fell on the floor holding his stomach. He was never able to make it to his seat right away due to laughing so hard.

Every morning since he'd been at the school, Antwan, the school's bully would taunt and abuse him and today was no exception. Why? Because, Tisa chose Madjesty over him. Here Madjesty was, quiet, dirty and without any friends, yet one of the prettiest girls in school liked him anyway. Antwan decided to make Madjesty pay daily.

Madjesty lifted his face and tasted the salty blood in his mouth. He was use to it now and as he had many times before, he swallowed it all. Turning around, he saw his brother who was staring at him with a sad look upon his face. There was nothing Jayden could do to help, he wasn't a fighter and neither was Madjesty.

"I love you." Jayden mouthed, hoping it would make him feel a little better. And for the moment it did.

"I see your head getting stronger, Phillips!" Antwan said sitting in his seat. "Maybe it's because of all that dirt around your neck!"

More laughter filled the room until the white male teacher walked in and placed his suitcase on his desk. "Settle down," he said. Then he looked at the twins and held his nose. "I sure do wish you Phillip boys would wash up before coming into my classroom. This is getting a bit ridiculous."

"I'm sorry, sir" Madjesty said, apologizing for his mother's failures."

"Me…me, too." Jayden added.

"Yeah well that's not good enough today." Mr. Magarey replied. "We have a serious test scheduled and I need my students focused. So get out of my classroom! You two reek!" The class fell out into more laughter before the teacher addressed them and said, "Settle down. This is not a circus!"

"Sir, what about the test?" Madjesty asked. "If we don't take it we gonna get a bad grade."

The teacher frowned in defiance. He hated when a child spoke back to him after he made a decision. Opening up his desk drawer he removed the brown wooden paddle inside of it and said, "Get over here."

"No, sir." Madjesty said shaking his head. "I didn't mean it. Honest."

"GET OVER HERE NOW!"

Madjesty reluctantly walked toward Mr. Magarey's desk. He felt off balance the closer he got to the teacher. Why was the world punching him in the gut over and over again? What was he expected to learn from all of this?

When Madjesty finally reached him, he bent over so that his rear was faced him. The teacher raised the hard wooden paddle and whacked Madjesty three times on the bottom.

The students looked and pointed but kept their comments to themselves. In Texas Corporal Punishment was allowed and since Harmony signed the necessary paperwork giving the school permission, Mr. Magarey took full advantage.

Madjesty held on to his tears. They were useless and he was tired of using them anyway. He felt as if he was a human punching bag for any adult who needed a release.

"Now!" He said placing the paddle back into the desk. "Don't make me say it again! Leave my classroom! You're being disruptive."

Sore, Madjesty and his brother headed for the door.

Before the boys left the room the teacher said, "I'm tired of you two coming in here like this. If you don't get it together, we'll have to teach you outside next to the dumpster where you belong."

●●●

Mr. Ramsey's House

Madjesty and Jayden walked home from school in a daze. Life for them was dreary, sad and depressing. So much so, that often times the days seemed to run into one another. It was a horrid life to be abused and they felt extreme pain every second of their young lives.

All Madjesty wanted was to be liked and loved. To feel like he'd always have someone in his corner who appreciated him, besides his brother. Yet life showed him that everyone didn't deserve a good home, family and friends. If it weren't true, he would have a happier life. There were many of nights he cried himself to sleep, wondering what he'd done as a child to deserve such a bad mother. His answer never came.

Walking into the house, they stopped at the door when they heard the sounds of their mother panting mixed with the noise of a male moaning. "Mmmmmm....open that pussy you dirty bitch. Open that pussy for daddy. Whose pussy is this, huh?" Slap of the ass. "Whose pussy is this?"

"Yours, daddy! This all your pussy."

Hoping they wouldn't get into any trouble, simply for coming into their own home, the twins tried to creep past the couple. From where they stood they could see Harmony's leg draped over the back of the couch and Mr. Bad Guy rising and falling into her body. When he came up for his last pump, he saw the boys and smirked.

"Shiiiit, I'm cumming," He said releasing his load into her waiting vagina, eyes still on the boys. He wouldn't allow anything to stop him from getting his rocks off, not even her young children.

"Don't stop now! I'm almost there!" Harmony said irritated. "I'm sick of you getting yours before I get mine."

"Bitch, get up!" He slapped her naked thigh but she kept pulling him back onto her body. "Come on now, get up." He stood up and his sweaty chest looked as if water was poured all over it. "Your sons are home."

"So, who cares," she said pulling him back onto her body again. "You got yours off but I didn't cum yet!"

"Stop being so horny," He laughed rising again. He wasn't about to fuck her again even if she begged. Her pussy was rancid and she needed to bathe. "I said they're home." He adjusted his pants and Harmony finally stood her wretched ass up.

Looking at Madjesty and forgetting in a drunken daze she hit him in the face with a cup she said, "Fuck, happened to your head?"

"Nothing, ma," he replied, slightly angry. After all of the pain he'd been in all day because of her, she didn't even know it was her fault. "I think I fell or something."

"Don't tell me nothing. Did that boy at school beat your ass again?"

"No, but something happened today." Madjesty handed the letter the school drafted on their letterhead. Harmony's eyes moved left to right as she read the words and grew angry. "They called but said no one answered the phone."

"So ya'll getting in trouble again?"

"No, mama. They said we stink and can't come back unless we take a bath and you wash our clothes." Jayden said. "They say we bein'...disrupt...disrupt..."

"Disruptive." Madjesty finished.

Harmony balled the paper up and threw it at them. It landed at their feet. "So ya'll went to school without taking a bath? Stupid ass niggas! Why you walk out of here like that? Have me looking bad in front of them people at school! You know I tell ya'll to wash up before you leave!"

"Sorry, mama." Madjesty said accepting responsibility. "But...we don't know how to wash our clothes."

"But you know how to take a bath, dirty ass niggas!"

Mr. Bad Guy walked up to the twins. "Harmony, don't be so hard on the boys," he said as he ran his hand through Jayden's bushy hair and softly hit Madjesty on the chin with a closed fist. Madjesty could smell the scent of his mother's pussy on his hand and his stomach churned. "They *just gotta toughen up. If Ramsey's punk ass would be harder on them and stop treating them like girls they wouldn't have this problem in school."* Then he looked at them with judgmental eyes. *"This one is a punk,"* he said pointing at Madjesty, *"and this one walks like a bitch. They're bound to get fucked with at school."*

"Fuck all of that!" Harmony said, still angry with them for interrupting her before she could bust a nut. *"If they would pay attention in class none of this would happen!"* She reached for her glass on the table and downed all of the alcohol.

Harmony was such a horrible mother and terrible human being that she didn't understand the purpose of the letter. All in all the school board decided that she was a bad mother and that her children were unkempt. Yet she associated every problem at school with them being trouble makers when the boys couldn't be further from it. If they were graded on their behavior they would be considered model students because the only area they lacked was education. They could barely read and were pretty much being passed through school because no one wanted the responsibility of dealing with their mother. On more than one occasion she came to the school drunk, cursing and making a scene. In the end it was decided to get the children out however possible.

"And I say its Ramsey's fault!" Mr. Bad Guy persisted.

"Stop talking shit about Ramsey. I ain't trying to hear all that."

"Bitch, you better listen! Ramsey ain't fittin' to raise no kids. I been knowing that negro since '72."

Although Ramsey was Mr. Bad Guy's friend he would often visit the Ramsey home twice a day, once to see his friend and again to see his woman. He was as despicable of a man as they came.

"Well Ramsey ain't here now is he?!" Harmony yelled. Snatching them both by the ears, she took them to the bathroom and slammed the door shut. *"Get undressed!"*

Once they were naked, she ran the tub of water and poured a lot of bleach into the tub. Once the tub was full she pushed them inside injuring Madjesty's head again, causing the fresh wound to reopen and bleed some more. Blood dripped from his head and fell into the water turning it slightly pink. Luckily outside of a bruised arm Jayden wasn't hurt too badly.

"Look at your head!" Harmony ranted. *"Stupid ass nigga let somebody hit you in the face."* She took the bleach and poured it over the wound.

"MAMA, NOOOOOOOO!" The sensation felt like fire against his skin and burned his eyes. He slapped water into his face to wash it away. *"IT HURRTSS!"*

She smacked him in the mouth silencing him immediately. "Cover your mouth and stop making noise in my got damn house!" Madjesty put both hands on his mouth and tears rolled down his face. "You ain't nothing but a punk ass nigga!" She threw open the bathroom cabinet looking for Band-Aids. Finding some she peeled the backings off of five and mashed it on his head.

"Owwww!" His screams echoed through even though he covered his mouth.

"Shut the fuck up!" She yelled smacking him in the face again. It was evident that she hated Madjesty the most. "I'm sick of your shit. You supposed to be a boy but you act like a bitch! Both of you! Now don't come back out until you're clean. I'm sick of them school people thinking I don't take care of my kids! Sick of it!"

When she left Jayden wrapped his arms around his brother. "It's okay." Then he took a wash cloth used to clean the toilet that was on the floor, and wiped his brother's wound. It was the only rag they could access. While adjusting Madjesty's band aids over the cut he said, "Mama, doesn't mean to be this way. She just be drunk sometimes."

Madjesty dropped his hands by his sides and sobbed. "Jayden, I hate mama, a lot."

"Don't say that," Jayden said shaking his head. "You don't mean it."

"I do mean it. I'm sick of her! She doesn't love us. Why doesn't she love us?"

"She'll be fine. We just have to pray harder. We have to always pray that God will change her from mother monster into a nice mommy...like we always wanted. She gonna change. You'll see."

"What if God doesn't answer our prayers?"

"Then I'll never talk to him again."

The boys stayed in tub, finding solitude in the quietness of the bathroom until Harmony called them for dinner. Smelling food, and wearing the same clothes they wore earlier, they rushed into the dining room to eat. After all, they hadn't eaten since the early morning of the day prior and their tummies were growling. The school long since stopped their meal privileges because Harmony didn't complete the necessary paperwork to get them free lunch. She may have taken the time to authorize Corporal Punishment, but feeding her children wasn't a priority. It was as if terrorizing them was her life's work.

When they got to the table Mr. Bad Guy was still there and they were slightly grateful because at least Harmony's attention wouldn't be solely on them. Taking a seat, they couldn't wait to bite into the over cooked fried chicken and burnt white rice she prepared. For them it wasn't about the taste of the meals, but a need to survive.

"Why ya'll sitting there looking all crazy?" Mr. Bad Guy asked digging into the bowl of chicken. He hadn't washed his hands since he dug into Harmony's pussy earlier and the crust from her dried vagina juice sat on the top of his fingers. "You hear me boys?" He asked devouring the food with his mouth open, "I know you not still mad at your mama for putting you in line." He paused. "She only doing it because boys like you might get fucked in your ass if you don't toughen up. You want somebody to put a dick in your ass thinking you a punk?"

"No," Madjesty said watching the food roll around in his mouth.

"Don't say no, boy if you don't mean it. That's why you getting your ass kicked at school now. You don't know how to open your mouth and stand up when its time."

Madjesty held his head down until Mr. Bad Guy, who was already on his second piece of chicken to their none, wiped his mouth with a napkin and stood up. "Okay, let me teach you how to be a man." Madjesty couldn't be sure if he was drunk before, but he could definitely see that he was drunk now. He wobbled a little where he stood but maintained footing. "I'm sick of coming over here and doing nothing. Rise, baby bubba!"

"Huh?"

"Huh, nothing, boy! Stand up." Madjesty looked at Harmony who wasn't paying any attention to either of them. She was engrossed into the bottle of liquor that Mr. Bad Guy bought her. "Don't look at your mother, boy. Get up."

Madjesty pushed the chair back, which made a screeching sound against the hardwood floor. Then he stood up and stayed in place, next to the table.

"Over here!" he continued. "And put your hands up." Madjesty walked away from the safeness of the table and stood in front of the four-time loser. "Hands in the air."

Madjesty put his hands in the air and when he did, he was met with a crushing blow to the chest. He flew backwards and landed against the coat closet. The doorknob hit the bottom of his head bruising it immediately. Jayden jumped up in his brother's defense until Mr. Bad Guy pointed at him and said, "Sit the fuck down! If you ain't help him fight at school don't help him now." Then he turned around to Madjesty. "Get up, boy. I ain't got all day!"

Madjesty was crying so loudly it irritated both Mr. Bad Guy and Harmony. "I'm tired of these niggas crying all the time. I told you they act like bitches!" She said.

"It's okay," Mr. Bad Guy said raising his hand to silence her. "I'm 'bout to teach these boys how to be men. When I get finished with them, you can get on your knees and give me something to say thank you." He paused. "But right now I don't need your lip service. Just know that when I'm done, they'll be as tough as nails." Then he turned his attention back to Madjesty. "Get up, boy." He did. "Now, put your hands in the air." Madjesty did. "Good...now aim and swing." He did. Stooping down low Mr. Bad Guy said, "Good, now try to hit me again." Madjesty aimed and swung but hit nothing but his own face, causing Mr. Bad Guy to fall into a serious laughter. "You can do better than that, boy." Again Madjesty aimed and again he missed. Getting irritated, Mr. Bad Guy hit him in his chest again, and again and again.

"Stop it!" Jayden yelled. "You hurting my brother."

Mr. Bad Guy heard his pleas but didn't care. He was an abusive bastard while he was there and an abusive bastard at home. With five kids of his own, he took turns using them as target practice whenever the liquor gave him muscles. Although lately he took a break on abusing his family because he was also taking a break from his wife to hang out in between Harmony's funky legs.

Mrs. Bad Guy knew her husband was a cheater due to the neighborhood rumors, but she was thankful because at least her children were safe. After fucking Harmony he was so tired when he got home that the only thing he wanted to do was sleep.

"Please stop," Madjesty said, his chest was on fire. With outstretched hands he begged for no more. "I...I can't breathe."

Seeing the tears run down his face and wondering how much damage he already caused Mr. Bad Guy decided to stop his lesson. Besides, if the boy had to go to the hospital who knew what he would say to the doctor's. He wasn't supposed to be there and he definitely wasn't supposed to be with Harmony over his friend's house when he was out of town.

"Get out of here! Both of you." Mr. Bad Guy said. "I can't do nothing with you two. You're going to always be faggies!"

"But we're hungry. We haven't eaten anything." Jayden said looking at his mother for support.

Hoping she would at least feel sorry for them and allow them to have a piece of chicken, they waited for a response. Instead she gripped her glass and poured more alcohol into her body. "Drink some water from the sink and go in your room. I'm sick of looking at both of you, too."

Once in the room Madjesty sat on the bed and said, "My chest hurts."

"Fuck you!" Jayden yelled from the top bunk.

Madjesty was shocked at his brother's response. "You mad at me?"

Silence.
"Jayden, you mad at me?"

• •

The Next Morning

The next morning the boys were still hungry. By now two days had gone by and they hadn't eaten.

Normally Madjesty would be sleep but worrying that his brother hated him because he didn't speak to him last night, he got up before Jayden did.

"Jayden," Madjesty said pushing him softly. "It's time to get up." Jayden stirred a little but eventually opened his eyes. "You mad at me?"

Jayden rubbed his eyes and said, "Naw. I'm not mad. Just hungry."

"Cool!" He smiled happy to have his brother back. The world could be against him if it wanted but he needed his twin and that really was the bottom line. Without him by his side he would go crazy. "Let's go find something to eat."

Doing what they did often, they looked for Pimp Fast Tony, but when they couldn't find him they decided before going to school to go door to door to get the ingredients necessary to make a sandwich. Back in the day it worked but because most of the neighbors hated their mother and her whorish behavior, they shunned the boys. Harmony managed to fuck half of the husbands on their block and was working on the husbands of the block over from theirs. So as far as the women neighbors were concerned, her children could keel over from hunger for all they gave a fuck. They were her responsibility not theirs.

Still starved and without a plan, the boys trudged on the way to school. They were almost there when they saw Antwan and a group of his friends standing in an alley. Waiting. They had a loaf of bread and a jar of mayonnaise with them.

"There they go." One of them said.

When the twins saw the pack of children their hearts dropped and they tried to run.

"Go get 'em!" Antwan ordered.

Madjesty and Jayden were caught and brought back to Antwan in the alley. Pushing them on the ground Antwan said, "So I hear ya'll came by my cousin's house begging for food."

"Ughh, I smell them already!" One of the boys said holding his nose.

*"Shut up!" Antwan yelled. "You messing up my concentration."
Turning his attention back to the boys he said, "Is that true? Did you go
begging for food at my cousin's house?"*

"Yeah." Madjesty said. "We hungry."

*"That's all you had to say. We got some stuff for ya'll to eat right
here." Madjesty and Jayden's eyes roamed to the bread and the mayo.
Their stomachs growled and their mouths began to salivate. "What you
waiting on? Make the sandwiches."*

*Madjesty and Jayden tried to pretend as if they didn't want the food
at first but their stomachs told them otherwise. Running to the spread,
they made mayonnaise sandwiches using the ingredients Antwan and his
goons gave them. But right before they put the food in their mouth's Antwan stopped them.*

"Wait!" he said holding up his hand. "Ya'll forgot one thing."

"What?" Madjesty asked.

*"You gotta sit down and eat." Both of them sat down and leaned
against the wall. They were about to finish their meals until he said,
"You forgot something else."*

*Antwan walked up to them, pulled down his pants and pissed on the
sandwiches as they held them in their hands. They tried to jump up but
the kids pushed them back down. When he was done the sandwiches and
their clothes were drenched with his urine. His friends laughed so hard
they couldn't hold their composure.*

"Now eat it!" Antwan demanded.

*"NO!" Jayden yelled, dropping the sandwich. "You gotta hit me! I
ain't doing it!"*

"Then your brother betta do it!"

"No!" Madjesty said trying to be brave like his brother.

*Antwan frowned. "If you don't eat it," he said looking at Madjesty.
"We gonna jump you."*

"So what! I don't care no more. I'm not eating it!"

"Then we gonna tell Tisa how you ate pissy sandwiches anyway."

"But I didn't."

*"But we gonna tell her and she gonna believe me over you. And she
ain't gonna like you no more either."*

*Being afraid of losing Tisa's friendship, Madjesty put the soggy
sandwich in his mouth and everyone laughed. "I knew you were a punk."
Antwan said before he and his friends punched him in the chest and arms
and ran away.*

*When they were gone Madjesty opened his mouth and spit out the
wet bread. "I HATE THEM!" He yelled! "I FUCKING HATE EVERY-
BODY!"*

"*Me too!*" *Jayden replied.* "*Why don't people like us? What did we do to them?*"

"*I DON'T KNOW BUT I'M SICK OF EVERYTHING!*" *He could still taste the urine in his mouth.* "*I'M SICK OF PEOPLE PICKING ON US!*"

"*What we gonna do for food?*" *Jayden asked. Having gotten only a few chews of the bread he said,* "*I'm still hungry.*"

"*Maybe we can go to that store again. And take stuff.*"

"*Without paying?*" *Jayden inquired.*

"*I guess.*" *He shrugged.*

Before going to school, they stole some chips from the store to feed their hunger. It temporarily fulfilled their pangs and they were able to make it to school on time. Once there, the entire school was buzzing about the pissy sandwiches Madjesty ate. Life was horrible and it didn't seem to let up. All the twins wanted to do was run away from it all but they had nowhere to go. However, hard times were causing them to be tougher and to see life differently.

As if that wasn't enough, being born to an alcoholic mother caused them to have learning disabilities and often they couldn't think straight. Still, they did the best they could, given their circumstances in school. They weren't adults and they couldn't make decisions for themselves. They had to endure and hoped they came out alive.

Sitting at his desk in class as always, Madjesty stiffened his neck and balled up his fists. He waited for what he knew was coming, and just like he did the many times before, Antwan whacked him on the back of his head with the heavy book, temporarily causing him to see stars.

••

Pimp Fast Tony

Madjesty and Jayden were looking out of the window of their room at Pimp Fast Tony and his three young whores. He was a fascinating handsome man who always wore a suit no matter how hot it was outside. One of his whores wearing a pair of short-shorts wiped down his car with a white cloth exposing her vagina with every move she made. Men would constantly honk their horns as they drove by and Pimp would proudly wave. The other whore stood next to him, fanning him with a pink fan to keep him cool. Pimp Fast was counting money in his hand while Crissa spoke to a man in a car a few feet over from where Pimp stood. The man seemed to be smitten with her and Jayden was entranced. What was going on? What was Crissa saying to the man in the car?

When the conversation was over, Crissa swaggered out of the car and the man handed Crissa some money, which she quickly gave to Pimp Fast. Afterwards the car drove out of sight.

"Why you think she did that?"

"Did what?" Madjesty asked.

Unlike his brother he was waiting for Tisa to come outside and wasn't paying Pimp or his bitches much attention. Madjesty wondered would Tisa hate him after hearing about the pissy sandwich story at school, too?

"Why she give him that money?"

"I don't know." Madjesty shrugged.

"You think that's his girlfriend or something?"

"I don't know." He responded. "I guess."

"But he got like three of them."

"Maybe he likes lots of girls."

"I think Crissa pretty." Jayden offered. "She prettier than the other ones."

"So finally you like girls." Madjesty laughed pointing at his brother.

"No I don't!" He said disgusted with the whole idea. "I like money!"

"Don't lie! You said she was pretty."

Jayden wasn't lying. He really didn't like her in that way. He was more interested in what looked like power. In Jayden's mind Pimp Fast got cash because he had the baddest bitches around him at all times. Jayden didn't know what they sold or how they sold it. He just knew the girls made the money and gave it to him and because of it, he had a shiny pretty car and money in his hands. Suddenly, he wanted to be just like him.

"There she go!" Madjesty yelled.

When Tisa came out of the house she kissed her father and then her mother Crissa. She looked so pretty wearing her pretty red short set with her long hair out. For her, life seemed great and that was the only thing that secretly Madjesty was envious of. He wanted Tisa to be happy, truly he did, but he didn't understand why life at his house couldn't be good too.

As he watched her talk to her parents he thought about them together. There was something he wanted to ask but could never muster the strength to do. He wanted to ask Tisa if she'd agree to be his girlfriend. But every time she got in his space, he could never pop the question.

After speaking to her parents Tisa approached Madjesty's window. Jayden frowned not liking the girl one bit. He didn't want anybody to take his brother away from him especially the fast girl across the street.

Madjesty waited on her to give him what he lived for and his antici-pation seemed like forever. When she was within a few feet of his window finally, she gave him what he lived for, a smile. A smile as wide as out-stretched arms wanting to be hugged. A smile so large that it showed both rows of her perfectly white teeth and a few missing teeth. A smile that was made especially for him.

"Hey, Madjesty." Tisa waved. She always spoke to him through the window because Harmony rarely let the kids hang outside. She was too embarrassed by their clothes and too lazy to do anything about it. "What you doing?"

"Nothing." He smiled.

"Why you worried? Go back 'cross the street!" Jayden yelled.

Tisa frowned and for the first time ever, Madjesty wanted to drop kick his brother. "Jay, go lock the door before mama come in here."

"She ain't gonna come. Mr. Bad Guy in the living room with her."

"Go lock it anyway."

Knowing he wanted his privacy, Jayden frowned and locked the door. Then he stayed on his top bunk knowing his brother wanted to be left alone. But it didn't stop him from rolling his eyes at Tisa every chance he got.

"I heard about what happened at school. Is it true?"

Madjesty looked at her glossy lips and wondered how they tasted. "No. They lying on me and stuff."

"If it ain't true how you know what I'm talking about?"

He got caught in his lies. "Cause I heard about it too."

"Good...I'm glad it's not true." She smiled. Then she handed him a box of Johnny Appleseed's. He would only eat a few at a time with his brother in case he got hungry. Tisa always brought him gifts and he wished he could do the same for her.

"Thanks."

Tisa frowned and said, "How come it always smells stinky in there?"

Madjesty was overcome with embarrassment. "I don't know. Guess 'cause its kind of dirty."

"Humph." Tisa said. "Well, I be glad when you grow up so you can be real cute. I know you cute right now but people can't tell, cause your clothes be dirty and stuff. But I think you cute anyway. Just not real cute."

"Tisa! Get over here!" Crissa said. "We gotta go."

Madjesty didn't know if Crissa liked him but it definitely didn't seem like it.

"Well...you heard my mama. I gotta go. I'll see you later okay?"

"Okay." Madjesty said. "Thanks for the candy too."

"It's cool. I got plenty more where that came from."
    Madjesty knew that he needed to marry her but first he had to find a way out of the house and into a new life.

MEETING MR. NICE GUY
TWO WEEKS LATER

After another tough day at school Madjesty and Jayden came home preparing to hate their lives and everything about it. But when they opened the front door, they smelled the scent of McDonalds in the air. The twins looked at one another in disbelief, neither expecting to get such a treat. Was the food for them? If not would who ever looks at them, take pity and share?

When they reached the living room, they were surprised to see the trash pushed against the walls as opposed to being scattered throughout the house. It was somewhat neater than it normally was and it shocked and confused the twins.

Through it all, nothing stunned them more than when they saw their mother. Harmony was at the dining room table humming and preparing the food for the boys on paper plates. She was dressed neatly and didn't seem as drunk. Was Ramsey home? He couldn't be, they thought. The summer hadn't passed and Ramsey normally would have to cuss Harmony out after he came home to get her to clean up the mess she'd made over the months. So what caused the sudden change?

"Boys, come over here and sit down." Harmony said in her fakest voice. "I want you to meet someone."

The boys walked slowly into the dining room, waiting on her to curse them out for God knows what. In that moment the most handsome man that either of the boys ever seen walked out of the kitchen. They knew then that if God could bless them with the same attractiveness that they'd want to look just like him when they grew up. It wasn't just the way his hair was neatly shaped, or the way his clothes hung effortless on his fit body, it was in the way love poured from his eyes. This man was kind. This man was confident. This man exuded love.

"Hello, fellas!" He said running his hand through their bushy heads. His voice was country but bellowed like the sound of the ocean. "We gotta get these cotton balls taken down for you now don't we?" he laughed. "My hand gonna get stuck."

Madjesty laughed so hard at his humor that you would've thought he was Eddie Murphy in 'Delirious'. He didn't know if the joke was really funny or if it was the fact that someone had bothered to take the time to make him laugh.

"How are you fellas doing?" He asked.

"Fine." Madjesty said looking at him briefly before looking back at his worn out shoes.

Jayden just waved. He didn't want to get too excited about another person, only for him to leave their lives within days.

"What's your name?" he asked, Madjesty first.

"M...Madjesty."

"Whoa!" He said. "Madjesty, huh? Well that means you're destined for greatness. That whether you know it or not, you will have the power to lead." Then he looked at him seriously. "You just make sure that you lead people in the right direction."

Madjesty smiled. "I will, sir."

"And your name?"

"Jayden." His eyes roamed to the dirty hardwood floor. He didn't want to do anything to make the man not like him so that Harmony would blame him for his quick exit.

"Ahhh...Jayden." He smiled. "Your mother sure did pick some great names.

"Thank you." He blushed.

Harmony winked at him and Mr. Nice Guy smiled.

"Let's see...well Jayden means to be 'thankful'. And that only God will be your judge."

"Sir," Jayden cleared his throat, still looking at the floor, "How do you know so much? You like really smart and stuff."

He laughed. "Smarter than some but not smarter than most." He paused. "But I know a lot about names because I study them. I was a writer for an old paper in Mississippi." The boys were amazed. "And I guess I just love names so much because of the people I've come across in my life, that I learned all there was to know about them. That reminds me!" He paused. "Always get education boys. Always. It's the difference between truly living and dying." Then he clapped his hands together and said, "Well I've ran my mouth enough tonight," he laughed, "so let's eat, boys!"

That moment...that night...was the best time they'd ever spent in that home together. It was the best time they'd ever spent with their mother and it was the best time they'd ever had in life. Unfortunately when Harmony Phillips is your mother, best times don't last always.

In Front Of Tisa's House

Madjesty snuck out of his house after having such a nice evening. Mosquitoes sucked his bare arms as he crept out but he didn't care. He was on his way across the street to Tisa's house. In a good mood, and excited about Mr. Nice Guy being in their lives, he got the nerve to ask the question he always wanted to know.

He knocked gently on her window to get her attention. And when she finally came to the window wearing a pretty pink nightgown, she looked behind her before acknowledging him. When the coast was clear, she raised the window.

"Hi." She said.

"Will you be my girlfriend?" He blurted.

"Okay."

"For real?"

"Yeah."

"Can I have a kiss?"

Tisa looked behind her and leaned in kissing Madjesty softly on his lips. His heart skipped beats. He knew then what he wanted more than anything. A girlfriend and a real family. Already at a young age he was articulating how he wanted his life to be and he couldn't wait to make that happen with Tisa.

"I gotta go before my mama comes. I'll see you later." She said.

"Okay. Bye." He smiled.

Madjesty ran back across the street and sat on the porch for a little while. He thought about life and he thought about his girl. Suddenly images of his mother ruining it all came to mind.

The Greatest Man On Earth
Some Days Later

As time went on, the twins discovered that Mr. Nice Guy purchased a home on the same block as Ramsey's, in the hopes of starting a better life away from racist ass Mississippi. Madjesty was grateful although Jayden was apprehensive. He didn't like getting close to people only for them to leave him with broken hopes and promises. But after seeing how he really seemed to care, Jayden put down his guards and opened his heart.

Days were better the day he entered into their lives. He provided the best food he could buy and even dug into his own pocket to purchase them decent clothing. Mr. Nice Guy wasn't rich so he had to take caution on the money he spent, but he did what he could. For whatever reason he gravitated towards the boys and it showed in his actions and the things he did for them.

One Saturday afternoon, he decided to take the boys to get haircuts. They never had a proper cut and most times Harmony would chop their hair off with a pair of dull scissors to keep them looking boy-like. So when they walked into the barbershop for the first time, both twins were amazed at the high spinning chairs and large mirrors. The sound of the clippers mesmerized them and they were interested in seeing how they'd look once they left. Everyday was an adventure with Mr. Nice Guy and today was no exception.

While Mr. Nice Guy was talking to the barbers, the twins sat down in chairs against the wall and took a moment to talk to each other alone.

"I love him," Madjesty said.

"Me too." Jayden whispered. "You don't think he gonna leave us do you?"

"No. He gonna stay." He paused. "If mama don't give her pussy to somebody else."

"MADJESTY! YOU CURSED!" Mr. Nice Guy looked at the boys, smiled and continued his conversation with a few barbers. He seemed proud to be their Ready-to-Love father.

"Why you so loud?" He frowned.

"How you know that word?"

"*Mr. Bad Guy says it all the time when he and mama stinks up the living room.*"

"*Well I don't like it. God don't like it.*" *Jayden persisted.*

Madjesty wasn't going to argue with his brother about his opinion. So he left the matter alone.

"*What you think gonna happen when Mr. Ramsey comes back?*"

"*I don't know, Jayden. I'm scared though.*"

"*Maybe Mr. Nice Guy can take the house from Ramsey.*" *Even at this point, the boys didn't know Mr. Nice Guy's real name and after so much time passed, they felt it would be rude to ask him. So whenever they were in his presence they'd call him sir.*

"*Mr. Ramsey might not give up his house.*"

"*He might do.*" *Jayden persisted.* "*And then maybe we can all live together. Me, you, mama and Mr. Nice Guy.*"

Madjesty's eyes were wide with hope and anticipation. He wanted a real family, he wanted a real father and he wanted real love. "*Maybe he can.*"

When Mr. Nice Guy called the boys over to get their hair cut by separate barbers, one barber across the room wouldn't take his eyes off of them. The entire time the boys received their hair cut, he looked at them with penetrating eyes. The twins felt so uncomfortable by his stares that they were five seconds from crying. Did he not like them? And if he didn't would he tell Mr. Nice Guy not to like them too?

"*Wagner, come here for a second man,*" *the strange barber said while a client sat in his chair. It was at that moment that they found out that Mr. Nice Guy's name was Wagner and Madjesty liked it immediately.*

Wagner swaggered over to the strange man to see what he wanted. Once there the strange barber whispered something in Mr. Nice Guy's ear, which caused him to step away, frown and become angry. Then Mr. Nice Guy did something that shocked both boys. He stole the man in the face with a closed fist causing him to crash into his mirror shattering it into a million pieces.

"*Get the fuck out of my shop!*" *the strange barber yelled holding his bloody nose.*

Always the southern gentleman, Mr. Nice Guy shook his hand and addressed all those present except the pervert. "*Sorry for the inconvenience, fellas.*" *He nodded at everyone.* "*I do hope you'll continue to have a nice day.*" *Then he paid the barbers who cut the boy's hair and softly patted the twins on their backs.* "*Come on, fellas. It's time to hit the road.*"

The twins hopped out of the seats and followed him out the door without hesitation. They never found out what caused Mr. Nice Guy to hurt the strange barber, and after the incident he acted as if nothing happened. He even took the twins to the movies before taking them to get some pizza and ice cream later that night. It was obvious that he took to the boys so much, that in a way, his connection with them was greater than it was with Harmony. He knew these were the impressionable years and he wanted to be the positive role model in their lives, that is if they would have him.

They would never discover that the strange barber knew, from the moment he laid eyes on the boys, that they were girls. So he wanted them sexually.

"Look, I know girls when I see them," *the strange man whispered in Mr. Nice Guy's ear.* ***"And I know you don't have kids of ya' own, you said it. Now I don't know why you pawning them off as boys and I don't care. I love me some little girl pussy too. So if you let me fuck one of them, I won't say a word about what you do to the other. I have to tell you, I got some friends though, who may wanna pay to play, but that's on you. I'm just interested in getting me a little taste now. So what do you say?"*** *he smiled licking his lips and groping his dick.* ***"Can I have one of them tonight?"***

The strange barber's words infuriated Mr. Nice Guy and although he didn't show it, hours after the incident, it still weighed heavily on his heart.

Were the boys girls? If so, why would Harmony make such a vicious lie? He decided to ask her when he spoke to her later that night, when the kids were asleep. He knew she wasn't the best person but her beauty, even with the scar on her face, intrigued him. She had more personality than any woman he'd ever met in his life. Plus, when she wasn't drunk she was charming and a pleasure to be around. So he never gave up hope after meeting her at a bar that with a little backing, she could be one of the greatest.

After their night of fun, Mr. Nice guy dropped the kids off home. "Tell your mother I'll be in, in a second." He said. "I got to make a few stops."

He saw the look of desperation in the twin's eyes and felt it on the deepest level of his soul. "Look, I don't know what you boys been through, but judging by the looks in your eyes I can tell it must've been a lot. But don't worry, I'm coming back. I'm a man of my word." He promised. "I will never leave either of you. No matter what."

Mr. Nice Guy always knew what to say. Hope entered their lives the day they saw his face and they appreciated God for it.

"Go on now," he smiled. "It's dark out here. I'll be back."

He didn't pull off until he saw the children walk inside. Mr. Nice Guy's words resonated with them and unfortunately it would be the last time they'd ever hear him speak directly to them again.

• •

In The House

When the boys walked into the house, they could smell the stench of another sexual escapade and they were devastated. How could a woman be so horrid that she would fuck up a good thing she didn't deserve? Mr. Nice Guy wasn't rich, but he was a provider and he would have gladly taken care of her and her two sons. Madjesty didn't understand. His mind couldn't wrap around what she was doing. As far as he could tell Mr. Nice Guy was great and most of all, he loved him.

What also bothered the twins, but especially Madjesty, was her apparent need to fuck on the family sofa as opposed to her own room, subjecting them to her lustful acts on a consistent basis. In her mind her reasoning was clear, she shared the bedroom with Ramsey, and she didn't want to take the chance of one of her male whores leaving something behind that Ramsey would later find once returning home. No. Sex in her room was out of the question and she didn't care what her children thought of it.

Trying to walk past their mother who was on the couch 'getting her life', hurt. But when they saw Mr. Bad Guy's face their hearts dropped. What was it about him that drew her? The answer was simple. He reminded her of every man who'd ever took advantage of her body starting with her uncle all the way to her current beau.

Harmony's knees dug into the cushions as her arms draped over the back of the couch as he pounded her relentlessly from behind. He scowled as he moved in and out of her pussy as if he hated the bitch. Madjesty was taken aback by the stone look on his face and wondered if he liked what he was doing to his mother. If he enjoyed what he felt.

The expression on Harmony's face was quite different. A smile kept her lips company as she backed into each of his heavy thrusts. When she wasn't getting it good enough, she spread her ass cheeks apart and demanded that he go deeper...and deeper...harder and harder. The tingling sensation running through her vagina held her attention and nothing else mattered. Then she saw her kids. The two fuck ups who always knew how to mess up a wet dream. Her lips turned upside down into a frown as she wiped sweat off her forehead.

They weren't supposed to be home.

They were early.

"*What are ya'll doing here?*" *Harmony said. Mr. Bad Guy peered at the boys saying nothing. He decided that both of them were faggies in the making and didn't want to speak to either of them. "I thought you were staying out."*

"*We were, mama.*" *Jayden said. He could feel his body trembling. Harmony didn't like to be interrupted during sex and they both knew it.*

"*Well why ya'll here then?*"

"*We just left...Wagner.*" *Madjesty offered.*

In that instant...in that moment...he wished he never learned his name.

Hearing Wagner's name, Harmony turned around to look at Mr. Bad Guy as he leveled a dark expression her way. Rising up, he stood over top of her like a giant. His eyes squinted closely together and the muscles in his arm buckled as he cracked his knuckles. The boys felt something awful was going to happen because the tension in the room went from dark to heavy in less than five seconds.

"*So you fucking that nigga?*" *He said slapping her with a backhand.*

Blood flew from her mouth and dampened the sofa. Harmony tried to hide from his next action but he kept her put with his presence. She didn't dare move another inch fearing what he might do next.

"*No...I'm not...*"

"*When we met him at the bar,*" *he interrupted, pointing a long finger in her face, "you said he was a friend of Ramsey's! Said he wasn't interested in you and that he was in love with his wife!*"

Harmony brought her knees into her chest and appeared to curl up into a ball. "He is, baby. The boys must be mistaken. I would never..."

He grabbed her by the shoulders and stopped any further words. "You fucked him!" He yelled in her face. The same face that held his dick for an hour a few moments earlier. "You fucked him didn't you?" He released her and crashed his fist into her face.

Harmony felt off balance as she tried to get away from him. Putting one of her feet on the floor, he stopped her before she could move another. Grabbing her by her hair he balled his fist up again, preparing to jam it into her stomach. "Please! Don't do this!"

"*Bitch, I told you I wasn't about to have another woman step out on me! Didn't I tell you that?!*"

The force of his fist entering her stomach had come so quickly she almost didn't believe it happened. And before she knew it she was met with a barrage of blows. The boys were so stunned; all they could do was watch.

"Not in front of my kids," she managed to say. *"Please don't do this in front of them."*

Madjesty wondered did she want him to truly stop for their sake, or was it an attempt to get free. Either way his heart pounded in his chest and he wished the mad man would stop before he killed her.

"Why you giving my pussy away? Huh?!"

Over and over he beat Harmony and there was nothing the twins could do but watch. Madjesty said the wrong thing, and as a result, a man who was drunk and incapable of knowing when he'd gone too far was killing his mother.

When Jayden saw her head move around loosely as if it were no longer attached to her neck, he could no longer remain silent. *"You're hurting her! Stop it!"* He yelled.

As the beating continued, Madjesty was too entranced to say anything. Because something suddenly overcame him, something he couldn't describe into words if someone asked. It started out as small flutters in his stomach and turned into a tingling sensation that moved throughout his body. Small bumps rose from his skin and a smile spread across his face. She was getting what she deserved, and he was pleased. In the midst of the violence, he found pleasure. He found the sweetness of revenge.

"STOP HITTING MY MOTHER!" Jayden continued to scream.

His pleas did nothing to stop his anger from festering. In the drunk's mind, Harmony's wretched pussy truly belonged to him, and he would beat her until she realized it.

Just when things couldn't get any worse, Mr. Nice Guy comes through the door with a bouquet of white roses and red wine. Madjesty was no longer smiling and now was extremely worried. He didn't want him getting involved in any of this mess and most of all, he didn't want him getting hurt. Things appeared to move in slow motion at this moment.

Seeing Harmony near death, Madjesty watched as the white roses dropped to the floor followed by the crashing of the bottle of red wine. The peddles on the flowers went from white to red as Mr. Nice Guy moved quickly toward Mr. Bad guy on a mission. At first Mr. Bad Guy didn't see him. How could he? He was focused on murdering Harmony Phillips. But when he attempted to collide into her jaw using his fist again, it was stopped by Mr. Nice Guy's massive hand. His fingers swallowed Mr. Bad's fist as if it were never there to begin with and his fit body shadowed Mr. Bad's like a building over a block. The two of them fought tooth and nail for a woman who was not their own. They fought for a whore, who wasn't fitting to take care of her own children. Yet they'd fallen under her spell and could do nothing about it now.

In all truthfulness it wasn't their fault. Harmony even in her drunkest state was a seductress with the ability to make a man feel like he was the only one in the world. That when he was with her, nothing else mattered.

Mr. Nice Guy was pretty good with the hands and was getting the best of Mr. Bad. Blood was splattered everywhere as Mr. Nice punished him with the use of several gut punches and a few more upper cuts.

When on hands and knees Mr. Bad Guy crawled to the recliner where his pants and jacket hung over the edge, Mr. Nice Guy let him go. In his heart of hearts he was a good person and couldn't beat a man who wasn't willing to fight him straight up. Unlike the animalistic behavior that Mr. Bad Guy exhibited moments earlier, he would not exact the same revenge. He was human and a good man and he would always play fair. Besides as long as Harmony was alive, he would let sleeping dogs lie.

"Get your things and go." Mr. Nice said, breathing heavily as he looked down upon him. "And don't ever come back here again. Ever!"

Turning his attention away from him, Mr. Nice Guy picked up Harmony's limp body off the couch. Blood weighed heavily on her eyelashes and he wiped it away with his large fingers hoping she would open her eyes. When she did, he smiled.

"You okay?" He asked, in that country voice the boys grew to love.

She nodded and smiled. "Thank you."

Mr. Nice Guy was preparing to take her to the hospital when he felt a pain shoot through his shoulder followed by another through his lower back. Unable to hold her anymore, she dropped to the couch as he fell to the floor. On his knees with wide eyes, he fell face first to his death. He died instantly.

Madjesty pissed where he stood, as Jayden passed out cold. Silence had stolen any voice Madjesty had and his lips trembled. He'd seen a man get murdered and he would never be the same.

Mr. Nice Guy's blood poured from his body and onto the filthy wooden floor.

"OH MY GOD!" Harmony sobbed, her face severely bruised. "YOU...YOU KILLED HIM!"

"Yeah but you made me do it!" He yelled pointing at her, gun still in his hand. "All because you're a fucking whore!"

"I didn't make you do nothing!" She cried harder. "You can't put me in this! I'ma tell the police! I'ma tell 'em what you did."

When she said that he aimed at her and pulled the trigger, but he didn't have any bullets left. She fell backwards onto the couch, holding her chest, knowing that she'd gotten away with her life. As a reminder of the blessing, she looked on the floor at the dead man to her left.

"You one lucky, bitch!" Mr. Bad Guy laughed walking up to her. *"Now go wipe your face. We got a body to get rid of."*

•••

The Next Morning

The next morning the blood was wiped piss poorly off the floor and Mr. Nice Guy's body was gone. The gentle man. The sweet man who had taken a liking to the boys, who genuinely cared about them and their well-being was now dead. This was a crushing experience. And it was also an experience that would affect each of them differently.

Instead of the usual silence after a night of Harmony's drunken escapades, they heard her busying about the house although she didn't come to their room.

Sitting on the bottom bunk, Jayden looked at his brother. "You think she gonna be mad with us?"

"I don't know." Madjesty shrugged. All morning his gaze remained on a yellow stain upon the wall, next to the door. He couldn't understand any of this and how people could be so mean to one another. "

"She gonna be mad." Jayden said. "I know it."

Both of them were riddled with fear when Harmony walked into their room frowning, looking like a monster. Once inside their space, she closed and locked the door. The whites of her eyes were blood shot red and around them were black. Tearstains rested on her bruised face and she smelled of alcohol.

"Because of you, Madjesty," she said plugging up an iron that was thrown in the corner of the room. "Wagner is dead." She tapped her fingers over the hot part of the iron checking the temperature. Finally she pressed her finger against her wet tongue and touched the iron again. It sizzled. "And now you gotta pay."

Madjesty cowered in the corner and Jayden screamed out, "Mama, no! Please don't!"

"Shut up you, little bitch!" She pointed in his face. Then she turned back to Madjesty. "Wagner would still be alive, if you hadn't opened your fucking mouth. That man loved me and I was going to leave Ramsey for him. And you ruined it all!"

When the iron was hot enough, she removed it from the wall and caught up with Madjesty. Overpowering him, she placed her knee on his throat and held him to the floor. The more he moved, the more pressure she applied until it was difficult for him to breathe. Taking down his pants, she placed the iron on his thigh. Loving the pain she was causing her son she smiled in delight.

Next to alcohol, Madjesty derived a strange pleasure from inflicting pain on her children. She wanted to make them hurt as much as she hurt on a regular basis. She wanted them to hate life as much as she hated life. In her mind, in her own sick way, if they hated their lives, she could make them feel one ounce of the mental torture she felt on a regular basis. Alcohol was the only way she conquered the demons she saw in her dreams. And abuse was the only way she got revenge. She knew very personally what the term, misery loves company meant because she operated that way for so long and more importantly she had no intentions on changing.

As the iron pressed against his skin, the pain Madjesty felt was overwhelming. Striking pain ripped through his flesh as if he was being skinned alive. His eyes rolled up into his head and Harmony smiled. Over and over she burned him on the thigh until the iron was too cold to do further damage.

When Harmony was done she stood up and looked at his pus-raised skin, "You better never tell nobody about this. If you do, I'll have you killed and dumped where Wagner is. You understand me?"

"Yes," he cried. "Yes."

For days on end, she would come into the room and burn Jayden once or twice but Madjesty the most. She wanted to scare the children into secrecy so that they'd never tell about what happened to Wagner when Ramsey finally returned home. She never, not once, saw that Madjesty was changing for the worse. How could she, she was in a drunken daze most of the time and mad at the world the rest.

The twins were out of school for a week before she finally let them return. The sun wasn't as crude as it had been in the week's prior but it would not have made a difference to them anyway. Their spirits were broken and they barely spoke to each other. They sauntered to their elementary school in silence. Troubled thoughts occupied their minds but there was one thing that Madjesty still looked forward to, and her name was Tisa.

After Mr. Nice Guy was murdered, Madjesty wasn't allowed to look out of his window, or leave his house during the entire week Harmony kept them at home. She was too concerned Mr. Bad Guy would come back to kill her and the boys. Even though he moved his family out of the neighborhood, fear held Harmony and her children hostage. Through it all there never was a day, ever, where Tisa wasn't on Madjesty's heart and mind. It was all he had to keep going.

When they walked into the school Madjesty couldn't believe his luck. Tisa was there, holding her book bag and laughing with friends. Madjesty was always amazed to see people laughing because he very rarely ever *did. What was she laughing about? What good things were going on in her home, that wasn't going on in his?*

When Tisa saw Madjesty in the hallway, she approached him. But after days of heartache and physical pain, Madjesty was waiting on it...waiting on the thing she did to make his day. Smile. And then she gave it to him. But there was something wrong. This smile was different because it didn't seem to make the complete upward motion it needed to expose all of her pretty white teeth and spaces. What was wrong? What changed?

Needing to be alone Madjesty said, "You can go into the class, Jayden. I'm coming."

Not liking Tisa anyway Jayden said, "Okay."

Tisa walked up to Madjesty who was dressed neater than he normally was. The night before Harmony washed a bag of clothes for them to wear at school for the week. She wanted to have as little attention on them as possible. She didn't need some nosey teacher pulling them into the office because of their dirty condition only to learn about the Mr. Nice Guy's murder. No, she was being careful these days...for now anyway.

"Hi, Madjesty."

"Hi." He smiled.

"You okay?"

"Yeah."

"Oh. Why you haven't been to school?"

"Not feeling well."

"Oh...I had a cold too." She let out two quick coughs.

"Feeling better?" He asked, genuinely concerned.

"Kinda."

Silence.

"Well...I gotta go to class." She continued. "But I can't be your girlfriend no more."

Madjesty tugged at the bottom of the white shirt he wore. Suddenly it seemed to itch against his dry skin. Suddenly it seemed to be too tight around his neck.

"Huh? But why?"

"Because I go with Antwan now. I'm sorry."

She walked away. She left him alone. She left him devastated.

The news of his first break up took all he had left. "Go to class, Madjesty." A teacher said.

Angry about losing Tisa, he spoke quickly to the woman. "I'm going! Wait!"

The teacher was stunned but left it alone. He wasn't her student. Madjesty was growing rebellious and anger was quickly becoming his best friend. In his mind adults were evil and didn't deserve to breed or take care of children and that went for all of them. The teachers, too.

"I go with Antwan now. I'm sorry." Kept replaying in his mind. "I go with Antwan now. I'm sorry. I go with Antwan now. I'm sorry. I go with Antwan now. I'm sorry." He couldn't stop it and it was tearing him apart.

Once in the classroom, Madjesty grabbed the encyclopedia that was on the wall and approached Antwan. He was pissed at the world and decided he wasn't going to be too many more of his punks. He wasn't going to be the kid who bit his tongue all the time. He wasn't going to be someone too afraid to talk. Besides, he'd done that already and it had gotten him picked on, beat and ridiculed. It was time to change and it was time to change now.

Although everyone was talking at first when Madjesty approached Antwan with the book, the room got deadly silent. Seeing something different in Madjesty's eyes, Antwan wasn't as cocky as he usually was. He was stunned by his boldness in even approaching him. "What you want, stupid? Another piss sandwich?"

Everyone laughed except Madjesty. Gripping the book tightly he could feel his nails digging into the fabric on the book's cover. He hadn't expected it to be so heavy and he wondered how Antwan held it so securely in his hands, the days he hit him repeatedly in the back of the head.

When Madjesty gripped the book how he wanted, he whacked himself in the front of the head. Then again...and again...and again, until the wound Harmony caused reopened. Blood poured down his face and Antwan's eyes grew larger. He was frightened and the other kids in the room including Jayden were too stunned and scared to make a sound. What had gotten into him? What could make a boy who was so quiet and so withdrawn so crazy at the moment? Life had fucked him up. Life had stolen the only precious moments he had to live for and life had taken both Mr. Nice Guy and Tisa.

When the teacher finally walked into the classroom, Madjesty was dripping in his own blood and a grin rested upon his face.

"What the fuck is going on here?" The teacher asked rushing up to Madjesty, removing the book from his bloody hands. He didn't even realize he'd used profanity in his classroom. Madjesty didn't allow his presence to move him either which way. As far as he was concerned, he could suck the dick he thought he had between his legs. His focus was razor sharp and zeroed in on Antwan with precision, never taking his eyes off

of him the entire time. He wanted him to know that what he just did to himself, he could have easily done to him.

Madjesty, in that moment wanted to make a statement. That you could never hurt a person who could easily hurt themselves.

"Are you crazy or something?" The teacher continued.

When the teacher said that Madjesty looked at him and said, "Fuck off."

"What you just say to me, boy?"

"I said fuck off!" The teacher anchored his arm and rushed him out the room thinking he was losing his mind. When in all actuality he was. But was it his fault? How could he be normal when life around him was anything but?

"You stay here and don't move. I'm calling your mother." The teacher said after they walked into the Nurse's office.

Madjesty sat in a seat too big for his small body. His legs dangled under him as he waited for the nurse to come in and do her job. An unrelated woman walked into the room and looked at the bloody little boy in shock. What happened to that small child? She said to herself as she kept it moving, as every other adult he encountered in life did to him. No worries though. He would simply add her to the list of adults who didn't give a fuck.

A blue baseball cap sat in the seat next to him and he lifted it up. Who did it belong to? Who had left it? Whoever it was they were short because now the hat belonged to him. He put it on his bloody head and smiled. It fit! The pressure against the wound stung a little but he was use to pain now. Something happened to him in that moment. The hat made him feel safe. It made him feel right. He pulled it down further to cover his eyes and his face produced a menacing smile.

That moment sparked a change in his mental direction. He was no longer afraid of anything and he was susceptible to pain. As he grew into a teenage boy, and eventually into a teenage girl, he would no longer move to the beat of another person's drum. He would be forever changed. He would forever be Mad.

PART TWO

PRESENT DAY
GREEN DOOR - ADULT MENTAL HEALTH CARE CLINIC
NORTHWEST, WASHINGTON DC

A puddle of sweat rested in the seat of Harmony's panties and her jeans were completely drenched between her legs. She could smell her own pussy and hoped the meaty scent didn't extend further than her own nose. The heat in the room hadn't missed Christina Zham either. The back of her shirt was clinging to her skin and she kept pulling it to allow small pockets of air to get inside in the hopes that it would cool her off.

"Harmony, I really am sorry about the heat in here." Christina said fanning herself with her chart. "Hopefully they'll fix it today."

"I don't care." She was starting to twitch a little and needed alcohol badly. A stiff hard dick wouldn't hurt either.

"Well, its time to talk about that period in your life."

Harmony rolled her eyes and sat back into the hard seat. Her eyes looked over Christina's and she wondered what she thought about her so far.

"I told you how I feel about that already. Not now."

"Harmony, I know how you feel...but we've covered everything else."

"I haven't begun to tell you everything that has happened in my life. Clearly we can find something else to talk about."

Christina rolled her eyes and threw her head back. She knew she was being unprofessional but it was hard to avoid when dealing with Harmony. After all of their sessions together, Harmony still didn't understand that she was there for help.

"I know we haven't spoken about your life in *full* detail, but now we have to talk about that *specific* time."

"You think you know everything don't you?" Harmony asked.

"Excuse me?" Christina leaned in.

"You sit over there with your little degree on your wall and make assumptions. You're not even trying to really understand me. You say you are but your actions show me different. I'm a drunk, Christina. A washed up fucking drunk but I've never been a fool."

"You don't know what you're talking about."

"Yes I do." Harmony looked down at her dirty nails. Then she balled up her fists and looked back at her. Christina took notice. Was she about to hurt her? "You just want more reasons not to like me. More reasons to blame me for the things that have happened in my life. More reasons to hate me."

Christina sighed. She hadn't realized she was so obvious. She would have to do a better job of 'faking it' if she was going to get through to her.

"If you feel that way I'm sorry." She said in a slow, soft tone, as if she were speaking to a child. "But unless we talk about what happened to you during those thirty days we can't move forward. The time really has come."

"Well, I'm not ready to talk about that. I want to talk about something else first."

"Like what?"

"ANYTHNG!" Harmony screamed. Then she repeated herself in a lower tone. *"Anything."*

Christina didn't want to push her but it was her job to force Harmony to delve into her emotions and she would stop at nothing until she did just that. Despite how she felt about Harmony, it was her job and she would do it the best she could. Truth be told, Christina despised Harmony. She despised her more than anything and had no more love for her than she did a homeless dog. Still, she needed to figure out how a mother like her came to be.

Before the doctor could say anything else, the maintenance man entered her office unannounced. He didn't bother to knock and that irritated Christina. "I'm here to check your thermostat," he said without apologizing for his interruption.

"Well I'm with a client now."

He looked at her and back at Christina. He didn't give a fuck. His wife called ten times already and wanted him home to explain the panties she found in his workbox. This was his last job for the day and although he dreaded seeing her, she knew he had to come home.

"Okay, well let me make it quick. I got orders to do this today, and judging by how hot it is in here, I'd think you'd want me to take care of this now."

"Hurry up."

As he fussed with the thermostat he kept looking over at Harmony. He'd seen her face all over the news and couldn't believe he was standing in her presence. And just like the rest of the world who watched the story unfold, he hated her guts. His face tightened and he looked like he was seconds from punching her in jaw. Like if she said the wrong thing, he'd be all over her as if he were fighting a grown ass man in the streets.

"Are you done?" Christina said putting a few loose strands of her brown hair behind her ear. Her white skin flushed because the heat in the room had risen with his extra body.

"Let me see if it works," he said, turning around to finish his job. After awhile with one flip of the switch, cool air blew into the room putting Christina at immediate ease.

"Aww...thank you." She paused loving the feeling. Harmony didn't care if it was on or not. She spent years in Texas, where temperatures stayed in the hundreds. "I appreciate that."

He grabbed his tool box and moved toward the door. Angry about the personal shit he was going through at home he decided to add his two cents. "I think it is awful what you did to your children and I hope you rot in hell for it."

Christina couldn't believe his gall. "YOU GET OUT OF HERE THIS INSTANT!" She stood, pointing at the door.

Having said his peace he walked out and she sat back down. Now that the air was on Christina was slightly chilly because her shirt was wet and she hoped she didn't catch a cold. "I'm sorry, Harmony. I didn't know he was going to do that."

"It's okay. I'm kind of use to it now. I think everyone blames me for all of those deaths. It's funny, I wasn't even there." She looked at her dirty nails again and flipped her hands over to the lighter side. She thought about the people she touched with them and all the people she hurt. Her mind went briefly to her kids and her heart ached. One sip of alcohol...and maybe a stiff dick could make her feel better instantly. Yeah that's it! If she hurried, she could run to the liquor store, maybe meet a stranger and get both. "You think I can go to the bathroom right quick? Or maybe we can take a lunch break?"

"Why now?"

"I really gotta go get something to eat. I'm really hungry."

"You sure you don't want to get something to drink? You sure that's not it?"

She thought about the bitter taste of vodka in her mouth and how it always warmed the back of her tongue before eventually reaching her throat. She thought about how moments later, the feeling would take over her body...that feeling when nothing or nobody mattered.

"I'm not going to get any alcohol. I just...I just gotta...leave. I just gotta go for a minute."

"You can't." Christina said. "These are required appointments. You know that." She paused. "Now, I really want you to tell me about your daughter."

"Which one?" She said through tight lips.

"Madjesty." She paused. "It's time for you to talk to me about Madjesty."

MAD PHILLIPS
OCTOBER OF 2003
FORT WASHINGTON, MARYLAND

I was downstairs, in the basement prepared to do whatever I wanted to this so-called mother of mine, when all of a sudden, I heard some noise upstairs.

"Hold up? Ya'll hear that?" I asked my crew.

They stood behind me, watching me, afraid to make a move. I had decided that she would be our first kill, a reason to bring us closer together; As a crew and hopefully as a family.

"Naw." Krazy K said, looking at my mother. His eyes so wide I thought they'd pop out of his head. The scowl he always seemed to have was even stronger. "I aln't hear nothing."

"Well I did." I tugged on my New York Yankees baseball cap to be sure it was over my eyes. I didn't like people looking in my face. I didn't like people looking at me at all. "Keep this bitch quiet." I said looking at the ceiling. "I'm gonna see what's up."

When I walked up the basement stairs and touched the cold gold doorknob, I caught my sister right before she entered. I didn't want her in on my plan. Didn't want her to know what I was going to do to Harmony. Didn't want her to stop me. Or at least try anyway.

But the moment I saw her face, I was thrown off. It was different. Not like how it use to be when we'd gone days without food. Not how like it use to be when we didn't take baths for days at a time, because we moved from house to house staying with one of Harmony's man toys each week. It was different in a good way...for her anyway. Her long hair hung down her back and shined against the ceiling light. I think she was even wearing a touch of makeup. She never worn it before because we couldn't afford it but now...now it was different. She looked, pretty...like one of them models in the Seventeen Magazine I saw when we were at the grocers stealing food. She was still my sister...still my twin, but different. Then it dawned on me, while life for me got rougher, shit for her just kept getting better. It was the story of my life.

"What's that noise downstairs?" Jayden asked trying to walk around me and down the steps. "Is mama here?"

"No…And that's the TV on." I said closing the door behind me.

Jayden followed me into the foyer but she kept looking at the basement door until I gave her a look which meant I would drop her ass if I had to. I just didn't give a fuck. Wasn't nothing, or nobody gonna stop me from completing my plans against that woman. A woman I hated more than anything.

"Where's mama?"

"She gone. Now what are you doing here?" I asked. "Why you not posted up in the hotel with some nigga?"

"I have something to tell you," Jayden said grabbing my hand. I snatched it away. "I'm sorry, sister; I'm not trying to invade your space. It's just that…well…Jace has something to tell us. I think it may be good, Madjesty."

"Mad."

"What?"

"I keep telling ya'll not to call me Madjesty no more. I go by Mad now."

"I'm sorry."

"And who the fuck is Jace?"

"Mama, use to be with him back in the day. And I think…Well, I think he may be our…."

Right before she finished her statement, someone pulled up to the mansion and walked through the doors. He was handsome…like in a drug boss type of way. He seemed to have some strange power and his eyes peered at me at first. He had two other men behind him and through the open doorway, I could see ten vans parked in the driveway.

"Is Kali here?" he asked Jayden, putting one hand softly on her back.

Who was he to touch my sister that way? Who did he think he was period?

"No. I don't think so."

"Is he?" He asked me.

I shook my head no. "Who are you?" I asked. "And what are you and all these vans doin' at my house?"

"You must be Madjesty?"

"Mad. I go by Mad now." I said looking at him and the other men standing behind him. "Now who are you and what are you doin' in my house?"

He looked at both of us sadly and dug in his pocket. Then he pulled out a little piece of white paper. It was crumbled like he'd been reading it and refolding it in different ways. Like he wanted to throw it in trash but couldn't.

"I have some news for you girls. It's the paternity test." He paused.

I shot Jayden a dark glare. Fuck did this nigga mean he had a paternity test on me?

"Don't be mad at Jayden," Jace said spotting the look I gave her. "I had her bring me some of your hair out of your brush. For the test."

"When was that?"

"It was a while back. I came into your room real quick and left back out."

"I knew it," I knew I couldn't trust this bitch. "You tried to say you weren't in my room when I asked you."

"Madjesty, please!" Jayden said.

"Mad! I told you to call me Mad!"

"Girls, this is serious." Jace said. "I have to tell you something. Both of you."

He unfolded the paper awkwardly in his hands and said, "Jayden, I'm...I'm your father." Jayden was so excited about the news that she wrapped her arms around him. And although she wasn't holding me I could smell the scent of her perfume as she moved toward him. She smelled like the girl Rocket I had a crush on in Texas. Her screeching voice was feminine and happy. She was so girly and I wondered how she could do it so easily when everything about me was all boy. We both grew up as boys, so what made her different?

Her excitement and the way his words replayed in my mind finally let me know what was going on. He said, '*I'm your father*'. After all of these years of not knowing who else we belonged to and all of these years of being in Harmony's miserable world we finally knew our other half. And unlike that creepy man who'd been staying here, the man before me seemed regal, like a boss. Like a real man.

Something came over me. It finally dawned on me. He was our father? I had a father who wanted to be in my life? If this was the case it changed everything for me. For a second I thought about Mr. Nice Guy and how he treated us. Was it possible for Jace who was claiming to be my father, to treat me the same way?

"So...so you our father?" I asked, hoping it was true. "So that means you gonna help us now right?"

Somewhere in the course of hugging him she was now hugging me. Her breasts pressed against my chest and I wondered was she happy with her titties because I hated mine. Hated the curves of my body and hated the girl I was becoming.

I looked at Jace again. He was my father. He was *our* father. Just looking at him and I could almost see our resemblance.

"I'm going to do whatever I can for you girls," Jace said. He didn't seem easy and his eyes seemed to miss mine when I tried to look into them. "But, Madjesty, you're not my...you're not my biological daughter."

"What are you talking about? You said Jayden's your daughter and we're twins." I said to him. Even though we weren't identical we were still twins. "So I have to be your daughter, too." I looked at Jayden and then back at him. "Right?"

"Honey, you aren't my biological daughter." His eyes roamed the floor and hung there for a moment. He wasn't looking at me anymore. Look at me! Fucking look at me!

"How is that possible?!" I said. "It don't make no sense."

"I didn't understand it either. But before coming over here, I talked to a doctor about it." He paused. "When you're mother was pregnant, she had a condition called, hetero...hetero...."

"Heteropaternal superfecundation." The dude with him interrupted.

I looked at both of the intruders in my home and felt like breaking both of their jaws. Why they have to fuck with my life? I didn't need nobody and here they were making a fool of me. I stomped around the foyer angry and embarrassed that I allowed myself to fall for this nigga. My feet seemed to swell in my shoes and my temples throbbed. I would never allow myself to trust another adult. Ever.

"What the fuck is hetero...whatever the fuck?!" I asked.

"It's when your mother had different sexual partners...at the same time."

Me and Jayden looked at each other. I remembered the many nights I saw her fucking this dude or that dude. So I believed it instantly.

"What?" I said.

"Ma, fucked two niggas at the same time, Mad. She was a fuckin' slut!"

Hearing this I snapped. Once again, Harmony succeeded in making me feel like an outcast. I didn't want another father, I wanted the father my sister had. I wanted us to be connected. Always.

"Do you know, who my father is?" I said wiping the last tear off of my face. Where did they come from? I'd been standing in front of them crying and didn't even know it.

"Yes."

"Who is he?" Jayden asked.

"Kali."

Hearing this put me off balance and I leaned against the pillar in the middle of the floor.

"How do you know?" Jayden asked.

I was too angry to say anything else.

"I had somebody pick up some of his hair from the barbershop. I sent it in with our hair. Just to make sure."

"I want to be by myself." I said evenly. "Please leave."

"Madjesty, we can take another test to be sure," Jace offered.

He gave me one of them half smiles. The one I remembered Tisa giving me when I was little. He was a liar. Just like all of the other adults he was a liar and I wanted him the fuck up out my face.

"Please leave," I whispered. I wasn't trying to hurt anyone but I would if they didn't leave me alone.

"I got you and your sister." Jace continued. He took a step in my space. "You don't have to worry about shit."

"I'm not a fuckin' charity case!" I screamed. "YOU DON'T HAVE TO TAKE CARE OF ME!"

"Mad, when you comin' back downstairs?" Wokie asked coming out of the basement's door fixing his pants. Seeing everyone in the foyer he said, "Oh…I didn't know you had company."

"Go back downstairs, Wokie. I'm coming."

Wokie walked back downstairs and I said, "Please leave. Now. I need to be alone with my friends."

Knowing there was nothing else they could say to me, they left the mansion; And finally I breathed. I don't think I took too many breaths when they were there. Then I breathed again because I knew exactly what I was going to do. I had a plan.

When they were completely gone, I walked down the stairs with the weight of the world on my shoulders. My feet seemed to swell in my shoes again and I wondered if I had stolen the wrong size.

I couldn't believe it. I couldn't believe what they said. The fact that she was a whore, had caused me even more pain. Now I dreamed of how hard I was going to make life for moms over the next thirty days before I finally decided to take her life. It would be my single purpose.

"Put her on the chair and tape her down," I ordered.

Everyone jumped to take care of the chore, seeing the anger in my face. When it was done I stooped down in front of Harmony, grabbed a knife that was on the floor and slid the tip of the blade up and down her inner thigh. At first it shined against the light and hit the blacks of her eyes. The members of my gang remained silent.

"I found out who's my daddy today, mommy," I said angrily before adjusting the baseball cap on my head. "I guess the saying's true. Like father, like son." With that I dug the knife into the flesh of her leg. She tried to cry but her voice was muted.

Look at this dirty bitch, sitting on the chair with her legs all open waiting for somebody to fuck her. She probably like this shit. I wonder how she'd like it if I rammed it in and out of her pussy. Nasty slut. I couldn't remember all the times I saw different niggas running in and out of this pussy. This nasty pussy. Or all the times she told us to be quiet when we were in the backseat of some strange car, while she was fucking some nigga in the front seat. Yeah this bitch was going to pay. And she was going to pay with her life.

KALIVE MILLER
WASHINGTON, DC

Kali sat quietly in the passenger seat, with his right arm gripping in pain. He wasn't sure where he hurt himself because life for him in the days preceding moved so fast. All he knew was that it hurt so badly that it temporarily took him away from his thoughts of revenge and hate. He removed the hatchet in the leather case, which rested on his back and set it on the floor of the truck. His cousin Vaughn, who was driving, continued to move silently and cautiously down the Maryland streets. Surveillance was heavy because of the recent meeting Kali had with Jace. They invited beef into their lives and knew it was just a matter of time before things popped off.

"You aight, man?" Vaughn asked. He looked at him through his dark shades and then back at the road.

"Naw. I'm still fucked up with this nigga Jace."

"Cousin, why do you give a fuck about this dude? He ain't even blood."

"He was like blood." Kali said. "We were like family before shit started jumping off. You know this nigga actually had the nerve to ask me about that bitch Harmony again? Why is he so green over that slut?"

"I never liked him."

That wasn't the response Kali wanted but he brushed it off as his truth. If Jace didn't want the friendship back fuck it, but he was going to give him his fucking money. After all, Jace owed him. He said he'd kill the dude Massive and he did but he didn't get his payday. Yet part of him, the part that loved him like family, was hurt by the whole shit. His only reason for going off on his own was so that he could prove to him that he wasn't a loose cannon, and that he could come through when he needed him. Now, since Jace dissed him none of that seemed to matter anymore.

"Well I loved that dude like a brother." Kali said. "But if he gonna break the bond we had, then the shit's on him. I'ma find away to get at him, I just gotta think." Kali rubbed his sore arm again. "So where you tuck the money I got from Massive?"

"It's at my crib."

Kali frowned. "Which one nigga?"

"You know, the one out Maryland." Vaughn said. "I know it's gonna be good there. Plus I put it somewhere where it can't be found."

"You don't think that bitch gonna fuck with it do you? Because I started to take it to Harmony's crib but that chick liable to steal it from me. Forcing me to break her jaw."

"Again?"

They laughed. "Yeah. Again."

"I feel you, but don't worry, the dough good there. She ain't gonna fuck with your shit and risk me killing her ass. She a young girl, in college and shit. All she care about is them books. That's why I keep her around."

"Good." Kali looked off into the distance and saw a few corner boys making secretive hand-to-hand motions. He couldn't believe they were doing the shit out in the open. Taking a blunt from the glove compartment he fired it up. The smoke filled his lungs and at first seemed to choke him. He released the air and leaned further back into the seats. "But you said you know somebody we could cop from right?" Kali looked over at Vaughn and handed him the fire. "I'm really trying to start my own shit and I wanna move on Jace's blocks too."

"Yeah, I know this dude. And with the hit you did on Massive, you got more than enough cash to make things happen." He made a turn on Indian Head Highway. "What you want though?"

"The white. I ain't fucking with nothing else yet."

"Then he's your man."

One minute he wanted to be a dope boy, the next minute he wanted to be a hit man and then he wanted to be a king pin. He was all over the place and he knew he needed to make up his mind.

"Cool, so how much you think we should get?"

"Let's see what he saying first. I wouldn't want you to put all of your money out there if you don't have to."

He didn't sound too confident and this bothered Kali. "Aight, set that shit up."

"I'm on it. So you really want me to take you back to that spot?" Vaughn asked. "Because I'm not sure if it's a smart move."

"I ain't staying long. Plus I left some shit over there I got to get back. After that, I'm done with that bitch's crib."

• •

Concord Manor

Kali walked behind the large mansion quietly. He crept in through the back door that he knew was open because Harmony stayed drunk and would always lose her keys. He had his gun there and a few other things he hadn't taken with him when he originally left. He couldn't get ghost without them. Walking into the kitchen, he was surprised to see Madjesty standing in the middle of the floor looking at him.

The black jeans and black shirt she wore made her look smaller than she already was, and the navy blue baseball cap hid her eyes. She didn't seem scared by his presence, just curious.

"Fuck is up with you?" Kali asked going for the cabinet which held his gun. "And why you standing in the middle of the kitchen floor?"

"Last I heard this was my house."

He smirked. "Yeah well, whatever."

Then he moved for another cabinet, grabbed a glass and turned on the faucet. Placing the cup under the lukewarm water he filled it completely before swallowing all of its contents. His back was turned toward her but he could see her boyish reflection from the window.

"So, is it true?" Her voice was somewhat feminine, but her tone was a little masculine. Almost like a rebellious little boy who thought he knew everything.

"Is what true?"

"That you my father?"

Kali turned around and looked at her. He always had a feeling he was both of their fathers but Harmony was such a whore that he couldn't be sure. "I don't know. I mean, your moms said it could be me or the nigga Jace." Then he walked up to her. "But I'ma be real with you kid, your mother's a whore. When we was coming up she fucked half the niggas on the block. So you could be anybody's baby." He was about to go to the room he used upstairs to grab his shit when her words stopped him.

"Jace came by here the other night. He said you were my father. He said my mother fucked you and him at the same time, but for some reason, we got different daddies. I ain't never heard of nothing like that, but I wonder if you think it's true."

Kali stopped, turned and stared at her again. "How would he know that shit?"

"He said he got your hair from some barber shop you went to, and tested me and my sister. My sister is his daughter, and he said you my father."

She didn't sound so standoffish now. She looked at her tennis shoes and he glanced at them also. He could tell they were the wrong size by the position of her toes as she moved them.

"So he took my hair?"

"That's what he said."

Kali squinted. He wasn't the smartest man but to him nothing the girl-boy just said made any sense. "I don't believe it."

"I'm just telling you what he said." Then she came out of her shoes and held them in her hands. "Jace seems to be real ready to be my sister's father. He talks to her on a regular and everything. I'm wondering if we could. I mean...I'm wondering if we could be like that, too."

"What make you think I want that?"

"I'm asking." She frowned. "I mean, if you don't want it that's cool."

"You sure about that?"

"I ain't never have no father, and I wanna know how it is. I be beefing with my moms but that's cause of the shit she did to me. If I had a father, like somebody who really wanted to be in my life, maybe I wouldn't be so mad at the world you know?"

Kali heard all of that and the only thing he could focus on was Jace. "When he came over, did he come with a rack of niggas?"

His dismissal of her feelings stung. "Yeah. I think they were looking for you too."

He saw her about to walk away when he said, "I don't know what them peoples talking about, but even if you were my daughter I wouldn't want one. I got my own problems right now and dealing with a kid just don't fit into my plans."

Madjesty's head dropped. Out of both of the dads, she would get the one who wasn't worth shit. "Fuck you!" She yelled. "'Cause I ain't want a father no way." She stopped the tears from welling up in her eyes. "I was just telling you what the fuck them peoples told me." Then she walked off, her voice trailing behind her. "You can see yourself out."

Kali stood in the kitchen for a second thinking about what she said. He wanted a family, always had, but he didn't know if he wanted her. She wasn't the type of girl he could imagine calling 'Daddy's little girl'. Had it been Jayden it may have been another story. But Madjesty, well, she was all nigga and he wasn't feeling it one bit. For now he would focus on getting money.

Kali got the shit out of the house he wanted and was about to leave out the back door when he saw some nigga in all black in the bushes. When he turned to the other side he saw another nigga. He gripped his weapon, dipped back into the house, and dropped to the floor, fully ex-

pecting all of the windows to come crashing in on him. But after forty more seconds, nothing happened. Why weren't they shooting at him? If they wanted him, he was sure they had him outnumbered. They could've ambushed the house and sent the nigga to meet his maker. So what was stopping them?

When he raised his head he saw Mad standing over him in her white socks. "You still here?" She paused. "And why you on the floor?"

"Yeah...uh, I ain't gonna leave right now. Where your mother at?" He remained cowering down.

"She ain't here." She lied. "Why?"

"Well I'm chilling here for the night. You cool with that?"

"Whatever," Mad said walking away again.

On his hands and knees, he crawled toward the room he stayed in upstairs. He knew it was a mistake coming into the house, but now he didn't have a choice. Once in the room, he locked the door and put the dresser under the knob. His mind was racked trying to figure out how he would leave, and more importantly, why he was still alive.

Lying in the bed he cocked his gun and aimed at the door. Whoever came in was gonna get the business...and that went for anybody.

MAD

HOOD HOUSE PARTY

After that last drink things seemed to move in slow motion as my body fell against the wall. I'm glad it was there because falling on the floor would've been embarrassing.

I saw people, lots of them even though things were blurred and I couldn't make out their faces, I did see her face clearly. My girl, Glitter. I saw the way her body seemed to fill the jeans she was wearing as she shook her hips to Jay Z's voice booming from the speakers. I noticed the way a little sweat formed right above her small breasts in the red shirt she was wearing. And I saw how she flirtatiously moved her long tiny braids to the left, and leaned into the dude she was talking to at the moment. Who was that nigga?

Every now and again her eyes would find mine, but I wanted them to stay on me all night. Why wasn't she over here when we came together? My biggest fear was that she'd leave me and not want me no more. See my plan for us was simple, we would find a place of our own, and she would somehow have my kids, and make me a father. It's the only thing I thought about every day and the only thing I constantly looked forward to.

He touched her shoulder and she looked at me again. In a way that begged me not to 'start shit' like she constantly said I did. I gripped the bottle in my hand tightly, so tightly that at first I thought I'd smash it under my fingertips. I reached what my friends called the "drunk zone" a long time ago. It's funny; the Hennessy bottle had become an extension of me. An extension that for good, bad or worse, I needed almost every morning now.

"This party is like that!" Sugar said easing in front of me. Her arms in the air and her neck moving crazily from right to left. She was in the drunk zone too. Her ass grinded against my joint like she was making circles in the crouch of my jeans.

"You think it was cool to leave her in the house by herself?"

"I don't give a fuck. I needed a night out." I looked at Glitter again and wondered if she minded Sugar dancing with me.

"You the boss." She yelled, trying to be heard over the music.

I took a swig of Henny from the bottle, pulled my black cap down and tried not to look into the red glasses Sugar always wore. Looking at her too much gave her the wrong impression. My lips were dry so I licked them and the hairs from her curly dirty ponytail stuck to my mouth. I wanted her away from me. She stunk. Like sweat and pussy and I wasn't feeling it one bit.

"If that nigga don't want it, I damn sure do!" Wokie said grabbing her waist and easing her in front of him. She gave me a disappointed look but didn't stop dancing as she eased in front of him, besides, she offered that ass up and now it was for the taking.

"Mad, is so fucking pressed over Glitter!" she yelled over the music. "She acts like she the only one in the world."

Wow. And her breath smelled like rotten fish too. "Why is that?" I said swigging again from my bottle.

"Because you never dance with me. You never dance with nobody but Glitter."

She noticed a lot about me. More shit than I wanted her to notice. Anyway why was she angry? They called us Mad Max, because we were friends and we shared everything, including her pussy. Not me though. She ain't my type of girl, but every member in my crew with the exception of me and Glitter fucked Sugar. I liked a girl who was wifey material and who wanted a family as bad as I did. Not a girl who gave it up because it was there. Sugar is my homie but for me that's as far as it goes.

Now the party was starting to get crowded and my neck was getting too heavy. That's how I'd always know I was officially in the drunk zone. Taking another swig when I looked across the room again, I saw the dude whispering in her ear. What the fuck? I told her to put a bra on because every time she rubbed up against something or somebody, her nipples got hard. I know this nigga wanna fuck her. All niggas wanna fuck my girl and it don't matter that she only fourteen either.

I was just about to step to them both when Kid Lightning stopped me. He looked at the bottle in my hand, then at Glitter and back at me. He said, "Give me some, fam."

He tried to take it out of my hands but I held on to it tightly. "Naw, it ain't that much left."

"Look like it's enough for me." He looked at the bottle and then back at Glitter across the room again. "I don't want nothing but a sip."

"And I said no." I looked into his eyes so he knew I was serious.

I figured he thought I was drunk. I was off the Henny and he knew once I finished an entire bottle, there was nothing I wouldn't do or nobody I couldn't be.

The music was pumping loud as shit but my anger was boiling over. Fuck this nigga. I'm about to turn this bottle right side up and hit this mothafucka in the head. I pushed myself off the wall and moved in their direction.

"What you doing, Mad?" Kid said grabbing me by the arm. "It ain't even like that? You know it's…"

I couldn't understand him. Shit was swirling around in my head.

"I don't want no nigga touching her!"

"She a girl, Mad. Niggas gonna try and holla. You know that. She…"

"I should bust her shit open. Matta fact…"

I moved to talk to Glitter but Kid kept the grip on me until I gave him a slow stare from his Jordans to the top of his head. I was about to crash this bottle in his face and get his own blood all over the new Hugo Boss shirt he just stole yesterday when he decided to release me.

"Aight, man. You on your own." He raised both of his hands and stepped off.

"Man, why niggas wanna fuck with my girl?" I said to myself.

"Cuz Glitter bad as shit." Krazy K said out of nowhere. I didn't even know he was near me.

The girls liked him because he had big ass feet and had a permanent scowl on his face. They figured the bigger the feet the bigger the dick but I couldn't call it. Out of all of Mad Max they were afraid of Krazy the most. The funny part about it was, out of all of us, he was the nicest. "You knew that when you bagged her."

I took another swig. "Where Wokie at?" I asked. Wokie was the most outspoken of my crew and I fucked with him tough. With Wokie what you saw was what you got and I trusted him with my life. "He was just dancing with Sugar."

"Fucking some bitch." He said. "But kill that bullshit wit' Glitter. We having a good time tonight. I ain't trying to start no beef if we ain't got to."

"Who the leader of this crew?" I asked Krazy. He didn't say anything he just backed away from me. "Anyway I'm not about to sweat no bitch. If she wanna be over there let her stay."

I looked back at Glitter and the dude and he looked like he was like twenty something. I could take him. I ain't never fought one on one in my life but I could take him. I knew it.

"Man fuck this. I'm stepping to." I said.

I felt hands on me pulling me back, I think it was my friends but I couldn't be sure. Anyway it wasn't working because in seconds I was in Glitter's face.

"Hey, baby. What you doing?" Glitter's eyes looked at me in a pleading way. And she held my hand. "This is my…"

"Why you dancing all on this nigga like that?" I looked deep into her big brown eyes. She can't leave me. She gonna leave me. I know she gonna leave me. I'ma kill her first. I'ma kill the dude first. How 'bout I kill both of 'em. "Fuck wrong with you, disrespecting me like that, Glitter?"

"Baby," she said softly. I was surprised I could hear her so clearly over the music. "What you doing? It ain't like that. Please stop."

"Fuck that shit!" I said grabbing her by the back of her hair. "You don't fucking carry me like that and expect me not to say shit. You coming with me."

I pulled her when he snatched her away from me and pushed me. Then I don't know what happened but I was flat on my back.

"Bitch, I will break your fucking jaw!" He balled up both fists and looked down at me.

When he did that all I saw was that Mad Max had come out of all directions of the party. I stood up and smiled when I saw the power of my crew. Krazy knocked the nigga down with a right and Kid stomped him in the stomach repeatedly as he coughed up blood. Sugar found a beer bottle and cracked him on the head and when she was done she kicked him anywhere her feet would land. I got down and stole him several times in the face and Wokie eventually got some of the action too. Before we knew it a full fight erupted and we were hitting anybody who looked like they were trying to get in our way. This is how shit always ended up for us, in a fight. Sometimes we got hurt sometimes we didn't but we always stuck together.

When the party went into "mob mode" we knew it was time to bail before the police got there and locked all of us up. We heard stories of Juvie and wasn't trying to get caught up there.

"Let's roll!" Wokie said grabbing me. He was laughing so hard he was holding his stomach with the other hand. "We set shit off so let's leave 'em to it."

"Come on ya'll!" I said snatching Glitter by her hand. At first she snatched away from me but I gripped it again and yoked her harder toward the door. If she played with me I would fuck her up out here. "Where's Krazy?" I asked.

"I'm right here!" He said coming behind us.

When we made it outside we could see from the windows in the house that the fight was in full mode. I loved when shit kicked off because of me. I was sweating and my tennis shoes seemed tighter than ever on my feet.

Once I got outside the night air was cool and put me at peace. At ease. I never got a chance to go out and be with friends or anybody when I was living in Texas with Harmony. Life was all about her and it was like we were never in it. So when I got the chance to do what I wanted these days I took it. At night I loved that you could be whatever you wanted. I believe in the right places you could be God or the devil. It was your choice.

"Man, this was a nice ass neighborhood before ya'll fucked it up!" Sugar said. "That's why I hate going places with ya'll."

"Stop playing," I said. "Bitch, you love us." I pulled her toward me and put my arm around her neck as we continued to walk down the block.

"Move, boy!" I loved it when she called me that. *Boy*. It was funny though, she only told me to move when Glitter was around and that's the only time I felt comfortable around her. "And give me some of that Henny." I thought about how her breath stunk a little back at the party and poured it down her throat myself so her lips wouldn't touch the bottle. She wiped the drops off of her face with the back of her hand and gave me that look again like she wanted to fuck me. Then she whispered, "Give me a chance. Fuck Glitter. I'll obey anything you say."

I took my arm from around her neck and put space in between us. As the days went by it was getting more obvious that friendship wasn't enough for her.

"Nigga, you crazy as shit!" Wokie said to me patting me on my back. "Why you always starting fights and shit?"

"It ain't me. And where was your ass anyway before everything happened, nigga?"

He put his fingers under my nose and I could smell a fishy odor and I hit his hand. "Fuck is that?" I frowned.

"Pussy! You just smelled some good ass pussy!"

I looked at Sugar and she said, "Don't look at me."

But it was her, I knew it. "Naw it was somebody else back there." Wokie lied. "A bitch I told I would meet down there."

"Yeah, whatever, nigga!" Kid said. "Your dick gonna fall off if you keep fucking with all of them hoes!"

We heard some screams back at the house. Apparently the fight had gotten wilder than ever and Krazy said, "Nigga, Glitter got you open?" He laughed. "Whoever own that house gonna be mad as shit when they come home and they got you to thank."

We were all laughing and having a good time except Glitter.

I put my arm around Glitter and said, "If she stop fucking with my head shit like that wouldn't happen." Then I lifted the bottle to pour some down her throat. "You want some?"

She pushed my hand away. "Baby, you gotta stop doing this shit." She was serious. "It wasn't even like that."

"So what, you mad?" I frowned.

"Yes! You playing yourself and me too!" She paused.

"I'm a dude, too, Glitter. I know how niggas think and I'm not gonna let them take you from me."

"You not a fucking dude!" She screamed. "Why do you keep saying that shit?"

I could feel my hair tighten and I pulled my cap down. When I looked at my friends they seemed to look elsewhere but Glitter's eyes remained on me. The embarrassment I felt by her lies was overwhelming.

I swigged from my bottle. "I don't like people touching you. I told you that."

"But you were wrong, tonight, Mad. You gotta stop drinking like that or I'm not gonna fuck with you no more. I'm serious. If you wanna lose me then that shit back there..." she pointed, "Yeah that's the way to do it."

"Glitter, don't talk to me like you crazy." I said.

"When you get drunk or high you act stupid. That's why my moms don't like me fucking with you."

Knowing her family didn't like me made me feel sick because she was close to her moms. "You act like you ain't the one who be bringing us the smoke and liquor. You just as guilty as me."

"But you go too far, Mad. You gotta push back sometimes." She paused, kicked a stone off the sidewalk and it flew into the street. "It's alright to get buzzed but not to where we gotta fight all the time."

"Whatever, bitch, you know niggas stay trying to fuck you." Sugar interrupted. "Mad be tired of that shit. I mean, show some respect."

"Sugar, shut the fuck up!" Glitter said. "You always jumping on Mad's side."

"Did you see when I banked the nigga?!" Krazy said jumping in front of me and Glitter as he walked backwards. "His eyes were all wide and shit." He imitated the look of the nigga we put on the ground. "He looked like he was about to shit on himself when he saw all of us." He laughed.

We all laughed. I fucked with my friends, tough. With them I felt like I could do anything. The only thing missing in my life right now was my sister and the love of a mother and father. I was starting to believe that the way my life was going, it wasn't in the cards for me. That's why

I held on to Glitter so much, if she left me, if she stopped fucking with me, I would wanna die.

"How we gonna get home?" Wokie asked. "'Cause I'm tired as shit."

"Stop playing," Kid said. "You know how we do."

"Well there's too many of us this time. We gonna have to catch two separate cabs." Sugar said. "And I'm in the cab with Mad because ya'll be faking when its time to dip." She laughed. "Mad, the last time we was about to jump out the cab and run why these niggas get scared and pay?"

"Stop lying, bitch!" Kid said. "I was ready to run but Wokie said his mother worked around there somewhere and he ain't wanna get in trouble."

"Nigga, I'm not trying to hear all that. Ya'll too scary." Sugar continued. "Like I said, I'm rolling with Mad and Glitter."

"You wanted to roll with Mad and Glitter anyway." Wokie said. "But I'm coming with ya'll too."

"Aight, but let me rap to my girl right quick before we flag the cabs down. Ya'll walk ahead of us."

When they went ahead, I looked at Glitter. She was so fucking pretty. She had the biggest brown eyes I'd ever seen in my life and her skin was the color of milk chocolate.

I didn't know how to fuck before I got with Glitter. I mean, my mother tried to teach me how to suck a dick with a carrot that one time but I wasn't having none of that shit. Just the thought of a man touching me, anywhere and in any way made my skin crawl. I would rather kill myself then to even go there.

Before Glitter, I didn't even know what pussy tasted like. Now that I had her, we fucked in every way imaginable. Even stole one of them dildoes we saw in a store one time so I could fuck her with it every now and again with my hand. She liked for me to eat her pussy while I fucked her with it. Truthfully I ain't like to do it, thinking if she wanted the rubber dick, what was stopping her from getting the real thing? Yeah, the dildo was Glitter's thing not mine and she never even put her hands or mouth on my joint because I would die if she touched me there. I can't explain it but I would die. I got mine off by rubbing on top of her and she could never understand how I always came. I couldn't understand either.

"You not gonna leave me are you?" I asked her. "'Cause I can't lose you, Glitter."

"Babes, why you always thinking somebody gonna leave you?" She asked looking at me. "You ask me five times a day seven days a week and each time I say the same thing. No." Then she paused. "But, if you don't stop the crazy shit I will."

"That don't make sense to me."

"How come?"

"I mean…I never had real love, but I figured it would be different…unconditional."

"I don't understand?"

"Like, if you love a person, you gonna love them how they are." I paused. "And yeah I like to drink, but this me. What happened to taking me the way that I am?"

"But you also change for people you love. Are you willing to do that for me?"

We stopped walking and looked at our friends who were now jumping on people's cars causing their alarms to go off. If they were caught, we were far enough behind them to go our separate ways and get the fuck out of dodge.

"All I know is I gotta have you. I want a life with you." Then I touched her stomach. "I want you to have my baby."

She pushed my hand away. "Mad, lets just enjoy our time right now. When you get so serious it makes me nervous. Keep it light."

She was gonna leave me I just knew it.

"Now give me some of that shit." She said talking about the bottle of Henny in my hand.

"Now that's my bitch."

"Whateva, nigga."

I poured the Henny down her throat and kissed her. She spit the liquor back in my mouth and our tongues fucked. My joint was throbbing like shit and I wanted to jump on top of her until I came.

"We got a cab!" Krazy yelled three blocks up the street. "There's another one behind it! Wokie holding it for you! Let's roll!"

• •

The Next Morning

When I woke up I was on my back outside and felt a dog licking my hand. At first I thought I was tripping until it lifted its leg and pissed in my face.

"Get the fuck away from me?!" I yelled backing away from the dog. It ran away and I leaned up against a dumpster. After wiping the urine off of me with a newspaper on the ground, I spit five or six times trying to get the taste out of my mouth. This shit was Déjà vu.

My head throbbed viciously and I knew once again last night must've gotten out of control. That was the only fucked up part about me.

When I drank, I drank real hard and would often lose time and not remember what I'd done the night before.

Eventually standing up, every bone in my body ached. It felt like I fought five or six niggas and I couldn't remember shit. For real the last thing I recalled was that we jumped in a cab after the party and that's pretty much it.

Reaching in my pocket for my cell phone I called all of my homies to find out where they were. When I couldn't get a hold of them, I walked down the block trying to find out where I was. There were a lot of stores in the area and I knew I was definitely in the hood. Somewhere on the Southside in DC.

"Hey, cutie!" Some girl called out to me. "You fine as shit. You got a girl?"

When I turned around I saw a washed up looking older woman in a long blue dress with big yellow flowers on it. Her teeth were missing and her mouth seemed to be mostly jaw.

"Naw. I'm good." I told her. "Thanks anyway though."

"As pretty as you are you must got somebody at home, huh?" She continued. "Is that it?" She asked. "That's why you don't want this pussy?"

When she called me pretty it dawned on me that my hat was missing. I never went anywhere without my hat because I hated being referred to as a female. Yeah I know what the doctor told me I was some months back, but in my mind, that wasn't the case. I was then and would always be a nigga.

"So you not going to talk to me?" She continued.

I ignored her. When I spotted a cab I decided to do what I did best. So I hopped into it without any money.

"Where to?" the black driver asked me suspiciously. He must've already known what I was up to.

I gave him an address not too far from my house when my phone rang. It was Wokie and I quickly answered.

"Where are you nigga?" He said. "We were looking all over for you."

"I'm in a cab." I said rubbing my head, still smelling the piss of the dog on my skin. "Why ya'll leave me and shit?" Then I paused. "Aye, yo, turn that air conditioning down some." I said to the driver. He rolled his eyes but he did it.

"Nigga, you don't remember last night?" Wokie continued.

I hated that question because it always meant they knew something I didn't. And if we were all together, they'd spend the next two hours laughing and telling me the story in different versions.

"Naw...I don't remember shit. So give it to me straight."

"First we go to the party right..."

"I remember the party." I said trying to prove I wasn't that far off.

"Well you remember getting mad because Glitter was talking to her cousin on the dance floor?"

"Her cousin?" I remembered her on the dance floor, but I didn't remember it being her cousin. Then again I didn't know what her cousin looked like. "Fuck is you talking about? She was dancing with some dude."

"My nigga, I'm telling you it was her cousin." He paused. "Anyway, you step to this dude and he drops you."

"He hit me in my face?"

"Yeah! That's when me and the crew banked this nigga on the floor! I'm telling you that shit was wild."

"Go 'head." *Damn! I played myself again.*

"Anyway, so after we caused a major fight at the party, we all went outside and hopped into a cab. We went to this restaurant and you and Glitter got into it there."

"Why?"

"Some nigga was trying to give her his number and you flipped. Even after she said she didn't want the nigga's number and told him to his face."

"I...I can't remember none of that shit."

"I know." He said. "Anyway, the dude starts busting off in the restaurant and we got out of there. I think somebody got shot and everything. We thought you were behind us but you went the other way. And we lost you."

"Fuck! Did anybody in Mad Max get hit?"

"Naw." He paused. "But Glitter had another seizure when we made it to my house. It was real bad too."

"Is she okay?!!!"

"Yeah, man. She's fine."

I was relieved. Glitter had seizures on a pretty frequent basis and sometimes it would happen out of nowhere. I always worried about her because she looked to be in so much pain when it would happen.

"I'm glad she's good, man. Damn!"

"Yeah she's fine." Wokie continued. "But she said she's tired of your shit. And that if I spoke to you to tell you it was over."

My heart dropped. "She said...she said like it's over for real? Or like, if I called her shit would be cool?"

"Sounds serious to me, homie."

"Like really serious?"

"I don't know how serious it gotta be for you, but she sounded like she was done."

When I got off the phone with him I knew I had to beg Glitter to take me back. Even if I had to stop fucking with the Henny I was willing to do that. Unlike some people I could stop drinking anytime I wanted.

Really.

To be with her, it wasn't even a problem.

It was me and her against the world and I had to prove it.

MAD
WILD COLORS

The bus sounded like it would break from the inside as it maneu-vered down the street. No matter how slow he drove it creaked and moaned. My book bag sat in the available seat next to me to prevent any-body strange from sitting too close. Bus rides always made me uncom-fortable because I hated people and hated the way their judgmental eyes moved over me. Was I a boy or girl I'd hear them say, and I'd just pull my hat down lower. It was none of their fucking business. This was the main reason I preferred jumping out of cabs, I loved my privacy, but to-night I needed my energy to beg my girl back.

Five minutes into the ride toward Glitter's house, a drunk wearing a dirty black coat with his toes hanging out of his brown shoes got on the bus.

"Can I sit here?" He said to me. The nigga wobbled and could barely stand up.

I ignored him.

"Scuse me. Can I sit down please?" His spit plopped on my lip and I wiped it off. Now I'm mad.

"We can't move the bus until everyone is seated!" The bus driver yelled looking at me through the big rear view mirror.

"I'm saying, can you please move your book bag, boy?!" A ghetto bitch asked that sat across from me. "I'm tryin' to see my boo! I'm just saying!"

I moved by book bag and he sat next to me. The bus started rolling again. The drunk smelled of alcohol and I thought about drinking the new bottle of Henny I had in my book bag. But ever since Glitter broke up with me, who I hadn't spoken to in two days, I ain't fuck with it.

"Where you going?" He asked trying to spark conversation.

I turned my head the other way and ignored him again.

"What...you don't talk or something?" I could see his spit crystals falling on my jeans and I wanted to scream. He was so close to me now, I could smell everything nasty about his body.

I still wouldn't speak. Instead I focused on the bus driver's dark ashy hands on the large black steering wheel hoping he'd speak to somebody else.

"Well fuck it then!" He yelled, before he burped what smelled like vomit.

Getting nothing from me, he turned around to speak to someone else and she straight out told his ass, "Get the fuck out of my face, drunk! I ain't got time for that shit! I'm going to work!"

I laughed to myself. He was mostly quiet after that. Then I tried to call my girl again but Glitter meant what she said and didn't except my calls. Why? I mean, we beefed before but she always took me back so what made this time different?

When my phone rang I saw a strange number and quickly answered. "Hello? Glitter?"

"No!" she giggled. "It's me, Rocket."

"Rocket?" I knew who she was but how did she get my number?

"Yes. You forgot me already?"

Silence.

"I knew you were drunk when you called me the other day." She laughed again. "So how you doing?"

I leaned up and looked out the large bus windows to be sure I didn't miss my stop. I wasn't close so I leaned back in my seat and said, "Nothing. On the bus."

"So were you serious?"

"Serious about what?"

"What you said to me. When you called."

It was official. I entered the drunk zone and called a girl I hadn't seen in months and now I was about to look stupid. And then it wasn't just any girl. It was a girl I liked a lot at school a few months back in Texas. A girl who always smelled pretty but looked prettier. A girl who's hair was so shiny black and long it didn't look real, except I'd seen her scalp when she ran her hands through it. And a girl who witnessed the day I found out I wasn't a boy, because I got my period and bled all over myself in class.

I was not about to embarrass myself again so I said, "Yeah. I'm dead ass."

"Okay. Well here's the number. You got a pen?"

"Uh…yeah…go 'head." I said grabbing a pen in my bag to write the number on the back of my bus transfer. She read off the number and I wrote every digit.

"Okay, they sell rooms for cheap in Texas like I was telling you and they don't care how old you are. These people got like ten houses and

they keep them for runaways, who are abused and stuff like that. Not saying you are but you may need the help. They're real nice." She paused.
"My cousin Sammy is sixteen and he got one already. The room is so big
and pretty, Madjesty. You'll love 'em!" She sounded so excited. "I'm
sure of it. You just gotta find your way back here. When you're ready."

"Thank you." I couldn't believe I told this girl I wanted to move during one of my drunken escapades. "I appreciate it." I folded the number
and put it in my bag.

"No problem."

"Hey, Rocket. Do you still mess with, Baisley? The football player?"

"Yeah...kinda, but I still think about you. That's why I was happy
when you called."

Since I didn't have anything to lose I said, "Even with knowing that
I'm a...that people are saying that I'm...that..."

"Yes...even with you being a girl."

She gave me all that and my only response was, "Cool." I sounded so
fucking stupid but I wasn't expecting this call. I wasn't prepared.

"I gotta go, Madjesty. But look...try being more forceful with your
girlfriend. Girls like that sometimes."

"Huh?"

"You said your girl playing you soft. Try being more forceful, she'll
respect that more than anything you do that's nice. At least I do." She
paused. "Well...I gotta run. Hit me if or when you move back to Texas.
Maybe we can hook up and catch a movie or something."

When she hung up I thought about her. A lot. And I thought about
our conversation. She sounded so cool and I was angry I couldn't remember speaking to her the other day on the phone. What else did we
talk about? I knew I had her number, I kept it with me everywhere I
went. But I also thought I would never call her because the way I left
school was a way I wanted to forget.

My heart thumped in my chest when I saw the bus approaching the
building Glitter lived in. Pulling the cord to ring the bell, I got off with
plans to win her back. I borrowed twenty dollars earlier from Wokie to
take her to her favorite restaurant, *Fridays* if things went good between
us. I wanted things to go good.

Before going in, I looked at the small red brick building in a southeast DC project. It looked kinda out of the ordinary because although all
of the other buildings were run down and flooded with trash, her building
had colorful flowers in front of it and the grass was the color of a green
crayon. I didn't see her mother's car out front and I was happy about that
because for whatever reason, she didn't like me. But I did see her ex-
boyfriend's brother car. His name was Nook. I spotted it anywhere be-

cause it was an older model Ford with rims. Nook went to school with us and Mad Max was real cool with him. I was cordial but I never really liked him because I always felt like his brother had an ulterior motive, to tell her ex-boyfriend what we were doing together, and to take her away from me. But I never let them know my real feelings because everybody went on about how cool Nook was. Now, here his car was, sitting in her parking lot.

I stole one last look at it before going inside of her building. I could smell food being cooked and that the hallway was recently cleaned with Pine Sol. Looking up at her door which was on the second floor, I saw Nook running out of her apartment with his head down. His keys jingled in his hand and he bumped into me knocking me back a step. He was definitely in a hurry.

"My bad, man" he said passing me, before rushing out of the door.

I looked at him as he disappeared. He didn't know who I was. Didn't even look at my face. I walked up to her door.

Standing in front of her door I took two breaths before I finally knocked. Some kid my age opened the door and he seemed irritated. Not irritated like I was bothering him, but irritated that he couldn't finish something.

"Yeah?" He asked eating a hot dog. Mustard from it dripped on his plain brown t-shirt and silver chain. "What you want?"

"Glitter here?"

"She on her way back." He opened the door wide. "Come in."

I walked into her apartment and looked around. It was my first time inside. The door closed behind me and I locked it. The apartment was neat in a boring kind of way and didn't have much life. As pretty as Glitter was, I'd think it would be a bit spicier and sexier. But this wasn't her place it was her mother's so I guess it made sense. The large screen TV on the floor seemed too loud and it smelled like someone had recently boiled a lot of eggs. When I looked at the table in the dining room I saw a yellow bowl of eggs and figured somebody was about to make egg salad or something.

"Sit down." He said.

I sat on the cloth brown sofa, and he sat next to me and grabbed a game remote. He looked neat enough and had an average face. But his eyes looked older than he probably was and he kept examining me.

He picked up the other game remote and said, "You play, man?"

"Naw."

"Damn! Why you don't play?"

"Where's Glitter?" I said looking him over. I didn't see a resemblance. Was this her brother? "I came to see her."

"She not here." He sat the extra remote down and played some fight game by himself. Why was the TV so loud? I wished he'd turn it down some. "So you really don't want to play? Most dudes that come here for Glitter wanna play."

"A lot of dudes come here for her?"

He laughed. "A rack of niggas. My sister has a lot of fans."

"So...so that dude that came out of here is a fan?" Please God don't let her be fucking Nook too.

"You wanna play with me? I'll let you beat if you play with me."

Before I could answer her mother walked into the house. She had gotten fatter than she did the last time I saw her although not real big. Shades covered her eyes and I was surprised that she didn't even look in our direction. It's like she knew where he would be sitting so she preoccupied herself with the purse in her left hand and her plastic bag in the right.

"Good, you boiled my eggs!" She put her purse on the table next to the door and I could see a money envelope filled with cash inside. She walked the bag into the kitchen. "I sure thought I would have to beat your ass for not listening to me. Did Nook bring my weed?"

"Ma!" He said. "We got company."

I was surprised that this was her brother. I didn't know she had a brother. But I knew she had a mother. And I knew she ain't like me.

She walked out of the kitchen and shot an evil glare in my direction. "What are you doing in my house, girl?"

"Girl?" he said. "This a girl?" Suddenly the game wasn't so important because he stared at me as if I was from another planet.

"Go to your room, Jerrod." She turned the TV off.

Thank you! I was about to go deaf.

"But I was playing..."

"Go to your room!" He didn't move. "Now!"

Jerrod threw the remote on the table and stomped to the back of the apartment. Then he slammed the door so hard, the remote hit the floor.

"When I finish with her I'ma come in there and bust you in the mouth. I'm sick of your shit!" She yelled to the back. "Ain't been back but two days from that group home and already you acting crazy!" She continued looking at me.

I wondered was she talking to me and if I was supposed to respond. Now I was alone with an adult. I hated adults because every one I'd ever met, always did me wrong.

When she finished yelling at him, she dug in her purse, pulled out a cigarette and stood in front of me. When she lit the cigarette she inhaled then blew grey smoke into my face. I coughed.

"What are you doing in my house?" She took her shades off and sat them down on the table in front of me. Her fingers seemed to cross over the cigarette like a pair of legs. "I heard about what ya'll did to my nephew at that party. Had him in the hospital for two days."

"It wasn't me." I said clearing my throat before standing up. "But I'll leave."

She moved for the kitchen and brought out a knife.

"Sit the fuck down!" She said pointing the blade in my direction. I did. "Now I said, what are you doing in my house?" She smashed the cigarette into the ash trey on the floor. There were about ten half smoked cigarettes in the ashtray. I've seen it before with Ramsey, she must've been trying to quit.

"I came to see Glitter. But I can leave. It's not a problem."

"What are you, some fucking dyke or something?" She looked at my shoes and then my eyes, which were the only things she could see because my cap was so low on my head. "Well are you?"

"No." I whispered. "I'm not like that."

"Then what are you?"

"I'm...I'm...like a..."

"Are you a girl or not?"

"Yes."

"So you're a dyke."

"It's a long story." I looked at the knife and the way she held it. She'd pulled knives on people before I was sure of it.

"You like to kiss girls and shit don't you?"

"I don't like to kiss them...I just like your daughter."

She sat on the sofa next to me. Then she looked at me in a way that threw me off. In a way that Glitter looked at me when things were good between us. In a way that let me know she wanted to fuck. Biting down on her bottom lip she put her hand on my knee and rubbed it softly.

"Mam, I'm gonna leave now, okay?"

"Take your hat off in my house."

"But I'm gonna leave...can you tell..."

"TAKE...OFF...YOUR...HAT." Her words were slow but serious. I took my hat off and placed it on the knee she wasn't molesting.

"Now..." she paused, "How do you kiss my daughter?"

"I don't understand what you mean?"

"How do you kiss her?"

"On the lips." I pointed at mine. Not sure why I pointed I just did. "Or wherever she wants me to."

"Wherever she wants you to, huh?"

"Yes." I nodded.

"Show me."

"Show you what?"

She sat the knife down in her lap and it made me a little more relieved. Then she massaged my knee harder. "I said show me how you kiss my daughter."

This was so weird that I didn't know what to do. Like…was she actually asking me to kiss her? She must have some camera in here and was going to use it against me. I couldn't risk losing Glitter plus I didn't want to kiss her. Although her eyes were like my girl's her actions reminded me of my mother.

"I don't think its right…"

"If you wanna date my daughter than you'll kiss me."

"Really?"

"Yes. I like you. I just need to know you're good for her. That's why I be so mad at you sometimes, because I'm not sure where you're coming from. What your intentions are. So kiss me. Like you kiss her. And I promise everything will be cool."

Thinking she would leave us alone, so we could really be together, I moved in for a kiss. I could smell cigarettes on her breath but there was nothing I could do. I'd already moved in and our lips connected. When her lips touched mine she pushed her tongue into my mouth like a snake and grabbed the back of my head. The tip of the knife touched my knee and I was afraid it would accidently stab me. But she was breathing so hard and so heavy, I was afraid to stop her too. The kiss lasted for a minute, maybe longer. It was so long my neck started hurting and felt stiff. Her body trembled like she was getting something out of it. Like this was really what she needed. And then she started panting heavily. Like real heavy. Like she'd just finish cumming. I think she did. I think she did cum.

When she was done, she opened her eyes, smiled and backed away from me. I awkwardly smiled back but then she frowned. The next thing I knew she slapped me. So hard that when she removed her hand I saw my mother. Not my real mother…but a flash of her.

"You dirty, dyke bitch! Kissing me and shit!" She yelled backing away from me. "Why would you do that?"

"You…you asked me."

"Get out of my house!" Then she grabbed the knife and in a stabbing motion moved for me. I jumped up and grabbed my book bag and hat right before the blade entered my leg. She ran behind me as I rushed for the door but she didn't catch me. She couldn't catch me. I was gone and I was still alive.

I kept running until I entered the parking lot. I thought she would come behind me but she didn't. When I was a few feet from her house I got mad. Why would she ask me to do that and then try to stab me? What would she tell Glitter? I knew after that she would flip the story around and I would never get her back now.

Going into the building over from Glitter's I went into the basement and sat on top of a washing machine. Then I opened my book bag and pulled out my Henny.

Right before I did anything my phone rang. I took it out of my pocket and saw it was Jayden. For whatever reason I decided to answer.

"Hello." She paused. "Madjesty?"

"What do you want? And how did you get my number?"

"You gave me your number remember? When I called you a few days back." She paused. "You sounded drunk but you said I could call you. Mainly for emergencies you said." Apparently that was my new shit, calling niggas when I was drunk.

"So what's the emergency?"

"I miss you. Can we talk? Please?"

"No. You got your new family. Just be with him."

"Madjesty, please."

"I gotta go. Bye."

I hung up on her, put the phone in my pocket and examined the bottle in my hand again. I wanted a drink now more than ever.

"I'm not going to do this." I looked at the label and how cool it felt in my hand. "I'm stronger than this." I looked at the bottle again. I love the way it was shaped. "Just a taste…I'll do just a taste…"

I twisted the cap and poured it down my throat and replayed what just happened over and over again. I couldn't believe what I'd just went through. I drank some more and before I knew it half of the bottle was gone. I felt warm all over. I felt good. I felt better.

So I went back to her building and knocked on her door. Glitter's mom opened it and frowned.

"You must wanna die?" She was still holding the knife.

She was crazy but so was I. "Shut the fuck up, bitch."

"What did you just say to me?"

"I said shut the fuck up."

She didn't look so bold anymore but she was still frowning. "What are you doing here? Huh?"

"Where your room at?"

She wasn't frowning anymore. "Back there." She pointed.

I walked in. She didn't follow me at first. "You coming or what?"

Once I was in her room I saw a rolled up blunt on the table and lit it with a lighter next to it. She walked in behind me and closed the door.

"Sit down." I said.

"What do you want?"

"Bitch, sit the fuck down!"

She did.

I revenge fucked this old bitch with all I had. I put everything in her pussy from the remote control on her nightstand to ballpoint pen. She was going crazy and couldn't help but call my name.

"Fuck me, Mad! Fuck me." She reminded me of my mother and I knew what she wanted.

I don't know what came over me. I wasn't even feeling this whore. I was just high off the Henny and mad at the world. When she came and fell asleep, I went through her purse and stole her money. Then I stole the weed.

Once I left, I took a bottle of spray paint out of my book bag and looked for her car in the parking lot. When I found it I sprayed the word dyke on the hood and the driver's side door. In red. Stepping back I looked at my work and laughed. I guess it's really gonna be over now. After Glitter sees this shit and finds out I fucked her mother she'll have nothing to do with me. Maybe it was the liquor, but for now, for some reason, I just didn't give a fuck.

HARMONY PHILLIPS
FORT WASHINGTON, MARYLAND

I sat in a metal gray chair for days, and I was tortured just like that bitch of a daughter of mines promised. To make shit worse, on a regular basis pain shot up from my ass and through my back in ways you couldn't imagine. She really didn't care about what she was doing to me. Even though I gave birth to her and carried her for nine months before Kali snatched her out of my womb, she still didn't care about what she was doing to me! I couldn't believe what she was putting me through just because she couldn't have her way!

She didn't know it, but I could hear her conversations upstairs and I was taking mental notes about everything they were saying. I knew names and that they all went to the same school. Daughter or not I had plans when I got out of here, if I got out of here, to prosecute this whore to the fullest extent of the law. *My* law.

I was just about to piss in the chair because they never let me go to the bathroom unless I had number two, when Madjesty came walking down the stairs talking on the phone. She had a silver mixing bowl in her free hand that was covered with a yellow towel and every time I saw her, I couldn't get over how much she looked like a cute boy. In my mind she was a boy even though when I changed her diapers I saw the split tail running from the front to the back of her ass. I know if I had a boy, if I had the sons I always wanted, none of this shit would have ever happened to me.

"Wokie, bring me some smoke when you come?" She said trotting down the steps frowning on the phone.

When she finished her call she walked up to me with a sly smile on her face. Setting the bowl down she pulled up a chair so that she was directly across from me. I think she got off on what she was doing to me, in fact I'm sure of it.

"Hey, ma." I couldn't speak because my mouth was taped so she snatched the duct tape off my lips. "I said, hey, ma."

My lips burned and I ran my tongue over them. "Baby, when are you going to let me go? This has gone on far too long. You know I love you,

-74-

and you know I never meant to hurt you. Please, baby. Let me go and I promise I won't say anything to anybody about this. You gotta trust me."

"I'm going to let you go after I kill you." She laughed. "Unless you want me to do it now."

I put my head down, it was useless talking to her sometimes and I knew it. "I know you don't mean to do this to me, honey. And it's okay that you did what you did. But it's not too late to make things…"

"I mean everything I'm doing to you, Harmony." I could smell the alcohol on her breath. "So if you think I feel guilty 'bout any of this shit, you betta think again." She interrupted me.

"Was I that bad of a mother that you would…"

SLAP! SLAP! SLAP!

She hit me three times in the face, sat back in the chair and smiled. "I deserved that. I should never have…"

This time she hit me in my stomach so hard, I pissed in the chair. Urine ran down my legs and onto the floor.

"You wanna say something else?"

I shook my head no.

"I hate you. I hate you for what you did to me when I was a kid. And I hate you even more now. You don't even feel sorry for the shit you did to me do you? You don't even know what it was like bein' fucked with at school everyday do you? You don't know how it feels to be a girl when your mind tells you that you're a boy."

I was afraid to answer. Afraid that if I said the wrong thing, she'd hit me again. Sensing my fear she laughed hysterically and in that moment, she reminded me of her father, Kali. Suddenly I could see the family resemblance because it was obvious that they both were crazy.

After I learned that I gave birth to twins, by two different men at the same time, my mind was wrecked. I mean, how was that even possible? Truthfully I don't believe shit Jace says until I read the results myself.

"You hear me talking to you, bitch?" Mad said looking for a reason to hurt me again. "You not gonna answer me?"

In a low whisper I said, "Can I answer?"

"Yeah."

"I *am* sorry for what I did to you. But I was young, Madjesty."

"I go by Mad and I know I told you before to call me that. Call me anything different again and I'ma make the rest of these days worse than I already plan to."

I swallowed hard. This bitch was really taking advantage of the predicament she placed me in and as of now, there was nothing else I could do but submit.

"Okay…I'm sorry, Mad." I looked at the floor and then back at her. "But I was young. And I didn't know what I was doing. Nobody every told me how to raise no kids. I was doing the best I could."

"The best you could? By starving us? By burning us with irons?" Each pause she made, each sentence she formed I could see caused her to grow angrier. And then it dawned on me, there was nothing I could say or do to change things. She only used my responses as a means to hurt me even more. I was putting the ammunition in the gun she held to my head with every answer I gave. "Just cause you young don't mean you can treat kids like shit!"

"You're right, Mad."

"And Mr. Nice Guy…he was so good to us, and you couldn't even let us have him could you? You couldn't even do that!"

"Mr. Nice Guy?"

"Wagner!" She screamed at me with narrowing eyes.

"I'm sorry, I didn't know you called him that."

"He was the best thing that happened to us, and you had to be the whore you was instead of giving him a chance. And then you blame his death on me!"

"Mad, please, I'm sorry. I didn't…"

"Do you remember that shit? HUH?!!!"

"Yes. But had you not said his name, he would have never gotten killed."

Suddenly she stood up, turned the camera on and sat back in the seat. Then she smirked and removed the cover off of the silver bowl. Inside was a corndog soaked in honey. My stomach grumbled thinking she'd give me some real food, instead of saltine crackers soaked in warm water I normally ate. But when she moved the corn dog closer, I could see it was swarming with ants and dirt.

"What are you about to do with that?" I asked with wide eyes. "Madjesty what are you about to do?" I tried to back up in the chair and it moved a few inches but she was right over top of me.

"I sat this outside all night. In an ant pile outside of the house." She laughed. "And since you like shit stuck inside of you, how about you take this."

"Please don't!"

She didn't listen. Over and over she jammed the corn dog stuck with ants inside of me. I could feel them running down my legs and biting at my skin.

"Madjesty, please stop! I sobbed. "Please, these ants are killing me!"

"Consider this payback for all of the roach bites that covered my skin when I was a kid." With that she dropped it at my feet and every second I could feel the biting ants nicking at my inner thighs, feet and ankles.

Looking at me squirming around in discomfort she laughed. I needed to get out of here and I needed to get out of here now. I couldn't imagine waiting out the completion of thirty days for my death, and I certainly couldn't imagine any more torture.

When her phone rang, taking her attention off of me for a moment, I was grateful. When I glanced at the screen on her cell I saw it said, 'Jayden'. This was my out. This was the break I needed to be saved. So the moment she hit the button to accept the call I yelled, "JAYDEN, HELP ME! SHE'S GOING TO KILL ME!"

Enraged, Mad ran up to me and kicked me in the chest with her Nike boot, forcing me violently backwards. The chair toppled over and my head banged against the concrete floor.

Now she was really angry.

MADJESTY
DROP KICK

After chest kicking that bitch, I ran upstairs hoping Jayden didn't hear her. I didn't even say hello again until I made it to the foyer area in our house.

"Mad," Jayden said. "Is everything okay? Was that mama? It sounded like mama!"

I was circling the middle of the floor like a shark. "Huh?"

"I said is everything okay?"

"Yeah, but what you want? I'm busy right now."

"Was that ma I heard in the background?" She paused. "Mad...you not doing nothing to ma are you?"

"Look...what the fuck you want? I ain't give you my number to be questioning me and shit. I gave it to you because you said you wanted it in case of an emergency. So is this an emergency or what?"

I paced the floor looking down at the tiles until I saw Mad Max come into the house. Over the days I held Harmony hostage, they slowly but surely started moving in. With them every night was a party. We went to sleep when we wanted, did what we wanted and there was nobody to stop us. The dude Kali stayed up in the room and only came down when he wanted something to eat. He was acting weird.

"Nigga, we got some smoke that's gonna knock your ass on your back!" Kid Lightning, yelled coming into the house.

Covering the phone I said, "Go downstairs and check on that bitch. My sister on the phone."

"My bad," he whispered as Wokie, Sugar and Krazy K followed him.

I was just about to close and lock the door when Glitter came in with her overnight bag. I could feel my stomach fluttering and I knew I was wide open. She was playing on her phone and was going to walk past me as if she didn't see me until I stopped her.

"You still mad at me?" I asked.

"Naw...but we still not together no more."

I wondered did she know that when I was drunk, I fucked her mother.

"Yeah, whatever."

"I'm serious, Mad. Until you can start treating me right and not embarrassing me out in public, I'm not fucking with you no more."

"Did your mother tell you anything?"

"Anything like what?"

Maybe she didn't say anything. "Nothing...you fucking some nigga?" I asked remembering the dude who left her house.

"I can talk to whoever I want remember? I'm not your girl no more."

"So what the fuck you doing in my house then?"

"You want me to leave?" She moved for the door.

Grabbing her by the throat I said, "Bitch, stop fucking with me."

She smiled, wrapped her arms around my waist and kissed me. "I love it when you get jealous."

"No you don't. That's why you stay fucked up with me all the time remember?"

She smiled and said, "I miss you, a lot." Then she pulled a bottle of Henny and a blunt out of the bag she was holding. "When you're ready. We'll be waiting."

I smacked her on the ass. "Go downstairs. I'm coming."

She switched down the steps and I couldn't wait to eat that pussy. Directing my attention back to the phone I said, "What were you saying?"

"Mad, I'm glad you got friends and stuff. But I really miss you. I mean, how much longer you gonna ignore me? We still sisters ain't we?"

"I ain't no female. I'm your brother and you my sister." I corrected her. "Anyway, I figured since you got your new pops you wouldn't be checking for me no more."

"I'm gonna always check for you, Mad. I love you."

When my sister said she loved me, I felt some kind of way. I can't explain the feeling. Its like, she was the only one on earth that could make me feel like nothing else mattered. Not even my girl could do that for me, and I loved that bitch to death.

"Okay, I ain't beefing with you no more."

"For real?"

"Yeah...but you gotta stop keeping secrets from me. It made me mad when you came in my room and took the hair out of my brush. I mean, why didn't you think you could tell me that?"

"Because we weren't talking." She paused. "Let's just start all over. Maybe I can take you out."

"What? You big money now?"

"I got a little something-something." She joked. "Now are you gonna let me take you out or what?"

"I don't know." I said feeling bad I couldn't do anything for her. Next to not being loved being broke was the worst thing in the world. I already spent the money I ganked from Glitter's mom and ain't have shit to show for it, but I had plans to come up soon.

"Pleeeeeeeeeaaaaaaase!"

"Aight..." I laughed. "Stop whining. Where we going?"

She got all excited and said, "Wherever you want to! But I was thinking we could grab something to eat. Maybe Red Lobsters or something." We could never afford to eat there so shit must've been looking good for her.

"Aight, when?"

"I'ma hit you."

"Okay. That'll work."

"Alright, Mad." She said softly. "I love you."

"I love you back."

When I got off the phone with her I had a smile on my face. I ain't gonna lie, with her in my life again things were starting to look up. Although I did have to admit, Jayden had a split personality. One minute shit would be cool with her and the next she would be different. Everybody always thought I was the crazy one but if you kept a long eye on Jayden you'd find out she wasn't too far behind me.

When I got downstairs, the music was loud and Wokie had raised the chair Harmony was in and had his dick in her mouth. The rest of the crew was sitting at the table smoking weed and drinking Hennessey like nothing was going on. I guess they saw it so much lately that in their minds it was normal.

Tapping Glitter on the back, she jumped up out the chair so that I could sit down. She sat in my lap. Without saying anything to me, she wrapped her arms around my neck and threw her tongue in my mouth and I ran my hands over her perky breasts. Damn this bitch was bad. To be honest, there wasn't another bitch that could fuck with her besides my sister.

When the kiss went on longer I couldn't help but think about her mother. I fucked that old bitch and I hoped it wouldn't come back to haunt me later.

"So where ya'll niggas been?" I asked looking at them as we periodically looked at the blowjob Wokie was getting.

"We stole some more shit out Game Stop so we can sell some games, but they putting the press on security now, Mad. We gonna have to find another way to make some cash." Kid Lightning said.

"I *been* telling ya'll that. It's just a matter of what we gonna do." I said.

"We gotta do something because these niggas stay eating all the food and shit in this house." Sugar said. "I mean which one of you niggas ate my last donut?"

"Sugar, stop playing, bitch!" Glitter said giving me a lap dance as the music boomed from the radio. "Everybody in this mothafucka know when you get high you eat like shit. So don't even try it."

I thought about Kali, who stayed upstairs for days never coming out. Maybe he was the culprit but I never told them. The house was so big we rarely saw each other.

"Fuck you!" Sugar said.

"So what's up, ya'll back together now or what?" Krazy said, looking at Wokie but talking to us.

"I don't know. Mad gotta stop tripping." Glitter said.

"Stop fucking around, Glitter. You wouldn't be here if you didn't want me." I took the Henny out of her hand and downed it.

"You acting different." She said. "More confident. Why?"

"Cuz I speak the truth."

When Wokie was done busting his nut, he buckled his pants and joined us at the table. Out of everyone in the crew, he was the only one who took full advantage of fucking Harmony. The other niggas would ask me if it was okay to go on in, but him, he just didn't give a fuck. The real messed up part about it was, I didn't feel anything about it either which way. My emotions when it came to her were dead! The worst she felt the better I felt and that was the bottom line.

"So what we gonna do tonight?" Wokie asked taking the blunt from Kid. "I'm tired of staying in the house."

"Nigga, we live in a mansion. For real we ain't got to go nowhere but here." Krazy said.

"We gotta be careful with staying out all night." I told them. "What if this bitch would've gotten out?"

They all looked at Harmony and than at me. Kid looked high when he asked, "You never told us what she did to you. You never told us shit about her."

"And I never will." I said looking at Harmony, who had sperm running down the side of her mouth. "Just know that I wouldn't be doing any of this shit if she didn't deserve every last bit of it."

When I looked away for a minute, and looked back at Harmony, I caught an evil look on her face. She tried to wipe the smirk away when we made eye contact, but it wasn't quick enough. I smiled, knowing that there wasn't shit she could do to hurt me anymore. And there wasn't shit she could say to me either. I ran shit now, and would continue to run shit until I decided I ain't want to no more. I was just about to get up and dance with Glitter when I heard a knock at the basement door upstairs.

"Who the fuck is that?" Glitter asked jumping up.

"Damn, I forgot his ass was here." I said. "Look, let me go wrap to this nigga right quick." When I stood up I said, "Glitter, give me your cell phone."

"Huh? Why?" She said frowning.

I was going to start handling her differently. When you're nice people don't respect you so I needed to change shit up.

"Bitch, don't make me ask you again. Give me your fucking phone." She dug in her purse and handed it over. "Next time I tell you to do something fast, do it quicker."

With that I ran upstairs.

Upstairs

"What's up?" I asked Kali coming out of the basement, locking the door from the inside before closing it.

"What you got going on down there?"

Kali had been here ever since the day he said he didn't want anything to do with me in the kitchen. He would eat up all of the food and disappear upstairs. Every now and again I'd come home and see him looking out of the window but he never left. I knew he was afraid of something and couldn't wait for him to leave, especially since he made it clear we would not have a relationship. I ain't want him going downstairs finding Harmony tied up even though the basement door was locked whenever I left and I had the only key.

"Why, nigga?" I said getting in his face. "You said you not my pops, so you ain't got the right to be questioning me."

Kali grinned a little and said, "If you knew the nigga I was...I mean *really* knew me, you wouldn't be talking sideways."

"I don't know about all that, but what you want with me?"

"For starters, where the fuck is Harmony?"

"She ain't here. She gonna be back in a few days I think." I said taking my cap off to scratch my head before putting it back on.

"Well grab your house keys, I need you to roll somewhere with me right quick."

"For what?"

"You gonna make me ask you again?"

Silence.

"Give me a sec. I gotta go tell me friends."

JACE'S GOONS
FT. WASHINGTON, MARYLAND

Sitting in a car a few blocks down from the front of Concord Manor's entrance sat Jace's goons ready to attack Kali. Kali had just hopped into a truck with Mad and they peeped that Vaughn was the driver. They staked out the house for days and he never came out. Jace figured he knew they were waiting to murder him and suggested that all of his men with the exception of the one car leave the premises. His plan worked because Kali thought the coast was clear but he didn't use his full vision.

The only reason they didn't barge in the house and take him alive the night he went in was because of Madjesty, they saw her from the window. Had it not been for his baby girl Jayden, he probably would've taken his chances anyway, even if it meant killing Mad. He took Kali's threat on his life seriously, and had all intentions of laying him down one way or another. But he couldn't think about himself anymore because he had a daughter now and he didn't want to smudge their relationship already by killing her one and only sibling. So he played it cool and he waited and finally the time to take blood had come.

"Oh shit, Paco! They coming out now!" Kreshon said, slumping down in the passenger seat. "Call Jace."

Paco pulled off slowly behind Vaughn's truck careful to keep his distance as he made the call. "Hello."

"I got the nigga in my sights right now, Jace. All you gotta do is give the word." Paco said as Kreshon loaded his weapon. Both men kept their eyes on the truck.

"Good! He by himself right?"

"Naw, he got Vaughn and some young nigga with him."

"A young nigga?" Jace said confused. "Well fuck it, kill all three of them."

"I'm on it!"

Paco was just about to pull up on the side of the truck and fire into it when Jace called back.

"Hold up, you said a young nigga?"

"Yeah." Paco said. "Why you ask?"

"You sure it ain't a girl? A young girl?"

"Naw, he look like he about fifteen or something. It's definitely a dude though."

"Fuck! Fuck! Fuck!" Jace yelled into the phone.

"What you want me to do?" Paco asked, confused at his response.

"Nothing. Don't do nothing."

"What? Why?"

"That ain't no young dude, that's Harmony's other daughter. And she the only reason we ain't run up in that bitch and take that nigga out."

Paco squinted and said, "You sure? The nigga came out wearing a fitted hat and everything. It looked like a dude to me, cuz."

"I'm sure it ain't no dude. Did he have on a New York Yankees baseball cap?"

"Yeah."

"Then that's Harmony's kid and my daughter's sister. Leave the nigga alone right now but keep your sights on him. The moment you catch his ass slipping, blow the back of his head off, but don't hurt the girl."

"Got it boss!"

MAD
SICK SHIT

My nose was cold and my fingertips felt frozen. Why did they have the air condition up so fucking high? Fuck was he doing, trying to freeze us to death? We were driving in silence for fifteen minutes before I realized I didn't know where the fuck we were going or what the fuck we were doing?

From the back seat I looked at Kali. He looked like me. His complexion was slightly darker than mine but the way he looked at people matched my look. He wasn't hard on the eyes when he was quiet and he seemed to always be deep in thought.

"You still see them behind us?" Kali asked Vaughn.

"Naw, we lost 'em a while back. What you want me to do?"

He looked out of the window. "Nothing. Keep driving until I come up with a plan."

"Can you tell me where we going? I mean, I thought we were hanging." I asked from the backseat.

He turned to look at me. "What you ain't happy to be with your pops?"

Vaughn looked at him and then at me. "Hold up, this your son?"

Kali frowned. "This my daughter, nigga. Look again."

Vaughn looked at me through the rearview mirror. "Damn, so you family, huh?"

"I don't know." I shrugged. "He told me he wasn't my pops the other day. So I can't be sure if I'm family or not. I do know I'm trying to get a bottle of Henny before I go back home though."

"You drink?" Kali asked.

"Everyday."

"Ain't you too young to be drinking?" Kali said.

"Nigga...don't act like you weren't drinking damn near everyday when you was a shawty." Vaughn said.

"That's 'cuz my mother was a fuck up." He said looking out of his window. "And I didn't have nobody to keep me straight. This my kid and I don't want her doing the shit I did."

"I know your mother was fucked up, man." Vaughn said. "That's why I still can't believe you..."

"Don't talk about that shit in the car with her, Vaughn." Kali said seriously. "What you about to discuss is my business. Remember that."

"You got it." Vaughn said. Then he looked at me again. "So this really your father huh?"

"Like I said, he told me I wasn't his kid."

"Well I gotta put you through the test first." Kali said. "Any kid of mine gotta be good at following orders. You good at following orders?"

"Depends on the plan." He laughed. "What's so funny?" I asked him.

"Cause anybody with an attitude like yours gotta be related to me."

"You right about that shit." Vaughn said as he and Kali started talking to each other about shit I didn't understand. It was something about a dude name Massive, some money and buying weight. When they were done Vaughn said, "So tell me what the fuck happen at the mansion. How they hold you up that long?"

At that point we reached a red light at an intersection and all I could think about was getting some Hennessey. While Kali and Vaughn continued with small talk, I saw a black four-door Ford sedan with tinted out windows slowly roll across our path at the intersection. Kali and Vaughn weren't paying the car any attention because they were talking about what happened at the mansion. When the back window rolled down on the Ford, some dude in the back threw some metal shit on the ground. Then he placed his finger over his mouth to tell me to be quiet and rolled the window back up. With that the truck pulled off and when the light turned green, Vaughn pulled into the intersection and ran right over the shit on the ground. The tires made a loud popping noise and he lost control of the wheel. The shit happened so quickly, that even if I wanted to alert them, it wasn't enough time.

"WHAT THE FUCK?!" Vaughn yelled trying to handle the car.

"WHAT HAPPENED?!" Kali replied going for his weapon. "WHAT YOU HIT?!"

When he said that two cars pulled up on the right and left and eight niggas jumped out and one of them, smashed the driver side window, and put Vaughn in a head lock before shooting him in the leg.

"AAHHHHHHHHH, SHIIIITTTT!" Vaughn screamed in pain.

"What the fuck is going on?!" I yelled.

The nigga who shot Vaughn ignored me and aimed the gun at Kali. But there were guns aimed in all directions of the truck. "You coming with us or you want me to kill this nigga?!"

I was trying to take everything in when Kali aimed his gun at me while the men continued to cover the truck.

"What you doing?" I asked. I saw a dead body once in my life, the night Mr. Nice guy got killed and even to this day that memory haunted me. I wasn't trying to end up like him.

"Nigga, I don't give a fuck about that bitch." The gunman said, with his weapon on Vaughn. "If you don't get the fuck out of that truck we lighting this nigga up."

Kali grinned and said, "You give a fuck about her, because if you didn't I would be dead by now." He smirked. "Bitch ass niggas, should've killed me at Concord." All of a sudden I started crying. I could deal with some shit, but I ain't never seen this much gun play in my life. "Stop crying!" Kali said. "And toughen the fuck up."

I heard him but I couldn't stop. I didn't want to die like this.

"You think we playing?" He said shooting Vaughn in the arm. "Get out of the truck and put your gun down or we killing this nigga."

"So it's like that, Kreshon? We been knowing each other forever and it's like that? You gonna kill my cousin?"

The gunman I knew as Kreshon shot his cousin in the other leg and Vaughn screamed again. "Kali, please!" Vaughn cried. "I don't wanna die. They may not even kill you, man. But if you don't go with them, they gonna kill me. Please!"

"I know it's fucked up, man," Kali said holding the gun to my head. "I know, but I can't go with them. I can't."

"Please, Kali! Please don't do this shit!" Vaughn said. "I got kids."

"So, what, you want me to just give myself up just cause you got fucking kids? I got a kid too, nigga!"

"Yeah but you holding a gun to her head!" Vaughn said. "I got a family I'm trying to go back home to. Just go with these niggas."

"If you come with us it's gonna be cool, Kali." Kreshon said. "You know the nigga Jace got love for you. Just come with me so we can talk."

"I can't do it!" Every time he spoke the gun pressed firmly against my temple and I was afraid to make a move. I was so nervous he'd shoot me that I threw up on my legs and his arm. Kali didn't seem to be phased one bit and held the gun steady.

"So you not coming with us?" Kreshon said. "You gonna let me kill your peoples?"

"I can't do it. Sorry, cousin."

"Please, Kali. This nigga serious!" Vaughn pleaded.

"Fuck this nigga!" Kreshon said before shooting Vaughn in the stomach. Then he aimed the gun at Kali. They all aimed at Kali.

"I swear I'ma let one off in her head."

When he said that Jace got out of one of the cars and walked up to the truck. Looking at me he said, "Let him go. We'll catch up with him later."

Jace's eyes found mine and Kreshon put his gun down although the men around the car were still aimed in our direction. "You gonna see me again, nigga." Jace said looking at Kali.

"Not if I see you first."

The men piled back into their cars and I could hear police sirens in the distance and I hoped they caught up with us. I didn't want to be with Kali anymore at this point. Kali went around the driver side and threw Vaughn's dead body in the back seat with me and said, "Get in the front." He walked back to the passenger side.

"What? I...I can't drive that good," I said, smelling my own throw up on my clothes. I jumped into the driver's seat anyway. Even though I use to steal the cars of the dudes who use to come over and fuck Harmony, that was a long time ago.

"You gonna learn today."

With the gun on me I turned the key and put the car in drive and it jerked hard. "I can't drive!" I cried. "Why don't you just do it?" I put the car back in park.

"Because you the only reason I'm alive and until I get another plan I can't risk you running on me." He continued holding the gun in my direction. "Now, put the car in drive and remember that the gas is on the right and the brake is on the left. I don't give a fuck what you hit just move!"

It took me fifteen minutes of dipping on back roads before he let me stop for a while. We couldn't even go that fast due to having a flat tire. Looking behind him he said, "I don't think they following us." He lowered the gun enough so that it rested on his leg. His finger remained on the trigger. "We may be good."

"I wanna go home."

"You ain't going home until I get to where I'm going." He pulled his phone out and made a call. Then he said, "Let's dump this body and change this tire. We going to my people's house after that."

• •

Thirty minutes Later

I could *still* smell my own vomit when we reached some lady's house Kali called Bernie. When the door opened some older black chick wearing a gold wig, red lipstick and a white slip came out. She looked a little washed out. A cigarette dangled in the corner of her mouth and she held tightly onto a glass with brown liquor inside of it. The thing was, to be older she was still kind of pretty. Just looked as if she had a hard life.

"Keefer," she said throwing her arms around his neck, not dropping an ounce of alcohol. Then she tried to dig in his pockets. "You got something for me?"

Who the fuck was Keefer and why was he making her call him that?

"What I tell you about going in my pockets?" He paused. "I don't know where you picked up that fucked up ass habit but you better lose it."

"Sorry." She said softly. "My last beau never came to my door without a gift."

"Well he ain't around no more now is he?"

She frowned a little and said, "Come in." We both walked into the house. On to the next thing she said, "And who's this handsome young man right here?"

"It's my daughter. Madjesty."

"Mad." I corrected him.

"This fine young thing is a bitch?" Bernie said. "Damn, I know men who would pay a lot for you." She paused. "So what's up, honey. You fucking?" She smiled slyly easing in my direction.

"She ain't here for all that." Kali interrupted. "She here with me."

"You got it, you got it," Bernie said. "I don't want no trouble."

Once inside the house I couldn't get over how neat her crib was. Based on how nasty she looked I would've thought her spot would've been nasty too. The white carpet didn't have a spot on it and the tan leather furniture looked brand new.

"Bernie, you got some clothes she can wear. She had a situation earlier."

"I ain't wearing no bitch clothes." I told him.

"You gonna wear what the fuck I tell you to wear." Kali said looking at me seriously. "Now go get her some of your shit!"

"Fuck that shit! I ain't wearing no female clothes."

"Bernie, give me a second with my kid."

"You got it, baby. Uh, when you done, I want to go see them peoples. I need a fix."

He looked at her and said, "Whatever." He threw her something in a tiny cellophane bag. She smiled. "I'ma go get good for you now." She disappeared into a room.

"You almost had me killed." I said when she left. "And you held a fucking gun to my head for about an hour! What type shit is that?"

He was quiet for a minute before he said, "I think you really my kid, the only thing is, you cried earlier, and I better never see you do that shit again."

"I was crying because I was scared."

"I don't give a fuck! I better never see you crying again." He paused. "Fuck was you scared for anyway? You act all hard and shit and then when the time comes to show and prove, you tense up. Relax or take that fucking cap off and put on a pair of high heel shoes." He paused. "Like I said, I better never see you cry again while you call yourself my kid."

I didn't feel like arguing so I said, "I wanna go home. Can I leave, or are you still holding me hostage?"

"You can leave. I want you to take the truck and come back for me tomorrow." He said.

"I'm not trying to get involved in this shit." I told him pacing the floor. "You beefing with my sister's father."

"What's your cell phone number?" he asked ignoring me.

"What?"

"I know you got a cell so what's the number?"

"When I give it to you can I get the fuck out of here?"

"Yeah, but like I said, I expect you back here tomorrow. I'ma call you when I want you to come get me. I don't give a fuck where you are or what you doing, when I hit you you better drop everything and come scoop me. I'm not the type nigga you want on your back." After I gave him my number I moved for the door and my phone rang. "Answer the phone."

"Why answer the phone? You right there."

"I wanna make sure the number is right."

I took the phone out of my pocket and said, "Hello?"

He hung up. "Good, I'll see you tomorrow. You on call so don't get locked up and don't forget what I said." He paused again. "Take your time on them roads. You still a rookie driver. Oh and keep your friends and your sister out my fucking business. Don't tell 'em nothing about this shit."

"Whatever." I just wanted to get as far away from him as possible.

"And another thing. Your shoes too tight. Go a size up."

"What?"

"You wearing the wrong size shoes." He said walking back toward the house. "I'll see you later."

When I got in the truck, I thought about what he said. I didn't even know he noticed my boots. When you have to steal your clothes it's sometimes hard to be picky and I didn't know my feet had grown.

I was just about to pull out when my cell phone started ringing again. Was he fucking with me? When I went for my phone I noticed it was Glitter's cell ringing instead. I forgot I took it from her because everything moved so fast. It was a voice message from the nigga Mark. Nook's brother.

"What the fuck?"

I hit the button to listen.

'Glitter...hit me so we can rap. I can't wait to fuck that pussy again. You got extra wet last night. Hit a nigga up. Oh, and you bet not be fucking with that bitch again. My brother keeping an eye on you.'

Click.

If this bitch thought she was gonna play games with me she had another thing coming. That goes for this nigga, too!

MAD

A RIFT IN THE CREW

When I made it to my house I parked the truck in the driveway and looked at the house. Today was a long day and all I wanted to do was step to Glitter about this dude and get in bed. Before getting out, I saw a car I recognized in the driveway. But what the fuck was this nigga doing at my crib? I didn't deal with him on a personal level and outside of talking to him at school; we didn't have too much to say to each other.

When I walked into the living room, I saw my crew sitting on the sofa and floor. "Who car is that in the driveway?" I asked interrupting their play on Nintendo.

"Baaaaaaaabbbbby," Glitter said running to kiss me. "Where you been?"

I pushed her away because we still had new beef to settle and I needed to know why her ex was calling her. "Fuck that...go put some ice in my shit." I said handing her the bag of Henny. Ever since Rocket kept it real with me I decided to change some shit up when it came to dealing with bitches. I can't believe I played myself by going over her house begging and shit. Never again.

She took the bag from me. "Did I do something wrong?"

"Do what the fuck I asked." I said pushing her toward the kitchen.

My crew stood up seeing the irritation on my face. "What's that smell?" Wokie asked.

I took my vomit covered shirt off and just kept on my white t-shirt under it. Then I looked around trying to spot the nigga I knew was somewhere in my house. "Fuck all that. Is Nook in my house?"

All of them looked at the floor and then at me. "He had some smoke, so I thought it would be cool to invite him over." Kid said. "I mean, we were broke and ain't have no money."

"Yeah, and I gave you all I had the other day when you was going to take Glitter out." Wokie added.

"So you let this nigga in my house? When you know his brother Mark wanna fuck my girl." *Or had fucked my girl? Again? I thought.*

"Mad, he cool. He ain't even like that. For real."

"Where the nigga at now?"

They all looked at each other and Sugar said, "Downstairs."

I took a step closer to them and said, "Downstairs doing what?"

Judging by the look on their faces I knew what was up. So I broke to the basement. When I was at the bottom of the steps, I saw that this nigga untied Harmony and was fucking her on the floor.

"Fuck is you doing here, Nook?" I paused. "That's my mothafuckin' moms."

He jumped up and said, "Nothing…uh, they said it was cool."

"Nigga get the fuck up the steps before I break your jaw!" He looked like he wanted to challenge me. "Or call the police."

He took one last look at Harmony and then at me before running up the stairs. When he was gone I put Harmony back in the chair. She had a blank look on her face, almost like nothing else mattered anymore. I had that look before a couple of times while living with her. When I had her tied back up, I said, "They feed you?"

"Yes." She said flatly.

I took a seat in front of her. "You know this is all your fault right?"

"Yes."

"So now all you gonna do is keep saying yes?"

"When are you going to kill me? I want to get life over with."

"I'm not done with you yet."

"But I wish you would be. If you hate me so much, why won't you just kill me instead of letting your friends fuck me for free!"

"You want me to charge?" I smirked. "Figures."

"I want to die."

I don't know why I didn't just kill her, especially after this Nook shit because if she got away, I knew she was going to call the police. Part of me wondered if I could even do it. I mean, torturing her was easy. Almost as easy as talking, after all she did it to me for most of my life. But now that I'd have to really kill her, I didn't know if I could follow through. Or maybe I could…and then runaway to live in Texas. In the place Rocket told me about.

"I'll kill you when I'm ready." I said. Then I looked down at the floor. "But…uh…I gotta ask you something."

"What, Mad?"

"Tell me about Kali. Like…who is he really?"

In a real dry tone she said, "What do you mean, Mad?"

"You heard me! Like…why is he beefing with Jace? Jayden's father."

An interested look covered her face. "Did something happen?"

Not being able to talk to anybody else about what happened earlier I said, "Yeah...like twenty niggas tried to kill him today. They surrounded the car and everything."

"You were with him?"

"Yeah...he been back here for a while now."

She shook her head. "I can't believe that nigga still in my house. Like he live here or something."

"He gone now." I frowned. "Answer the question, though. Why did they try to kill him?"

"So they weren't successful? In killing him?"

"No."

"How come?"

Irritated I said, "I don't know, but I think it had something to do with me. It was like, the dude Jace didn't want to kill him with me in the car."

"Figures, Jace was always soft." She shook her head. "He should've blown his face off. Now all he did was piss Kali off which will make shit worse. I knew that nigga was part weak the moment I laid eyes on him."

This bitch went on a rant. "What kind of man is Kali? Like really?"

"He's dangerous and careless. He acts off of emotions and often without thinking straight." Then she smiled. "Just...like...you."

I was angry. "Fuck is that supposed to mean?"

"Look at you, and what you're doing to me." She paused. "You've had me tied in a chair naked for days while your friends rape me all because you're angry, Madjesty. I mean really! How sane is that shit? Huh?"

I stood up and stole her in the face. "You too stupid to know anything about me, bitch!"

I grabbed the camera and moved for the stairs when she started laughing. "The thing is I'm not stupid. I know exactly what I'm saying." She paused. "You're just like your fucking father. I don't know how I never saw it before. It's so clear now."

"I'ma see how clear shit is when I leave you down here for two days without any food."

Silence.

I knew that would get to her.

"Please! Please don't do that."

"Fuck you!"

* *

Back Upstairs

When I got upstairs I locked the basement door and Nook was gone. My crew was in the living room talking until I walked in. Glitter handed me my Henny and I sat in the recliner.

"Why would ya'll let the nigga downstairs?" I asked.

"Like I said, Mad, he had smoke." Kid said.

"Now he know we got somebody hostage. You don't think he gonna tell somebody at school?" I drank all of my Henny and handed my glass to Glitter. She went to make me some more. "How could ya'll be so fuckin' stupid?"

When I asked that there was a knock at the door. It was my sister, Jayden. She was carrying mail and I didn't know if it was from here or not. The moment she walked in Wokie, Kid and Krazy's mouths dropped.

"I'ma fuck ya'll up!" I said. "I told you 'bout looking at my sister like that."

"My bad." Wokie said as the others walked to the living room and sat on the sofa.

She was wearing a tight pair of jeans and a tight t-shirt. The curves of her body were outrageous and now she looked more like a model. It's amazing, a few months ago we were inseparable, now we were living different lives.

"What you doing here?" I asked. "I thought we were hooking up later."

She looked at my friends who kept stealing looks at her from the couch and said, "Can we talk? In private?"

"Let's go in my room." I looked at all of them and said, "We leaving in about an hour and we not finished talking neither."

When we made it to my room I put the camera on the dresser.

"Who truck out front?"

"Mine." I paused. "I'ma take a shower. Give me a minute."

"Okay...can I wait for you? In here?"

"I guess."

After my shower I remembered I put the video camera on the dresser we used to tape what we did to Harmony. When I came back she was looking at it. I ran up to her in my towel and snatched it away. I checked her eyes for a minute to see if she looked like she saw anything. She didn't.

"Why you stay going through my shit, Jayden? That's the one thing I hate about you."

"I'm sorry, Mad." She said softly. "At one point we didn't have any secrets from each other. And now things are so different."

"Whose fault is that? Yours or mine?" I got dressed under the towel. Sliding on my boxers before my jeans.

"It's nobody's. It's just that I miss you and it seems like everything I do makes you angry all of a sudden. We use to be so close and I guess I just want that back. Don't you?" She looked so pretty and smelled so good.

"Well if you stop snooping in my shit we wouldn't have this problem." I grabbed a new white t-shirt from its pack in my drawer and then grabbed a new blue Hugo Boss t-shirt from my closet. "Give me a second and stay out my shit."

I walked into the bathroom and put the shirts on. When I came out I put on a pair of butter colored Timbs. I didn't like 'em at first because I thought they were the wrong size but the moment they got on my feet I had immediate comfort. Kali was right.

"Can we talk?"

"About what?"

"Mad, where is ma?" She said softly. Then she handed me a welfare check with Harmony's name on it. I guess the mail she had in her hand did come from here. I handed it back to her.

"I don't know."

"Well I'm worried. Mama would never not cash a check. You know that."

"Drop it."

"Daddy told me a lot of stuff that happened when she was younger." She said ignoring my comment. "To me it kind of explains why she did the things that she did to us. I mean, it don't make her no angel, but it does help me understand."

"You calling that nigga daddy already?" I smirked. "You couldn't wait to bow down to a dick."

"He's my father, Mad."

I wanted to tell her about what happened earlier but I didn't trust her and Kali told me not to. We hadn't really been talking so I didn't want to take the chance. Plus I wanted to see if she would open up to me, and tell me what she knew. It was crazy, our fathers were beefing and the only thing standing in the middle of us was them.

"I don't give a fuck what your daddy said," I grabbed another baseball cap. My black one and pulled it all the way over my eyes. "That bitch don't give a fuck about us."

"I'm still scared, Mad. I mean, she got shit with her but she's still our mother. What if somebody killed her? What if she's hurt somewhere and needs our help? You know how crazy drunk, ma use to get. She done broke damn near every bone in her body from falling down at one time or another."

"You can't be serious, Jayden. I bet you if something happened to you she wouldn't give a fuck. Matta of fact, I don't even remember that bitch asking about you."

"What you mean? You don't remember her asking about me?"

I slipped up. Fuck! "Why should you give a fuck about her?"

"Because I love her."

"Jayden, sometimes I think you're crazy. It's like you got a split personality or something. One minute you saying one thing and the next minute you saying another."

"I don't have no split personality."

"Look…wherever the bitch is, leave her there." I said firmly. "Now if you ain't got shit else to talk to me about, I'm out. Me and my crew 'bout to hit the streets."

"We still on for our date?"

"Yeah."

"Okay, well I'ma hang around here for bit, while you're gone. In case ma come back."

Jayden was pissing me off. Fuck she care about Harmony so much for? This bitch sent us through hell when we were kids, and now she all worried where the fuck she at. This shit is stupid and it was making me angry. I didn't feel like any of this right now. I was almost killed, my father held a gun to my head and I walked in on some unassociated nigga fucking my mother. Jayden was only adding to my problems whether she knew it or not.

"So you don't trust me? You think I know where she is and I'm lying to you or something?"

"No, Mad, but why are you acting like this? I mean technically this is still my house too. All I wanted to do was hang around in case she shows up. You can lock your door if you think I'ma go through your shit. It's not that deep."

"I know but you making it deep." She looked like she was about to cry. "Jayden, I don't want to fight about her." I grabbed her hand. "You my favorite sister."

She laughed. "I'm your only sister."

"I know, but you still my favorite." I softly hit her on the chin with my fist. "We been through a lot together, and although for whatever reason you care about ma, you gotta remember what she put us through. We went through stuff in our lives as kids nobody should ever have to go through. Or have you forgotten about the fact that she had us thinking we were boys until this year. Until a few months back actually." I was getting through to her. I saw it in her eyes. "Look, if she comes through I'll call you. Until then I'ma see you soon. Maybe tomorrow." I paused. "We still on right?"

"Fuck yeah! I gotta hang out with my brother." For some reason, when she said brother it made me smile. Even now, when I looked into the mirror I didn't see a girl. "But meet me at my house." She grabbed a pen and pad off my desk. "This is my address." She paused. "So meet me there when you can and we'll go out." She paused. "You need money for a cab?"

I had Kali's truck so I said, "Naw...I'm good." Then I paused. "So you leaving or you staying here?"

"I'm gone." She giggled. "Plus I can tell you don't want me here."

I was relieved. "It ain't that I don't want you here." I lied. "I just don't want you to worry about her. Now I'ma rap to you tomorrow."

"Alright and when we hook up we gotta talk."

"About what?"

"About Kali. Jace wanted me to tell you some things he says you gotta know about him."

MAD

WASHINGTON, DC

The window was broken on my side and rolled down on the passenger side in Kali's truck. We had the music on blast and the entire block was feeling our vibe. The cool nighttime air rushed inside and brushed against my face. She was wearing my baseball cap and she looked so fucking sexy because she had it pulled all the way over her eyes. The way I wear it.

My hand was under her dress and my finger was inside her pussy as I looked outside the truck to make sure nobody saw what we were doing. My joint was throbbing and she was getting wetter and wetter by the second. Her body was leaned against the door and her feet rested in my lap. I noticed that each time I moved across her button with my thumb, her toes that were painted pink, would spread slightly. She was just about to cum.

"You better stop before they see you," she said in a hushed tone as she guided the motion of my finger by pushing and pulling on my wrist.

"Like you give a fuck." I smiled loving the squishy sound her wet pussy made.

"You right." She smiled. "I don't give a fuck. So please don't stop!" She bit down on her bottom lip. Like her mother and for a moment it gave me the creeps. I actually fucked her mother. How crazy is that shit? "I'm almost there."

We were outside of a DC project and I was drunk and high out of my mind. We were waiting on Wokie's cousin to come outside so we could go to this party at this restaurant in Maryland. At first I wasn't with it, believing somebody needed to watch Harmony after what happened with Nook but like most nights we went out, I ain't give a fuck.

The rest of Mad Max was outside of the truck to the right, dancing, drinking and talking shit. The brick building Wokie's cousin lived in always had something going on outside whenever we came over. There was never a dull moment and since I liked trouble, I loved her crib.

"Mad, please don't stop." She begged. "I'm almost there."

She was just about to cum when somebody walked up on the passenger side door. I pulled my fingers out of her pussy careful not to touch my face and she pulled down her dress. It was Krazy K.

"Damn, man!" Krazy said holding a lit blunt. "Ya'll doing it like that?"

"Fuck you want, nigga?" I asked.

"I wanted to see if you wanted to hit this?"

"Naw you got that."

He palmed Glitter's head and backed away to rejoin the crew. Kanye West's voice blasted from the speakers now and everything felt good. Everything felt right.

I was about to go back under her dress when she said, "Naw...we'll save it for later."

"Scaredy cat!" I joked.

"You mean scardy pussy!"

I laughed and wondered what I could wipe my fingers on. Since she was looking at what I did with my hand and I didn't want her to think I didn't want her juices on me, I decided to let the shit air-dry. Fuck it!

"You still mad at me?" She asked.

"Naw...you said we weren't together so I gotta believe you really fucked the dude because we weren't together." I said doubling up on my words.

"You sure you not gonna revenge fuck a bitch? To get back at me?"

"Naw. That's not my style. But if I find out you still dealing with this dude I'ma lose it, Glitter. You gotta put these niggas in check." I told her. "Plus you fourteen. Why you letting these old heads fuck you anyway?"

"Why you driving when you don't have a license?"

"Bitch, answer the question."

"Baby, I don't fuck with niggas like that and I'm not fucking with my ex no more. I told you that. After I came over your house and we got back together I cut him off." She played with a black thread that was loose on her dress. "His dick was trash anyway."

"Yeah whateva."

"I'm serious." She looked me in the eyes. "I mean, you believe me right?"

I took a sip of my Henny and looked into her eyes. I could smell the scent of her pussy on my hand. It had a scent but it was slight. Not nasty. "You know I believe you." I paused. "You still got your face don't you?"

She laughed. "You talk to me different now. Why?"

"I feel different now I guess." I took another swig. "I seen a lot in my life." I remembered Vaughn's dead body. I took another drink. "I guess after awhile you just change how you deal with people. I don't know."

"Why you drink so much?"

"It's hard to explain," I shrugged. "I guess it helps me forget about the parts in my life that hurt the most."

"Like what?"

"I'm not ready to open up about the kind of stuff I been through. Let's just say I came up hard."

"See, that's why I feel like we'll never make it. Until you're ready to be real with me about everything, it's like we just faking it."

"We gonna make it, Glitter. I love you. And when you look at me I can tell you love me too. I need that in my life and I don't want to lose it."

She looked at me seriously. "Why you love me so much?" She asked. "I be seeing them girls trying to holla at you all the time at school. Especially now since you got your gear together and you wear your hair short and curly."

"School?" I laughed. "Like I ever be there."

"When you do go they be on you hard. But you never give them no play. Why?"

"Why, you want me to get with 'em or something?" She kicked me in my side lightly with her foot. "Ouch!"

She laughed. "Don't get fucked up, Mad."

"Babe, I don't give a fuck about none of them bitches at school. I want a shawty by my side I can be loyal to. I was raised by a whore. It's not a good look. I want you to have my kid. I want us to raise a family. Together. Marriage and all."

"But how? You a girl and I'm a girl."

Whenever this question came up it fucked me up because I didn't have an answer. All I knew was that I wanted a family and I wanted to be the father of that family. "I'm not a girl." I told her. "I told you to stop saying that."

"I know you don't like me to call you a girl but you are, Mad. And you a pretty one, too. Even with all them scars on your face."

"Stop saying I'm pretty! I'm serious."

"Mad! I hate when you talk like that. I love everything about you. Even when you angry with me and your nose flares up." She joked nudging my arm. "But, baby, you are a girl. You gotta remember that shit because that's why I'm feeling you."

"I ain't trying to hear that shit, Glitter. All my life I was raised like a boy. I ain't no girl. Just because some doctor tell me what he sees between my legs don't make shit different!" I took another pull off of my bottle. "I been a boy all my life."

She raised her eyebrows and leaned in toward me. "What you mean you was raised like a boy?"

Damn!

I fucked up and now she was going to press the issue even further. "I didn't mean that. Just drop it okay?"

"You gotta hear me, baby," she paused. "I love *everything* about you. Even that pussy between your legs." When she said that it made my skin crawl. I hated having anything related to a woman on my body, especially a pussy. "So despite what you think in your head, you are a girl. And you're my girl. And I love you."

"Let's just focus on me and you and eventually getting a place of our own." I said skipping the subject.

"Yeah okay, Mad." She paused. She reached for my bottle and I gave it to her. She took a quick sip and handed it back. "Why we gotta leave the mansion? I like it there."

I didn't think about it before. I guess I always believed at some point someone would lock me up after they found out what we did to my mother. I still wasn't sure if I would kill her or not. I'm so fucking confused. If I let her go she gonna tell. I just couldn't.

Remembering what Rocket said about them rooms in Texas I decided to ask another question. "Would you move to Texas with me? If I left?"

"Why you wanna leave?" She frowned.

"You not answering the question."

Silence.

"Damn, you gotta think that long, Glitter?"

"No!" She said. My heart dropped. "I mean yes."

"What's wrong? You don't wanna be with me for life?"

"Yes. But I really like it here." She looked out of the window at all of our friends. Only Sugar was staring in our direction. She was always looking in *my* direction. "I really love our friends." She waved at Sugar. Sugar waved back and when she wasn't looking rolled her eyes.

"You not answering the question." I grabbed her warm hand. "If I had to leave, would you go with me?"

"Yes. I'll go with you anywhere." She paused. "It's just that I really hope shit works out because I love it at the mansion." After she bopped her head to the music she said, "Why he give you this truck again? And why the window busted out like that?"

"I don't know why he wanted me to hold on to it." I lied. "I guess I'll find out tomorrow. He wants me to come back and scoop him up."

"You always…"

All of a sudden, everybody to the right of the truck moved in a wave like motion away from it. Their faces looked extremely scared and at that moment it was as if time stopped. What had everyone so fucked up?

"MADDDDDD, ROOOOOLLLLL OUUUUTTTTT!" I heard Wokie's voice call out to me from the outside of the truck even though I didn't know where he was.

Glitter quickly moved her legs off of me and looked behind her out the window. Not knowing why everybody was running, I tried to put the car into drive but I couldn't remember which way to turn the key. When I finally remembered, I was too late. Some niggas ran up on her side of the truck, put a gun through the window and blew her brains out. Blood and meaty tissue splattered on my face, hair and clothes. My heart pounded in my chest and I felt like I would black out. My shawty was actually dead! Some niggas killed my fuckin' girl!

When her body slumped frontwards, the gunman took the cap off of her head and looked at what was left of her face.

"Oh shit! It looks like a bitch!" He said to another gunman who approached my side of the truck.

Now there was a gun pointed at me on both ends ...from the passenger side and driver side window.

"Man, it's not Kali! FUCK!" the passenger gunman said hitting the top of the truck. "What we gonna do now?!" Then he paused. "We gotta kill this other bitch!"

They had taken her away from me. *My Glitter*. I put my finger against my nose and inhaled. The scent of her pussy was still on me. This couldn't be real. After everything I'd been through in life I didn't even get to keep my girl. I didn't care about anything. What did I have to live for anyway? I hated the woman who gave birth to me, my father wanted nothing to do with me and my sister seemed like she was moving on in life without me. So what did I care if I died today or tomorrow? I was going to be more reckless if I made it out of this shit anyway. It was best to put a bullet in my head. No fuck that put two to my head to make sure the shit is done right. I want no mistakes.

When he said to kill me I leaned my head against the barrel of the gun through my side of the window and said, "Squeeze twice."

"Oh shit!" the passenger gunman said. "She said kill her so do it!"

The driver side gunman looked at me and then back at the other gunman. Putting his weapon down he said, "Naw...he told us to leave her alone if she was with him. We gotta go."

"Man, kill this bitch! She a witness. Jace ain't gonna say nothing if we tell him it was an accident."

Jace was involved. I hated this nigga on the deepest level now.

"We can't! Now let's get the fuck out of here!" With that they ran off leaving me alive and alone.

The block was quiet when their footsteps faded away. I never got what I wanted...even if it was death. My life couldn't be more fucked up then what it is right now, and I have all intentions on making the world around me feel me on this shit too.

PRESENT DAY
GREEN DOOR - ADULT MENTAL HEALTH CARE CLINIC
NORTHWEST, WASHINGTON DC

"Whoa," Christina wiped her face with a napkin. Although the air conditioner was working, Harmony's story was getting crazier by the minute. "Did she talk to you after everything happened? I mean, how did you find out about her friend? And how she died."

"She told me some stuff. She used it as an excuse to hurt me more."

"Did she always seem so angry? I mean based on your version of the story, she seemed to always be angry with you."

"She was always mad with me about something or another. I don't care what I did to do right by that girl, she never was grateful."

"She never was grateful?" Christina smirked. "Ms. Phillips, what did she have to be grateful for? You were drunk half the time and for the longest your children thought they were boys!"

"She should have been grateful for life! For breathing." She paused and then lowered her voice. "She should have been grateful for life."

Christina shook her head in disgust. "If what you're saying is true, that your children should have been able to overcome all obstacles and be grateful for life," she paused, "shouldn't you have been grateful too?"

"What do you mean?"

"You make a lot of excuses for things in your life, Harmony. You say nobody ever cared about you, or loved you, yet you turned around and treated your children the same way your abusers did you...if not worse. You're not taking your own advice and you're still playing the victim. Even now."

"That's not true."

"It is." She said in a low tone. "That's why so many people roam around the world killing and hurting each other. They don't know how to stop the vicious cycle. To combat hate you MUST LOVE. It's the only way. You had a duty to love your children and you didn't do it." She paused. "Why?"

"I never fucked my kids! Ever!"

Christina was confused. She lowered her head, sat back in the seat and sighed. "I just said a mouthful, and that's what you got from my statement?"

"Well what you saying?"

"There are lots of reasons that people grow up and treat their children badly, and it seems that the main reason you gave was that you were abused as a child. So what I'm saying is that if you wanted to, if you really desired to be different, you could have broken the cycle."

Silence.

"Well none of that matters anymore now does it?" Harmony said. "Because during this time, after her girlfriend died, even if I wanted to change she would never forgive me for the past. Ever."

"You know there was a study done on monkeys some years back, and basically it showed that if monkey babies weren't held, and given love, they would grow up to be cold and calculating. Disassociated. Turning that study to humans the same remains true. Touch and love establishes trust. Without it, individuals can't feel empathy for one another. They don't know how to gage true love versus lust, etc. They don't know how to show compassion."

"So you trying to call my kids monkeys?"

"I'm not saying that, Harmony." She sighed. "What I'm saying is that when you don't show love, hold your children and show general affection, they can't express it effectively to other people. They don't know how because they haven't been taught. So when they do come into contact with someone who gives them any type of attention, if it isn't real, they won't know the difference."

"I'm not trying to hear all this shit."

"You don't have to hear me. Just look at your life. It's proves my point."

"Whatever."

Christina wrestled with the papers in her lap. She said, "Okay, let's take it another route. How did she react when her girlfriend was murdered?"

With an attitude Harmony said, "Things went to a whole nother level when that girl died. I always knew Madjesty was angry with the world and me, but when she died she started to drink more and be real mean. She became real cold. Like steel. I think the only one who could calm her down at that point was Jayden."

"Okay, so what did she do after the murder?"

Silence.

"Harmony…" Christina paused, "How did she do after the murder? Mentally?"

"It was like...it was like...everything that happened to her after that night was my fault and I started to pray that God would just take my life because if he didn't do it, I had plans to do it myself."

"Okay, Harmony," she sighed, "Continue with your sob story."

HARMONY
CONCORD MANOR

The basement felt like a tomb. I could hear life go on around me outside, but I didn't feel a part of it anymore. It had to be about four in the morning and I was surprised the kids weren't running around in the house or raping me. Most times I'd think about my life and why I wasn't able to be regular or normal. And when I wasn't thinking about shit like that I'd think about fucking, drinking and eating. Since my life was not my own, usually I just went to sleep.

I was asleep when Madjesty came down the stairs. Her hair was matted with blood and her eyes looked wild. She looked like she was drained and I became immediately afraid. What would she blame me for now? It seemed that everything bad that happened to her was all my fault, but what about me?

As always she pulled the chair up in front of me and sat down. She snatched the tape off of my mouth which meant she wanted to talk. She only did that when she wanted to talk.

"They...they killed my girl." Tears rolled down her face although she didn't make a crying sound. "They killed her right in front of me." She looked at her bloody hands. Turned them over and over examining them. Then she smelled her finger. One finger.

"I'm sorry, Mad. I really am. Are you okay?"

"I don't know why stuff keeps happening to me, but I'm not gonna be right after this shit." She said pointing to the floor. "They should've fuckin' killed me and let me be with her." She continued. "I'm not gonna be right at all."

I knew from dealing with her in the past that I had to be careful. Usually anything I said, if I didn't say it right was flipped around on me. So I was slow about saying anything and I chose my words carefully. It's amazing, when I wasn't drunk I could think clearly.

"What I'm gonna do without her? What I'm gonna do without my girl?"

"I don't know."

"Mama, please. Tell me what to do. Tell me how to make this right."

She hadn't called me mama in weeks. And I couldn't lie, for some reason it felt good.

"Mad, you gotta be a good person, baby. You gotta stop the violence." I said softly. "Too much is happening right now and you gotta do right starting with this shit you doing to me. Let me go. *Please*."

"What you talking about?" She frowned. "This shit with you ain't got nothing to do with me losing my girl. All you care about is yourself."

"I care about you too, Madjesty. You're my daughter." I said softer.

"Don't call me that!" She pointed at me. "Don't call me that ever again."

"What?"

"Your daughter. I'm not a...I'm not your daughter."

I didn't know if she didn't want me to call her my daughter because of anger, or because she didn't feel like a girl. I always felt that unlike Jayden, she didn't take the idea of being a girl too well.

"I'm sorry." I said. "But I love you."

"You don't love me." She cried. "You don't love me."

"I do. Baby, I swear I do."

She shook her head and tears rolled down her face. "Why did you do me like this? Why did you make me this person?"

"I don't understand."

"This person." She said hitting herself in the head with both fists. "This fucking person! That hates everything and everybody! Huh? Why?"

Silence.

"I'm sorry." Sorry felt like the right thing to say so I said it again. "I'm sorry, but you gotta let me go. I can help you deal with what's going on, but not if I'm like this. And not if you kill me."

She stood up, grabbed a bat and walked toward me. Then she hit me in the head with it as hard as she could.

I can't remember much after that.

All I know is, I woke up in a different place.

Ursula Givens
My Daughter's Dead Day

Ursula led the way in her car on the way to her daughter's funeral. She almost couldn't afford Glitter's going away service and she definitely couldn't afford to ride in a limo. Madjesty had stolen all of her money and she was dead broke. Because of it, she would have to take her car, which was still painted with the word dyke on it everywhere. She knew people would be pointing and gawking, and questioning her sexuality, which made her hate Madjesty even more.

Not only that, but word had gotten back to her that Madjesty was somehow involved with Glitter's murder and she wanted blood and revenge. Her son Jerrod and Nook, her weed dealer, rode with her but they knew better than to say a word when she was like this. She seemed to be more entranced with Madjesty then anything else.

"What ya'll know about this girl?" Ursula asked.

"Not much." Jerrod said.

"'Cause of her I gotta gotta go to my daughter's dead day! Fucking bitch!" She yelled. "I can't stand dykes. Kissing other girls and shit. What type shit is that?" She paused. "God meant for man and woman to cohabitate. Not man and man. Or woman and woman!"

Nook and Keith remained silent. There was no greater homophobe on planet earth than Ursula Givens. She hated homosexuals so much, that she used every five minutes to talk about them, even if they weren't the subject. She didn't realize that people who hated on homosexuality so much, were suspect. Straight people need not speak on others because they're confident in their own. She didn't care. She was confused and she held hate in her heart. Madjesty played her and now her daughter was dead. She wanted revenge and that's all she cared about.

"Well put the word out that I'ma raise some money, for the first person who can prove this bitch killed my baby girl." She paused. "If that's not gonna work, any other dirt they can dig up on this bull dagger will do too. And I'll put five hundred on it if they can bring her to me!"

HARMONY
BLACK HOLE

It was very dark. So dark originally I thought I was still dreaming. When I woke up my head was throbbing and I felt like my right leg was broken. When I tried to move my toes I didn't think my leg was broken. I knew it was broken.

"Ahhhhhh!" I screamed out in pain. "Helllllllp! My leg is broken!!! Please!" I couldn't do anything but cry and beg her to let me out since she didn't want to let me die. "Okay I was wrong, Madjesty!" I screamed. "I was a horrible mother and I treated you badly! Now please…please let me out of here. You're going to kill me!"

She didn't answer but I felt she was listening. I felt her presence. There was not much room to move around and the smell inside this space was putrid. I couldn't even breathe. Where was I? My question was answered when Mad finally opened the door. I was in the crawl space.

Under the stairs.

In my own house.

"Morning, mama." Madjesty said. She still looked crazed. Like she wasn't the same. This meant trouble for me. She didn't have a bra on under her shirt and I could see her breasts. She never wore less than two shirts since she started stealing her own clothes. She completely lost it and no longer cared. It was evident. "You were saying something?"

"Madjesty, I think my leg is broken. You gotta let me out."

"Why I gotta do that?"

"Madjesty, please…you gotta let me out of here. I'm hungry and injured." I sobbed. "Please let me go."

"Why?" She smirked. "I would think you'd like it under there, being as though you put me there so many times. Remember when you grabbed me by my hair and threw me inside? Without food or drink?" Then she laughed. "As a matter of fact, you forgot I was even under there. The lady in the wheelchair had to feed me." Then she paused. "Hey, what happened to the lady in the wheel chair anyway? I was starting to like her."

"Madjesty, please." I continued. "I know I was wrong for how I did you. You proved your point but you must let me out of here now. This is too much."

"Don't worry, I'm not gonna do you like you did me, mama. I'm gonna do you right."

She was calling me mama more which meant trouble. She was saying it in a condescending sort of way. Like she really didn't mean it. She stepped away from the crawl space door but left it open. The front door was about ten or fifteen feet in front of me. If I ran, if I ran quickly, maybe I could save my own life.

When I remembered I couldn't run because my leg was hurt she returned with a bowl of chowder in one hand and my stomach rumbled. She kept the other hand behind her back and I knew she was hiding something. Also judging by my hunger pains, I figured I must've gone two or three days without eating. I was starting to know how different pains felt when I didn't eat regularly. Basically the way I felt meant it had been two to three days since she hit me over the head with the bat. It was a wonder I was alive. She slid the bowl across to me. I tried to snatch it but she snatched it back.

"I got to put a little salt in it first, mama."

My mouth was salivating. "I don't need no salt. Just give it me. Please."

"Oh yes you do." She laughed. Then she took whatever she had behind her back and dangled it in front of me. "This was my girl's. I found it in the trashcan upstairs. She left it there when she used my bathroom."

"What are you going to do with that?" I frowned.

Without responding, she put the dirty tampon in my food. It was old and smelled foul.

"Here you go, mama." She laughed. "Now it's good enough to eat." She slid the bowl in my direction and I saw the creamy white color turn a little red where the tampon rested.

I cried.

"It's your fault my girl is not here and you cry?" She said tearing up too. "You deserve everything you're getting, bitch."

"Just kill me, Madjesty. I'm sick of this shit."

"You gonna eat the food or not?" She said reaching for the bowl.

I snatched it from her quickly. I was gonna either eat this or die.

I looked down at the bowl and despite the dried tampon could smell the scent of food. I was hungry. So without a spoon I closed my eyes and sopped up the soup handful after handful. The smile was removed off of her face as I satisfied my hunger.

I smiled.

She frowned.

"Let's see how much longer you can last after three more days without food."

• •

More Days Later

I can't know how long I'd been under here. My mouth was dry and I felt extremely weak. My end was near and I was grateful. I lived a long life. A *really* long life. I don't know if I would've made it in the world if I was free. I probably would kill her. I probably would kill both of my kids.

I closed my eyes preparing to drift into a permanent sleep when she opened the door. The light hit my eyes and hurt. She smirked at me. Grabbed my hair and stabbed me multiple times in my arm, legs and shoulders. I felt the pain but would give her no satisfaction.

I was done.

She was going to kill me slowly. She was going to drag it out as long as she could.

• •

The Next Morning

I was still alive. But why? So much blood left my body that I could barely lift my head. I was weak and drained. The strange thing is, the longer I lived the more I wanted life. I needed to get this bitch back for everything she'd done to me. It couldn't end like this. But I knew I wouldn't be alive long if I didn't get help. But how could I? I was hidden under my stairs. And then I heard a voice. A different voice. So with everything I had in me, and with all of the strength I held inside, I screamed to the top of my lungs.

"HELLLLLLLLP!!!"

JAYDEN

PIMP FAST JAYDEN

Jayden's face-hardened and her lips stiffened as the two-time Grammy award winning gospel singer's voice boomed from the speakers upstairs. She hated gospel and any mention of the Lord. She'd been in a battle with him ever since she was a kid and every prayer she threw up to heaven was ignored.

"Fuck God!" She spat walking around her room. "Just leave already!"

Knock. Knock. Knock.

Jayden stopped in her footsteps and looked at the closed wooden door.

Her chest filled with air before she let out a breathy and irritated, "Yessssss?"

"I'm about to leave for work. Can I talk to you for a minute?"

Jayden stomped her foot put her hand on her hip and flung the bedroom door open. "Yes, Ms. Nadine?"

Nadine, her landlord, wearing a light blue housekeeping uniform that made her look larger than her actual husky build, smiled. Her yellowing teeth and thinning black hair layered in dandruff flakes gave character to a face that was growing older than its fifty-year-old age. Yet her disposition was so mellowing that most people smiled when she entered a room.

"I see you didn't touch the food I made you yesterday. It's still in the fridge." She reached to touch her on the shoulder but Jayden moved back. "Is everything okay?"

"I wasn't hungry." She frowned.

Nadine smiled awkwardly and removed a black withered bible with gold lettering from her brown purse. The strap on her purse was coming off and was held in place by a staple and a lot of silver duct tape. "I wanted to pray with you before I left for work." She paused. "Xion told me you haven't been able to get in contact with your mother or sister and I wanted to offer you some words of encouragement."

"And I told you I don't believe in God, His Son or the Holy Spirit."

Her words made Nadine's face, which was covered in a net of wrinkles, tremble as if she were a child who had just gotten smacked by her mother.

"Just a few lines, Jayden. Please."

"Nadine, maybe I should move."

Silence.

"Please don't!" She placed the bible in her purse and backed out of the room. Yet she remained in the doorway. "I really need the money or my house will go into foreclosure. Xion can't help me like he use to. He don't have that job in construction no more." She continued, not knowing he use to work with Shaggy in the drug business.

"Then you have to let me have my privacy, Nadine!" she yelled. I don't want to hurt your feelings, but if that fucking God of yours was any good, you wouldn't be broke and I wouldn't have to be here."

She slammed the door in her face.

It took a moment before she could hear her white work shoes click clacking up the steps. It took even longer before the ceiling creaked, indicating that Nadine was now upstairs. But it wasn't until the music was shut off, the floor moaned, the keys jingled and the door closed, that she knew she was finally gone. And she could get down to what was bothering her the most.

Grabbing the house phone, she dialed a number and waited for Gucci, one of her girls, to answer. In the weeks passed she had spent over a thousand dollars on them collectively, to buy their friendships and eventually their pussy. And now that the day came for them to make good on her gifts, none of them were answering their phones. They had a meeting at 6:00 PM that evening and it was now 5:30.

"Where the fuck are these bitches?" She frowned, talking to herself.

When her feet grew tired of walking, she plopped on the queen size mahogany bed that Xion bought her within the small cramped room. She could see her reflection in the large mirror on the matching dresser. She looked older than she had just a few months ago. But it made sense, a few months ago she thought she was a boy, now she was a teenage girl. A few months ago she was living under her mother's tyranny and now she was trying to run a successful sex operation. A lot of shit had changed.

When her personal home phone line rang she jumped up, picked up the receiver and answered. "Hello?"

Silence.

"Hello!"

More silence.

She looked into the receiver as if it would show any indications of being broken.

"Hello! Who is this?"

She heard a click and hung up. Sitting back on the bed she bit her nails until they bled again. A habit she picked up in the weeks preceding. Calls like that came all the time and she was starting to worry about her safety.

Glancing at the six chairs against the wall that she kept aligned to hold meetings with the members of Thirteen Flavors, a sex operation disguised as a baby-sitting service, she wondered if any of it was worth it. Her mind raced back to having to steal from the grocers just to survive when she was back in Texas, and how she was always picked on about her dirty clothing at school. When those childhood memories resurfaced, she answered with an overwhelming, yes. It is all worth it.

Since she left home, Jayden was finally starting to get in a business state of mind. The only problem was, she could barely read and she wasn't all that good with money if it was in large quantities. So in order to create the flyers, and advertise and keep things in line she relied heavily on Passion. She deemed Passion her assistant and bottom bitch.

She was too embarrassed to ask for Xion's help because she didn't want him thinking she wasn't smart, knowing that any weakness could be used against her in the future. She didn't even let the girls know she could barely read, count or write. Whenever something required those skills, she would suddenly act as if she didn't have time for those matters. In her own time she would study elementary school books to learn the basics. Despite the learning curve she was under, she was determined to make money. She just needed to find a way to keep her girls in line first.

Looking at the Gucci watch her father bought, his first gift to her, she frowned when she saw it was now fifteen minutes before her meeting and not one of them had bothered to confirm.

Reaching into her brown Gucci purse, she saw she had six missed calls on her cell phone. With the advertisements they placed mostly in grocery stores and on Craigslist, they were getting calls everyday. It didn't take dirty men long to read between the lines when they saw her flyers. Besides, the ad was subliminal but sexy enough so that a horny man, if nothing else would be persuaded to place a call, even if he didn't have children. They occasionally got real babysitting offers and they would claim to be booked up for those specific dates.

The ad showed a picture of Passion, Foxie, Na Na, Gucci and Queen with three neighborhood kids in the living room upstairs. The girls were all wearing tiny jean shorts with colorful t-shirts as they posed in various parts of the living room. To play off of the name Thirteen Flavors, they held ice cream cones in their hands and looked innocent although slightly seductive. Underneath the picture was a message that read, 'Let us tame the bad boys and girls of your life. Thirteen Flavors babysitting services…our girls are available anytime of day or night.'

They received so many calls that they weaved out a lot of crazies be-fore finally settling on six different clients for the weekend and one for Passion tonight. But before they did anything, Jayden wanted to meet with them about her expectations. That's why the meeting was so impor-tant.

Frustrated that more time passed, she placed another call to Gucci, who despite secretly not liking her, always answered her phone when Jayden called. She didn't want to call her but now she had no choice.

"Hello…hello?" Jayden yelled.

"Yes, Jayden." Gucci said sarcastically.

"I didn't expect you to answer. I mean…I been calling everybody all day."

"Well I'm not everybody now am I?"

"Look…where are you? And everybody else? We have a meeting in less than five minutes."

She sighed. "We not coming."

"What you mean you not coming?"

"Just what I said. Na Na's mother sick so we at her house. Plus we not really serious about all that 13 flavors shit. I mean, you cool and all, Jayden, but you taking this prostitution shit too far."

"Oh really? After all the money I gave ya'll and after all the shit I bought?"

"We thank you for it." She paused. "But like I said, Na Na's mother is sick."

The thought of not making money with her business bothered her greatly. She played with the strap on her purse as she struggled with what to say next. "I'm sorry to hear about Na Na's mother. Did ya'll want me to come over?"

"No."

"Well let me speak to Na Na."

She sighed. "Hold on. Let me see if she can talk."

Jayden heard loud music and boys talking in the background. In her mind it didn't sound like they were in Na Na's house because her mother didn't allow them to turn the TV up let alone have boys in the house.

Jayden stood up and waited for Na Na to get on the phone when sud-denly the background noise stopped. She took the phone from her ear and saw that either the call disconnected or that Gucci hung up. She called back several times before someone answered.

"Why the fuck you hang up?!"

"Jayden…this Na Na. What's up?"

"What's going on? Is your mother sick or not?"

"She is, but we decided to come to the meeting. Gucci got stuff messed up when you called earlier. We in front of Passion's house now trying to pick her up."

Jayden felt sick with how they were treating her all of a sudden. What was with all the games?

A few more seconds passed of silence. "Is Passion there?"

"I don't know yet." Then she paused and yelled, "Go to the back door and knock hard, Gucci! She may be sleep!"

"Who driving?" Jayden asked, interrupting their search.

"We in my mother's truck."

"She ain't there!" Gucci yelled.

Jayden heard her. "Fuck! Let me see if I can get a hold of this bitch again!" She paused. "But you tell her if you talk to her before me that I'm sick of this shit and we ain't gotta be friends if it's like this because I'm all about my money." Jayden ended the call and called Passion's cousin house.

Her uncle answered the phone. "Hey, Mike, is Passion over there?"

"Who is this? Jayden?"

She sighed. "Yeah."

"When you gonna let me taste that pussy?"

"Fuck you talking about?"

"Every time I see you walk up in this bitch I be thinking about the same thing, eating that pussy." He paused. "I know that shit good to ain't it?"

It sure is, nigga. I ain't fucked nobody and even if I did it damn sure wouldn't be you. She thought. Jayden never had vaginal sex and as far as she was concerned, there was no need. She got her rocks off every other night by fingering her pussy until it was wet, before running over the tip of her clit with slick fingers. Once she figured out how to get an orgasm, she never stopped.

"How come every time I call there you coming at me sideways?" She paused. "Where your wife at anyway?"

"She not here. But fuck her!" he paused. "You gonna come over here or not? 'Cause just the sound of your voice got the veins on my dick pulsating."

"Look, I ain't got time for all that," she glared, "tell her I called and I'm looking for her."

"You tell her yourself." He said. "She hitchhiked over that boyfriend of hers house since she couldn't steal my car. I'm sick of her taking my shit and I think she got a key made."

"Where is her car?"

"It's broke again. So now she think my shit belongs to her."

She slammed the phone in his face and was about to call Xion. When she picked up the phone Passion's uncle was still on the line. *"You young bitches are all the same! Dumb!"* He yelled before hanging up.

She shook her head and dialed Xion's number. The moment she heard his voice she said, *"I need you."*

"Finally you gonna give me some of that pussy?" He laughed. *"'Cause I'm tired of fingering you while you beat my dick."*

"All that?" She laughed. *"On the phone? Really?"*

"You know I'm serious."

"Later, for that, daddy. I gotta find Passion first. You mind taking me to her boyfriend's house?"

"Is something wrong?"

"It's just girl business." Xion had no idea about Jayden's hustle and she didn't intend on telling him either. *"Nothing you need to worry about, daddy."*

"Aight...but don't she fuck with the nigga Coop?"

"Yeah. So?"

"You know he half crazy right?"

"You scared?" Jayden questioned.

"Yeah aight." He laughed. *"I'm on my way."*

Fifteen minutes later Xion pulled up in his new white Yukon with rims. Jayden walked out the house and turned around to lock the door. He eyed the way her round ass filled the pockets of her jeans and her shiny black hair rested in the middle of her back. When she turned around she smiled at him and sauntered seductively to the car.

When she got in she eyed him. Xion was sexy all the way around the board. The sun bounced off his vanilla colored skin and she loved the way his white t-shirt hugged his muscular arms.

"You hungry?" He asked pulling down his red baseball cap.

"You look good." She said eying him again.

"Good enough to fuck?"

"Xion!" She playfully hit his arm. *"Stop talking to me like that."*

"I'm serious. When you gonna let me make you feel good?"

"You do it every night you come over and flip my clit." She smiled. *"Let's get over one step at a time."*

He frowned a little and said, *"What you want to eat?"*

"Nothing heavy right now. Maybe some nuggets or something."

He took her to get the food and she shared a twelve-piece nugget box with him as he drove. Dipping sauce on one she placed it into his mouth and he ate it, gently sucking her finger.

"Xion, please stop." She said through tight lips. "We'll fuck when I'm ready."

He shook his head. "You know Shaggy at school telling niggas I stole his bitch right?" He chewed. "I had six different niggas approach me about that shit yesterday."

"And you care about that 'cause?"

"'Cause that was how I use to get my money. Now that I don't work for him no more, I gotta get my shit elsewhere."

"Why you telling me?"

"Truthfully?"

"Yeah, Xion." She paused. "I hate when you beat around the bush with me because I know something's up."

"'Cause I wanted to see if you could talk to your pops. Maybe he can put me on. If nothing else, holla at Shaggy for me. I'm use to a certain lifestyle, Jayden and a nigga been broke since he cut me off. I can't even help my aunt Nadine out no more."

"Aight, X. I'll see what I can do." She was wondering what she could possibly say to her father. Although their bond was growing by the day, it was still new. "I can't make no promises though."

He winked at her. "Thanks, ma."

When Xion got to Coop's street they saw people looking in one direction. The closer they got they could hear Passion and him fussing before the car even stopped. Their voices were so loud, that neighbors looked out of their windows while others walked outside and straight stared at the house.

"You sure you wanna knock on the door?" Xion asked looking at the window. "This nigga's a handful."

"I'm sure." She smiled. "Plus me and Passion got business and I need to rap to her tonight. It can't wait."

"Aight, let's go." He said parking.

"Naw, baby, you chill here. I'm going in myself."

With the car in park he looked over at her and said, "I just told you this nigga be wilding out. And you trying to go in by yourself?"

"Please, X. Let me do this. If I need you I'll holla." He hit the steering wheel and looked out the driver's window. She put her hand over his. "I promise. I'm gonna be okay."

He smiled on one side of his mouth. "I know you gonna be good. When I met you, you were fighting." He smirked and gripped her hand. "I see you getting more independent by the day too."

"I can't be a baby no more, Xi. My mother and sister are missing. I really may be on my own out here."

"No you not. How you on your own when you got me?"

"I hope you mean that."

"I do, Jayden. And I know you got to handle your family affairs by yourself," he paused, "for whatever reason. But I'm still here and I got your back. So don't tell me you out here on your own when you not."

"I'll hurry back." She opened the truck door.

Xion wasn't feeling letting her roll by herself but he didn't push the issue. Besides he wasn't her man although he was trying to be. He saw the strong woman she was becoming and crowding her too much could be bad for his ultimate plan of making her his girl. He'd seen first hand where that got Shaggy. Nowhere.

Jayden walked slowly up to Coop's door. Her palms sweated and she wiped her hands several times on her jeans to dry them off. After taking a deep breath, she knocked on the door. Coop flung it open and gave her an evil look.

"You lost?"

"No."

"Then what the fuck you want?" He asked. His stomach rose and fell and his goatee although neat had cat hairs all throughout it and she wondered how they got there. He was twenty-five years old, cute but at the moment extremely angry. Still, Jayden could immediately see why Passion went for him. He was a bad boy, a nigga who always got what he wanted and if he didn't get his way people suffered. Everything in Jayden's young body said run but she decided not to because there was no way she could go back home to Harmony. In her mind, it all came down to this moment.

"I said what the fuck do you want?" He looked her up and down.

"I'm here to see Passion. Can you tell her I'm out here please?" She paused, her feet moved nervously under her body. "Uh...we...we got...some stuff to do today."

"Some stuff to do today?" He said sarcastically.

"Yes."

"Well she got other plans tonight."

"I can't go until I speak to her."

"Bitch, get the fuck off my steps." He said slamming the door in her face.

Jayden took a step back and looked at Xion's car.

"What happen?" He said with a screw face from the car. Then he cocked his gun. She didn't see it but she could hear it. Every neighbor who was near looked at what would happen next. *"That nigga disrespect you?"*

"I got it, baby." She waved him off. Then she pointed at everybody. "Stay in the car and be cool. A lot of people watching."

A few of them stopped looking in her direction and pretended to care for their lawns and other fake shit after hearing her comment. But some folks didn't give a fuck and kept their eyes on the house.

"I don't know about this shit, babes. Just come on."

"Please, Xi! One second."

She turned around focused on the door again and with all of her might, banged heavily on it. Everyday she gave herself tests, to be stronger and harder. The old Jayden was still inside of her and told her she was a fool for even trying to run a sex operation but in her mind she couldn't see herself doing anything else. She knew what she wanted to do the moment she laid eyes on Pimp Fast Tony, especially after years later, when she learned what he actually sold.

When Coop didn't come back to the door she knocked even harder, until it sounded as if she was about to kick his door down.

Hearing the sound of his door rattling as if it was about to come off of the hinges, he threw the door open.

"Don't fucking slam the door in my face again, nigga." She said before he could say anything.

"What you just say to me?" He was shocked at her response.

"You heard me!" She paused. "Now you got my bitch in your house, while she's in your house, I can't make my money. I put a lot of money into her ass, and that's why she look the way she do to you. Now either give me the five hundred dollars I spent on that bitch, or tell her to get her shit and come on, because I'm not leaving without one or the other."

He laughed and said, "What are you, her fucking pimp or something?"

Jayden stood her ground. "Go get her!"

He knew he could choke her in one instant, but looked at all of the witnesses who were staring in his direction. In his mind none of this would've happened if Passion hadn't popped up over his house while he was fucking another bitch. The girl left after Passion threatened to bust the windows of her brand new Benz. Coop tried to get Passion to leave until she threw his yellow cat in his face and it scratched him on the mouth. When she did that shit hit the fan and they'd been fighting ever since.

"You know what," he said looking at his neighbors on the left and then the right, "you can take this bitch with you because I'm tired of her shit anyway."

He was preparing to slam the door in her face again before she blocked it from closing with her foot. "Leave the door open."

He looked at her, smirked and walked into the house.

A minute later Passion came outside rattled. Her long hair was all over her head and her face was bruised. The blue t-shirt she was wearing was ripped and when she saw the neighbors looking at her she tugged at the black mini skirt she was wearing so that no one could see she wasn't wearing any panties. She came over panty-less in the hopes of seducing Coop but her plan was foiled and instead of dick she got her ass whooped.

Jayden wondered how much money she'd have to reinvest to get this bitch up to par again. She was still sexy and pretty, but she looked abused.

"What are you doing here?" Passion said looking behind her worried he'd snatch her up at any moment. "Now he's gonna really be mad."

"Passion, get your shit and come on. That nigga passed mad a long time ago."

"Girl, he be like this all the time."

Jayden shook her head. "Passion, I got a client set up for you tonight and you can't be fucking with my money."

"But I can't do it tonight!" She said looking at her seriously. "I caught him cheating on me girl. Shit got out of hand."

"I don't give a fuck about all that! You agreed to do the job now it's time to make money."

She pouted and folded her arms. "You came all the way over here to tell me that?"

"Yes! And you're my friend and I care about you. You don't need to be messing with him, girl." She paused. "You said yourself he had another bitch in the house. I mean, how much proof do you need?"

When she called her a friend Passion's heart lightened up. She saw Jayden as someone who was fly and had it all. Always. That's because recently Jayden developed a habit of lying. She told everyone who would listen how wonderful her mother was and how close she and her sister were. But whenever Passion wanted to meet them, she'd make an excuse. Truth was she was ashamed of Harmony and Madjesty and wanted to keep her new friends/whores out of her personal life as much as possible.

"I'm your friend?" Passion asked.

"Yes. But we also got business together. You don't need to be around this type of dude, Passion. We gotta go. Now!" She said grabbing her hand pulling her toward the truck.

Passion shook her off. "I'm sick of you acting like I'm property, Jay. I mean, damn, you taking stuff too seriously with all of this Thirteen Flavors shit." She paused. "I was just trying to make a little money so I can get some clothes and get high. I ain't trying to be fucking for the rest of my life."

"You so fucking pressed over these niggas! When you gonna understand they just playing you? The least you could do is make some money if you gonna give the pussy away."

Passion placed her hands on her hips and smirked. "What you know about fucking niggas? They telling me you still a virgin."

Jayden knew her virgin status made her look inexperienced but she wasn't going to fuck before she was ready and that was the bottom line.

"And that makes your point how?"

"What you mean?"

"I haven't had to fuck a nigga ever. Yet I got more paper than you?"

"Whatever."

"Bitch, look at your fucking arm." Passion did. "You wearing the gold bracelet I bought." Jayden frowned. "Now bring that ass on now. Because contrary to what you believe, that pussy belongs to me."

"What you just say?"

"I said bring your ass on. Because there ain't but one pussy that can be in charge at a time and it damn sure ain't yours!" Words just flowed from her mouth as if she was her mother and it shocked her at first. But when she took a few steps away from the house and Passion wasn't following her she got serious. "If I reach the car and you not behind me I'ma tell Xion. Then he gonna get his heat, get out that car, and put that bird in your mouth. Let's go. Now."

"You really do got more than one personality."

"What?"

"They told me you have split personalities, and now I'm starting to see that."

"Fuck all that. It's time to roll."

Passion hesitated one second before dipping out of the door and behind Jayden. Besides, Jayden was right and Passion knew it. The niggas she fucked most of time didn't give her shit but dick. Passion was tired of being used, she wanted more out of life and Jayden could give that to her. She wanted to have fun and she wanted to be taken care of and thanks to Jayden she had jewelry, kept a fresh hairdo, fly clothes and a steady supply of any drug she wanted. If Jayden cut her off now she knew she couldn't keep the lifestyle she was use to since she entered her life. They were almost at the car when Coop ran outside.

"Bitch, where the fuck is my money?"

Passion stuffed it in her bra earlier but didn't think he would notice right away. Passion and Jayden ran to the car but he caught Passion and grabbed a large patch of her hair.

"Get the fuck off of me!" She yelled hitting him on his arms, her punches bouncing off as if they were never there to begin with. "You're hurting me!" Her body dragged against the ground as if she was a lifeless doll.

"You gonna come in here, start shit and then steal my money? Fuck that!" Coop said pulling her toward the house as quickly as humanly possible.

"Let's go, Jayden!" Xion yelled. "Don't make me get out of the car. I'm not coming alone."

"One second!"

Coop almost had Passion inside of his house until Jayden caught wheels and ran in their direction. She wasn't a fighter by nature but she turned into one when necessary.

Right before Coop slammed the front door, Jayden pushed it open using her body weight and Xion hopped out of the car to help them out. When Coop saw Xion rushing in his direction, he pushed Passion inside and grabbed Jayden. Once he had both of them, he slammed the door in Xion's face and locked it.

"OPEN THIS DOOR, NIGGA!" Xion banged with a closed fist. "OPEN THIS FUCKING DOOR RIGHT NOW!" The gun rested in his waist and he was waiting for the perfect time to pull it out and start busting.

Inside the house Coop had knocked Passion to the floor. With his attention off of her he grabbed a handful of Jayden's hair before hitting her in the face with a closed fist. She held on to her face and tried to fight him back. She was no match for the man's brute strength and it wasn't until Passion got off of her ass and helped out that together they were able to overcome him. Having been beat in the past by her mother Jayden made up in her mind to go the distance.

The young girls hit him everywhere blows would land and although he wasn't hurt much, it was difficult to control two teenage wild women.

Sirens rang in the background and it was obvious the police were on their way.

"I'ma kill you bitches!" He yelled.

Hearing this, Passion grabbed his vase off of the counter, and smacked him in the head with it. She cut herself in the process. When he fell to the floor she and Jayden ran out of the house and into Xion who was about to kick down the door.

"Ya'll okay?" He asked looking behind them into the house. He grabbed Jayden and checked her over. The sirens were getting closer. "This nigga hit you in the face?"

"It's okay, baby," Jayden said trying to catch her breath. "I'm fine." She looked behind her hoping Coop wouldn't run out at any moment. "But let's get the fuck out of here. The cops are coming."

Xion was preparing to ignore her and go into the house anyway. "I'm bout to go crush this…"

"Please, let's just go!" Jayden said grabbing his hand pulling him to the car.

"I feel like killing this dude."

"And if you really want to you can handle that later," Jayden said. "For now I'm trying to get home. I got some business to handle and the more time I'm here, the more time my money is being fucked with."

Xion reluctantly ran to his truck with the girls following him. It was silent for fifteen minutes as they approached Jayden's house. "I'm sorry, Jayden." Passion said breaking silence.

"Prove how sorry you are by doing what you gotta do." Jayden looked over at Xion hoping he wouldn't catch on. "Because that shit back there is gonna cost you."

"I know, mami. I'ma make it up to you too."

Jayden loved it when she called her mami.

• •

Back At The House

After everything was all said and done, she held the meeting with her girls. It went off without a hitch and at the end of the night outside of Passion's hand being cut, and her face being bruised things between them were fine. After the meeting Jayden was clear that the girls knew their duties as far as Thirteen Flavors was concerned and they were going to handle them or she would cut them all off for good.

Jayden hadn't expected things to go the way that they had with Coop but she needed her. Why? Because there wasn't a thing Passion wouldn't do in the bedroom, and that included licking ass, sucking toes and anything else Jayden could think of. When it came to Passion she was all game.

Passion was a goldmine and Jayden needed to keep her mind on business and out of the different niggas that ran in and out of her pussy. For free. Picking up the flyer they created she stared at it deeply. Passion looked like Crissa, Tisa's mother. She was just as pretty and seductive and she may have even been the age she was the last time Jayden saw her.

After she held the meeting with the girls, she sat on the sofa and thought about her mother. She thought about her sister. She thought about life. Before spending time with her father, she hated Harmony and everything she put her through. But it was Jace who told her that Estelle was murdered in front of Harmony and that her father, Cornell was killed in jail. Jayden never knew any of these things because Harmony didn't open up to them, ever.

She was just about to catch a nap. After all of the events of the day she was tired and wanted to be up around the time Passion had her session later that night. She was about to close her eyes when her phone rang. It was Mad.

"Hello."

"Jayden, can I come over? I really need to see you."

"Madjesty, where have you been? I've been calling you for days."

"I know...I been through a lot. I just need to come over and talk to you. Is now good?"

"You still got the address?"

"Yes. I'm on my way."

So much for her nap.

When Madjesty got there she smelled of alcohol and her hair was dyed red. The hair color change symbolized the blood that fell in her hair when Glitter's life was stolen. Jayden noticed immediately that her eyes were slightly pink and she looked like she'd been crying.

"Mad, what happened?" She said, opening the front door for her. "Are you okay?" She held her tightly. "Are you hurt?"

She stepped inside using slow motions, her head was hung low and she looked beat. "I'm fine. Just had a long couple of nights."

"Come downstairs. My room is there." Jayden locked the front door and walked toward the basement with Mad following her.

"Who house is this?"

"A friend of mine's aunt house. She works in the evenings and is hardly home. It's almost like I have the whole place to myself."

When they made it to her room she said, "Come sit on my bed."

"It's small in here." Madjesty noticed. "You like it better than Concord?"

"It's mine."

"I feel you." Emotionally torn down, Mad flopped down on her sister's bed. "They killed my girl some nights back, Jayden. They fucking killed my girl right in front of me and I wanted them to kill me too."

"Your girl?" Jayden was confused by her comment.

It was then that Mad realized she never expressed that she was what some people considered a lesbian. Personally Mad hated the tag because in her mind she was always a boy, and would always be one.

"Yeah...we were sitting in the truck and they fucking ran up to it and killed her. What I'm gonna do without her?"

"Was it the girl Glitter? The one I saw you with at the house that day?"

"Yeah. She gone!" She sobbed harder. "She fucking gone!"

"I'm so sorry, Mad." Jayden hugged her again and rocked her like she did when they were boys on the bottom bunk in Texas. "It's gonna be alright. I promise."

Mad fell into her sister's embrace and wiped the tears off of her face. Suddenly, for the moment anyway, everything seemed okay. "I need you, Jayden. I really need my sister back. I can't do life without you no more. You know?"

Her strong embrace made Jayden uncomfortable. It didn't feel right. "I know, Mad, and I ain't going nowhere. That's why I wanted to talk to you. So we could repair our bond."

Madjesty held onto Jayden tighter. "Please mean that shit, Jayden. 'Cause you said that before and the moment that nigga came into the picture, the one you met at the McDonald's, you rolled out on me. We were always together before then and you left me."

"Madjesty, ma said I had to get money if I wanted to keep you out that hole. I did what I had to for you." *She paused.* "Plus I don't even talk to that nigga no more."

"I thought he got you this room."

"Naw, his friend got me this room." *Jayden corrected her.* "It's a long story."

"Jayden, don't be no fucking whore." *Mad said seriously.* "I know what these niggas be wanting and you can't play yourself like that. Nobody likes a whore. If that nigga didn't come into the picture we would never be beefing right now." *She was definitely drunk and it was changing the way she talked to her sister.*

"I'm not a whore and I never left you!"

"You did, Jayden. And it fucked me up because I didn't have anybody until Glitter came into my life. Now she gone and I need you back. So you gotta step up and be everything I need. Without you in my life I'ma lose it on these niggas, Jay. I'm serious!"

"I know, Mad." *She pried herself away from her sister's heavy alcoholic smelling body.*

"I think Harmony may be dead. I just wanna prepare you for that." Madjesty said, knowing it had been a day since she left after stabbing her. She wanted her to die slowly. *"Just letting you know."*

"Until they find her body, she's still alive to me." Jayden paused. *"But let me go get you some coffee. We got stuff to talk about."*

Jayden went into the kitchen to make some coffee. When she came back Madjesty was sleep and balled up like she use to when they shared a bunk. For a moment Jayden looked at Mad from the doorway. A small part of Jayden, although tiny, was afraid of her. She'd seen her snap and knew if you were in the way when that happened, you could end up hurt.

Walking into the room and closer to the bed she said, *"Mad, wake up. You gotta drink this."* Mad swung almost hitting Jayden in the face. Jayden jumped out of the way moments before she caught blows. *"OH, MY GOD!"*

"I hit you?" Mad asked.

"No! But you almost did."

Waking up fully she said, *"I'm sorry."* Then she looked at the coffee cup. *"What's this?"*

"The coffee I was making you. Remember I told you I was going to get it?"

"My head fucked up right now, Jay. I don't remember shit except the fact that my girl is dead."

"I understand, but you gotta drink it so we can talk."

Mad rubbed her head a little, accepted the coffee and said, *"About what?"* She drank as much as her stomach could handle.

"We gotta talk about Kali."

"Kali?" She removed the cup from her lips. *"Why we gotta talk about him?"*

"You gotta stay away from him, Mad. He bad news."

Mad's eyebrows rose. *"Why you say that shit?"*

"My father told me about him and the relationship they had as kids." Mad moved a little from irritation and placed the coffee cup on the floor. *"Don't be angry."*

"I'm not angry, Jayden. I'm just not trying to hear this shit."

"But it's important."

"Is this the reason you wanted me to come over?"

"No. I miss you! But you still gotta listen to what I'm saying." She paused. *"I know you don't like Jace, but he told me to talk to you about this because he's worried."*

"That nigga don't know me to be worried. He's your father not mine."

"He's worried about, me."

Mad was angry he cared so much about her because it proved once again that she was alone in the world. "Fuck that got to do with me?"

"Kali is not a good person, you gotta stay away from him."

"So let me get this straight, your father is telling me to stay away from mine?" Mad laughed. "That shit don't even sound right."

"Tell me something, does your girlfriend's murder have anything to do with Kali?"

Mad didn't want to say yes because she didn't want to give her the satisfaction, so she lied. "Naw. It didn't."

"Well Jace told me that some niggas are after him and they won't stop until he's dead. Kali got a price on his head and they'll kill anybody who stands in the way of that."

"Did he tell you that he's the nigga with the price?"

"No but I had an idea. I mean I'm not stupid, Mad." Jayden sat down on the bed next to her. "They fucked the same woman at the same time, and got her pregnant. How could they not have beef?"

"From what I saw, the beef is deeper than that. I don't believe your sweet father would shut down a whole city block because somebody fucked Harmony's nasty ass."

"A whole block?"

"Yeah...he ain't tell you that huh?" She laughed. "He trying to make it like he's so nice and he's so concerned about me. Well he ain't. They killed a nigga in front of me. Shot him three or four times, Jayden. The nigga Vaughn. Then they killed my girl."

"How you know my father had anything to do with that?"

"I saw the nigga get out of the car with my own eyes the night Vaughn got killed." Madjesty paused. "And the dude who killed Glitter said Jace's name." Mad paused. "They were trying to kill my father but hit Glitter instead!"

"Your father?" Jayden repeated. "Now who's claiming daddies?"

"Say what you want but I know the nigga Jace ain't no angel."

"Mad, you're my sister, and I don't want you hurt. Please, stay away from him okay?" She waited on Mad's response until her phone rang. "Give me a second." She stood up and answered the phone. "Hello."

"Hey, Jay, I'm at the hospital." Passion said.

Instead of being concerned Jayden was irritated. "Passion, why are you at the hospital?" Jayden looked at her watch. "You got a babysitting job in an hour and I don't want you fucking around. After that shit to-night you owe me big time."

She sighed. "I know, but I needed stitches in my hand because after I left the meeting, the cut started bleeding more. When I hit Coop over the head with the vase it must've really been deep. I won't be here long though."

Jayden rolled her eyes and put her hand on her hip. "Man..."

"You know it wouldn't be too bad if you asked me if I was okay right? Since we friends."

"Sorry...are you okay?"

"Yeah."

Jayden rolled her eyes again. "Good. So what's up? I got company now."

"Your mother is here."

Silence.

"My mother?" Jayden said. "Why would my mother be there?"

"I don't know what happened but I saw them bring her in a minute ago. She looks really bad though. Real thin and she's badly beaten. Everybody been talking about it."

"Wait a minute, is she alive?"

"Yes."

"Good...well how you even know what my mother look like? You never met her before."

"This gossiping ass nurse was talking about how they found her in some hole in a house. She was almost dead and she's not conscious." Jayden placed a hand over her heart. "The nurse said they picked her up from Concord Manor and how when she was a kid she remembered when some big time drug lord name Cornell Philips got arrested from there. Anyway, somebody tried to kill her." Jayden looked at Mad who had fallen back to sleep on the bed. "But thank God they didn't' get away with it."

"Look, I gotta...I gotta go. Is there anything else?"

"Yeah, Shaggy is here too. He keep asking me about you. What you want me to tell him?"

HOSPITAL

HARMONY

When I opened my eyes, I could feel the wide catheter cord digging inside of the small peehole in my pussy. I told them it hurt earlier, but no one bothered to listen. Now they were going to have to take it out, or else I was going to rip it out myself.

The hospital room was deathly silent until I yelled, "NURSE!!!!! NURSE!!!!!"

I waited for her to come into the room. To hear the sounds of her hospital shoes screeching across my doorway. I hoped the white nurse would come. Her name was Elizabeth and she always told me things would be okay, and I believed her. She'd check my issue, give me medication for my pain and stay with me until I drifted off to sleep.

If it was the black nurse, name Shonda, she would come in talking on the phone, only to tell me that I looked fine, without even checking my problem. Behind my back and to the other nurses she would say I complained too much. I heard her say that a lot of times in the hallway when she thought I was sleep. I hated that black bitch the most.

"NURSE! NURSE!" I screamed again.

Nothing.

Nobody.

All of a sudden the room felt colder. Did they forget I needed help? After what Mad put me through I thought I was going crazy. I hated to be alone. And it seemed like I had cords hooked up to every damn part of my body although the catheter hurt the worse. It had been hours since someone told me what was going on with me. Was I gonna live or die? If I was going to die, the least they could do was bring me some vodka and let me fuck the orderly who secretly comes into my room, lifts up my gown and plays with my pussy late at night. At first I pretended to be sleep, but sometimes he did it so good, I would moan and move my hips until I came all over his fingers. Now he'd come in the moment his shift started, sometimes earlier, and wake me up. I'd open my eyes and he'd finger fuck me until I begged him to stop. Kali use to do that to me. Finger fuck me when he thought I was sleep. I loved it then and I loved it now.

"NURSE!!! NURSE!!!"

Where are they? I need a drink. Bad. I want out of here! I'd been feening for alcohol ever since that daughter of mine took me against my will and tortured me. Hateful bitch. She gonna pay seriously for what she did to me.

"Ms. Phillips, I see you're up," detective Bernard Tassel, said entering my room.

FUCK! I didn't feel like dealing with this cop. He'd been bothering me from the moment they rolled my ass through the door.

"I'm sleep." Under the covers, I held on to the catheter preparing to pull it out.

"If you were sleep you wouldn't be talking right now, would you?" *Bastard!* "We have some more questions for you."

Detective Bernard Tassel stunk badly. He wore too much Old Spice. I remember the smell because Ramsey loved it when we were together. It stunk then and it stinks now. I'd rather smell fifty sacks of detached balls than that cologne.

"I told you I don't wanna talk."

"And I said I have questions."

I turned away and with the hand that wasn't about to pull on the catheter cord, reached from under the covers and turned the TV on using the remote connected to my bed. "I don't have any more answers for you. I told you that already."

"And we understand that," he walked up next to my bed and turned the TV off, "but we need to be sure. There has to be something you remember."

I moved a little and the stab wounds throughout my body stung because of my recent stitches. And my hairline fractured leg, in a walking cast, felt weak. Then I remembered the pain pump they gave me so I tapped it a few times. Hopefully it will help ease the uncomfortable feeling of this catheter also.

"I wish you leave me the fuck alone." I tapped the button again.

"Easy up on that pump," he smiled. "I don't want you to pass out before we get some answers." He sat down in a chair next to my bed. "They have me on this case and I must tell you, I have a 90 percent close case ratio. Which means I always get my man, or woman."

"Congratulations." I said rolling my eyes.

"Ms. Phillips…"

"Detective, please," I said interrupting him. Then I pushed the covers off of my body. Exposing myself I opened my legs and pulled the cord out. Urine splashed on his face and dampened my bed.

"WHAT THE FUCK?!!!!!!" He yelled removing a napkin from his pocket to wipe piss off of his face.

"Maybe you should leave." I told him trying to hide my laughter. Then I yelled. "NURSE!!!!"

He walked up to my bed and I thought he was about to hit me. I squinted preparing for the blow. Then he pushed the button on the remote that looked like a little lady. I heard it beep.

"That's how you get the nurse into your room."

"Well...thank you."

He threw the piss soaked napkin in the trash and said, "Thank me by helping me solve your case. What do you remember?"

Wanting him to leave I decided to tell my version again. "The night everything happened, I was in my room, preparing for bed. I had just made dinner for my daughters when all of a sudden, I was hit in the face with a closed fist. When I came to, I was here."

"So you don't remember how you got the wounds on your body, or who gave them to you? Your daughters don't remember either? Maybe I can talk to them."

"I can't remember nothing and they don't either." I looked at the door for the nurse. Where the fuck was she? "I don't understand why you don't believe me, I'm the victim."

"Ms. Phillips, we know you're the victim. But you do realize that over time, memories can be recalled. And when those memories come up, it's my job to bring them out of you." He paused. "I don't want what happened to you, to happen to anyone else."

"Like I said, I don't remember shit."

He sighed. "Oh well, I've done all I can for now. You have my number."

When he finally left the nurse came in. I didn't recognize her. She wasn't mean or nice, just somewhere in between. "Why did you take the catheter out?" She asked.

"It hurt."

"You should've asked for help. We could have moved it a little."

"I don't want it back in."

"It has to go back in, mam. If it doesn't go back inside you'll get an infection and you'll have to stay longer."

I let the bitch put it back and finally met with the doctor. He gave me my status, told me I was doing better and to try to get some sleep. The catheter wasn't as uncomfortable because I think the medicine was taking hold of me. I was feeling high and relaxed.

The moment I closed my eyes, someone I hadn't seen in weeks walked into my doorway. At first I couldn't tell how bad I looked, until I saw the expression on her face. I figured she'd love to see me like this, after everything I supposedly put her through.

I couldn't get over how much she looked like me when I was younger. She took my face and was probably out there trying to take my life. Where did she get fly clothes from? Somebody was taking care of her like Jace once took care of me. She had my eyes and the body I had when I was her age. She looked so much like me it was crazy. But it wasn't me, because I was in the bed, cut up not knowing if I was going to live or die.

"Mama, can I, can I come in?" Jayden asked. I nodded and she walked in slowly.

"I been here everyday. Did they tell you?"

"No."

"I spoke to some nurse name Shonda."

I shook my head. "Nobody told me nothing."

"Mama," she paused looking me over, "what happened to you?"

Silence.

"Too much."

"Mama, did…did…Madjesty do this to you?"

I stared at her like she was the dumb bitch that she was. Why the fuck would she ask me something she already knew the answer to? This is why I always said when I was younger, before I even had any kids that I didn't want to deal with girls. This bitch was as stupid a bitch as they came.

"What do you think, Jayden?"

"Oh, my God!" She started trembling. "Why would she do this to you?" She started pacing the room and tears fell out of her eyes by the pounds. "I…I can't believe she did this!"

"Jayden, calm down."

"Why?!!! Why would she do something so mean? I asked her! I asked her over and over again did she do anything to you and she told me no!"

"Jayden," I said softly. "I didn't say she did this." I was trying to diffuse the situation because I had plans for Mad I didn't want her ruining. She couldn't handle the truth and I needed things to remain calm for my plans to work. "Relax, baby. Please."

She seemed confused but she stopped walking. "But…I came over the house to ask about you and Mad said you weren't there." She seemed calmer. "And then I saw your mail and your welfare check wasn't picked up. So none of it made sense."

"Jayden…she didn't know. It wasn't Madjesty. I mean…Mad."

"Mad?" She paused. "You sure Madjesty didn't do this? She kept making me call her that also recently."

"I'm sure."

"But when I talked to a nurse downstairs, she said you were in the house. Mad stayed in that house. So how didn't she know you were there?"

"You got my check?" I asked ignoring her question.

"It's in your room at the house, ma."

I was about to go off if these bitches fucked with my check but luckily she put it up for me. "Jayden, your sister didn't do this to me. She was so busy with her friends in the house that she didn't know what was happening

"But it seems strange that she didn't..."

"Jayden, it's true. She didn't do this."

She seemed relieved and I could see her exhaling. She walked closer to the bed and said, "Well who found you?"

"Katherine Sheers, the caseworker from the department of Child Services." I paused. "Remember...you met her when you came back home that day. With Trip's son?"

"Oh. Yeah." She paused. "You mean Shaggy. But ma, how come they don't like you? Trip...Shaggy's mom?"

"Don't care and not interested." I lied. "But I hear you girls haven't been going to school and Katherine wanted to check on you. When she came in the house, she said the door was cracked open. I heard her walking inside and I gathered enough strength to call for help. Had it not been for that woman I probably wouldn't be here." Then I looked at her. "Why haven't you been going to school, Jayden? If ya'll don't go to school it could mess up my check because they'll take you away from me."

"All you care about is a check?" She frowned.

"You know that's not true. Well, at least you should know."

"I missed a few days, ma. It wasn't a lot though."

See this is why I use to smack this bitch upside the head all the time. Her not going to school caused problems for me. "You gotta go to school, Jayden. And you have to move back home."

"No!"

"Jayden, you have to move back home." I was firm. "You're not going to be by yourself when you move back, Madjesty will be there."

"But why I gotta come back? I got my own place. I can pay you more."

"Because this caseworker will find you and put you in a foster home. Do you want that?"

"No!"

"Well that's what will happen. She told me herself." I paused. "Now I'll give you a few weeks to get your things together, but every night you have to sleep at Concord. I can't have this woman coming back to my house and getting into our business. Okay?"

"Okay." She paused, "And mama I'm sorry, about everything. Had I known you were hurt I would've been there for you."

Now here is the part of the plan I was going to find hard to fake. I had to convince this bitch that I gave a fuck. That I still didn't hate her as much as I did the day she was born.

"Jayden, all of this is my fault. When I almost died, in that house, all I could do was think about my kids. I wasn't a good mother and I know it now. So if anybody should be sorry it's me." She gave me a strange look. "What's wrong?"

"Nothing, you just remind me of the day I came to the house and met the social worker." She said in a low voice. "The day Shaggy brought me over."

I frowned a little. "So you're saying I'm faking it?"

"No...No!" She shook her head. "I'm not saying that at all. I really just want to make sure you're okay and that you mean everything you say." Then she looked at me as if she didn't see me before. "Are you in a lot of pain?"

"No. Not a lot."

"Mama, I know, I mean I know we haven't been on the best of terms in our relationship." She paused. "I was kind of angry with you for what you did to me and Mad."

"Jayden, please..."

"No listen, mama, I was mad at you for that. But I talked to daddy, and he cleared some things up for me. I never really knew how hard of a life you had growing up. And he helped me understand that."

"Daddy?" I repeated.

She smiled. "Yeah, we are getting to know each other now."

"Jayden, you can't tell him about how I treated you when you were a kid."

"Why?"

"Because we're starting all over. Me and you." I gripped her hand. "And he might tell Katherine Sheers."

"But if something ever happened, and they took me away, instead of going to a foster home, couldn't I live with him?"

"No...he's a drug dealer, Jayden." I said sternly. "And I know you know that." I paused. "Don't you?"

"Yes."

"She'd never allow you to stay with a person like that." I touched her long hair and wanted to cut it off. "Listen, what happened back in Texas is the past. We need to leave well enough alone if we're going to have a future."

"Ok. I...I understand."

"I know this is a lot, but believe me when I say it's for your own good." I paused. "Now does he know I'm here?"

Just when I asked that Jace walked through the hospital door. It looked like not a year had passed since I last saw him. His tall body hung in the doorway and his beautiful eyes widened with pity when he saw my face. I must really look bad. He ran his hand threw his soft curly hair, which was cropped real low, and then he rested his hands into his True Religion jean pockets. Even though I could tell he was at a loss for words he looked so fucking sexy and all I could think about was the days he use to hold me and love me. After quickly looking him over, my stare settled on his eyes again. This time he looked a little angry.

"How are you, Harmony?" He said in the doorway. "Long time no see."

"I've been better, Jace."

He smirked. "So have I." he looked at me seriously. "Consider yourself lucky though."

"Why's that?"

"Because when you have the privilege of breathing, after everything you've been through, you should never take for granted that you're still alive."

I smiled lightly. I knew where he was coming from immediately. "I don't take anything for granted, Jace. And I'm a changed woman these days and not the same person I use to be years ago. I'm not even the same person I use to be a few days ago."

"That's good for you. Although sometimes you have to answer for your past."

"And so do you. Besides, how's Kali? I heard a lot has been going on lately. I thought he was your friend?"

He frowned and I saw his jaw jump. He balled his fists up but looked at Jayden.

I could tell Jayden was feeling slightly uncomfortable and so was I. She cleared her throat and said, "Mama, do you need anything?"

"You're about to leave?"

"Yeah. I have something to take care of." She paused. "But I'ma be back everyday until they let you go."

"How did you get here?"

"Daddy, brought me." I looked at him but he was smiling at her.

"Give me a few seconds alone with your mother." Jace said. "Then we'll leave."

When she left he stepped into the room and said, "I could kill you, bitch. For everything you put me through over the years."

My heart rate sped up and I hoped he wouldn't hit me. "What are you talking about?"

"You kept me away from my kid for fourteen fucking years. I been searching the world high and low for your ass, even had to kill a few niggas in the process! And then you rob me the night of my party. The only reason you still alive is because when I look into my daughter's eyes, I know she's mine."

"I heard you did more than just look into her eyes, Jace." I paused. "I heard about the paternity test."

He walked up, grabbed my neck and squeezed my throat. "Don't fucking play with me, bitch."

I put my hand over his and whispered, "I still love you."

"What?" He squeezed harder.

"And you still love me." I said softer.

"Fuck you."

"You're hurting me, Jace. Please let me go."

He released me and I coughed several times. "I don't fucking love you!" He said. "Probably never have."

That hurt. "Jace, I just been through hell. Now I might not have been the best mother, but Jayden is alive, and she has all of her limbs."

"She may got all her limbs but she can barely read. I've had to help her pick what to eat on menus and sometimes when I give her money, if it's a lot, she can't count it."

"It's not my fault she wasn't doing well in school."

"Something else is wrong with her, Harmony. She doesn't seem like everything is all together sometimes." He paused. "I know she's gone through a lot because she finds it hard to talk about her childhood, but if I find out you abused my kid or some shit like that, I'ma add that to my reasons to kill you. And I wouldn't give a fuck if you was in a coma."

When he said that Jayden walked back into the room. "Is everything okay?" She asked looking at me and Jace.

"Yeah. Everything's fine."

"Okay, well we're about to go, ma." She paused. "I'ma call the doctor to see when we can come get you. And then I'ma help you get better."

Out of Jayden's sight, Jace stared me and leaned up against the doorway. The thing about Jayden helping me was this, I was just as irritated with this bitch as he was with the whole situation. Why she fake love me so much if I did her so wrong? If I was such a bad mother she wouldn't be here doing all of this for me. It's obvious I had to do something right.

"Thank you, Jayden." She was about to walk out with Jace when I said, "Can you do me a favor?"

"Yeah, ma. What you need?"

"Call, Mad. Tell her I need to see her as soon as possible. We have a lot of talking to do."

MAD

WICKED

I was a few blocks away from Kali's house. The back of this cab stunk and whenever I moved my feet on the mat under my sneakers, it sounded sticky. The grey vinyl seats were worn out and holes were everywhere. He didn't give a fuck about this cab and I wouldn't give a fuck about not paying him either.

I was sitting back, drunk out of my mind. Losing Glitter…I mean…losing my bitch killed me. I felt like everything I did from here on out, anything at all, didn't matter anymore. I had a mother who hated me who I hated back and I had a father who didn't want me as a daughter. I felt alone. I didn't even know what I wanted to do in my life and lately all I had to look forward to was getting the news that Harmony was dead. I left her in the crawl space days ago, and stayed with a girl I met the day I rolled out. She had her own place and a part time job at the Laundromat. I wasn't feeling her because she reminded me of my mother…kept wanting me to eat her out and shit like that. Every time I'd do it, I would have to be drunk. That's when I knew she wasn't the one.

But the days flew by and every time someone would knock on her door, I thought the police were coming to arrest me. That they found out I killed my mother and were about to put me in jail. At some point I thought about going to the place in Texas, the one that kept runaways. The one Rocket told me about, but it didn't seem worth it since Glitter was gone. So I just roamed. Around. Not giving a fuck.

When my phone vibrated in my pocket, I took it out and saw Wokie's number. My friends kept calling me but I wasn't ready to talk about what happened with Glitter. She was dead. She was gone and thinking about it still made me angry. When was shit gonna start looking up in my life? I didn't ask for shit, not even to be born, yet I constantly felt like I was being punished.

WHAM!

I didn't even know I hit the back of his seat that hard until I heard his voice.

"What the fuck?!" The African cab driver said after my fist crashed into the back of his seat. I eyed his license on the visor and saw the letters

T H A B O. I can't read too well but I think it said Thabo. He looked at me in his rearview mirror with a screw face. "Why you do that?"

My head wobbled a little due to feeling my buzz. "I'm…I'm sorry. I didn't mean to do that shit." My voice was deep and hoarse from all the screaming and crying I had been doing over the past few days.

"Look, do you have money for the cab?" He asked. "Because I don't have time for games."

I sat up and said, "I got your fucking money, nigga! Just drive!"

"Don't fuck with me! I want my money!" He said shaking his finger.

"And I said I got your shit!"

My heart was banging in my chest because he seemed rougher than the other cab drivers and I knew what I was about to do…run. I ain't have no money on me and the little cash I did have I spent on the liquor in the bag I was carrying.

"You are sad, son! Really sad!"

"Fuck you talking about?"

"A young man shouldn't have such a terrible mouth like that. It's really pretty pathetic if you ask me." He was staring at me through the rearview, like he was better than me.

"Well I ain't ask you shit now did I?"

At least he got something right by calling me a young man. I tugged on my baseball cap to cover my eyes even more. Then I drank the entire bottle of liquor, put my book bag on my back and prepared to dip.

When we reached three blocks from where Kali was staying I said, "Right here."

He stopped the cab and I opened the door and bailed. I got two blocks up but when I turned around to see where he was I was surprised to see him still chasing me. What the fuck? Normally they couldn't catch up when we hopped out of cabs but this driver wasn't giving up.

"I'M SICK OF YOU NIGGAS RUNNING OUT MY CAB!" he yelled as he gave chase.

I couldn't believe how hard he was going! He was actually chasing me and left the door to his cab open just to try and catch me. Because of the Henny I wasn't my normal self and couldn't run as fast. After awhile, I felt like I was moving slower and slower. I guess my body was giving out on me at the wrong time. I was just about to give up and fall on the ground when a girl in a black Ford bucket pulled up on me.

She rolled down her window and said, "Get in!"

"What?!" I asked looking over at her.

"Boy, you gonna get in or get caught?"

Without thinking twice I jumped into her car and the cab driver kicked the back door so hard I heard the metal dent. She took off and my head snapped back.

"BITCH!" She yelled hitting her steering wheel. "HE FUCKING KICKED MY CAR!!!!"

"Sorry about that!" I looked behind me to see Thabo in the middle of the street yelling and throwing up his middle finger.

"I BETTER NEVER SEE YOU AGAIN!"

"I can't believe his ass almost caught me!" I said as she sped down the road. She looked behind her repeatedly and I could tell this whole thing made her uneasy. It kinda fucked me up that I put her in this predicament. "I can't believe you stopped."

It wasn't until two minutes in the drive that I really looked at her. My adrenaline must've been pumping or something. When I looked over at the girl who probably saved my life I noticed she was so pretty. Her skin was brown, like a new paper bag and her lips were very pink. I was immediately relaxed around her. She was wearing tight jeans and I could see the fullness of her thighs as her foot moved from the brake to gas peddle. Her face was innocent and she had the longest eyelashes I'd ever seen before on a girl. Were they real? It ain't matter. Fuck it! She was definitely my type.

"I don't know why I stopped either." She said.

"I'm glad you did." I told her tugging at my cap again.

"Boy, what are you doing ditching cabs? He could have killed you."

"What he gonna kill me with, his hands?"

She laughed. "You must be use to jumping out of cabs and shit. You don't even seem like this shit bothered you."

"Naw, I got money. I just ain't wanna give it to him." I lied. "I ain't like how he was talking to me in the cab. That's why I rolled out."

"You wild as shit. But I like that." She looked out at the road as she drove down the street. "So where you going?"

I didn't want to tell her to drop me off at Kali's yet, besides we past his crib a long time ago. For some reason, I was feeling her and I wanted to spend a few more minutes kicking it. Even if I had to walk a long way back to Kali's spot, it was cool with me. If I had money, I would've taken her out to eat, but as it stood now I was flat broke.

"Uh...I'm going five more blocks up the street. You can let me out here if you want." I said.

"Why, so you can jump out of another cab?" She laughed.

"I'm through with that shit."

She giggled. I swear this bitch was so fucking pretty. "So what's your name?" She asked me.

"Mad. What's your name?"

"Amber."

"Amber, you got a man?"

"No. I mean, I had one but I'm single now." She smiled. "But I know you got somebody." She laughed. "As cute as you are."

"Naw...I don't." I thought about Glitter and felt bad. Like I was cheating on her or something. "I'm single."

"Stop playing. How many baby mothers you got? Two, three?"

She really thought I was a dude, and it felt good to talk to her. Then it dawned on me, God had fucked up by taking my girl and he sent me her to make shit right. So I decided at that time to forgive him and accept Amber as a gift.

"I ain't got no kids. I want some though."

"I don't have no kids either. I guess I'm looking for the right person." She looked at me real sexy.

"Maybe you found that person." I said.

"Not if you get locked up."

"I told you I'm done with that cab shit. It was my first and only time."

She brought the car to a slow roll and said, "Which house you live in?"

I pointed to the first one I saw. "That one right there. With the blue Honda in the driveway."

She stopped the car and popped open her glove compartment. Then she took out a pen and paper and wrote a number down. "This my cell number. You got one?"

I wrote down my number but changed the last digit because I needed to change my voicemail first. I didn't want her calling and hearing a change in my voice. I knew I probably sounded more masculine to her now because my voice was hoarse from all the crying. And even though I didn't sound like a bitch on a regular, my voice wasn't as deep as it was right now.

"Here. Call me when you can."

"Aight, boy! This ain't no blank though is it?"

"Why would I give you a blank when you just saved my life?"

She smiled again. "Saved your life? You the one who told me he couldn't do anything to you with his hands."

"You remember everything." I smiled, tugging at my cap even more.

"Naw. I got a bad memory. I just remember the stuff about people I like." Then she paused. "You real cute though. I hope you not playing games with me."

"I don't play games." I told her. "What you see is what you get."

"How old are you?" She asked.

Figuring if she was driving she had to be at least sixteen I said, "Sixteen. You?"

"I'm seventeen." She smiled again and said, "Okay…uh…well…if you wanna hang out later, call me."

"Aight, if I finish what I have to do early, I'ma do that."

When I got out of the car I waved at her and she smiled. She smiled a lot and I liked that about her. She reminded me of Tisa. The first girl I ever loved. She was definitely somebody I wanted to get up with when shit settled down for me. For now I had to go to Kali's crib to break the news to him that I left his truck with my dead girlfriend's body. And to make matters worse I didn't give a fuck.

• •

Bernie's House

When I got to Bernie's house the door was open and I walked inside. Niggas were trying to kill him yet he left the door open. Amazing.

"Kali." I said softly, trying not to disturb anybody. "Ms. Bernie." The sound of my feet pressing against the wooden floors caused it to creak.

When no one answered I walked deeper into the house until I heard a lot of panting and moaning. When I came to a door it was cracked and I saw Ms. Bernie bent over on the bed while Kali licked her ass as he beat his dick. She was moaning like crazy and I couldn't believe how gross the scene was. Why was he doing that old ass lady like that? What really fucked me up was that it smelled like shit in the room. I backed away from the door and walked into the living room. Tired, I plopped down on the sofa. On the table was some Henny and I poured myself some in a dirty glass already there. Drinking everything in the glass, I leaned back into the cushion and looked up at the ceiling. All I kept thinking about was Glitter. When thoughts of her got too hard, I thought about Amber, and about how much I liked her smile. I pulled the cap further on my head and drifted off to sleep. When I woke up I felt something pointing in the back of my head. I knew from instinct it was a gun.

"Take your hat off."

I did.

I looked up to see Kali standing behind me.

"That's the second time you pulled a gun on me. Either shoot or leave me the fuck alone."

He smiled, tucked his weapon in his waist and walked in front of me. "How long you been here?"

"Long enough". I told him.

Wearing his boxers he smirked and rubbed his stomach. "Oh yeah?"

"Yeah…and I see you already ate. You full?" I asked referring to the ass eating I saw him do earlier in the bedroom.

"I'm good." He laughed wiping his mouth. "What you know about that?"

"Nothing." I said thinking about the old lady. "You got me all day on that shit." Then I thought about Glitter's mother and bit my tongue.

"I got you on a lot of other shit too." He said seriously. "Anyway, why it take you all them days to get over here?"

"A lot of shit happened to me."

"At least you're here now because we got some shit to handle to-day."

"Okay, but I got some bad news. I couldn't drive the truck back over here."

He didn't seem too mad when he asked, "Why not?"

"My girl was killed a few nights back. Jace was looking for you and killed my girl instead." A tear fell down my eyes and I wiped it away.

"What I tell you about crying?"

"I'm sorry."

"Fuck that sorry just stop crying. If you gonna hang with me you got-ta toughen up." He paused. I pushed back anymore tears. I'd cried enough at Laundromat Girl's house anyway. It was time to move on. "Now why they kill her?"

"Because she had my baseball cap on and they thought it was you." Then it dawned on me that if I had the cap on, I'd be dead now but I wasn't relieved.

"Look, I'm sorry about your peeps but shit gonna be alright." He sat next to me. "We can get another truck. We probably wasn't gonna have that one too much longer anyway. Them niggas was gonna stay on me as long as I had it."

"Why is Jace trying to kill you?"

He rubbed his head and said, "A long story. Let's just say we got beef we haven't squashed yet."

"You think you can squash it?"

"Jace is like a brother to me." He paused. "And basically he fucked me out of some money for a job I did for him. So if I wanted shit to be settled, I could let the debt go and all would be forgiven."

"Why don't you do that?"

"Cause I like the drama."

Silence.

For a moment I thought about the conversation me and Jayden had, and how she warned me that he was trouble. For whatever reason though, the fact that he was crazy made me want the connection even more. We were just alike.

"My sister told me he doesn't want me fucking with you. Said to stay away from you."

"What you tell her?"

"Told her to get the fuck out of my face with that shit. I'm my own person and can't no nigga tell me how to run my life."

He smiled. "Look, I wanna say I'm sorry about that shit I said to you, at your crib." He looked away. "I wouldn't have ripped you out of that bitch's womb if I didn't think so."

"You really did that shit? Why?"

"Because she wasn't a good mother and didn't deserve you." I liked him even more.

"So you are my father?"

"Yeah. And I was going to tell you when you got here. I want you to call me your father too. No more of that Kali shit. We blood and I want people to know it."

"For real?" I smiled.

"Yeah. I ain't gonna lie, your mother got around so at first I didn't know if you were really mine. But the more time we spend together, the more I'm sure of it." Then he stood up. "You ready to prove you family?"

"Yeah." I smiled. "What I got to do?"

"For starters if I ask you to do something, you gotta do it, no questions asked." He paused. "And I never wanna see you cry again either."

"Done."

For some reason when he said that I was his kid, I felt a huge weight lifted off of me. I felt like I belonged to somebody and I was going to do my best to show my loyalty.

"Kid, did you see anybody following you on your way over here?"

"Trust me, nobody knows where I am. I haven't been home in days."

"You ain't answer the question."

"Nobody followed me."

"Good, kid. That's good."

"I'ma call you pops. That's okay with you?"

He smiled and said, "Yeah. But let me get dressed. We gotta stop past somewhere right quick."

"I'm ready when you are." I smiled. "Pops!"

• •

On The Road

Bernie was quiet as she drove us to another location. She scratched her head and her gold wig moved a few inches. She seemed to be in her head as she chain-smoked and drank the liquor out of the cup I used earlier. Had I known it was hers I would not have used it. On second thought...I probably would have. I wanted a drink and didn't care who I was drinking from.

"There the house go right there." Kali said pointing at a house in some part of Maryland. "Stop right here, B."

"You not gonna be long are you?" Bernie asked. "I need a fix."

"Naw...but you gotta wait for me aight?" He said leaning over to kiss her.

"You know I ain't going nowhere."

He smiled, looked around the car before getting out and said, "Come on, kid."

When we got out of the car and approached the house I could smell weed before we even hit the front door. Off the break I hoped he was friendly enough with whoever inside that they would share.

Kali looked behind him and then at me and said, "Whenever we go anywhere, we always have each other backs."

"I got your back."

"Good."

He knocked at the door twice before somebody opened it up.

"WHO THE FUCK IS IT!?" Some chick yelled from inside.

A black girl in a pair of high heels, little jean shorts and a purple bikini top opened the door wide. When she saw it was Kali she tried to shut it back. But he pushed the door so hard, she fell on the floor, holding her bloodied nose. I shut the door behind him and ran through the rooms within the house. We were alone.

"Nobody's here." I told him.

He smiled. "Real smart, kid." Then he turned his attention to her. "Now don't fuck with me, bitch!" he yelled over top of her. "Where the fuck is my money?"

She scooted backwards on her elbows until she sat on the couch. "What money, Kali? I ain't got nothing of yours in here."

"Bitch, don't fuck with me!" He yelled. "Vaughn told me my shit was over here. Now go get it!"

"But he dead! I don't know where he put your stuff. I'm for real, Kali."

"Bitch, if you think you can keep a million dollars worth of my money you got another muthafuckin' thing coming. Now go get my shit."

A million dollars? What the fuck was he in to? I thought.

"I ain't got no money, but I got some bags that Vaughn brought over here before he died. I never went through them so I don't know what it is."

"How you know it's not money then?"

"I just know its bags. That's it."

"Fuck you think I'm talking about?"

"Okay, give me a second. I got to think about where he put it because it's been a long time." She continued to hold her bloodied nose.

"You think it's a game?" He asked.

"No. I really can't remember." She paused. "If you give me a sec..."

Kali rushed up to the couch, grabbed her by the hair and stole her in the nose. If it wasn't broken before it was definitely broken now. Then he hit her again and again until her face was so red it didn't look real and her nose spread out like jelly on a sandwich. For some reason, shit like this was starting not to bother me anymore. Since Kali entered my life death and gloom had been nonstop and I decided to just go with the flow.

"Now, bitch, I'ma ask you again, where the fuck is my money?"

She pointed to the couch she was sitting on and he threw her body to the floor to get her out the way. It made a loud thump and he told me, "Help me look for my shit."

I moved the pillows off the sofa with him until we got to the handle of a sofa bed. When we pulled it out we found two duffle bags full of money. Kali smiled, dug into one of the bags and handed me a stack of hundred-dollar bills.

"That's for the shit you been through. Tuck that."

"This mine?"

"Yeah, call it child support." He winked.

"It's got to be at least five hundred dollars here."

"Five hundred dollars?" He said. "I gave you a full stack of hundreds. That's five thousand." He frowned.

"Five thousand!!?"

"Yeah...what you can't count or something?"

I stuffed it as best as I could in my pockets. "Yeah...I'm just tripping that's all."

I never had this much money in my life. I was going to go wild with Mad Max!

Once back in the car he told Bernie, "Take me to get something to eat." Then he looked back at me. "You hungry?"

"Yeah, but I'ma need some more liquor first."

He laughed and my phone vibrated in my pocket. It was a voice message from my sister. I'd been ignoring her calls ever since I left her house. I remember that day and it played over in my mind constantly. I hated that she was letting Jace come in between us.

That day, after we had our conversation about me staying away from Kali, she got on the phone. It seemed pretty important so I went back to sleep. When I woke up she was gone. I took a few dollars I saw on her dresser and went about my business. But now it was time for me to stop avoiding her and my friends so I listened to her message.

'Mad, mom is in the hospital. So much has happened and I really wish you'd answer your phone. I'm not mad at about the money you stole from me." She paused. *'So stop dodging my calls.'* She continued. *'The social worker found ma in the house and ma says we have to go home or they'll put us in a foster home. I don't want that, Mad. Please call me. Oh...and she wants you to go see her. Call me when you get my message, if you want, I'll have Jace take you to the hospital. I Love you.'*

My heart dropped.

She was in the hospital?

But that bitch was supposed to be dead!

MAD

WASHINGTON DC

After I left my pops I got up with Mad Max at the Holiday Inn in Downtown D.C. I didn't want to go back to my crib until I found out what was up with Harmony. Was she gonna tell the police what I did or what?

With the money he gave me, I rented the room, got him to buy me some liquor and ordered enough pizza for me and my crew. We were sitting in the room, which had two twin beds and we were kicking shit. Sugar brought some weed over and we were smoking and drinking.

"Where Wokie at?" I asked sitting on the bed with my head against the wall.

"Fucking with people's cars."

Five minutes later Wokie came in with two cans of spray paint. "I just fucked somebody's shit up!" He laughed.

"You better stop fucking with people's cars." Sugar said.

"What you do man?" I asked.

"I spray painted Mad Max all on they shit!" he laughed. "Like five niggas cars."

"That's some dumb ass shit!" Sugar said.

"Yo, shut the fuck up!" Kid said. "You been complaining ever since…"

"Glitter died." Krazy said.

Smoking on a blunt Sugar said, "Ya'll remember when Glitter smacked the hell out of that teacher when she tried to carry her that day in class?" She laughed and coughed the smoke out of her lungs. "I couldn't believe she really did that shit."

"All because we dared her." Krazy laughed. "She ain't give a fuck. She would never pass up on a dare."

"Man, ya'll wasn't even there. I saw that shit and was like, did she just hit this bitch in the face?" I said pulling on the weed. "I knew then that she was the bitch for me. I fucking miss her, ya'll. Like, she was gonna have my baby and everything."

"We miss her too." Kid said. "Like it's not even real yet."

-152-

"It's real." Wokie said. "That's the fucked up part about it. We can't see her no more."

I tried to hold back my tears because I was tired of crying. She was gone and I was going to move on starting with the Amber. Drunk back, I decided to hit her up to see if she wanted to hang out with me and my crew, but she didn't call me back after I left a voice message. I already had in my mind how we would be together and stuff if she gave me a chance. And how pretty she would look when she carried my baby. Even though I just met her, I was feeling her and for some reason I think I was in love.

"I love her." I said out loud.

"You love who?" Sugar asked chewing pizza with her mouth open.

"The girl I met today."

Silence.

"Mad, how you love her when you just met her?" Wokie said. "That's some quick shit."

"What you saying, I'm lying or something?"

"Naw…I just think you may want to get to know her first."

"If nothing else hit the pussy." Krazy laughed.

They all laughed.

I looked at Sugar and she was pouting. I knew where she was coming from. She didn't want me to be with anybody, let alone another girl.

"So why we here?" Kid said eating a slice of pizza. "We was living it up in the mansion and now we at a hotel."

I looked at them seriously and said, "I ain't wanna tell ya'll but Harmony got out. She in the hospital now."

They all looked at each other crazy.

"She got out?" Wokie said. "How the fuck that happen?"

"I think I left the door open and this social worker bitch walked in. Me and Jayden ain't been going to school so she wanted to check on us."

"Damn, you think she gonna say something?" Wokie asked.

"What you mean, about you fucking her?" Sugar asked. "I told you that was dumb but you wouldn't listen. Plus you was the only one hitting the pussy on a regular."

"Sugar, sometimes you act like you ain't even a part of this crew." Krazy said.

"Right! I bet if something went down you'd be the first one to talk." Wokie said.

"You got me mixed up with you, nigga! Can't nobody in this crew hold water tighter than me."

"Everybody shut the fuck up!" I yelled. "To answer your question, Wokie I don't know if she gonna tell. I mean, she ain't say nothing to Jayden and it sounded like shit was cool."

"How you know?"

"Because she my sister for one, nigga, and for two she woulda said something to me. As of now, I don't think Harmony said nothing. Plus if they take us away, she not going to be able to collect welfare and my mother never had a job in her life."

"Hold up, ya'll live in a mansion and collect welfare?" Sugar asked.

"Yeah!" I paused. "So?"

"I'm just asking." She said sitting on the floor grabbing another slice of pizza.

"Man, I'm not trying to get in trouble for fucking that old ass lady." Wokie said. "What we gonna do?"

"Right now we gonna relax, smoke this shit, and drink this liquor." I said. "Trust, we gonna be fine. Plus I ain't trying to think about that right now. Shit been happening to me like crazy and I just wanna have fun to-night."

"But what if…"

"Drop it!" I said cutting off Wokie. "I don't wanna talk about it." My phone rang and I picked up when I saw it was Amber. "This the girl I was telling ya'll about!"

"Answer the phone, nigga!" Wokie said.

"Hello." I said putting the phone up to my ear.

"Can I speak to Mad?"

"This me."

"This Mad?" She sounded confused.

"Yeah…why you say my name like that?" I said deepening my voice.

"No reason, at first you sounded like a girl."

"Stop fuckin' around." I paused. "I ain't hardly no girl."

Eavesdropping Wokie said, "What the fuck?" Then he laughed. "Why you trying to sound like a nigga?"

I threw my shoe at him and it missed his head and crashed against the wall. "Shut the fuck up!" I said covering my hand over the phone.

When he was quiet I said to Amber, "How I sound like a girl?"

"I don't know. You did at first though."

"Yeah if I pulled this dick out you wouldn't be saying that shit." I said.

Sugar laughed real hard but stopped when I looked at her seriously. My friends knew I didn't consider myself to be a girl, but I guess they always thought I was playing.

"So you being nasty now?" Amber giggled.

"Just telling the truth."

"Well if you're nice enough to me, maybe I'll see how good your dick really is. That's cool with you?"

"Yeah." I said thinking about fucking her already. "So you got my message? About coming to the hotel? We got food and stuff over here."

"We?"

"Yeah, me and my friends."

"Your friends?" Immediately I thought about kicking everybody out until she said, "But maybe it'll be cool. Give me the address. I can hang out for a little while."

"You sure? You sound mad or something."

"Naw...I was just hoping we could be alone."

"We can. So come hang out and when you ready to be alone, I'll throw them out my room." They frowned. "Or get another one." They smiled. "Cool?"

She laughed. "It's cool. But why you give me a blank? Truthfully that's why I ain't call you back when you hit me earlier. I thought you were running game."

I did change one digit off my number and now she was calling me on it. "Look, if I gave you the wrong number it was by mistake. But I'm not about to kiss your ass. What you trying to do?"

"I'm on my way."

I gave her the info and made my friends clean up a little bit. Fifteen minutes later Amber came in looking like a dime. Wokie, Kid and Krazy K had their mouths dropped when they saw her ass. She was wearing some tight jeans and a cute pink top. She looked so fucking sexy that immediately my joint started throbbing.

Sugar got up and bumped Amber on the way to the door. She left without speaking.

"What's up with that bitch?" Amber asked.

"It's a long story." I said.

"Hey," she smiled waving at everyone else. I walked behind her. "Ya'll look like ya'll were having fun."

We walked over to the bed and Wokie was chilling on it like it was going to be a threesome. "Get the fuck off the bed, nigga!" I said kicking him.

Wokie jumped up and moved to the other bed with the rest of my crew. "Damn, all you had to say is excuse me."

I rolled my eyes at him and focused back on Amber. I hated when new people came around because somebody was bound to show off.

"So, what ya'll doing?" She asked plopping on the bed. "I'm not interrupting anything am I?"

"Naw we be doing whatever we want." Kid said. "So you cool. We MAD MAX, baby!"

We all laughed. "Yeah...we do anything we want." Krazy added. "Without parents to bother us."

"What's Mad Max?" She asked.

"Another long story." I interrupted.

"Well you must be the leader if the group has your name." She said looking at me.

"I'm always in charge, baby."

She laughed. "Well pretty soon if you want to be with me, you gonna have to start telling me some of these long stories."

"You got that." I winked.

"You smoke?" Krazy asked her.

"Yeah." She shrugged. "Sometimes."

I gave her the bob, she inhaled and coughed. "You aight?" I asked. "Want some water or something?"

"Naw." She coughed a few more times. "I'm good." She smiled again. "It's just been a long time." Seemed like every time this girl smiled my joint throbbed.

We kicked it some more and before I knew it everybody was talking shit and having a good time. Eventually Sugar got out of her attitude and came back into the room. We ain't give her a hard time because as much as she was getting on my nerves, she was my friend and I fucked wit' her.

It was three in the morning and me and Amber climbed in the bed together while the music played in the background. I was drunk but was feeling so good with her. I never thought I'd feel another female so quickly. Maybe Amber could be my girl and I could start all over.

We were lying on the bed face up with pillows under our necks. "I had fun with you and your friends tonight." She was rubbing my leg. I lifted my head and saw Wokie, Kid and Sugar on the floor sleep. Krazy was in the other bed knocked out. "They seem to care about you a lot."

Dropping my head back down I looked at her. "They do, but I'm looking for more."

"Like what?"

"I mean, my friends are cool, but I'm looking for somebody I can make a life with. I want family. I never really had that coming up, so it's always been a dream of mine."

"When you say you want a family, what do you mean?"

"I'm talking about a wife, and a kid." I paused. "That kind of stuff."

"You act like you real old or something."

"Naw. I know what I want though."

She smiled. "You sound like it."

"That's because I'm dead ass."

"And why you ain't got no girl? You so fucking cute."

I thought about Glitter and the way we had so much fun together. "I had one, but we ain't make it."

"What happened?"

"She died."

"I'm sorry to hear that." She seemed sincere. "How did it happen?"

"It was unexpected." I paused. "And I want to leave it at that." Amber rolled over and got on top of me, and then she stared into my eyes. The rim of my cap stabbed her forehead but she didn't seem to mind. "What you looking at?" I pulled my cap down some more.

"You." She paused. "And how come you always pull your cap down when I look at you?"

She moved to lift it up a little and I grabbed her wrist. "Don't do that. It makes me uncomfortable."

I released her arm. "Sorry. I like the way you wear it anyway." Then she leaned her head to the left to prevent my cap from hitting her face and kissed me on my lips and my shit throbbed again. "I like you a lot, Mad. A whole lot. I hope you not playing games like some of the boys at my school."

"I do know them niggas but I don't play games." I paused. "I'm feeling you too."

She kissed me again and I threw my tongue in her mouth. I was rubbing her arms and back and then she took her pants off. I couldn't wait to fuck her. Stuff was moving so quick and the drink and the smoke had my mind wrapped. The way she ran her hands over my body got me ready. I was so into her that I didn't feel how quickly she went into my pants. When her fingers hit my stuff and went into my hole, her eyes popped open and she jumped out of bed.

"What…what you…what are you?" She asked stepping on an empty box of pizza. Then she wiped her fingers on the bed. "You got a…"

"What you talking about?" I said jumping up with her, looking at my friends who were still sleep. I was glad they weren't awake because this would have been embarrassing. "Why you being all loud?"

"But you a…you got a…pussy."

"Lay down," I said pushing her on the bed. She sat back on the edge but she looked at me like something was wrong and I grew angry.

"Why didn't you tell me you a…"

"Just stop it for a second. Let me explain." I said.

I pushed her back down and she was laying face up...real stiff like. "Explain what, Mad. You a girl! You a fucking girl!"

"I know...but all my life I thought I was a boy." I smiled trying to calm her down. I lay next to her and she scooted away from me. "I didn't find out I was anything different until this year."

"But, I can't fuck with a girl!" She said getting angry. "I'm not like that."

"Please don't act like this." I cried. "I could treat you so good if you let me. Better than any of them boys at your school. But you gotta listen to me."

"But I'm not gay."

"Me either." I said shaking my head putting my hand on my chest. "Like I said I'm a boy, I just don't have a..."

"Bitch, you got titties!" She yelled cutting me off. "I'm not fucking with you."

I couldn't believe this. We had a good time and I was feeling her like I thought she was feeling me. I know people don't understand what I went through, but if she just gave me a chance to explain things would be better. I had to try harder. That's it. Try harder.

"Please, give me a chance." I cried reaching into my pockets. "I got money. You can have it all if you want it." I laid the crumpled bills on her stomach. "I'll buy you whatever you want if you don't leave me. I don't care what I got to do to get it for you." I wiped my tears away with my hand. I was crying! Why was I crying? "I just don't wanna be alone anymore. I need somebody I can be with. Somebody who can love me."

"NO! YOU SO FUCKING NASTY! YOU GOT TITTIES AND A PUSSY AND YOU TRIED TO MAKE ME THINK YOU WERE A BOY!!! YOU COULD NEVER FUCK WITH A BITCH LIKE ME!" She yelled pushing the money on the floor.

I couldn't deal with this now. I couldn't deal with this kind of rejection. I wanted to keep her to myself. I wanted her to stay with me and now she wasn't. So I grabbed the pillow behind her head and put it over her face. She tried to fight me but I held it down. My friends were still sleep and moved a little but nobody got up to see what I was doing. They were drunk and this bitch had me fucked up if she thought she could talk to me like she was crazy. Why she even stop her car if she was going to embarrass me? Why was she even nice to me? I was going to treat her so good...better than I treated Glitter.

I don't know what came over me, but all of a sudden I was crying harder and it made me angrier. Who was this bitch to come into my life and play games with my heart? I pressed the pillow harder and could feel her movements getting lighter. She gave up. It took awhile but eventually she gave up the fight completely. She wasn't built to last. And she wasn't moving anymore and I couldn't hear her screaming at me telling me I wasn't any good. Amber had to be...she had to be dead.

I lifted the pillow and jumped out of bed. Her eyes were open and she looked scared. What the fuck did I just do? What the fuck did I just do? I leaned against the wall and looked down at her. She looked like she was looking at me but I knew she wasn't. I couldn't believe I killed somebody. It happened so quickly. What was I going to do now?

• •

The Next Morning

I didn't go to sleep and one by one members of my crew started waking up. When they saw the stone look on my face they knew something was up. I was sitting on the bed, with my head against the wall looking down at Amber, hoping this was all a dream. Hoping she would wake up and be like, *'I'm sorry for calling you names and I wanna give you a chance'*. It never happened.

Wiping the crust out of his eyes Kid said, "Fuck wrong with you?"

"She dead." I said.

Silence.

Sugar stood up and walked over to her. "Stop fucking around, Mad. You know how scared I be."

"And I'm not fucking around! This bitch is dead! Look at her!"

Sugar ran to the corner of the room I guess trying to get away from the dead body or me. I couldn't be sure.

"How she die?" Krazy asked looking at me then at her. "Did she drink too much?"

"I killed her."

Their mouths dropped.

"Why...why you do that for?" Sugar said standing in the corner crying. "Why you kill her? I'm not trying to get tied up in more shit. We already on the hook because of your mother."

"This ain't about my mother."

"I'm just saying...when you said you wanted to get your mother back I could see that. But this girl didn't do anything to you. I don't understand why you had to kill her."

"And you thought you could be with me?" I said to her in a low voice. "You thought you could be my girl? With a heart like that?" I shook my head. "Naw, shawty, you too weak for me. You could never be on my arm." I don't know where that came from but it was real talk.

She didn't say anything else.

"What she do?" Krazy said.

"She crossed me. Now kill all that other shit!" I said looking around at them. "Because just like that shit with my mother, we gotta keep this between us. If we do that, things will work out. It always does."

"FUCK! I'M GONNA GET PUNISHED!" Kid said.

"Fuck punished, if this shit gets out you gonna get locked up!" I told him. "But don't worry, I'ma get us out of this."

"How?" Sugar said.

"I'ma call my pops." I paused. "He got my back. Always!"

HARMONY
OUT

"Ann, I'll be home when I can. You gotta stop pressing me out!" Jace said.

Silence.

"If you make that move, it'll be the stupidest shit you've ever did in your life. But it's on you."

Silence.

When he hung up the phone he looked at me like whatever argument he had with his bitch was my fault. "Don't get mad at me because you beefing with your girl."

"Don't say shit else to me." He said.

I was riding in the passenger seat of Jace's silver Hummer and I was angry. There was something in his eyes that told me one wrong move and he would throw me out on my ass. I didn't ask him to pick me up from the hospital and I damn sure didn't ask him to put me in his truck. He let his daughter whine and beg him to do this for her but none of this shit was for me.

"You talk to your sister?" I asked Jayden. When she was silent I looked back at her. I could tell she was thinking about something. "You hear me?"

"Yes."

"Why didn't you answer?"

"Because I was thinking. What you want?" She snapped.

I shook my head and said, "Did you talk to your sister?"

"No, mama. When I do I'll let you know. I did tell her she has to come home though on her voicemail."

Jace looked at me in disgust. "Losing your kids." He said. "How fucking motherly of you."

"Not now, Jace."

When we passed a few stores, I noticed an "Everything Market". You know the kind of place you could get beer, pads, medicine and anything else you wanted at any given moment.

"Can you stop at that store over there. I wanna go in and grab something right quick." I asked pointing out of the window. "I'm only gonna be a second."

"Stop there why?" Jace asked. "The doctor said if you were going home you had to be on bed rest, since you were pressed to leave the hospital early. So that's exactly what I'm doing, taking you home."

"If you been in a hospital as long as I was, you would've been pressed to go home too."

"Well, I'm not stopping. I ain't got time for all that shit." He persisted.

"I'm asking you to stop at the store." He didn't seem to be slowing down. "Please, Jace." He finally stopped in the store's parking lot and I smiled.

"Don't smile at me, Harmony. I don't know why you do this type shit." He said shaking his head. "You can never be regular, even after all these years. Always gotta keep up shit."

"I know." I paused, "But I'll be right back."

"I can go for you, ma. You shouldn't be moving around too much on that leg especially." Jayden said from the back seat.

"I'm fine, I been cooped up in a hospital for days. I really wanna start helping myself."

Jace gave me an evil stare but fuck him. I was gonna do me regardless. "Harmony, why you tripping? The fucking doctor said you shouldn't be moving around. Let me or Jayden go grab what you need."

"And I said I wanna do it myself. I am self sufficient you know?" I paused. "Just because you found your daughter don't make you my daddy too."

"Whatever, Harmony. Do what you wanna do."

I was about to leave when I realized I was broke. "Can I borrow some money?"

He rolled his eyes, reached into his pocket and handed me a one hundred dollar bill. I smiled and he said, "Bring back my fucking change. I'm not taking care of you no more."

"For now." I smiled.

Slamming the door on my way out, I limped into the market and went straight for the cooler. I could already feel an ice-cold beer going down my throat before I even bought it. I couldn't wait. I grabbed a 40-ounce Budweiser and went to the counter to pay for it.

"Anything else?" the woman asked me.

"Naw. Just this for now." When she rung up my purchase I said. "You got a bathroom in here?"

"Yeah…over there in the corner."

With the beer in my hand I went into the bathroom, closed the door and popped the top. Then I downed the beer without taking one breath. I leaned up against the stall door and let the intoxicating feeling take hold of me. Next to busting a nut, there was nothing like having a cold one when you haven't had it in months. Deciding I was still thirsty, I left the bathroom and did the same thing four times. On my fourth time out of the bathroom, when I opened the door I was met by Jace at the doorway.

"Fuck are you doing in here? You got your daughter out there worried like shit about you." He grabbed me by my arm and my stitches felt itchy.

Damn, this nigga could fuck up a wet dream. "Jace, please." I said snatching away from him to walk around him. "I done told you already that you not my father."

I was almost away from him when he grabbed my arm, sniffed and said, "Hold up, you been drinking?"

"Jace, don't be ridiculous."

He tried to go into the bathroom but if he did he would see four empty bottles sitting in the sink. "What are you doing?" I said blocking his path.

"You were in there drinking wasn't you?" He yelled. "You so fucking reckless! Damn!"

"Please stop it, Jace! You doing too much."

"What the fuck is wrong with you?! You just got out of the hospital and you up to your old shit already. I mean, are you that fucked up in the head?"

The way he yelled at me told me he still felt something for me. "I haven't been drinking, Jace. Okay?"

"So what you in here for?"

"I came to get some Tylenol."

"You got a pharmacy bag full of hard hitting drugs out there, and you wanna get some Tylenol?"

"It's my life! Not yours."

"Where the Tylenol?"

"What?"

"Show me the fucking Tylenol."

"I didn't get a chance to buy it, Jace. I had to go to the bathroom."

"Okay, give me my money and go to the car. I'ma get the Tylenol for you."

"I'll do it, Jace! Damn!"

"Bitch, give me my fucking money."

I dug in my pocket and handed him about eighty-six dollars and some change. He put the shit in his pocket and frowned.

"I knew you were a lying ass bitch."

"Fuck you."

"Listen, I don't give a fuck about you no more. But I'm in my daughter's life, and for whatever reason she loves you more than anything. But, bitch I will kill you before I let you fuck her up more than I'm sure you already have. Do you understand what I'm saying?"

"Yeah, Jace. I understand."

This is why I hated Jayden. She took my life and now my fucking man. And no matter how hard I tried I couldn't get nobody to understand my point of view. I was always blamed for shit and it wasn't fair.

"Now either you come on, or you getting left." He paused. "It don't make me no never mind."

JAYDEN
CONTROL YOUR BITCHES

Friendly High School hallways were crowded with teenagers when Jayden walked in with her Gucci purse. She hadn't been to school in days, but after talking to Harmony she realized that if she didn't go back, the social worker would come snooping around the house again and she could possibly be placed in a foster home.

A lot of things plagued her young mind these days. Like the fact that her mother was almost murdered, her sister may have been responsible and that her friend Passion, who was also her bottom bitch wasn't answering her calls. Thirteen Flavors was starting to be a big waste of time because she couldn't control her girls long enough for them to be consistent.

She reached her locker and was entering her combination when Xion walked up behind her, put his arms around her waist and rested his head on her shoulder.

"Hey, you." He said rocking with her. She could smell the scent of Double Mint gum in his mouth.

She smiled, turned around and looked into his eyes. "No...hey you."

They kissed each other before separating. "I ain't think you still went here no more, ma."

"Well you thought wrong." She laughed, turning around to open her locker. She grabbed her book and her book bag. She faced him again. "Anything new happening?"

"The same old." Then he paused. "But I wish I was making money." He kissed her on the cheek. "Were you able to talk to your father about me?"

"Not really. I'ma do it though. My moms been sick and she's our focus right now."

"When you gonna holla at him, babes? I need to make money now."

"I wish you stop asking me that shit! You gotta give me a chance to..."

Her sentence was cut short when she saw Shaggy rushing up to them in the hallway. The way he looked, you would've thought he caught them cheating. His brows creased the closer he got to her. She hadn't seen him since he put her out of the hotel and she didn't want to see him now.

"So ya'll still trying to throw this shit up in my face?"

Teenagers looked at the scene in the hallway and this made Jayden angry. It was tough enough going to school, she certainly didn't need to be getting in trouble or causing a scene.

"Throw what shit in your face?" Xion asked stepping closer to him.

"The fact that I cleaned this bitch up and now you with her." He was about to swing on him when Jayden blocked him.

"Why you tripping all of a sudden, Shaggy? Me and you were never together."

"Bitch, don't fucking act like you ain't know what time it was. Now you think you gonna run around school with this dude. I should..."

"Hold up," Xion said putting his hand out to prevent him from getting any closer to Jayden. "I ain't about to let you touch her."

"Nigga, did you just put your hands on me?" Shaggy frowned knocking him up against the locker. "You must've lost your mothafuckin' mind."

"Stop it, Shaggy! Fuck is wrong with you?" Jayden asked stepping in the middle of them both.

"If it wasn't for me you wouldn't be looking like you do! Now you posted up in the hallway with this nigga?"

When the principal walked in their direction, Jayden got nervous. Most of the crowd broke and Jayden was trying to think quick. After stabbing Toni and her friends she was trying to remain low key because the principal made it known that if she got in trouble again she would be expelled. Grabbing Shaggy's hand she said, "Come with me so we can talk in private."

"Fuck you talking about?" Xion asked. "This nigga tripping and you want to go with him?"

Jayden pointed down the hall at Mrs. Crimply who was moving closer. "I can't get into trouble again, Xi. Give me a second to talk to him. I'ma call you later I promise."

Shaggy was now so mad he was pacing. When Xion walked away after one last frown, Jayden and Shaggy dipped into an empty classroom. When the door was closed she peeked out the rectangular window on the door. She didn't relax until she saw Mrs. Crimply's cotton ball hairstyle walking past the classroom. When she was out of sight Jayden turned her attention to Shaggy.

"What is wrong with you?" She asked stepping up to him.

"I told you what the fuck is up with me."

Jayden not feeling his answer, pushed him into a desk. "You could've gotten me in trouble!"

"Don't push me again, Jay. Because the way I feel right now I could fuck you up in here."

"Can you tell me what's wrong with you all of a sudden? And why were you at the hospital with Passion that night?"

"She called me." He paused. "Said she needed a ride. Now why you fucking with this dude?"

Jayden was confused. Not only was Shaggy acting in a way he never had before, he was acting as if he wasn't the one who told her over and over that he was not her man. Yet here he was, trying to check her about a dude who offered to help her when she needed him the most.

"We not together, Shaggy. We never were! So why you tripping now is beyond me." Then she put her purse down on the desk next to him and said, "You wanted it this way remember?"

"You know how I felt about you."

"How? You told me everyday you came into that hotel room that I wasn't your girl. And I respected that each time."

"That's because you had a lot on your mind. And I ain't wanna put more on you by trying to fuck you."

She frowned. "So in order for us to be together we gotta fuck?"

"Stop playing with me." He smirked. "If a nigga do for you what I did for you, he wanna fuck." He paused. "The first time I break my rule to always fuck first, I get carried."

"Then if you didn't get the pussy that was your fault. Because I damn sure got the money."

His jaw flexed. "So you fucking Xion?"

"I haven't fucked nobody yet."

Shaggy smiled a little and said, "Then why he doing all this shit for you? I heard he put you up in his aunt's house and everything."

"The same reason you did." She said slyly. "He looking out."

Silence.

"I don't want you hanging with him no more. He think it's funny that I backed you financially and now you look the way you do. If anything you owe me that. I was there for you when nobody was."

"I'm not property, Shaggy." As if she remembered something she said, "Hold up...were you the one playing on my phone?"

Silence.

"I knew you were!" she continued. "Stay the fuck away from me! Or else!"

Angry he couldn't break her, he hog spit in her Gucci purse. Her eyes widened and she smacked him in the face.

"Why you do that nasty shit?!" She yelled looking in her bag. Spit rested on her shades. "That was so fucking gross!"

"I bought it for you so I can do whatever I want to it."

She took her cell phone and wallet carefully out of her purse, trying not to get the phlegm on her hand. When she got what she wanted, she left it on the desk.

"If you think just because you gave me that purse you control me, you can carry it yourself, faggy ass nigga. Because I'm my own person now and a long way from the broke bitch you met at McDonald's. So fuck off!"

When she walked out of the room her phone rang and she saw it was Olive. It was ironic that she called the moment she went in on her friend Shaggy in the classroom. Stomping down the hallway she decided to answer the phone.

"Hello." She said holding the cell to her ear.

"Oh, my God. You answered." Olive joked.

"Yeah, I just had a problem with your friend."

"Well what you doing now? Trying to get high and talk about it?"

Realizing she couldn't sit in class all day without being angry she said, "Yeah. It's Friday anyway so I might as well start the week off fresh Monday. I'm on my way."

• •

Over Olive's

Jayden was lying on Olive's bed with her smoking weed. They were face up looking at the blue-sky mural that Olive had painted on her ceiling. Jayden forgot all about how good weed made her feel because she hadn't had any since she met Olive.

"So what's up?" Olive said looking at her. "You look like you got a lot on your mind."

"A lot of shit is up."

"Did things get better back at your house?"

"Not even close. My mother was almost killed and my sister hasn't been home in weeks. Stuff just seems to be falling apart."

"What you gonna do?"

"Take one day at a time I guess."

"Anything else bothering you?"

"Yeah...my friend Passion been tripping too."

"How?"

"Well I gave her some money so she'd do some things for me. Now that she got the money she ain't been doing shit and she ain't answering my calls. Her or her friends."

"You gave all of them money?"

"Yeah. It was a strange arrangement but they broke it."

Olive rolled over on her side and said, "Next time don't give a bitch shit until after the work is done." She said. "That's rule number one in the game. Any game."

Jayden took notes. "I guess you're right."

"I know I'm right." She paused. "Now what's up with you and Shaggy? Why you guys beefing?"

"He didn't tell you?"

"Naw, ever since Toni and them came into his mother's party on some bullshit, he been mad with me. That's why I don't fuck with them bitches right now."

"Really? I thought ya'll were close."

"Who?"

"You and Toni."

"Not really. She mad because I told her even if she was beefing with you, I wasn't getting involved and that she should've never carried shit like that over Shaggy's house." Then she paused and said, "So why are you and Shaggy not talking?"

"I don't know. I mean...for the longest he kept telling me he didn't want a relationship, so I didn't press him. And then out of nowhere, he puts me out of the hotel he was paying for just because I hung out with Xion one night."

"You hung out with Xion?"

"Yeah."

Olive shook her head. "You know you can't do no shit like that, Jayden. That boy was feeling you."

"I don't understand." Jayden frowned. "He kept telling me he wasn't my boyfriend and that he didn't want a girl. How was I wrong?"

"Jayden," Olive said playing with a few strands of Jayden's hair, "boys do stuff like that all the time. But you gotta know when they feeling you despite what they say outta their mouths. Girl, if every bitch took what a nigga said at face value all the time nobody would be in a relationship. Or procreate!!! Shaggy the type of nigga who wanna know you want him!"

Olive stared in Jayden's eyes seductively and it made her uncomfortable. She'd seen Harmony look at men like that so she was pretty sure what it meant. "Olive, I gotta tell you something."

"What's up?" She smiled.

"Uh...I'm not like that." She said softly. "I mean, I like when you touch my hair and talk to me real nice, but I'm not into girls. Will never be in to girls."

Olive released her hair strands and laughed. "If you took it the wrong way by me playing with your hair, I see you don't know how to read women or men."

Jayden smiled from embarrassment, "I guess not."

"Don't worry, Jayden, I'm not into women either." She paused. "At least not anymore. I use to be but they too much trouble and keep up too much shit." Then she played with Jayden's hair again. "And I touch you because I think you're pretty and I think you need it from me."

"Need what?"

"Love. Attention. All that." Olive shrugged.

Jayden stood up. "I'ma call a cab."

"Did I do something wrong?"

"Naw...I think its time for me to go. I'm high enough as it is." Jayden made the call and sat in a chair within the room.

"What is wrong with you, Jayden? You different from anybody I ever met before and that makes you unique. Because I've met a lot of people." She paused. "But, don't you want people to love you?"

"No! I don't want love anymore. I use to."

Olive sat up straight in the bed and said, "Why not? Without love you might as well die."

"I can't love. If I love, and it's taken from me, I don't know how I would react at this point in my life. I just wanna make money and take care of myself. I don't want people promising to do stuff for me and taking it back. I don't want to depend on anybody."

"Your life must've been some shit." Olive said shaking her head. Then she got up and stood in front of her. "But if you gonna live, Jayden, you gotta learn to love and let people love you back. I'm just letting you know." Then Olive popped an ecstasy pill and smiled. "God is love."

"Fuck God!" Jayden spat, forcing Olive's eyes wide open. "I use to pray for God every night when I was a kid. I prayed that he'd love me and prayed that he'd take care of me and my sister when our mother burned us with irons, but it never happened. So God can't do shit for me but stay the fuck out my way."

Her anger startled Olive. "You more fucked up than I thought." When Olive's phone rang she left Jayden where she stood to answer it. Looking at the number she said, "Hey, Shaggy." She saw Jayden's expression change at the mentioning of his name. "Yeah I'm home." She paused. "You're here?" She paused again. "Alright, let me open the door for you."

When she hung up she looked at Jayden. "That was Shaggy. He called out of the blue and is at the door."

Jayden got her phone and her wallet. "I'm 'bout to leave." She heard a horn and looked out the window. Her cab was there. "My ride here anyway. I'ma talk to you later."

"Okay, but make sure you call me, girl. I don't like the way this conversation between us ended."

"Aight...I'll hit you later."

Jayden hoped she'd be able to leave without running into Shaggy but when Olive opened the door Shaggy was there and he had Passion by his side.

MAD

THE BOND THAT DOESN'T BREAK

Me and all of my friends were on the Washington DC subway's (Metro) red line for over two hours, just riding it back and forth like we always did when we were bored. I was trying to feel them out. See if anything changed since my father came to the hotel and got rid of Amber's body. I could always tell when something was up because we were all quiet. But that wasn't the case. We talked about stuff, like we always did still, something felt off. I felt like after I killed Amber that now they held something over my head and I had nothing over theirs. That would have to change.

"What's your worst fear?" Wokie asked me.

We were sitting on the metro in our seats in a way that we could all see each other. Our backs leaned against the windows and our feet pointed toward the aisle. The five of us were taking up full seats so that no one could sit next to us. Sugar kept looking at me. In a way that made me nervous. Then she'd look at Krazy, Wokie and Kid, and I knew they held a secret behind my back. What was it?

"I don't know. I don't have no fear." I told them.

They all looked at me. "Well she did kill somebody." Sugar said. "So we got to believe when she say she not scared of nothing."

"Why you being all hot?" I asked, sipping the Henny I poured in a Coke bottle earlier. There were two more bottles of Henny in my bag ready to go.

"We all got fears." Wokie said. "I don't care what she say."

"Right, nigga. We all got fears, so since you asking the question, what's yours?" Krazy asked.

Wokie looked at the white lady with the red hair and tight blue dress that he'd been eyeing since she got on fifteen minutes earlier. She looked like she popped right out of a fashion magazine. She was beautiful.

"I'm afraid of dying. I guess." He looked at us.

"That's too easy!" Kid said.

"Why?" I asked him.

"Because everybody's afraid of dying."

"Not me." I looked at all of my friends. Then I poured some more Henny down my throat. "Not me."

"Pick something else," Krazy said. "And when we all get the question nobody can say death. And we can't pick what somebody else picked either."

"So what's your greatest fear, Wokie?" Kid asked. "Because you can't say death, man."

"I'm afraid of drowning." He paused.

"Ain't that death?" Sugar asked.

"Naw…it's a way of dying. So shut the fuck up and listen." Wokie said. "Anyway, when I was a kid, I saw this baby drown before."

"Where?" I asked.

"I was at my aunt's house in Atlanta for this family reunion cookout. She had this pool in her backyard. Anyway, after the cookout nobody wanted the party to be over. We were having too much fun even though the mosquitoes was fucking us up! It was nighttime and all the adults were inside the house, having a party. My cousins, about six or seven of us around the same age, and me, were sitting by the pool drinking beer. We weren't supposed to be out there but the adults were so busted that we knew they wouldn't know."

"How old were you?" Kid asked.

"'Bout thirteen I think.

"Nigga, that was last year! You fourteen now!"

"Shut up, Kid! And let him finish the story." I said.

"Shannon, my girl cousin, use to be real close with us, but shit changed. We didn't even know she was pregnant before she brought her baby to the cookout. Then, nobody really wanted her around. Anyway, that whole night she kept trying to hang with us, but she'd bring her baby and it made us uncomfortable. The baby wouldn't stop crying." He swallowed. "Anyway, 'bout five beers later, we convinced her to put the baby in the pool. Saying it could swim naturally like in the womb. She didn't want to do it at first but I could tell she wanted to fit in, even though we were younger.

"After five more minutes the baby was in the pool, swimming. She was so amazed that she left it in the pool because we all thought it was funny the way it seemed to move. After a minute though, the baby wasn't swimming no more. It wasn't even moving. It was like, it just floated or some shit." The train stopped and more people got on. I could tell Wokie didn't want nobody but us hearing the story, because it took him a while to restart.

"Like I was saying, after awhile the baby wouldn't move. It just floated." He paused. "I'll never forget the look on my cousin's face when she took her dead baby out of the water. It was blank. Like, she died too. I wanted to hold her and tell her I was sorry but I was in the drunk zone. She just held on to the baby like it was going to wake up. It didn't."

Tears came down his face and he quickly wiped them away. We looked elsewhere to pretend we didn't see that shit. Crying amongst the crew was a no-no.

"What did ya'll do?" Sugar asked.

"Me and my cousins went into the house, but didn't tell the adults. Nobody wanted to be the one to say they witnessed the baby die. After about fifteen minutes one of my aunts went outside to do something when all of a sudden she started screaming. Me and my cousins knew what was up. We were there and saw the whole thing. Anyway, when we went outside," he swallowed, "when we went outside…we saw the baby and my cousin Shonda floating in the water. She killed herself too." He looked at all of us. "After all this time, I never understood how she could purposely kill herself by drowning. She wanted to die that bad that she took her own life. After that shit I don't even go to pools no more. I can't stand 'em."

We all looked at each other but remained silent.

"What's your greatest fear, Krazy?" Wokie asked trying to get the attention off of him. I felt him on that shit too.

Krazy looked at Wokie and I could tell suddenly the conversation got serious. This was the deepest we ever got with one another. I wondered if it was because Amber's death brought us closer.

"I don't know," he shrugged. "Mad, give me some of that Coke." I handed him the Henny disguised as Coke and he took a large swallow and gave it back. "I guess it would be, to get locked up. I mean half of my family in jail. My mother, my father, two of my aunts and most of my cousins. I got so many family members in jail that if I went there, I might be alright."

"So how is that your greatest fear?" I asked.

"Because the idea of not being able to do what I want fucks me up. That's why me and my foster mother don't get along right now. That bitch keep trying to tell me what the fuck to do. I'm like, old lady bitch, I'm fourteen!"

We all laughed.

The train stopped and a pretty Spanish girl walked on and sat in a seat next to Krazy.

"So I don't give a fuck about jail! You know. Because for real I'm not scared of nobody. I just like freedom. If they locked me up, I'd probably still be on the run like that dude in the news."

"Right! I can't believe they haven't caught him after all this time." Wokie said.

"They wouldn't catch me either. I'm too smooth for that shit." He was showing off for the girl and we knew it. We let him live though. It was considered rude to announce a show off in our crew amongst somebody else if you could help it. "But if I had to pick something," he paused, "a fear that is, that would be it."

He smiled at the Spanish girl and she waved.

"What about you, Kid?" Krazy asked.

"Me...my fear would be not having shit. You know...like not having a fly ass ride, no whole bunch of money. Shit like that." He looked at all of us. "I mean...I like getting high and chilling with ya'll. But what would happen if we grew up and the same shit was going on, and we still didn't have no money?"

"So what you gonna do about it?" Sugar asked.

"We doing greatest fears! Not greatest questions, bitch."

"Nigga, fuck you!"

"Bitch, suck my dick!" Kid yelled back. "Anyway, if I had to pick a fear it would be that, because I don't want to be broke. I don't wanna grow up not having shit. You know?" Then he looked at Sugar. "And I guess I'ma sell dope to make my come up."

"What about you, bitch?" Kid asked Sugar. "What's your greatest fear?"

She rolled her eyes and said, "Being alone." Then she looked at me. "Not having ya'll in my life. Even though everybody in this crew treat me like shit."

"Girl, you know we be just fucking around with you." Kid said. "You the only bitch in the crew now. You gotta toughen up."

She put her head down and said, "But sometimes ya'll go too hard."

"Man, relax and answer the question." I told her.

She looked at me and said, "I don't wanna be alone. Ever." Then she scooted in and looked dead into my eyes. I took a swig of my Henny and tried to act like I didn't feel her focusing on me. So I looked at Krazy. But he was booking the Spanish bitch next to him and Kid was now busy with the contents of my book bag. I guess he was looking for the bob we rolled up earlier even though I told him I left it. He wasn't gonna find shit. Now I had to look back at her.

"What you just say?" I asked. "I ain't hear you."

"I said I don't want to be alone, Mad." She paused. "I want you to know, that you were right at the hotel. About me not being strong enough. And not having enough heart to be your girl." She played with her fingers.

"Don't do it, man." Kid said still looking in my book bag. I didn't even know he was paying attention. "I told you on the phone not to do it, Sugar."

"Yeah...we told you it was a bad idea." Wokie added. "Leave it alone."

She waved them off. "Mad, I love you."

Everybody in my crew did the *Mad Max Drop*. It's when somebody says something so stupid that everybody puts one hand on their forehead and falls back. Sometimes we would go too far and hit the floor but most times we would just fall back.

"Please stop! You killing us, Sugar!" Wokie said.

"Mad, I love you. And I know I could never replace Glitter. But I'm asking if you could be my girl."

"Then she asks this nigga to be her girl!" Wokie said. "You wrong on all levels!"

"Have you been listening to anything Mad says?" Kid asked. "She's a dude! She could never be your girl!"

I was stunned.

Embarrassed.

Shocked.

How could she ask me to be her girl? I wasn't feeling her like that. Cause of her, we had people listening who weren't even part of our crew. They were waiting on me to answer and I stumbled. On one hand I didn't want to hurt her feelings and on another hand I didn't want to be alone either and now I was. So I looked at her, long and hard before answering her question. Sugar was cute no doubt. I was even feeling the signature red glasses. But I didn't like how strong she was coming at me. I didn't like that she fucked every member in our crew and I didn't like her style.

"Sugar...you're my friend and I..."

She got up and stormed out before I could finish answering. We all got up to catch her but the train doors shut in our faces. We sat back down in a different place, so we could get the extra ears out of our conversation.

"That went over well." Krazy said stuffing a folded piece of small white paper in his back pocket. "But let's look at the brighter side, fellas. I just bagged the baddest bitch any of you niggas have ever seen in your life."

"Fuck that, bitch. Her eyebrows was too thick." Wokie said.

"Hatersssss!" Krazy smiled.

My mind was still on Sugar. I wondered how she was doing. I didn't want to hurt my friend. I loved her but we could never be. And then I wondered if that's how I came across to bitches I bagged. *Desperate.*

RAUNCHY 2 | T. STYLES

Pressed. I realized after this I was going to change my whole approach. No more coming at bitches at 100 miles per hour with that romantic bullshit. I was just gonna be me and if they didn't like it, fuck it. Only when I knew they wanted me would I change shit up and show them the nigga I really could be.

"Just because Sugar pulled that hot wet shit don't mean you getting out of it." Kid said to me.

"What you talking about?"

"Your greatest fear. What is it?"

"Oh." My greatest fear was also being alone but the rules were made and we stuck by our rules. No one in the crew was allowed to say another fear somebody already said so I'd have to pick something else. It showed me that we all had more than one fear in life. "I guess I would have to say fucking another dude."

"What?" Krazy laughed.

"I would rather die than to have another dude put his dick anywhere near me."

"So, Mad, real talk, you never, *ever* fucked a dude before?" Wokie asked.

"Why don't you ask me that again after I drop your ass on the floor." They all laughed.

"Just asking," he said putting his hands up and backing into his seat.

"Why?" Kid asked.

"Why what?"

"Why you never fucked a dude?"

"Because I don't find niggas attractive. Maybe if I hung around a better looking group of mothafuckas shit would be different." They all laughed. "Naw, all jokes aside, in my mind I'm a nigga. Like, I don't see myself as a girl until I look in a mirror. That's why I hate mirrors. I see myself as a dude. And it be fucking me up when bitches like Amber don't see that sometimes."

"That's why you killed her?" Wokie asked.

"That bitch was wilding out. Talking about how she ain't wanna fuck with me because I had a...I have a..."

"We got you." Wokie said and I appreciated them for not wanting me to say the word.

"And I snapped." I continued. "I just snapped and I smothered her with my pillow. Until she was dead." I looked at all of them.

"I probably would've killed that bitch too." Wokie said.

"Fuck is you talking about, nigga?" Kid asked.

"You ain't see how long she held onto the loud when we was passing that shit around. Puff...puff...give!" Wokie said. "She act like the shit was all hers. Damn near smoked it to the nub."

We bust out laughing.

"I love ya'll." I told them. "On some serious shit this right here, is my family."

"You telling us something we already know." Wokie said.

• •

Outside

I could see the pinks of my eyelids but I couldn't open my eyes fast enough. The noise. The noise was so loud it was drowning. When I finally popped my eyes open, I was in the driver seat of a truck, and my crew, was looking at me with wild eyes. I had fallen asleep behind the wheel of a truck and we were about to crash.

To prevent hitting a tractor-trailer, I whipped the wheel to my right, and we slammed into three cars sitting in the driveway of a house. The truck I was driving rolled up onto a small car and stopped. Smoke poured out of the engine and I looked at my crew. We were all gripping different parts of our bodies.

"What the fuck is going on?" Someone yelled coming out of the house.

"We gotta go, ya'll!" I said holding my arm. The house owner looked mad.

"My shit hurts!" Wokie said holding his back.

"Fuck that, man lets roll!"

We got out of the car slow at first until the man yelled, "Wait! You gotta pay for my shit! I'm calling the cops."

"Suck my dick, nigga!" I yelled.

When we finally got out we heard him say, "Sic, 'em boys!"

When we looked behind us four pit bulls were running in our direction.

"Oh shit! We about to get bit!" Wokie yelled.

"Nigga, shut the fuck up and run!" I said.

On a straight up chase, the dogs were gaining on us quickly. We were out in the open and would need to put shit between us if we were going to survive.

"Dip behind that house!" I said pointing to my right.

We all ran behind the house, opened a wooden gate when, like a white bitch in a bad horror movie, Kid fell to the ground. One of the pit bulls got inside the gate, and bit him on the leg. The other dogs were barking on the other side trying to get in.

"Awwwww help!" Kid yelled.

We all stopped what we were doing and turned to help Kid. I heard about pits locking their jaws so I decided to see if that was true. I found a rake and hit the dog in the head with it. It cried and let him go. We all helped Kid off the ground and ran as fast as we could. I was on Kid's right and Wokie was on his left as he hopped on one leg.

I couldn't believe all of this was happening. The last thing I remembered was getting drunk on the train. How did we get here?

We didn't stop running until we came into a small diner. I couldn't read really well but was okay with some words. I eventually saw a sign and knew we were in Virginia. But I heard Virginia was so big that we could be miles away from home.

"Are you okay?" I asked Kid.

He lifted his pants leg and examined the bite. It was bloody and flesh hung everywhere. "Yeah. It hurts like shit though."

"What the fuck happened?" I asked as everybody was trying to catch their breath. "I mean, I don't remember none of the shit after the subway!"

"I'll tell you tomorrow. Now I just wanna get home." Wokie said.

"Me too. This bite is killing me!" Kid said.

I was just about to suggest we flag a cab when my phone rang.

I pulled it out of my pocket and said, "Hello?"

"Madjesty, when are you coming home?"

I knew that voice and I hated it on the deepest levels. Why the fuck was this bitch calling me. "Who is this?"

"It's your mother. Now it's time to bring your ass home! We gotta talk."

URSULA
TATTLE TELL

Ursula walked into Friendly High School with one mission...to tell. She learned from Nook that Harmony was being held hostage at Concord Manor, and now she decided to do something about it by talking to the school's principal, Mrs. Crimply. Nook conveniently left out how he raped Harmony, but Ursula would not have cared either which way. Her mind was on Madjesty. She could have easily reported her money stolen to get pay back, but then she would have to explain how she fucked a fourteen year old child and got her money stolen after falling into a sex induced sleep. She was humiliated enough with the writing on her car and she couldn't subject herself to any more ridicule. No...Snitching would have to do for now.

"Mam, if what you're saying is true, we must call the authorities!" Mrs. Crimply said.

"Yes we must!" Believing Nook she said, "I know for a fact that this woman is bound and gagged in her own basement. And by the hands of her own daughter at that. This is ridiculous!"

"Okay, let me call her home first. Just to see if she answers the phone. If what you're saying is true, we'll call the authorities afterwards."

"Yes. Let's do that." Ursula continued. "Because I believe that bitch had something to do with my daughter getting murdered, too. She must be taken off of the streets."

Mrs. Crimply allowed the phone to ring twice before Harmony answered. "Hello."

"May I speak with Ms. Phillips?"

"Who the fuck is this?"

"I'm sorry, mam. I didn't mean to bother you. This is the principal at her twins' school and I'm told that Ms. Harmony Phillips is in trouble."

Silence.

"Mam, I don't know what you're talking about, but I'm Harmony Phillips I just got back from a cruise and I'm great." Mrs. Crimply remembered her voice from the past and knew it was her.

"Oh. I see." Mrs. Crimply said eyeing Ursula. *"Well...I'm sorry to bother you."*

When she hung up she said, *"Ms. Phillips is home and fine. You must be mistaken."*

"I'm not!" Ursula yelled. Nook seemed to be so forthcoming and she didn't believe he was lying when he said she was being held hostage. *"I have first hand information from a reliable source."*

"And I just spoke to Ms. Phillips myself." Mrs. Crimply persisted. *"She's okay. Just came home from a cruise and everything."*

Ursula was furious. She was all ready to run tell that and came up short. *"I'm sorry to waste your time."*

"Not a problem." Mrs. Crimply said. *"But if Madjesty is out of order, maybe I can let her social worker know instead. I mean, I have had problems from her in the past."*

"She has a social worker?"

"Yes. And I call on her whenever there's a problem. Maybe she can check into things."

"Sounds like a plan to me." Ursula smiled, feeling like she was closer than ever to getting revenge.

HARMONY
OLD MAMA

"Jace, thank you for the TV. I appreciate it." I said talking to him on the phone.

His voice sounded thick with sleep. "It's eight o'clock in the morning. And you calling me to tell me that?"

"Well I wanted you to know how much I appreciate it."

"Fuck you, bitch. I didn't do that shit for you. I did it for my daughter."

"But she's not watching it now is she?" I asked.

"Jace who is that on the phone?" Antoinette asked in the background. *"It better not be Harmony again."*

"Shut the fuck up!" He told her.

"One of these days I'ma leave you!" She continued.

I thought it was funny that she was still in the picture and that after all of these years, he still loved me.

"If that's how you feel make it today." Jace said to her.

Silence.

I waited patiently for her response but heard nothing.

"Harmony, there will never be a me and you again. I need you to understand that."

"Why don't you come over here and let me suck that dick. The way I use to. I know you'll like it."

"I've been with Antoinette for fourteen years and we never had a fight. Now that you've come back in the picture you're keeping shit up. I'm not fucking with you. It's over."

"Well I don't want to fuck Antoinette, Jace. I'm trying to fuck you. And you're still on this phone because you're considering it." I laughed. "Don't you realize the more you hate me, the more you love me?"

CLICK.

I laughed. I had him right where I wanted him, and it was just a matter of time.

The air conditioning blew comfortably in my large room and it felt good to be on my huge soft bed. For a minute I thought about my father, and Estelle, and how they must have felt coming home every night to this room. After going from a dirty dark basement, being fucked by kids and then entering a hospital for days I was finally getting my life back to normal. This was my life. Now all I had to do was settle old scores by tying up a few loose ends.

"Mam, everything is set in place, will you be needing anything else before I leave?" the technician asked me entering the doorway in my room. His brown skin was sweaty despite the air being on and he was carrying a work case tightly in his hands.

"Did anybody see you come in here? Or see what you were doing?" I asked looking behind him.

"No. I was careful."

"Good."

"So when can I get paid?" He asked walking deeper into my room.

I grabbed the remote on the bed and turned the TV on. "Bill me."

He frowned and angrily replied, "But that wasn't the arrangement. Had I known this, I would've charged you full price."

"Look, either you wait until I pay you or you get nothing. Now get the fuck out of my room. You're making my head hurt."

He stood a few moments in silence before saying, "I'm coming back here for my money, and if you don't have it, there's gonna be problems."

"Yeah, whatever."

When he left I focused back on the TV and my plan for my little girls. I been in the house for a few days and had relied on Jayden for everything. The funny part about it was, whatever I needed she gave me willingly. Whether it be washing my pussy, or buying me something to eat she did it all without batting an eye. She was my personal bitch slave. I had to give myself credit, even though I hated both of my daughters with a passion; I was able to play it off.

Fifteen minutes later when Jayden walked in, my room was a little uncomfortable. It was always uncomfortable whenever I saw her face. She managed to always look like she breezed out of a magazine. New everything. She was carrying a silver breakfast tray and on top of if it was pancakes, fried eggs with cheese and a glass of orange juice. She sat the tray next to me and opened the large cream curtains in my room to let the sun in. I stirred a little before sitting up straight.

"Good morning," she smiled, "I made you breakfast."

"Thanks, baby." She lifted the tray and put it over my lap. I picked up the fork and ate some of the eggs. "It tastes good."

"Thanks, I can cook a little something-something." She blushed. "Breakfast anyway."

"Really? I never knew you could cook like this."

She was silent before saying, "That's cuz there wasn't ever that much food in the house for me to show you."

I dropped the fork and looked at her slowly. "I'm sorry, Jayden. I guess everything I say or do will remind you of the mother I never was to you."

"Maybe at first, ma, but I really want us to get along better. I want us to have the relationship I know we can have."

"Even after everything I did to you?"

"Especially after everything you did to me." She paused. "I don't want you holding this over your head forever. I forgive you, ma. I really do. And I know when we speak to Madjesty together, she will forgive you too."

"Fuck her!"

"What?" She asked confused at my outburst. "I thought you said things were good between you two."

Damn it! I let her catch me slipping. "What are you talking about?"

"I'm talking about what you just said. About Madjesty." She paused. "I thought you said things were cool."

"Wait, what did you think I just said, baby?"

"Fuck her." She repeated.

I shook my head and laughed. "I knew you heard me wrong. I didn't say fuck her, Jayden. I said *I fucked up*." I paused. "*I fucked up* because my daughters will never know how sorry I am for ruining their lives." She didn't seem to buy it and neither did I so I kicked my plan into full gear. "Come here. Sit next to me on my bed."

She sat next to me and I reached in the drawer to my right. Then I handed her the gold earrings with the word Princess in the middle of them. They were the same earrings I'd stolen from Ebony and tucked in my pussy when I was a teenager. "These have been with me for a long time, and I want you to have them."

She held them in her hand and examined them. "Really? But why?"

"My daddy gave them to me when I was a kid and they mean a lot to me." I touched her hand. "You mean a lot to me and I want you to have them."

She looked confused. "But...these are big earrings," she paused examining them, "and I thought daddy said that granddaddy died when you were a kid. How could you wear them?"

This bitch makes me sick. Why couldn't she just go with the flow? "He did die when I was a kid. But he bought them for me before he died, so that when I got older I could wear them." I continued. "When I was a teenager I wore them everyday and now," I paused, "I want you to have them. This way you'll have something that you know meant a lot to me. It's a peace offering from mother to daughter. Do you accept?"

She held the earrings in her hand and wrapped her arms around my neck. "Yes, mama! I do."

Her embrace caused my stomach to churn but I held it together. I was just about to push this bitch away from me when Madjesty walked into the room half drunk and stumbling.

She looked at Jayden removing her arms from around my neck and said, "Did I interrupt? You two look like you're about to fuck or something."

"Madjesty!" Jayden said walking up to her. "Why would you say something like that?"

"Because I can't believe you in here hugging this bitch. After everything she's done to us."

"So I get no thank you for arranging a pick up for you and your little friends in Virginia?" I ask. "You see me and the first thing you do is call me a bitch?"

"You having the man whose dick you made Jayden suck come get us doesn't make you a model parent."

When Madjesty called and said she was stuck in Virginia, I called Abdul who lived in DC but close to Virginia. He agreed to pick them up for me as a favor, especially after the treat my daughter gave him. So what Jayden sucked his dick, at least she was home and in one piece. Because from what I heard from Abdul, one of the kids could barely even walk due to a dog bite on his leg.

"You had Abdul pick her up?" Jayden asked.

"It was the only thing I could think of last minute." I paused.

"See, Jayden, this bitch isn't sorry for anything she put us through."

"Mad, mama is sorry for everything. And she admitted that how she treated us when we were kids was wrong. We were just talking about it and everything and to tell you the truth, I believe her."

Madjesty walked up to me. "Well I don't believe her." Then she took a swig of the Hennessy in her hand. Then she looked at me. "So you asked to see me. What do you want? To have me locked up?"

"Locked up for what?" Jayden asked. "You didn't do anything to get you locked up. Right, mama?"

"Jayden, give me and Madjesty," I paused, "I mean, me and Mad a few minutes alone."

Reluctantly she said, "Okay. I'll be in my room if you need me. Just call."

When she left I looked as compassionately at Madjesty as I could, "Mad, I'm not going to tell the police what you did to me. And Jayden doesn't know what you did and I want to keep it that way."

"What?" she asked stumbling again. "Why?"

"Because it was my fault."

"Your fault?" She paused. "How?"

"Because had I not done you so wrong as a child, you would never have had to do what you did to me. And as horrible as that experience was in the basement, I'm realizing now it was all my fault."

Madjesty walked closer to the bed. "How come I don't believe you? How come I believe you're up to something?"

"I can't tell you why you feel the way that you do, but I'm coming to you as honestly as I possibly can, Madjesty. I was wrong for how I treated you when you were a kid, and because of it, I had everything you did coming to me."

"So you really aren't going to tell the police about me and my friends?"

"No, I'm not."

Madjesty took a swig of Hennessy, smiled and sat down on the bed. I wasn't a brown liquor girl but the bottle had my mouth watering. "You mind if I have some?"

She shrugged and said, "Are you supposed to be drinking? With you coming from the hospital and all."

"I won't tell if you won't tell."

She laughed and handed me the bottle. "It's your funeral."

I took the bottle and poured the liquid down my throat. She quickly took it back. I guess we had more in common than I wanted to admit. We both favored liquor. I was immediately relaxed even though the brown makes me frown. I was about to ask for some more when Jayden came running into the room.

"Ma, somebody's at the door!"

I sat up straight because her anxiousness put me on edge. "Well who is it?"

"It's three women. One of them is old and she says…"

"She says what, Jayden?!"

"She says that she's your mother!"

PRESENT DAY
GREEN DOOR - ADULT MENTAL HEALTH CARE CLINIC
NORTHWEST, WASHINGTON DC

Christina seemed uneasy the more Harmony told her story. Yet she'd be lying if she didn't admit that it was also very interesting.

"I'm confused." Christina said going over the notes on her chart. "I thought you said you were tortured for 30 days by Madjesty."

"I didn't say that."

"You did."

"No, I didn't." She paused. "I said that for thirty days I was tortured like you couldn't imagine."

"I'm still confused."

"What's there to be confused about? I was tortured for that amount of time."

"But it seems like you were only held hostage by Madjesty for days, maybe a few weeks at the most. Unless I'm missing something."

"I was down there, in the basement, for a few weeks."

"Ms. Phillips, your time frame doesn't add up. I mean, how can you be tortured for 30 days, yet you were rescued by the caseworker within a matter of weeks?"

"There are many different ways to be tortured."

Christina sighed. "Yes there are, but I'm speaking specifically of the ways you claimed you were tortured by your daughter."

"She wasn't the only one who tortured me." Harmony paused. "Because life for me got worse after that knock on the door."

"Okay. But how did Madjesty assist in all of this?"

"She had a part in it and if you let me finish without any further interruptions, you'll understand more."

"Okay, before we go there, how did your mother showing up make you feel?"

"Angry."

"Why?"

"It reminded me of everything I hated about myself." Harmony paused. "Because had she'd been there...had she been in my life, everything may have been different."

"It's true but things may have gone worse. It's hard to say what things would have been like because life didn't present itself to you in that way. I think you're supposed to learn from your past to uplift your future."

"You're just an outsider looking in. You'll never understand."

"Maybe not, but for now, please continue."

PART THREE

MAD

PINK

I was sitting in the living room, looking at the woman Harmony said was my grandmother. Beside her were two twenty something year old Spanish chicks that they said were my aunts. It seemed like shit just kept getting weirder and weirder in my life ever since we moved to Concord Manor.

"Irma, I don't know what you want from me." Harmony said, sitting bent over slightly on the couch looking in her direction. Irma sat next to her and her daughters stood behind Irma as she sat on the couch.

"I want to make amends, Harmony. Like I said, I'm dying and I wanted you to meet your sisters. They are your family." Harmony looked at them and they smiled. "I want to tell you why I did the things that I did to you in the past. I want to tell you how I loved you. How I always loved you."

"Well shit is too late for me, Irma." She paused. "My life is fucked up and can't nobody do anything for me at this point but leave me the fuck alone."

I thought it was funny how Harmony wanted forgiveness from us, but wouldn't accept it from her own mother. I'm telling you, this bitch is up to something.

"Harmony, please. Just give me a chance. And if you still want me to leave after that, I'm gone, and you'll never hear from me again."

"Ms. Irma," Jayden interrupted, "are you really my grandmother?"

"Yes." Irma smiled. "I am. And you don't know how good it feels to finally meet you."

"All of this is bullshit!" I said interrupting the fake ass ceremony.

"And you are?" One of her daughters asked me.

"She's my other daughter." Harmony said.

"Daughter?" One of the aunts asked. "I thought it was a boy."

"I'm Madjesty, and if what this bitch says is true, that means I'm her other grandchild."

"Don't call my mother out of her name again!" the aunt said.

"Fuck that shit! I'm so sick of people asking for respect without giving any." Then I sipped on more of my Henny. "I respect those who respect me."

"What has happened to you, Madjesty?" Irma asked looking at me suspiciously. "You look like you've been through a…"

"Fucked up life?" I said.

"Yes."

"Well I have."

Harmony looked at me in disappointment. Not anger, but disappointment. "Irma, if you want to talk, let's go upstairs and talk alone." Harmony interjected. When Irma's eyes remained on me she said, "Please."

Harmony, Irma and her two daughters went upstairs to the room leaving me and Jayden alone.

"Mad, why are you acting like this?" Jayden asked.

"Fuck you mean?"

"I thought after talking to mama upstairs, shit was cool between you two." She paused. "Then you come down here and embarrass mama in from of her mother. Why?"

"Well shit ain't cool. I mean, I just feel like something is up."

"If you wouldn't drink so much maybe you wouldn't feel that way."

"What you trying to say?"

"I'm saying you drink too much! Open your eyes!" Jayden said. "That's your grandmother."

"But she Spanish. She don't even look like me." I paused. "And since when do you allow new people into your life? You're usually the first one who's suspicious."

"And I still am." Jayden said. "But right now, I need you to calm the fuck down. I don't want that social worker taking us away, Mad. But you sure about to give her a reason acting the way that you are."

"The last I heard we weren't conjoined twins." I laughed. "So if I fuck up they'll just be taking me away. Don't worry; you'll be able to stay with your precious little mother."

She slapped me in the face and I laughed.

"I'm sick of you talking like that, Madjesty!"

"Finally you got some balls. You just showing them to the wrong person."

When I said that, my phone rang and I noticed it was pops. So I walked a few feet away from her and answered. "Yeah."

"I need you to meet me at my house."

"I can't do it right now."

"I thought we had an understanding. You family, and when I need you to have my back, you betta get it."

"I do have your back, pops. It's just that some shit just happened over here. And I can't leave."

Jayden looked at me and shook her head. "Still fucking with Kali." Then she walked away. "I hope your stupid ass get exactly what you deserve."

I shook my head and focused back on my call. "Are you there?"

"Yes. Its really not a good time though, pops. Social workers been hanging at the house saying if I don't start being home more, and if I don't go to school, they gonna put me in a foster home. I gotta chill. "

"When you needed me to dump that young bitch at the hotel I was there."

Silence.

"My house in thirty minutes, Madjesty. Catch a cab, I'll pay for it."

"I'm on my way."

• •

At Bernie's House

When I got to Bernie's house Kali was sitting on a sofa smoking a blunt. The house was filled with a grey haze and I could tell he'd been puffing one after the other.

"Where's Bernie?"

"She not here."

He stood up and the hatchet he took everywhere with him was on his back. "But we gotta move without her. Her car out front."

He walked toward the door and then to the car and I followed. "So where we going?"

"I need you to talk to this chick and get her to walk back with you to my car. She's a good friend of mine but we had a misunderstanding in the past. I know if she sees me things will be good but there can be no mistakes, Mad. You gotta do what I'm telling you."

"What's her name?" We got inside the car and he started driving.

"Don't worry about all that."

When he finally stopped driving, we were in front of nail salon. From the large window I could see a lot of women inside and I wondered which one he was trying to reach.

"You see that bitch right there." He pointed. "The one at the register? With the long hair and tight white t-shirt on."

"The pretty one?"

"Yeah." He paused. "I been following her for days." He looked in her direction. "I finally got her. She is never, *ever* alone even if she comes here. But today, for whatever reason, she happened to come by herself." He looked at me seriously. "Do what you gotta do, but I need you to get her to come to my car. She's a friend of mine."

I looked her over and knew it wouldn't be easy. "Should I say you are in the car? Waiting on her?"

"I know you not that stupid!"

"Well what can I say? She don't look like she'd even listen to me."

"That's your problem. Just do it." He paused. "And if you do it and do it right, I got a bottle of Henny for you and some smoke when you get back. But if you don't I'm cutting you out of my life for good."

My heart dropped and I wanted to prove to him that I could do what he wanted.

"Okay...I got you." I said moving for the door handle.

He laughed.

"What's funny?"

"Nothing. I use to say that when I was a kid."

"What?"

"I got you. Except for when I said it, I meant it." He grabbed me by the wrist and the pressure he put on it hurt so bad I thought he would break my arm. "This shit is important. You understand?"

"Yeah. I do."

"Bring her to me."

When I walked out of the car I walked into the salon. I was tipsy as usual but was trying to think of what I could say to convince her to come to the car with me alone. She just finished paying and was in front of a wall of nail polishes.

"Can I help you?" The Chinese receptionist asked once I was inside.

"Uh...how much for a manicure?" I glanced over at the woman I was there to lure outside. She was holding a bottle of red polish."

"You want tips?"

"What?" I frowned.

"Do you want me to make your nails longer?" The receptionist asked.

"Fuck no! Just a manicure."

She frowned back and said, "Okay. Pick your color and wait over there in the seats. We'll call you when its time."

When she said that I went to the polishes. She was still there but she looked at me and moved. When I looked out of the window I saw the car but my pops was leaned back so no one could see him. But I knew he was there and I didn't want to let him down. Out of everybody in my life, he was most like me. When there was nothing else I could think of to convince her to go anywhere with me, I decided to just walk over to her. She was looking at the pricing chart on the counter.

"Can I ask your opinion?" I said to her. She turned around and I couldn't believe how pretty she was.

"Yeah. What is it?" She said looking back at the pricing chart.

"What color do you think I should get?"

She looked me over, smirked and said, "You look like the clear polish type."

"What does that mean?"

"You're a boy right?" she laughed.

"Yes."

"Okay we'll unless you're gay you look like the clear polish type."

I picked the clear polish out and sat in the seat to wait my turn. She decided against red and had chosen pink instead. With the polish in her hand she sat next to me. My mind wrecked trying to find out what I could say to her to strike up a conversation. She looked rich; like she'd been kept and like she'd never have anything to do with me. Her hair hung down her back and she had a diamond watch on her wrist and an engagement ring on her finger that looked like it cost thousands. I really liked that ring. If I ever had a fiancé I would want one like that to give to her.

"What do you do for a living?" I asked her.

"Nothing anymore." She said examining the color of the polish she'd chosen. "I use to take care of myself and my man. Not any more though."

"Did you like it?"

"Like what?"

"Being a stay at home mom."

"Who said I was a stay at home mom? I don't have any kids"

"Sorry," I said swallowing hard. "I just assumed."

"Naw, he never wanted any kids. Not with me anyway." She paused. "The funny thing is, even if I could have them now, I'm too old. He ruined that for me." Then she looked at me. "I told him I'm leaving him today and that's its over. I'm sick of his shit."

"His loss." I said. "I know he'll be sad to lose you." I continued. "And you don't look so old that you can't have kids."

"Well I am."

"Why do you say that?"

"Because I'm almost forty." She looked at me and said, "Why all the fucking questions?"

Her attitude caught me off guard. "I'm sorry. I just never met anybody that looked like you before."

Her face still held a frown but when she looked at mine her expression softened a little. "Look, I don't know what you want from me, but I'm taken." Then she paused. "And even if I wasn't you couldn't afford me."

"I don't want to be with you." I paused.

"Then what do you want?"

"Actually what I wanted is kind of silly."

She shook her head. "I should've known you wanted something. So what is it?"

"I'm trying to go to college. I don't have a family or anything like that to take care of me. If I don't sell enough of the cookies in my car I won't even have a chance. So I figured I'd ask you if you could buy a couple of boxes. It will help me out a lot."

"How many cookies do you want a bitch to buy?" She laughed. "Because you'll need an awful lot sold to go to college."

"Just some. I'm asking everybody I meet to buy some."

"Well I don't eat cookies. You don't keep the kind of nigga I had by eating bullshit. It weighs on your hips."

"I understand." I said under my breath. "I wouldn't expect you to do anything for me anyway." I paused. "I mean, why should you? You don't owe me nothing and you don't even know me."

After I said that I moved a few seats away from her. She looked at the busy nail technicians and back at me. "What kind?"

"What kind of what?" I asked her.

"What kind of cookies you selling?"

"Chocolate chip, raisin...stuff like that."

"Okay, go get the boxes and I'll buy them."

"You can't go with me to the car?"

"Why?" She asked suspiciously.

"Because I have more than one flavor."

"No. I can't. I don't want to miss my place and I'm only buying them for you." She paused. "It's been a long time since I've given charity, so I might as well start today."

"Please go to my car with me."

"Look, let me just give you the money." She reached for her wallet and opened it wide.

"I don't want your fucking money!" I yelled.

Silence.

"Then how are you going to college?" She asked suspiciously. "It doesn't make any sense if you don't want my money." She put her wallet back in her purse. "Who are you?"

"I mean...I want." I swallowed. "I mean...I want to..."

"Look, just leave me alone. Okay?"

Fuck. If she didn't go with me my plan wouldn't work. And then, I thought about Glitter and how she use to have these bad seizures and everybody would help her. If I acted good enough, maybe that would work. It was settled. I didn't want to let my pops down so it would have to work. Sitting in my seat, I started shaking. Starting with my feet and then my legs. After awhile I trembled all over the way I saw Glitter do it back in the day.

"Are you okay?" She asked as everyone in the nail salon looked on.

"I'm...I'm having a seizure."

"OH MY GOD!" She stood up and screamed. "SOMEBODY CALL 911!"

I dropped to the floor and she knelt down beside me. I was shaking my body as hard as I could. "Can you...can you please tell my father. He's in that black car outside."

"Which one?" She rose a little to look out of the window.

"The one directly across the street."

"I see it. Give me a second!"

She ran outside toward the car and I wanted to go with her. But because I was supposed to be having a seizure, and other people surrounded me, I stayed where I was.

"Are you okay?" a nail technician said holding my hand. "The paramedics are on their way right now. Just relax. Everything will be okay."

I didn't say anything because there was no need in me faking around them so instead of continuing my act, my trembles got slower and slower. I waited until a minute passed before I sat in the seat and pretended to feel a little better. I wanted to give her time to get to the car and time for him to grab her. When I glanced out the window, I didn't see her and she hadn't came back into the salon. Hearing the ambulance I stood up and move toward the door.

"Wait! The ambulance is coming." The nail tech said. "Please wait. We want to make sure you're okay."

"I'm fine!" I dipped nervously out the door.

Once outside I ran as fast as I could toward Kali's car. I got into the passenger seat and looked at him. I was nervous, sweaty and scared. He pulled off quickly forcing my head backwards. I hated when people did that.

"Did you see your friend?" He nodded behind him and I saw her passed out lying on the back seat of the car. "What...why did you do this?"

"It's a long story!" He said entering a busy intersection.

Looking at the ring I admired in the salon, I took it off her finger and put it in my pocket.

"I see you're warming up to the idea of this shit real quick."

"I guess so." I said as we headed down the road.

When we drove in silence for another twenty minutes I said, "So you gonna tell me or not?"

"Tell you what?"

"Who she really is."

"Her name is Antoinette, she's Jace's bitch."

MAD
FIST FIGHT

After the kidnapping of Antoinette, I knew shit would probably get realer with my pops and Jace. So I bought me a bottle of Hennessey to keep my mind off of shit and dipped into a 7-Eleven to buy some blunts. I was meeting Mad Max later that night before we went to another party and Sugar said she had some bomb ass smoke.

I was about to step to the counter to get the blunts when I saw the sexiest bitch I'd ever seen in my life. Her hair hung down her back and the jeans she wore clung to her ass and hips. I could tell her waist was small because she was wearing a red t-shirt that clung to her back and landed at the tips of the jeans. She had an hourglass figure. I knew I had to have her so I pulled down my cap, lowered my voice and stepped to her from behind. Then I smacked her on the ass before squeezing it.

"What the fuck you doing?!" She yelled, turning around to look at me. I guess she liked what she saw because her frown softened. "Boy, you almost got fucked up! Why would you do some raunchy shit like that? You don't even know me."

"Please excuse my hands," I said feeling the alcohol. "I thought my eyes were playing tricks on me. I wanted to make sure that ass was real!"

"You still think it ain't real?" She said smiling through her frown.

"Baby that shit right there," I said examining her ass again. "Is realer than a mothafucka."

"Whatever," she said digging into her purse for money to pay for a honey bun, Doritos and a Pepsi. "You betta watch that shit. If I was with my friends they would've stomped your ass for that shit."

"And they would've gotten murdered by mine."

She laughed. "You must be high."

"Naw, baby. I just feel good." I paused. "But since I disrespected, let me get that for you." I turned my attention to the cashier and said, "Give me a box of cherry blunts and put her stuff in with mine."

The girl smiled and the black girl cashier rung everything up. I still had money from what Kali gave me so, trying to impress shawty, I paid with a hundred dollar bill. The cashier took the bill out of my hand and ran a black counterfeit pen over it. She frowned at the bill and took it to a white male employee behind the counter.

"What is this?" She whispered holding the bill. "I never saw it do this before."

"Who gave this to you?" He asked.

"He did." She said pointing at me.

He ran another pen over the bill again and it did the same thing. Change black. He walked up to me, slid the bill on the counter and said, "I can't take this."

"Fuck you mean you can't take this?" I asked.

"The money isn't real."

"Fuck you telling me my money not real?! I got that from my father."

"And I'm telling you it isn't real." He said seriously. "This black mark shows its fake money, if it was real it would have stayed yellow." He paused. "Now either pay using another form of payment, or leave the line."

"But it don't make no sense!" I was embarrassed and angry that he was telling me something that wasn't true. I just spent some money in the liquor store so I know it was real. And then it dawned on me, they never ran the pen over the money. They never ran that pen over any money I'd used.

"Don't worry about it," the girl said, "I can pay for my own stuff."

"Naw...I got it." I reached into my pocket and grabbed the change from the one hundred dollar bill that was broken at the liquor store. Giving the cashier forty dollars, he ran the pen over each bill. It stayed yellow. He gave me my fake one hundred dollar bill back along with the change from my real cash. I didn't even want to hang out at no party after this shit. I was blown.

And I knew the girl didn't want to have anything to do with me after that so I was about to leave the store until she said, "After all that grabbing of my ass, you gonna just leave me hanging?"

"I ain't feeling up for shit right now."

"Naw, nigga, after that foreplay in there, you owe me." She paused. "Now where we going?"

"Home." I said walking out the door about to catch a cab.

"I'm ready when you are."

"You really coming with me?"

"Fuck you think?" She smiled.

"Let's roll." I paused. "You drive?" I continued still blown about the fake money but happy I still got the girl.

"Yeah. I got my friend's car." She pointed at a black Acura.

"Cool," I said pimping to the car. "What's your name?"

"Denise." She paused. "Yours?"

I don't know why I decided to lie I just did. I guess there was too much emotion around my real name so I didn't want to give it to her. So I thought of a name I respected. A name that when I said I'd feel proud about.

"Wagner. But everybody calls me, Wags."

"Well I guess I'm going with you, Wags."

"You betta know it, baby."

• •

At Bernie's

Mad Max wasn't feeling me dissing them for a girl again. I'd gotten with so many bitches since Glitter died that they felt I was doing too much. To me it felt liberating, not to give a fuck about what a bitch said or thought. I was fucking more bitches then them and that was the bottom line. I'd lick a few pussies, finger 'em and rub my joint on they shit through my boxers to bust a nut. I wasn't sure if any of the bitches I'd been with after the crash knew I was a girl and I had all intentions of keeping it that way.

Kali and Bernie wasn't home when I walked in the house with Denise and I was glad because I really wanted to be alone. We were on the couch kissing so hard my lips felt swollen and cracked. Her kisses were sloppy, the way I liked it and they made my joint throb. She knew how to kiss and how to run her tongue into my mouth. Damn this bitch turned me on.

The only problem was every time we got deep into it, Denise would try to touch my body but I didn't let her. Sometimes with them other bitches I'd let them run their hands over my chest. Now I don't have no big chest or nothing like that, but I know some of them broads may have known I was a girl when they touched me but didn't care. I didn't care either because I was trying to cum. So if they started screaming about me being a girl instead of a nigga I'd just leave. Luckily that never happened after Amber. But this girl…Denise…I was conscious about. I liked her already, and for the first time since Amber, I think I was in love and I wanted her to love me back. So I had to be careful to keep my secret. Careful to not let her touch me even though I wanted nothing more.

"You got a condom?" She asked sliding out of her jeans, followed by her red panties. Her pink pussy opened in front of me like a rose. She was dripping wet. "I wanna feel you inside of me."

I leaned in. "Let me eat that first." I said licking my lips. "We can fuck later."

"Please say you got a condom though," she begged. "I wanna fuck you so bad, Wags. Eating pussy is okay, but if you want me to get mine, daddy, I'ma need that dick."

"You don't like your pussy ate?" I asked sticking a finger in her pussy as I looked into her eyes.

"Mmmmmmm," she moaned moving her hips. "Yeah I like it, sometimes. But I need dick in my life. If you can't fuck me right," she moaned again, "then you can't do shit for me, baby." Then she looked at me seductively as I placed four fingers in her pussy. "You can fuck me right can't you, Wags?"

"When I give you this dick, you gonna know it."

She opened her legs wider and I had all four fingers inside of her and a thumb.

"Ball up your fist, Wags."

I did.

"Fist me, baby. Fist me hard too."

I ain't never have no bitch this wild. My boys were not gonna believe this shit. So I fisted her ass as hard as I could. Everything but my wrist was in that pussy and she was loving it.

I got on the floor and placed a pillow between my legs as I fisted her harder. Then I moved my joint on the pillow as I looked at her wet pussy like it was a good movie. The more she moaned the wetter my joint got.

"Yes, daddy! Fist me! Fist me like I like it."

I pounded her harder and harder until her cum dripped all on the couch and I busted a nut on myself using the pillow.

She opened her eyes and looked at me. "I see you've done that before."

I really hadn't. "Yeah."

Then she reached for my chest and I grabbed her wrists again. Even though I wore a sports bra and my breasts weren't that big, I knew if she felt them she'd be able to tell the curse I was forced to live with...that I was a girl.

"I ain't trying to treat you like no slut and fuck you on the first night. So let me eat that pussy."

She smiled and said, "Since you made me bust once it's cool." She paused. "But remember, if we gonna have fun I need to fuck."

"I got that."

"Alright...you pop pills?"

"Naw."

"You wanna try?"

I shrugged because all I wanted to do was taste her. And if that meant I'd have to pop a pill than so be it, that's exactly what I was going to do. "Yeah. Whatever."

She reached in her jeans, and gave me a pill. I swallowed it with the Hennessey on the table and waited for it to take hold. And instead of swallowing hers, she rose up off the couch and stuffed the pill in her ass.

"What you just do?" I frowned.

"You never heard of that?"

"Naw."

"It's call shafting." She smiled. "And it gets me really horny."

When she said that the feeling from the pill I took was starting to take over me. I felt hornier than ever. Stuff moved in slow motion and I felt tingly all over. So I spread her legs apart and licked her pussy softly but she moved to pull me on top of her again. She made it known she wanted to fuck.

"Please fuck me, Wags."

"Not today." I pushed her legs open and ate her pussy harder.

She touched my arms and her touch felt different. More heightened and it got me hornier. This pill was the truth. Now she was moaning so heavily that I knew she was about to cum.

"Take your cap off," she begged. "I wanna feel that head."

"Naw, ma. I don't take my cap off for nobody."

I don't know what it was, but for some reason, I wanted her to be my new girl. I was in love with her and I knew with some more time I could get her to love me back.

"Don't stop, Wags," she said. "Keep licking that shit. You feel so good. I wanna cum in your mouth."

Once I located the tip of her clit I flicked my tongue over and over as she grew wetter. Then I put my fingers in her pussy and fisted her as I licked it. She was going crazy and I loved it. I rubbed my joint harder on the pillow and busted another nut. And then another. This was the best sex I ever had with a pillow, ever.

"Damn, your pussy taste so sweet." I told her.

"You 'bout to make me come, daddy. Keep licking that shit right there."

She gripped one of the pillows on the sofa as I stayed on her clit.

"Baby, I'm about to cum, you wanna see me squirt?"

"Hell yeah."

I backed up but kept my fist inside of her and white shit shot out of her clit. Damn that shit was sexy! I ain't never see no shit like that before.

"That was so fucking good," she said breathing heavily.

"You tasted so good." I took my fist out of her and licked her clit one last time.

I slid up on top of her body and lay my head on her chest. Her breaths were heavy and she wrapped her arms around my body.

"You know how to do that shit too good." She said. "You know, eating my pussy."

"I think that's a compliment."

"It is." She laughed. "But you sure you ain't got no small dick?"

I rose up and looked into her eyes, making sure to keep my voice deep and my cap down. "Fuck no! Why you ask me some shit like that?"

"Because most boys who can lick pussy real good can't fuck and got a small ass dick." She paused. "And I need dick." She said. "I can't even see how these bitches be fucking with each other out here. There's too much dick in the world. And if a nigga gonna rope me he got to fuck me twenty-four seven, ya heard?"

"Let's just say when its time for me to dig into that pussy, I'll make you eat your mothafuckin' words." She giggled. "Now open back up. I'm trying to lick that pussy again."

The next morning when I woke up I was lying on top of her body and she was snoring. But for some reason I could feel her body move lightly even though she was dead sleep. When I turned around, I saw Kali had his fingers in her pussy as he was beating his own dick.

"What the fuck?"

"Shhhhhhhh." He said putting his finger over his lips. "I'm almost done."

I turned back around. It was gross enough seeing my father's dick but now he was fingering my girl. I know I should have woken her up to tell her what my pops was doing but I didn't want to run the risk of losing her. So I stayed on top of her until the small jerks of him finger fucking her stopped all together.

When he was done he smelled his fingers, smiled and walked into the kitchen to wipe his hands. I followed him.

"What did you just do that for?" I frowned.

The moment I stood up my stomach churned. Alcohol stopped giving me hangovers like this a long time ago. I would always feel a major headache in the morning but never a stomach churn this badly. I went into the bathroom and threw up in the toilet. Every time I tried to approach him about what he did to my girl, I'd throw up again. It took me about fifteen minutes to get my shit together. It had to be the pill and I wasn't fucking with it again. Ever.

I walked back into the kitchen, wiped my mouth with the back of my hand and whispered, "Why would do some shit like that? And where is Bernie?"

"She ain't here," he said grabbing a beer out of the refrigerator. "And as far as me playing in your girl's pussy, you brought her in my house without asking, so that means I can do what and whoever I want."

"But that's my girlfriend. And I love her."

"I thought you said your girlfriend was killed."

"That's my new girl."

He shook his head. "And you can keep her," he smiled slyly. "I wasn't trying to take her from you. I just was taste testing." He smirked. "And she was getting wet as shit too. I don't know, son, but I think she knew your pops was up in that shit."

"Don't ever do no shit like that to her again. I'm feeling her."

He laughed. "You real mad."

"I'm serious!" I yelled.

He wasn't laughing anymore. "Consider it done. But never bring somebody in my house without asking. We got that bitch downstairs and don't need no unwanted company in here."

"Okay. I'm sorry." I said wishing my stomach would stop swirling.

"You look fucked up," he opened the refrigerator and handed me a beer. "Drink this. You'll feel better in no time."

Eager to get this sick feeling away I drunk half of the beer. "Oh, and that money you gave me the other day is fake."

"I know." he laughed.

"What you mean you know?"

"That's why we grabbed Jace's bitch. Had he given me the money he owed, I would've never been out of my cash."

"Why he owe?"

"Because this nigga name Massive was after him heavy. His father Rick couldn't stop him from coming at his son and he couldn't protect himself. I took care of it though. The same nigga who was trying to kill him helped me escape from prison."

"You escaped."

He smiled. "They don't know I escaped because there was a fire and we placed somebody with my body size in my prison uniform. So they think I'm dead and the grilled dead nigga escaped."

"That's the escape shit I been hearing on the news?"

"Yes." I was so interested now. My pops was go hard. "And you better keep that between us. I got something over you," he said referring to Amber, "and you got something over me."

"Now since this money is fake, I can't make no moves. So either he gonna give me what he owe, or his bitch is as good as dead."

"How much he owe?"

"Half of million dollars. Although the price may go up."

When he said that Denise woke up and covered her pussy with one of the couch pillows. She looked directly at my pops and smiled. I think he was right. I think she knew he finger fucked her earlier.

"Morning." She smiled looking at me. "Hope I didn't get you in trouble." She looked at pops again.

"Naw. You good." He said putting his finger under his nose so I could see him. Then he smacked me on my back. "But you gotta go now. Me and my…"

"Son!" I said before he said anything else.

He looked at me slyly and said, "Like I said, me and my son got shit to talk about." Then he looked at me. "Give her cab money so she can go home."

"I drive. But thanks anyway."

He smiled. "I'm going downstairs, son." Then he whispered in my ear. "I'll be back upstairs in five minutes. I'm about to go downstairs and get some of Jace's girl's pussy."

HARMONY
FAMILY AFFAIR

We didn't know what to say to each other. So I kept looking at the spread before me. The pancakes, sausage, eggs and grits looked pretty against the plate set I didn't even know we owned. The mahogany dining room was filled with delicious breakfast food along with fresh fruits and juices yet no one was eating.

"Everything looks nice, Ramona." I said forking my food. "Thank you for cooking.

"It's not a problem." She smiled. "I'm the only one who cooks back home. I love it though. It's very relaxing."

"Well I deem you my personal cook while you're here!" I said.

Everyone cleared their throats. Had I said the wrong thing? "We'll see." She said.

"You know this plate and silverware set are family heirlooms." Laura said. "Mama left them here thinking you might appreciate them." She scooped out food and placed it on Irma's plate. Then she dished her own plate.

"I didn't even know it was here." I looked at them and then down at my food. They didn't seem to be happy about my response.

"I bet Mama, will use them now," Jayden said looking at me and then at them. "They're beautiful."

I guess everybody was thinking the same thing, how was all of this shit gonna pan out. It was me, Irma, my sisters Laura and Ramona and Jayden. Although it was mostly silent in the dining room, the main thing heard was Irma's repeat hacking cough. It was irritating and I wished either she shut the fuck up, or roll over and die already.

"Are you okay, grandma?" Jayden asked looking up from her pancakes. "I mean, can I get you anything?"

She smiled, covered her mouth with a bloodstained tissue and said, "It feels so good to hear you call me grandma. You seem like you turned out to be a very beautiful, respectful young lady." Then she turned to me. "Harmony, you did really good with her."

"Thanks." I shrugged.

I could feel Jayden's eyes on me but she didn't say anything.

-206-

"Do you have a boyfriend?" Irma asked Jayden.

"No. I don't really believe in that kind of stuff."

"What, you got a girlfriend?" Ramona questioned.

"Aunt Ramona, no!" She said shaking her head. "That's so nasty. I'm just trying to focus on my life and school."

"Why don't you believe in boyfriends?" Laura said as she soaked a white paper towel into a glass of cold water and pat Irma's forehead. "You're so beautiful."

"Thank you." She smiled. "But I think love is scary. And I don't want to feel vulnerable to another person."

"Why?" Laura asked.

"I don't know the kind of person it would make me. I just wanna focus on making money and doing well in school. I'm having trouble with that school stuff though."

Irma looked at her lovingly and said, "I'm sorry to hear that, Jayden. I really am. Because when you love someone, as much as I loved your grandfather, your mother's father, life can be so great." She paused rubbing my hand softly before I snatched it away. "I'm sorry, Harmony. I just wanted to touch you."

"I'm not ready for that." I told her. "You gotta give me some time before you push yourself on me like that."

Ramona and Laura looked at each other and shook their heads.

"I understand," she coughed again. "But Jayden, give love a chance at some time in your life. It'll break down barriers."

"Maybe." Jayden said playing with the food on her plate.

"Where is Madjesty?" Irma asked as Laura rubbed her back. "I was kinda hoping to get to know her too."

I called Madjesty five times this morning and she didn't return my calls. I was getting sick of her shit and needed a way to break her down.

"She comes and goes as she pleases." I said. "But she should be here soon."

"You allow that?"

"There ain't much I can do about it right now. I'm just getting my health back to normal. I'll get a handle of her soon."

"Don't loose her into the streets, Harmony. Because once you do, you'll never get her back."

Just when she said that Madjesty came inside the house with her crew. "Mama, I'm home!" she said sarcastically.

They were loud and I could tell that even though it was early in the morning, they were drunk. Madjesty walked up to the table and without asking, grabbed a piece of bacon off a tray along with a pancake. She folded the food and stuffed it in her mouth then squeezed syrup in it. She

THE CARTEL PUBLICATIONS

stared at me while chewing and it was obvious that she was trying to work my nerves as her friends hung around the table like vultures.

"Don't just stand there," Madjesty said to them. "Grab some food. I told you Jayden called me and said that they were cooking." Then she looked at me again. "You don't mind if my friends eat now do you, mama?"

I felt like strangling her. After everything they'd done to me she'd bring them into my house again.

"Of course you don't mind." She continued. "You wanted me home so here I am." Then she looked at her friends. "Eat up, fellas and Sugar!"

"Man, I ain't wanna just eat they shit without asking!" Kid said.

"Mad said we could!" Krazy replied.

"Nigga, wasn't nobody talking to you," Wokie said slapping him in the face, afterwards laughing.

Before I knew it Madjesty, Kid, Krazy and Wokie were slap boxing around the dining room table. I was so embarrassed I felt like executing each one of them at gunpoint. Irma and everyone else just stared at them with their mouths open.

"Ya'll over there acting all stupid. But I'm eating." Sugar said grabbing some food.

Following suit, all of them grabbed food off the plates and stuffed them into their mouths.

"Madjesty, why didn't you and your friends wash your hands first?" I asked trying to remember my ultimate plan included being patient with this bitch.

"'Cause I ain't want to," she said. Then she turned to Irma. "What's up, Grandma? You still alive?"

"Madjesty!" Jayden screamed. "What is wrong with you?"

"Nothing." She smirked. "I'm just here to change some clothes and grab something to eat. I'm bout to roll back out and leave ya'll to it." Then she paused. "But don't worry, mama. I know I got to sleep here at night for the evil social worker you keep talking about gets me. I don't want you not to get your welfare check."

"Are these children drunk?" Irma asked me.

"Yeah, grandma," Madjesty smirked. "We drunk then a mothafucka." They all laughed. She turned to her crew and said, "Let's go to my room."

Her friends all waved at me and I could tell by the looks in their eyes that they wondered what my plans were for them. I remembered everything they did to me. Everything. Out of all of them I remember Wokie the most.

I stood up. "Wokie, come talk to me in the kitchen. Alone."

He held onto the banister and looked up the steps at Mad. "Go see what she wants." Mad said. "And then come upstairs."

Wokie came back down the stairs and we walked into the kitchen. I poured myself some orange juice and leaned against the counter for support. "How are you, Wokie?"

"Mam, I really am sorry for how I acted…"

"You mean you really are sorry for how you fucked me?"

"Yes. I…I thought it was cool."

I stepped closer to him and grabbed his balls tightly. "Well it wasn't cool and now I own you. And anything I need you to do, I don't care how big or small, you better be at my beckon call before I tell the police about your little act. Do you understand me?"

"Yes, mam." He said softly. "But can you please let my balls go, it hurts."

I finally released him and he held himself between his legs. "That's the fucking point." Then I wiped my hands on the jeans I was wearing because I could tell he'd been drinking but not washing his ass. "You can leave now, but remember what I said."

When he disappeared upstairs, I went back into the dining room and standing by the table was the electrician. I didn't even hear the doorbell ring. Madjesty must've left the door open as usual when she came home. I was about to be angry when I remembered that her keeping the door open was how the caseworker was able to find me alive.

"Mam, I'm here for my money. And I'm not leaving without it."

I sighed. "And I said I didn't have it when you called earlier."

He was getting on my nerves about this shit. All he did was install some fucking secret cameras in specific areas in the house. To make matters worse he was blackmailing me by threatening to hang around my house and tell my kids about where they were hidden. I tried getting the money from Jace the moment he told me he'd tell, but Jace never answered his calls. And the time he'd called before that, he wanted to speak to Madjesty instead of Jayden and he sounded pretty upset. Jayden didn't even speak to him and that was odd because over time the two grew very close.

"Well you not having my money is not acceptable."

"You can't take what I don't have!" I told him. "Give me some more time and I'll get it for you though."

"Either give me my shit now, or I'm undoing my work."

"Harmony, what's going on?" Irma asked.

If things couldn't get any worse, Katherine Sheers, the caseworker from the department of Child Services walked into the house. Everything was happening at a fucked up time.

"The door was open," she smiled. "And after the last incident with your life being in jeopardy, I decided to let myself in."

"Who are these people?" Ramona asked.

"Everyone this is my electrician and this is our caseworker."

Everyone looked at the electrician and the caseworker wondering what I would do next.

The electrician smiled slyly and said, "You sure you don't wanna give me my money?"

"Anybody got two hundred dollars on them?" I asked desperately. The last thing I needed was him opening his mouth now.

"Go get my purse, Ramona." Irma said. Ramona gave me a look but returned with her purse. She handed me the money. "Don't worry about giving me the money back."

"Thanks, Irma."

I handed the money to the electrician and he left.

Bastard!

When he closed the door Katherine said, "I'm here to check on the kids."

I turned toward Irma, Ramona and Laura and said, "You mind if I talk to her alone."

"Of course not," Irma said. "We'll be upstairs."

Then I looked at Jayden. "Go get your sister."

Irma, Ramona and Laura left the dining room and ten minutes later Madjesty came down the steps.

"Well, well, well," Katherine said. "I haven't seen you in weeks, Madjesty. How is it going?"

Madjesty tugged at her baseball cap, pulling it further over her eyes. "Cool."

"How is school?"

"Cool."

"Okay, that's good to hear." She said. "Because your principal called me and said that someone implied that you were responsible for what happened to your mother. And I know that couldn't be the case correct?"

Madjesty looked at me. "Oh...naw." She looked back at her. "Who told her that?"

"I believe she said some lady name Ursula Givens. You know her?"

Madjesty looked mad. "Naw. I don't."

"Well as long as you're doing well in school and everything is okay here." Then she looked at Jayden. "What about you?"

"School is fine."

"Great. Great." She paused. "Well everything appears to be in order here, Ms. Phillips, but I'll be getting records on their attendance and academics later."

"Well...they just started going back. Things might not be perfect yet."

"As long as we see effort, that's all we ask for." She smiled. Then she clapped her hands. "Well, let me be going. I'm sorry to have ruined your breakfast." She walked toward the door.

"Mrs. Sheers," Madjesty said, stopping her from leaving.

My heart thumped in my chest. What was she about to say?

"Yes."

"What happens if things aren't good? In school I mean."

"Then we'll have to look into the situation further. And if things aren't right, we'll have to put you in a home where things will get better." She smiled one last time and said, "Well, good afternoon. Enjoy the rest of your day."

When she left I looked at my kids.

"You see how serious shit is?" I asked. "We have to work together, girls. We have to."

"Why?" Madjesty laughed. "I don't give a fuck about them taking me away from here. All I'll do is run away."

"But I care, Madjesty." Jayden said. "I want us to stay together."

"And I do too." I said.

Madjesty laughed in our faces and said, "My friends are upstairs. I'll get up with ya'll later."

Jayden ran off crying and too be honest I was glad because after that shit, I needed to go to the liquor store to cash my welfare check and get some Vodka. The shit with my electrician and caseworker was too heavy.

The only thing was, since Jace wasn't over the house fussing over Jayden, I didn't have access to a car and had to walk to the bus stop. So I grabbed my house keys, my jacket and took the hike down the street. It's funny, even when I was a kid I never caught a bus. I was going to have to come up on some money soon because this shit wasn't working.

Once the bus came, and dropped me off a block from my destination, I walked up the street. Then I went to the store, cashed my check and grabbed two bottles of vodka that could fit in my purse. Not even out the door yet, I twisted the top off of one of them and downed over half of the bottle. Fuck! That shit feels so good. Once outside I was almost to the bus stop when I saw a familiar face pull up on me as I was finishing off the first bottle.

"Harmony Phillips? Is that you?"

"Yes." I said taking the bottle from my mouth and putting the top back on. "Who are you?"

"Oh my God! I can't believe it." She said pulling up in front of me in a black Navigator. "Get in."

"Who are you?" I said putting the mostly empty bottle of vodka in my purse.

"It's me, Mrs. Duncan. Your high school teacher."

I frowned because I did not feel like listening or talking to this bitch because she was always in my business. "I really got somewhere to be, Mrs. Duncan." Then I stood in front of the bus stop and looked anxiously down the street.

"Harmony, you're at a bus stop." She persisted as a few cars honked behind her, wishing she'd just drive away.

"I know where I am and like I said, I'm fine."

"Please. It'll be my pleasure." Looking at the pile up of cars behind her for whatever reason, I decided to get into her truck.

"Thank you," I said smacking my tongue as I eased into the front seat.

"No problem." She turned the air on higher. "So, are you going to the wedding?"

"What wedding?"

"The young lady who was in your class is getting married today. Ebony." She paused. I hadn't seen Ebony since she snatched her princess earrings out of my ears. "She's marrying a doctor and they have a beautiful home in Virginia."

My heart sank. This bitch was doing well and outside of my mansion, I didn't have shit to show for my journey in life.

"Ebony and I aren't friends anymore."

"That's such a shame." She said looking me over.

"You can tell her I said hi, though."

"I will." She paused. "Where are we going?" I gave her my address and she keyed it into her navigation system. "Ebony's a lawyer now, you know? She's doing really well for herself because she stuck with school."

I rolled my eyes. "Isn't that the Beez Sha-Neez?"

"What?" She frowned.

"I said that's good." I rolled my eyes again and yawned.

"So, how has life been treating you?" She asked looking me over again.

"I been doing pretty good."

"Really?" I couldn't get over how pretty she looked. It was like time hadn't touched her one bit.

"Yeah, I live in a mansion in Fort Washington." I opened my purse and eyed the corner of vodka in the bottle and wanted to finish it off. Knowing her square ass though, she'd probably have a problem with it. "It's a really nice place."

"Oh...so what do you do for a living to afford a mansion?"

"What, you thought I'd be living in the projects or something? Just because I ain't finish school?"

"I'm just asking what you do for a living, Harmony. I always took an interest in your life, you know that."

"I do a little bit of everything, Mrs. Duncan." I said taking the bottle out of my purse. Fuck her. I was drinking this shit. "But mainly I do consulting work."

"You shouldn't drink that in here. I'm driving, Harmony."

"Well let me out." I told her. "You picked me up remember?" I swallowed the last of the corner. "Anyway it's gone now. See." I said showing her the bottle.

She shook her head. "Are you sure life is treating you well?"

"Yeah, why you say that?" I smirked. "You gonna give me yours?"

"I'm asking because you don't look so well, Harmony."

"Damn, this is why I couldn't stand your ass back in the day! You too fucking nosey."

"I don't mean to be. It's just that this is the lifestyle I was trying to steer you away from. This is the lifestyle I feared you would have."

"What lifestyle is that?"

"A lifestyle of prostitution. Of alcoholism and personal abuse. You look older than the years you are. Have you looked into the mirror lately?" She paused. "And what happened with that scar on your face?"

"Wait." I laughed. "You think I'm a prostitute?"

"After everything I said, that's all you heard?"

"Well do you think I'm a prostitute or not?"

"Yes. I do."

"Why you say that?"

"Look at how you're dressed." I looked down at myself. The short black dress I had on was skimpy but not too bad. After all, I just ate breakfast with Irma and met the social worker so I was trying to keep low key. "What else would you be?"

"Let me out."

"But you aren't home yet."

"Just let me the fuck out!"

When the truck stopped I jumped out. "You know it's never too late to start all over, Harmony. And I really hope you know that."

When she pulled off some man pulled in front of me seconds later. "You wanna ride sweetheart?" From the look he gave me I knew what he wanted. Sex.

I hadn't fucked in awhile and as far as I was concerned, he was as good a candidate as any. "Yeah. But after that, you gotta take me home."

"Take care of me and I'll take care of you." He paused. "Get in."

JACE
SHIT IS SERIOUS

Jace roamed around the deli and he was an emotional wreck. Days passed since he seen or heard from Antoinette and he wondered what could have happened to her. So he called a meeting with Kreshon, Paco and his bodyguards Antony and Kevin. They were sitting in Gee's Deli avoiding the pink elephant in the room. That if Antoinette was missing, it was very possible that Kali had her.

"Boss, I know you said she was going to leave you." Antony said. "You sure she didn't just do it?"

"Naw. She wouldn't. She ain't got no place to go for real." He said. "Something else is up."

"Well I had two different bitches I fuck with ask about Antoinette at the salons she went to and they didn't hear shit." Paco said.

The disappointment of the news showed on Jace's face.

"What about you, Kreshon? Were you able to find out anything?"

"No, man. I'm sorry."

Jace paced the deli before Kevin broke silence. "I think Kali got her. As a matter of fact, boss, I'm sure of it."

Jace looked at all of the men. "You think the same thing?" *He asked eyeing all of them.*

One by one each of his men nodded. "I was afraid of this shit. I mean, don't this nigga know what I would do to him if he put his hands on her?"

"Yeah, but we killed his cousin," Paco said. "He might not give a fuck about none of that shit. He wants revenge."

"Or his money." Antony said.

"I don't know how he caught Antoinette. I always told her to be careful. And I always had somebody on her because I knew this nigga was lurking. She was so mad at me that she threw caution to the wind and now this shit!"

"When was the last time you saw her?"

"When she went to get her nails done." *Jace paused.* "And I asked around that salon and nobody wanted to answer my questions. I had a *feeling Kali got to them before I did. He probably threatened them or something."*

"He got her, man." Paco said.

"Have you been able to get a lead on Kali again, Pac?"

"Not since he was at the mansion." Paco said. "I know he not stay-ing there no more. That would be stupid." He paused. "Plus the day I did pop up there, the only people I saw was your daughter and three Spanish broads. Oh, and that bitch that looks like a dude."

Jace thought about Jayden. He hadn't seen her in days and wouldn't answer her calls because he had a lot on his mind. And the times he did call the house he was trying to reach Madjesty but she was never home. He figured she'd know something if he could just get her on the phone. Maybe throw a little money her way for some information.

Part of him blamed Harmony for Antoinette's kidnapping. Spending time with Jayden also allowed him to see her daily and because of it, his attention was taken off of home. There was something he found alluring about Harmony and she was truly the most interesting person he knew. He was falling for her scandalous ass again and there was no stopping him unless he put space between them. He made a decision that if things worked out with Antoinette, and he was able to bring her home, that he wouldn't be over Concord Manor so frequently. If Jayden wanted to see him she would have to come to his house.

Jace wished Tony Wop wasn't out of his mind because he could real-ly use his advice right now. But ever since he was poisoned at that party and tried to kill himself with a hammer, he was in a mental institution and his condition went from bad to worse. Outside of his physical body that was deteriorating by the day, Tony was not the same man. He didn't know Jace, his friends or even himself.

Jace also thought about his father Rick, who he wrote off after disco-vering that he lied to him about his gambling habit in Mexico. Shit in his life was fucked up and things around him were falling apart. He was big on trust. And looking at his men, he couldn't be sure that there was one amongst them that he could say without a doubt he trusted. Essentially he felt alone.

"Yeah, he's definitely not at the mansion no more." Paco continued.

"I'm there all the time anyway." Jace assured them. They looked at him strangely. "My kid is there. It's not even about that bitch no more."

They didn't believe him.

"Somebody told me he hangs out at this spot in Maryland. Not too far from Oxon Hill. I can check it out if you want." Kreshon said. "I mean, I rode past myself a few days back and never saw nobody. It's worth another try though."

"Yeah. But if you find him, don't kill him. I need to get Antoinette back safe first."

"You got it."

<hr>

Bernie's House

Kreshon was sitting in his car a few feet from Bernie's house watching Kali and Bernie walk toward the house. When he saw them together, and how they handled each other his mouth dropped. He was kissing her as they walked side by side and he had his arm around her neck.

He couldn't believe what he was seeing as he rushed for his phone. Dialing Jace's number he said, "I found out where he rests his head, man. You want me to take him out."

"No! I need to see if he got Antoinette first remember?"

"Okay, but there's something else."

"What?"

"You remember Bernice? From D.C.? From when we were kids?"

"Dope Head Bernice? From around the way? Who use to get high?"

"Yeah..."

"He finally found her?" Jace asked.

"Yeah, but their relationship doesn't look like it's supposed to, man."

"What the fuck you talking about?"

"You heard me, Jace. I think this sick ass nigga is fucking his own mother!"

JAYDEN
CHECK 'EM

Jayden was in class trying her hardest to understand her math lesson. But no matter how hard she tried, she couldn't get it like the rest of the kids. When it came to learning she failed miserably and she didn't understand why. She would never know that because her mother drank alcohol throughout her pregnancy, she affected both of her daughters mentally for life. They may not have shown the physical signs of being born to an alcoholic mother, but they certainly exhibited mental deficiencies.

As she scribbled meaningless drawings on her notebook paper, she thought about how she finally got Madjesty to agree to ditch her friends for a day and spend some time with her after school. Yet her mind was on Passion who was sitting a few seats in front of her. She'd been distant and Jayden didn't understand why she was so some timey. Still there was something unnatural that drew her to Passion and it had nothing to do with sex. Jayden was all girl but not having Passion in her life made her feel slightly empty and she didn't understand why. She just wished she could control her, and understand where her mind went on the days she decided that she didn't want to be her friend.

When the last bell rang for school, Jayden gathered her things and rushed behind Passion. Catching up with her she said, "What is up with you? Why you been acting so funny lately?"

Passion frowned a little and said, "Jayden, its nothing." She walked up to her locker and entered her combination. "I just have stuff to do before my client tonight. Don't worry though, I'm gonna fuck main man real good for you. You're gonna get your cash."

"So now that we work together, our friendship is over?"

"That's how you wanted it right? Don't forget Gucci and them are my friends too, they let me know the shit you be saying behind my back."

"What you talking about?"

"Didn't you tell them that you're sick of my shit and that we ain't gotta be friends and that it's only about your money?"

"Oh my, God! That was a long time ago."

"But you said it though."

"*Passion.*"

"*My friends call me Passion. You call me by my real name.*"

"*Uh...I...*"

"*You don't even know my real name.*" *She said shaking her head.*

It pissed her off that they talked behind her back but there was nothing she could do. "*I don't just want your friendship because you can make me money, Passion.*"

"*Well that's how it seems.*" *Passion smiled slyly.* "*You my pimp and I finally get that now.*"

"*Can I ask why you came to Olive's house with Shaggy that day?*"

"*He asked me to. It's not that deep.*"

"*Since when have ya'll been kicking it like that?*"

"*Recently.*"

"*Don't get all wrapped up into him. It's not a good look.*"

"*I got several friends. Shaggy just one of them.*" *She said.*

Just when she said that Shaggy walked up to Passion, put his arm around her waist and kissed her in the mouth. She didn't seem to want to kiss him but she went along with him.

"*You ready, babes?*" *He asked although he was looking Jayden square in the face.*

"*I didn't know you were picking me up today.*" *Passion said.*

"*So it's like that?*" *Jayden asked.*

"*We get up from time to time if that's what you mean.*" *Passion responded.* "*He's good to me and I'm good to him.*"

Jayden was so angry her face was turning a shade red. "*So you this pressed to get back at me that you'll fuck my friend, Shaggy?*"

Shaggy looked at her, smirked and walked toward the school's door holding Passion's hand. Right before leaving Passion turned around and said, "*Don't worry though; I'll be able to make my appointment tonight. We all know how you feel about your cash, boss.*"

● ●

After School – At Jace's House

Jace and Jayden were enjoying dinner in silence at his house. He had things on his mind and so did Jayden. But he called her after school to talk about Madjesty.

"*Baby girl, have you talked to Madjesty about Kali?*" *He asked forking some of his spaghetti.*

"*Yeah, but I don't think she's listening much. I think she's gonna do what she wanna do, dad. I'm starting not to like her.*"

Frustration showed on his face. Part of him wanted to get this nigga so bad, that if he had to kill his daughter's twin sister he'd gladly do it. The other part of him wanted nothing more than for Mad to heed his warnings and stay away from her own father.

"Well I want you to stay away from her if she's with Kali." He looked into her eyes seriously. "Never be alone with him."

"Okay...but I really don't see him anymore."

"That's good." Then he smiled at her. "We have to talk."

"Okay."

"There are some things you don't know about me, baby. I'm a..."

"Drug dealer."

He looked into her eyes looking for some ounce of disappointment. It wasn't there. "That doesn't bother you?"

"No. You gotta get your money how you gotta get your money." Her mother was right. She needed to do the right thing with school and obeying Harmony, or else she could be removed from home because she doubted the mean Katherine Sheers would allow her to stay with him if he was breaking the law.

He smiled. "You definitely my girl."

"I knew that the moment you came into my hotel room." She smiled. "Your eyes are like mine."

Going off point Jace said, "Jayden, I'm gonna kill Kali and I'm gonna kill him soon. You need to tell your sister to stay the fuck away from him and she needs to know that I'm not gonna ask her again."

"She not gonna do it, daddy."

"Well she'll be in my way." He said seriously. "Do you understand what that means?"

Jayden looked into his eyes, "I understand. But can you talk to her yourself one last time? For me please?"

He exhaled and said, "Okay." He paused. "Do you need anything? Any money?"

Although Jayden could have anything her heart desired from him, she always feared that if she got too comfortable with handouts, they would be taken away from her. So she made it her business to try to remain independent. Besides, Thirteen Flavors was earning that paper so she was doing pretty well. She planned that when she turned eighteen, she'd be able to buy a house of her own along with a new car. If things folded, only then would she call on daddy dearest.

"No I'm good. I don't need any money, dad."

Jace looked at her worried face and saw something was bothering her. "Jayden, you know you can talk to me about anything right? Even your past?"

"Daddy, I'm not ready to talk about my life when I was younger. Plus me and mama really trying to work things out. We're doing good now."

"Why won't you talk to me about your life back then? If you are doing so well now it shouldn't matter. How was life with your mother growing up?"

"Daddy, please. I just want to leave it alone." She couldn't bring herself to tell her father that for the longest time she and her sister thought they were boys.

"Just be careful, Jayden. She can change up on you just like that," he snapped his fingers, "I know."

"I know." She smiled. "But she's still mama."

Silence.

"Is there anything else bothering you that I should know about? You seem a little out of it."

"Kinda." She paused. "My friend is with this guy and he gets her to sell her body and stuff for money."

His eyebrows rose. "Really? How old is she?"

"My age."

"Is he some kind of pimp or something?" He said growing angrier by the minute.

"I think so."

Jace grabbed his phone and said, "Give me his name and number and I'll have it taken care of."

"No!" Jayden said extending her hands. "I don't want you to do that. But I want to know how is it possible that he got her to do what he wanted so easily? My friend always seemed so strong and I can't imagine somebody breaking her down that far."

Jace put the phone down and said, "So you want me to tell you how he possibly pimped her out?"

"Yeah. Kinda."

Jace smiled because he thought his daughter was trying to be one step ahead of them knuckle head niggas out on them streets and that made him proud.

"Well first he probably gave her anything she didn't have before he met her. If she's young, that's usually clothes and money in her pocket. Then when she got used to the good life, he probably threatened to take it away from her after some small fight. And at this point in the game, if he was good with his shit, she couldn't live without him. So she'd beg to be back in his good graces by doing anything he asked. He wouldn't take her back right away though. He'd make her beg a little and when he finally agreed, he'd demand that she prove her love."

"How?"

"By selling her body." He paused. "That's when the pimping would get started."

Jayden thought about the process. She'd done almost everything he said but break her down. She reasoned that if Passion wasn't fucking with different niggas including Shaggy, she'd have her right where she wanted her. But Passion had too many men willing to do whatever she asked.

"Wow." Jayden said.

"Too much for you?"

"No. Its just amazing how somebody can get into another person's head so easily."

"Yeah, there are other ways to do it to."

"Like what?"

"Beating her." He paused. "Or by pitching two girls together. Shit like that. See if he favored one more than he did her, she'd do whatever she could to regain position. This is usually if she acts up after it's understood that she's being pimped."

Jayden immediately thought about Foxie and how she'd start throwing all of her attentions toward her to get Passion jealous. She figured if she did her job right, Passion would come running back to her in no time.

"I answer all your questions?"

"Yeah, dad. Thanks."

"So are you still seeing Evan?"

"Evan?" she frowned.

Jace laughed and said, *"Shaggy. Paco's son."*

"No." She shook her head and frowned. "We barely speak at all."

"Good, because he's not good enough for you and I don't want you hanging around him."

"But I thought he works for you."

"He does. I trust him with work but not my daughter." Then he touched her hand. "You're precious cargo as far as I'm concerned and I want only the best for you."

"Thanks, daddy." She smiled. It felt good to be loved in that way.

"What about Xion, daddy?"

"What about him?"

"Is he a good dude?"

"I guess."

"Because Shaggy cut him off and now he's not working anymore. Is there something you could do for him?"

He was immediately angered. *"Did he ask you to ask me that?"*

"No!"

"Good, because a nigga who would put his girl up to asking her father some shit like that is no good."

"Oh."

"Baby girl, you need to stay out of that kind of shit." He said seriously. *"I don't want you talking to anybody about drugs. You never know who's wired and who's not. You hear me? You gotta always think smart."*

"Okay." She said sadly.

"Don't be sad. If he's a man and worthy enough for you he'll find his own way in life. As a matter of fact, ask him to do something to prove himself to you."

Jayden thought about what her father said when her phone rang. It was Madjesty so she answered.

"I waited here for over an hour for you and you didn't show." Madjesty said into the phone.

Jayden stood up from the table and said, *"Oh my God! I forgot all about us hooking up today."*

"Don't even worry about it," Mad paused.

"I'm with daddy. I can come later."

"It figures. You always putting that nigga before me."

"Madjesty, please! Don't be angry. We can hang out another time."

"I blew my friends off for you tonight. I should've known better."

"Where are you? I'm leaving right now."

"Stay the fuck out of my life, Jayden."

MAD
BANG BANG

I was in the kitchen at Concord Manor getting some ice for my Henny. I can't believe my sister stood me up again. Since we got here, she changed so much and I'm starting not to like her anymore. Leaning against the counter, I downed the liquor in the glass and was about to drink some more when Harmony walked up on me.

"What?" I asked looking at her. "I know you not about to play mamma and tell me I can't drink in your house."

"I know it's too late for that," she said. "I am surprised you're even here."

"Why you say that?"

"You usually gone by now." She paused. "But can I have some?"

I slid the bottle across the counter to her and said, "Help your self."

Without using the cup she swallowed some, frowned and slid it back toward me. "I can't see why you drink that shit."

I laughed and said, "You got your poison, I got mine."

I grabbed my bottle and walked into the living room. She was on my heels even when I sat on the sofa. She sat next to me.

"Where's your mother?" I asked, sipping some more Henny.

"You mean Irma?"

I shrugged. "Yeah…whatever. Where she at?"

"They took her to the hospital for some more tests. She's not doing too well."

"Oh." I drank some more until I noticed she was still staring at me. "You sad?"

Her head hung low and she said, "I don't care about that, bitch." Then she looked at me again.

"So you can ask us for forgiveness yet you won't give it to her."

"She abandoned me. And even though I was a bad mother I never gave up on you. Either of you. I deserve credit for at least that."

She wouldn't stop looking at me. What was up?

"What? You want some more Henny or something?" I asked frowning. I was thinking about hanging out with Mad Max or the girl I met the other day so right now, all I was doing was killing time. But I didn't want to kill it with her watching me. "Because I really wanna be by myself right now."

"Do you think we could ever start over?" She asked with raised eyes. "I mean, really start all over?"

"I don't know." I said drinking some more. "Because right now every time I see your face I want to kill you."

"Shouldn't I be the one with all the hate in my heart?" she paused. "I mean, you let your friends rape me, you stuck me with a corn dog filled with ants which it took the doctor days to clean out of my body and you tried to kill me."

"A normal person wouldn't do something like that unless they had a fucked up childhood." I said. "Now who do I blame for that?"

"Madjesty…"

"No seriously. Because if I started talking about how you burned me with irons, never washed my clothes, didn't feed me for days," I paused, "what you went through for them weeks downstairs couldn't even compare. Oh…and don't forget the biggest shit yet. That for years you had me thinking I was a boy."

"I don't know that you would've been any different, Madjesty. Quite honestly." She said. "I think you would've always looked and felt the need to be a boy."

"So that makes it right?"

"No it doesn't." She paused. "And I really am sorry about everything, Mad."

"I'm so fucking tired of people saying they're sorry." I said rubbing my temples. "If you really sorry, you wouldn't keep doing the things that you do. So you not sorry you did me wrong, you're sorry that I'm big enough not to take your shit no more."

Silence.

"I know you're angry, but it looks like something else is on your mind." She paused. "Something happened with you and Jayden?"

"How you know?"

She laughed and said, "She's the only one who can get to you, because I never could."

"She stood me up tonight again. Every time we make plans to hang out, she with the nigga Jace." Harmony shook her head. "What?"

"I was afraid this would happen."

"Why?"

"Because Jace can be very manipulative. So if he's in her head, anything could go wrong now. Jayden is going to change for the worse, not the better, Mad. And I know you love her, but you gotta be aware."

"For real?"

"Yeah…and with Jayden being impressionable she might not know what he's doing. He'll try and pull her away from her family. Her real family." I looked at her like she was crazy. Because although I may have been family, she hadn't been anything close to it since we were born. "By family I mean you."

"You don't know what you talking about," I said.

"Listen, you and I both know that Jayden is naïve. I've been telling her that for most of her life. It's not her fault, but she doesn't have her own mind. Quite honestly you may be losing your sister."

"Don't say that shit to me!" I yelled, standing up to look down at her. "I will fucking kill you if you talk to me like that! I could never lose my sister!"

"I'm sorry," she said backing down a little. "You're right. I went too far. I was just telling you so you'd know the truth. That's all."

When I sat down, she got up and moved for the staircase. "One of these days you'll see that we have more in common than you realize, Mad." She paused. "I'm not your enemy anymore. I'm your mother and I love you."

When she walked upstairs I thought about what she was saying. Jayden was acting differently and I didn't know how to take it. I was just about to call Mad Max and see what was up for the night when my cell phone rang. It was Denise.

"Hey, you busy?" She asked.

Her voice was like music to my ears. "Naw," I smiled sipping my Henny. "What's up with you?"

"I was wondering if I could get some of that dick you were telling me about the other day. Especially since you left me hanging last time."

Her comment took me off guard. "Yeah, if you ready for it I got it."

"I was ready the moment I laid eyes on you. But you were so bent on tasting this pussy." She giggled. "So can I come over?"

I knew I could have company because Harmony couldn't control me anymore. But with Irma and her daughters staying here for a while, shit was too crowded and I needed my own space. Not to mention Denise didn't know I was a girl.

"How 'bout we get a hotel?"

"What…you don't want me to meet your mother or something?" She laughed. "She don't like bad girls?"

"My mother is a bad girl."

She laughed. "Well, a hotel works for me."

"Aight, let me hit you after I get the room. You can catch a cab and I'll pay for it."

"I drive remember?"

"Oh yeah. Well give me a minute and I'll hit you back."

To be ready for her I ran upstairs to get my gear together. Then I jumped in the shower. Every time my hands ran over my breasts or vagina tears rolled down my face. I hated my body more each day because it seemed like every second I was developing into a woman. When I finished showering, I did something I never did, walked into my bedroom and looked at my naked body in the mirror.

My breasts…bigger than I wanted them to be. My hips…too curvy. And my vagina, all reminded me that I wasn't what I knew I was in my heart. A boy.

Feeling disgust with my shape, I opened my dresser drawer and pulled out a roll of Ace Bandages. Then I wrapped my breasts tightly over and over with the bandages until you couldn't see its form. I wanted them cut off and I couldn't wait until I had enough money to do just that. In fact I couldn't wait until I had a sexual reassignment surgery I read about in a magazine because I would never have to do any of this shit ever again.

After I bound my breasts I put a plain white-t shirt over it followed by a grey Hugo Boss t-shirt. With my shirts on, I grabbed a black fitted baseball cap and pulled it over my eyes. My hair was growing more now so it was red and curly and I liked it to hang out the sides of my cap a little.

When I was done with that I grabbed the black strap with the dick attached to it that I bought the other day and put it on. I smiled when I saw the long brown dick hanging between my legs and I put on my white boxers. With my t-shirts, hat, strap on and dick I looked like how I felt inside.

I let the dick hang out through the slot in the boxers and stroked it in my hand. It was as close to my complexion as possible and I couldn't wait to fuck her with this joint. As long as I didn't let her touch it or my body, I knew it could pass for the real thing once I was inside of her. Yeah…finally shit was coming together for me. When I got dressed, I grabbed my wallet and dipped out the door.

•••

In The Hotel

I was able to rent a hotel with the funny money my pops gave me. I decided that whenever I had a chance to spend it, I would so that it could be broken down into smaller bills and they could give me real money back. My plan was working but my cash was dwindling.

I waited fifteen minutes for her in the room and when she finally came over she was crying and looked upset.

"What's wrong, Denise?" I asked opening the door. Once it was closed, I walked her to the bed and we sat down on the edge.

"I hate my life. It seems like the moment I get stuff together, more stuff happens to me."

"Talk to me. What's bothering you?"

"A little bit of everything. I mean, I got more stuff going on with me than a little bit. You know?"

"Like what? I saw you walk through that door and I was like damn, she sexy as shit." I said examining the cute black boots, dress and leather jacket.

"I can't do nothing for myself. It's like, I got to depend on everybody else to take care of me."

"What happen...I mean, do you need something?"

"Yeah...my car was acting up and I needed about two hundred dollars to get it fixed. And if I don't come up with three hundred, I'ma get thrown out of my house."

"I thought you said two hundred."

"Oh...yeah...I meant two hundred."

"Ok...go ahead."

"I live with a friend and stuff is all messed up over there, it's the only place I got to live. The man in the house stay coming on to me and I hate him."

She seemed so sad and I understood what she was going through. Before my pops I never had money to do anything. So I decided to give her all that I had left. "I got that." I went to my wallet.

"You got what?"

"The money."

"I can't take money from you."

"Yes you can! I want you to have it." I handed her three hundred dollars. "But I'ma keep it one hundred, this money ain't real. So you gotta break it down until you have two hundred. Use it carefully you feel me?"

"Thank you so much, Wags! I really appreciate you for this." She smiled.

"Now, look, if you fucking with me you don't have to worry about nothing no more. I don't care what I gotta do, I'ma always take care of you."

"Why?"

"Because I think I love you."

Silence.

"How could you love me? You don't even know me." She seemed a little freaked out.

"It's hard to explain, Denise. I just look at you and feel like you could be the mother of my babies. I feel like you're the right one. And if you knew how my last serious relationship ended you'd take this as a compliment. I love you."

"You like me that much already?"

"Yeah."

She tucked the funny money in her purse and got on her knees in front of me while I sat on the edge of the bed.

"What you doing?" I asked.

"I wanna show my appreciation by sucking your dick." She said, rubbing the crouch of my jeans. "Damn, and you hard already."

I stood up pulled her up before pushing her to the bed. "Tonight I'm gonna be in charge. And every night after this I'm in charge. So you gotta always do what I say."

"Okay…" she giggled. "You like to be in charge. I respect that."

"I'm serious. If you with me, then I own that pussy."

She wiggled out of the dress she was wearing and then the panties. "Well welcome home, boss."

Before fucking her I closed all the blinds and cut off all the lights in the room. I wanted it to be as dark as possible. When it was almost pitch black, I made my way back to the bed and only took off my jeans. I left my t-shirts and boxers on. Then I crawled on top of her and she grabbed for my t-shirt.

"Take all your clothes off," she begged. "I want to feel you."

I grabbed her wrists. "What did I just tell you?"

"That you were in charge," she said in the darkness.

"Then shut the fuck up and open your legs and don't touch me unless I tell you."

She did and I pulled the dick out of the boxers and eased slowly into her pussy. Her moans were driving me crazy.

"Ahhhhh….you feel so good, Wags!" She paused. "I didn't know your dick was so fucking big. Shiiiiittt! Fuck this pussy, baby."

I eased in and out of her over and over again. The more I pushed, the more the part of the dildoe connected to my joint throbbed. I realized that by fucking her with the strap, the dildoe rubbed against my joint and was making me cum. Had I known I could bust like this I would've strapped up a long time ago.

"Mmmmmmm...fuccccccccckkkkkkkkkkkkk!" I called out after I came.

"You came?" She asked. "Inside of me? Because you can if you want to."

"Naw," I ain't come yet." I lied fucking her harder. "I'm worried about pleasing you right now."

After five minutes of hitting her from the front I took it from the back. She was clawing at the headboards as I rammed into her pussy over and over again.

"I'm about to cuuuuummmmmmmmmmmm, Wags! Please don't stop!"

I fucked her the best I could. I imagined this dick was mine and that she was my wife. Her body was so soft and she smelled so sweet that I didn't want to stop pleasing her. When she finally came, we drifted off to sleep.

••

The Next Morning

When I woke up the next day we were under the covers and she was looking at me. The moment I saw her eyes I realized it wasn't a dream and my joint was still wet from fucking her. I pulled my cap down, to cover most of my face and smiled.

"Why your hair red? I never saw a guy with red hair before."

In a low voice I said, "I saw my girlfriend get murdered in front of me." Her eyes widened. "Her blood got in my hair. It's been red ever since."

"I'm sorry."

"It's cool."

"Why you always wear that cap? Even to sleep?"

"Because I like how it feels and I got a big ass forehead."

"Let me see." She said reaching for the cap.

"No! Don't do that." I said. "Have you forgotten about our conversation last night?" I paused. "You gotta fucking listen to me or you'll lose me."

Making that 'losing me' statement was a huge gamble but I thought about what Rocket said. That most girls loved to be controlled.

She sighed. "I'm sorry and you're right. You are in charge."

"Right." I winked. "Don't forget it again." Control felt so fucking good.

"Were you serious about wanting kids and stuff? Because I always wanted a family."

"Yeah. I'm dead serious." I said my heart racing a little. "And if we connect like this, you gonna be the mother of all my kids."

"I want that so much. Really."

"I'm glad," I smiled. "But look, I gotta meet up with my crew so I'm 'bout to roll. But we boyfriend and girlfriend right?"

"What? We just met."

"So we not together? I just fucked the dog shit out of you and that's it?" I asked. "I mean, I thought you were feeling me."

"I am…its just…"

"You don't want to be with me?"

"I do." She paused. "You know what…I like you, and if you want me to be your girl than I guess I'm your girlfriend."

I kissed her and said, "Good. Now you betta get in the shower before me. I take forever and may use all the hot water."

She sat up straight, moved the covers off of us when all of a sudden she screamed. "OH MY GAWD!!!!!!"

"What?"

"There's blood all over the bed!"

When I looked under the sheets I saw a puddle of blood rested in the middle of the bed and my boxers were completely red. Now I realized I wasn't wet when I first got up this morning. I got my period. She would know for sure that I wasn't a dude now.

"I'm so sorry." She said. "Your dick must've been so big that you caused me to bleed."

She didn't know. She blamed herself. "Uh…I…"

"It's all my fault! All my fault!" She was hysterical.

I held her hand. "It's okay. I'm not tripping off of this shit."

"Yes you are! Look at all of this blood!" She cried. "It's all over your clothes."

I grabbed her shoulders. "Look, just go wash up. I'm fine."

"You don't want to see me no more after this do you?"

"Yeah I do but not if you don't get in the shower, baby." I laughed. "Everything's cool."

"You sure? You not gonna leave me are you?"

"No. I'm gonna be here when you get out. Now go get in the shower."

When she went into the bathroom I knew even more that I was going to have to be careful. Something like this could never happen again. Ever. My cover could have easily been blown not to mention that this was the second time I got my period out in public.

While she was in the bathroom, I jumped up and looked at my boxers. Blood was everywhere. I tried to find some tissue or something to put between my legs before she came out but I couldn't find anything. So I took a pillowcase off of the bed, put it in my boxers and around my dildo, which was dripping with blood. Then I put my jeans on.

Going into the hallway I found a maid who had a cart fully stocked with supplies. I grabbed a roll of toilet tissue and dipped back into the room. I looked at the bathroom and heard the shower running so I figured she wouldn't be coming out anytime soon. With my back faced the bathroom door I took the bloody pillowcase out of my jeans, dropped it to the floor and made a pad with a rack of toilet paper. I put the homemade pad between my legs and zippened my pants. I felt it would hold me for a little while but I had to get to the store and home.

When I didn't hear the shower, I turned around she was staring at me. I wondered how much she'd seen.

"What you doing?" She asked looking at the bloody pillowcase on the floor.

"Nothing."

"What's that?" She asked pointing to the case.

"A bloody pillow case."

Silence.

"Where did it come from?"

"I used it to get some of the blood off of my body."

When I said that she broke out in tears again and I ran up to her and said, "What's wrong now?"

"I'm so fucking nasty! I got my blood all over you and now you'll never want to talk to me again."

I held her tightly in my arms. It was the first time someone cried because they were afraid of losing me. Usually it was the other way around and I knew I couldn't let her go.

"Don't worry, Denise. I'm not leaving you. It was a mistake. Shit happens."

"You just saying that."

"I'm not. I fucks with you and it was an accident. Let's leave it at that."

"You sure?" She asked looking into my eyes.

"I'm positive." I said seriously. "Look at you, you think I'ma let you go because of a little bit of blood? You a bad bitch! And we in love."

"I'm so happy you're in my life. I need you so much, Wags."

I was wrapped up. This girl had my mind gone.

JAYDEN

BOSS BITCH

Jayden was in her room at Xion's aunt's house pacing and waiting on Passion. She kept the room despite having to move back home and she was glad she did for privacy's sake. It would be next to impossible trying to run Thirteen Flavors with her nosey ass mother around.

Jayden scheduled a big job for a client who requested five girls and since he used Passion before, he demanded that she'd be present. Although Jayden was about her money, the fact that she was beefing with her sister fucked up her head and caused her not to think straight. It seemed as if whenever she made headway, something would happen which would ultimately set their relationship back further. So when Passion called about the job, she took her frustrations out on her and now she wasn't sure she'd show.

The girls of Thirteen Flavors were spread out in the room. Some were sitting on the bed and others were leaning against the wall wondering if they would make some money tonight since Passion once again fucked it up for everybody.

"She ain't answering." Foxie said holding the phone in her hand.

"I think she with Shaggy again. Folks saying they serious." Queen added.

"Call her again," Jayden said to Foxie, disgusted by the entire situation. "And keep calling until she answers."

"She not coming." Gucci said, leaning against the wall, filing her nails. "I don't know why you don't get it through your head." She paused. "You act like Passion is the only bitch who works for you or something. I mean damn, get off her pussy already."

"Who the fuck you talking to?" Jayden said stepping to her.

"You! I'm sick of you pimping us around anyway! You don't fucking own us!" Gucci said. "And if we wanted to, we could do this shit by ourselves."

"You have one problem, I have the number the men call when they want business. Which makes it my business."

"We can start all over fresh." She laughed. "That shit won't stop us one bit because I heard you can barely read. Without us you lost."

"Get the fuck out my house!" Jayden snapped.

"What about the job?" Na Na said. *"The guy wants five girls, Jayden. If Gucci leaves, we may not make our paper."*

Gucci smirked and continued to file her nails.

"Well he's gonna have to deal with four now." Jayden said looking into Gucci's eyes.

"Four?" Foxie said. *"How you figure we got four?"*

"You heard me," Jayden said grabbing her purse. *"With Passion gone I'm gonna have to step in and step up."* She paused. *"And since this bitch right here don't wanna make no money, he's gonna have to work with four girls. Me, Na Na, Queen and Foxie. What part don't you understand?"*

Gucci stood in place contemplating what to say next. *"I'm just fucking around with you. I'm coming."* She said with an attitude. *"You better be lucky I got some shit I'm trying to buy or else you would've been short."*

"Bitch, one of these days you gonna realize you ain't doing me no favors. You were washed up before you met me." Jayden added. *"Now let's go make some money."*

• •

Client's House

When the girls showed up at Mr. Hopkin's house Jayden's mouth dropped when she saw the client's face. She remembered him clearly, and the confidence she exhibited earlier diminished. He was the same man who offered her a ride the day her mother sent her out into the world to make that money. The day she met Shaggy and Xion at the McDonald's.

"Wow, I haven't seen you in a while." He said opening the door. The girls piled inside not noticing their connection. Their minds were all about their job and making money like this was second nature. *"This is such a pleasant surprise."*

He'd stolen Jayden's words by his presence and she didn't know what to say.

"Well, you ladies can freshen up." He closed the front door. *"And when you're done, meet me in my basement."* Before he walked down the steps he said, *"And whose idea was it to name the company Thirteen Flavors?"* The girls pointed at Jayden.

"Mine." She said softly.

"I knew you were smart the day I first met you." He paused. *"Now let me see what other skills you got. Hurry up and meet me downstairs."*

When he disappeared into the basement Gucci approached Jayden. *"Are you okay?"* She asked. *"'Cause you don't have to do this if you don't want to. Everybody know you still a virgin and nobody will…"*

"I'm fine." She snapped, *"I'm about my money and I don't give a fuck what I got to do to get it."*

"Well let's go." Gucci replied.

"Yeah, the sooner we started the sooner we'll be done." Queen added.

Gucci looked at the girls. *"Alright, bitches! You know the routine. Let's get paid and let's get out!"*

When the girls put on their skimpy outfits, they walked downstairs to the basement to find Mr. Hopkins naked in a black leather recliner. He was holding a Guinness Stout beer in his right hand and his dick in the other. He was an attractive older man however he was certainly freaked out.

"Wait! Where is Passion? The main girl I asked for?" His eyes scanned the girls for that sexy face.

"She couldn't make it." Jayden said.

He frowned and said, *"But I told you that's who I wanted. And you said you would bring her."*

"I know what I said," Jayden said slightly more confident. *"And Passion, couldn't make it but Foxie right here, can do whatever she can could do but better."*

He examined her body and her fat ass. *"We'll see."* He paused. *"Get over here, and suck my dick."* Foxie without missing a beat walked over to the man and knelt down in front of him.

"I'm gonna take real good care of you." She said. *"You're not going to even remember Passion's name."*

He smiled loving her confidence.

"What do you want us to do?" Jayden asked dreading the question.

"While she's sucking my dick, I want you bitches to fight each other in pairs."

When Foxie started going down on him, he didn't like her flow so he immediately stopped her. *"No! I want you to do it like this."*

In a sitting position, he bent his upper body until his dick was in his own mouth. The girls were totally disgusted and it was obvious he'd done that many times before. He had a nerve to make it sloppy wet too.

"Do it like that!" He said. *"Lots of spit!"*

Foxie looked at Jayden, and did what she was told.

Pushing the freakiest shit she ever saw out of her mind she went back to his original request. "You want us to fight?" Jayden repeated. "You get off like that?"

"Yeah. You got a problem with that? I mean, I thought you were here to make money." He said pawning the back of Foxie's head as she gave him an appetizer.

"I am, but I'm not going to ask my girls to fight each other."

"So these are your girls," he laughed. "Just some months back you were running off like a scared bitch and now you running shop?" He giggled. "Either fight or get the fuck out my house." He paused. "It's your call, boss."

Wanting to save face in front of her girls Jayden said, "Then we leaving. Come on Foxie!"

Foxie stood up and walked over to Jayden. The women huddled together. "I know you use to collecting the paper and that you never went out with us before. But trust me, we've seen way freakier shit than what he's asking us to do. Outside of sucking his own dick. I ain't never see no shit like that." She paused. "Anyway let's do what he wants, Jay. I need this money. That's why I'm here."

"Yeah, you did say we was gonna make three hundred dollars a piece after your cut. I'm trying to get paid." Na Na said. "Let's just get it over with."

"We ain't doing shit if he wants us to fight each other." She looked at all of them. "And you shouldn't want to either."

"We big girls," Gucci said. "This is the nature of the beast and I ain't come out here for nothing."

"Come on, Jay. Please." Queen said.

"You better listen to your girls, boss," he said. "Do it, and there's one hundred dollars extra in it for you."

"Come on, Jay. Let's do it." Foxie begged. "I need this."

Although Passion didn't show up, she was glad that she'd come in her place. Because at least she'd be able to stop shit before it got too far out of hand because it was obvious that her girls didn't give a fuck. They were all about making their little coins.

"And take all that shit ya'll got on off. I want you completely naked."

Foxie went back over to the Mr. Hopkins and the girls got completely naked. Then Gucci stepped up to Jayden and smacked her in the face while Na Na and Queen faced off.

Although it was for the money, Jayden was sure the fight with Gucci was related to their beef earlier in the day. So Jayden smacked her back harder. The two of them started rumbling on the floor as Queen and Na Na's fight got underway. Seeing their titties swinging and their fists throwing, got him more aroused. He pawned the back of Foxie's head with force as she was handling her business on the dick-sucking tip. The wilder they fought the more excited he grew.

"Make noise! Scream! Fight!" He offered.

The girls got wilder when out of the corner of Jayden's eyes, she could see Foxie with cum all over her face. Judging by Foxie's expression, she knew the rest of the cum went down her throat. That would cost him extra.

"Don't stop," he said encouraging her to suck his dick again. "Get it back up for me." He whispered. But Jayden read lips.

"I can't do that. You only get one bust." Foxie said.

Jayden saw Foxie try to get up when he pulled her back down. He was trying to get another nut when this event only included one. Anything more would run him.

Rising up off of Gucci Jayden said, "Girls, get up. We 'bout to go." She watched Na Na and Queen stop fighting as they looked at Foxie. They had to admit she had major skills if she could get him to cum that quick. "You're done, Fox. Put your shit on."

Jayden walked up to the John and said, "You got what you wanted, now where is our money?"

"You're not done." He said. "She was about to suck me off."

"You already came!" Jayden said putting her clothes on. "Now where's my money?"

He laughed and said, "If this bitch don't suck my dick again, you ain't getting shit from me because I didn't cum yet." He paused. "Ask her."

Jayden didn't have to ask because she saw with her own eyes that he'd cum and that Foxie swallowed. It was just a matter of where Foxie's loyalty lied.

"Fox, did he bust?"

Foxie looked at Jayden and back at him. "Yeah. He did."

Jayden smiled. "Like I said, we want our money so we can leave."

Mr. Hopkins dug under the recliner, pulled out a weapon and yelled, "I want all you young bitches out of my house!" When they didn't move he screamed, "NOW!"

Upon seeing the gun the girls' eyes widened. "Okay, we gone," Jayden said softly, her hands up in the air. "Come on girls. We gotta go."

"But what about our money?" Gucci cried.

"You heard the man. Let's get the fuck out of here."

When they were completely dressed, they left his house and got into the car with their skimpy outfits on. They didn't have a chance to change *into regular clothing. Gucci in the backseat couldn't wait to use the opportunity to question Jayden's leadership.*

"I can't believe we got you running this operation." She laughed. "You can't even defend us if something happens. Not only that, you haven't fucked before. So what you know about pimping? Huh?"

"The nigga had a gun, Gucci! What was I supposed to do?"

Foxie remained quiet as she drove down the block.

"You were supposed to defend us!"

"I can't go up against no gun. I'm not crazy."

"Whatever, all I know is that we need to have a meeting." She paused looking at her. "Without you."

"So I'm not apart of this business no more? Even though I started it?"

Jayden looked at all of the girls. "Is that what ya'll want? Me to be out of the group I started?"

Silence.

"You gotta remember, Jay, we were friends before you came into the picture. And we can't lie, the money is good, but shit like this is gonna happen every time we go out unless you got a plan. And unless you can protect us. Like a true pimp would." Foxie said.

Silence.

"Give me a few days and I'll get your money and a bodyguard. And if shit don't work after that, ya'll can cut me out for good."

Gucci looked at the girls and they all seemed to be in agreement even though she didn't want any parts of the Jayden any more.

"You got a few days. But after that, you cut."

HARMONY
YOUNG BOYS

Jace was in my house all night trying to calm Jayden down. Apparently something happened to her that night and she was really upset and decided against talking to me. I asked him why he ain't take her to his house since it was obvious he was trying to avoid me too but he ignored me. Fuck both of them.

When I went into the kitchen I noticed I was out of vodka so I decided to make a run. I had some in my bedroom upstairs but that was my nighttime potion. My only problem was, I didn't have a car and the buses weren't running anymore. Walking into the living room I thought about asking Jace to take me but knew that would never fly. When I glanced at the table by the door, I saw his keys and decided to take his shit.

At first his truck was a little too big for me to handle, especially since I never owned a car even though I borrowed many. But after awhile, I had my flow and moved smoothly down the streets. Once I made it to the liquor store, I bought a bottle of vodka and downed half of it in the parking lot when I saw this cute chocolate boy eyeing Jace's ride. He was tall and was wearing a pair of khaki pants and a white t-shirt. From where I sat I could see his muscles bulging from under his shirt and figured if he wanted we could have a good time together. The only thing was that he was young. He must've been about seventeen but after witnessing personally the sex drive Mad's young friends' were capable of, I decided it might be worth the bait.

When our eyes met he winked at me and my pussy got wet. "You gonna wink or you gonna come over here and make me feel good?" I said out the window.

He pointed to himself and said, "Are you serious?"

"I'm looking at you ain't I?"

Why he thought I was playing was beyond me. He had three other kids with him so he said, "I'ma catch up with ya'll later."

"Man I know you not about to holla at no old ass lady!" One of them said.

Who the fuck was he calling old? Nappy headed niggas. The one I like threw up a fuck you sign in their direction and hopped in the truck.

"I like your ride. This nice." He said looking around. He smelled like he'd been outside all day and for whatever reason that turned me on.

"Thanks." I pulled off on a mission to find the perfect spot.

"What year is this truck?"

"I don't know but what you trying to do tonight?"

"Whatever you want."

I drove a few blocks looking for a private place to fuck. When I finally found the dark parking lot of a closed down market, I stopped and handed him the bottle of liquor.

"You drink?"

"Yeah."

"Drink up."

He poured the liquor down his throat and frowned a lot. I knew then that he wasn't use to the taste but his lips were black so I figured smoking was his preference. If the dick was good I had plans on getting him real acquainted with fucking and drinking so he could last longer.

"What's your name?" He asked.

"It doesn't matter. Can you fuck?"

"Yeah!"

I crawled in the back seat of Jace's truck thinking he would follow me. But when I got back there, he was looking at me like I was crazy from the front. "What you waiting on? Come on!"

He came in the backseat and I pulled my pants down. He was hesitant to take his clothes off and I said, "Look, if I'm gonna let you get some of this good pussy, you gotta be a little bolder. Now take your jeans off."

"What happened to your face? You fuck with somebody's man?"

"Are you somebody's man?"

"Yes."

"Do you give a fuck about her at this moment?"

"No."

"Then stop fucking around little boy before I put your ass out." I paused. "Now take your shit off. Consider this your final warning."

He finally came out of his jeans and I admired the length of his dick. I laid him down and got him real hard. Then I spit on his dick over and over until it was slippery wet.

"Oh shiiiiittt!" he said. "That feels so fucking good."

I wasn't checking for him. It was all about the rod. I put his entire shaft into my mouth and made it wetter. He had so much spit on his dick it fell on Jace's seats.

Ready for the world, I got up, bent over in the back seat and he slid his wet dick inside of me. Grabbing me by my waist I was pleased immediately with my pick. I always had an amazing ability to spot a good fuck from miles away.

"Damn, this pussy feels so good."

"You like this baby?" I asked pushing back into him. "Tell me how much you like it."

"I love this fucking pussy! Man…work that shit, bitch! Work it!"

I winded my hips until I could feel my clit throbbing. I was there and I knew automatically that he was going to be my jump off.

"I'm about to cuuuummmmm…" He said.

"Me too!" I paused biting down on my bottom lip. "Give me a few more pumps and we there. Make 'em count, son."

He did and I could feel his cum filling my body the moment I came all over his stiff dick. I needed this shit so bad that we went five more times before I took his young ass home to his mama. Now I love young niggas. They were always great for a good long fuck if you found one you liked. Next to liquor, there was nothing better.

After I dropped him off home I drove back to my place. I hoped Jace wasn't waiting on me or noticed I'd stolen his shit. When I opened the door slowly, the house seemed quiet and I saw no signs of him anywhere. Good. I'd gotten away with taking his truck and would be able to keep my life.

When I passed Jayden's room, I could still hear her crying and Jace consoling her. Creeping toward my room, I was blown when I saw Irma lying on my bed.

"What are you doing in here?" I asked closing the door.

She turned the TV off with the remote and patted the bed. "Come. Lay next to me."

This was the last thing I needed or wanted, to have a conversation with her about anything. Still, I got in bed and lay next to her. The least I could do was give a dying woman her last wish.

"How do you feel?" I asked. "You look better."

"I'm not doing too well." She coughed. "That's why I really wanted to talk to you. I've been in here since you took Jace's truck trying to stall him for you."

"You saw me?"

"Yeah, but don't worry. I won't say anything to him."

"Thank you." I smiled. "I appreciate that. I just wanted some air you know?"

"I do." She smiled. "Harmony, I went to the doctor's today and they said I don't have much more time."

"You told me that already," I said trying not to think too much about it.

"Harmony, please. Have an open mind, and an open heart." She said softly. "I'm begging you."

I noticed something over the time she'd been here. That when I looked into the mirror, I was starting to see her face. A younger face, but her face all the same.

"Okay. Go ahead."

"When your father and I got together, we were in love. Very much in love. I remember looking at him when he came to that Poker game hoping he'd crap out, so he'd play even longer. Your father hated to lose." She paused. "Anyway, one day Massive saw him looking at me, and when the game was over he beat me badly. I was use to it by then of course, because the beatings were so regular. What made this beating different was that I had something to look forward to. I knew even though he was beating me, that he'd never be able to break the connection I had with Cornell. Ever. The moment I laid eyes on him I knew it was love. Real love. After some time we were able to sneak off and consummate our relationship and I got pregnant on our first time with you."

"Sounds like you really cared about him." I said, trying to think of something to say. Hearing my father's name caused me to want to drink again.

"I did. Very much. And when I found out I was pregnant, I loved you from the start before I even saw your face. Unlike some kids who are brought into this world unwanted, that wasn't the case with you."

"Why are you telling me this now?" I frowned turning the TV on.

"Because I think you need to hear it. I can't imagine the things you went through, with me not being in your life. Estelle was supposed to love you not hurt you. That was our agreement. When I killed her, I seriously thought you would be better off without me. I thought Shirley would take care of you, and raise you better than I ever could."

"How?! When you were my mother?"

"Because I thought someone saw me kill Estelle, and I figured my life would consist of me always running. Understand, Harmony that I had no intentions on going to jail. I would kill myself first. And I couldn't see you going place to place with me never having stability. I wanted you to have a chance at life. A stable life."

"Why didn't you ask about me? Write me? Or something?"

"I asked about you all the time and sent you money once a month. You never got it?" She seemed really surprised. "The money I mean."

I looked at her like she was crazy. "Hold up, you're saying you sent me money?"

"Yes. You didn't get it?"

"Stop lying to me! I didn't get anything from you. Ever!"

"I gave your aunt Angela money once a month. And she said she would make sure she gave it to you. Even when I caught up with her recently, she told me she'd carried out my wishes."

I wanted to kill that bitch! "Well she lied."

Irma seemed upset and I believed her. "Listen, Harmony, I'm sorry about that. I really am. But I sent money for you, and even made sure that this house would be in your name after signing it out of mine. The paper work is still in the process but it's started."

"Well, I'm thankful for that I guess. I always loved this house." I said looking around the room my father slept in.

"Harmony, did you know I named you?"

"No. I didn't."

"Cornell and I talked about a name that meant 'an agreement' because we were in agreement that we both wanted you no matter the circumstance. That's how Harmony came to be."

I could feel tears filling the wails of my eyes and I needed a drink. Remembering the bottle in the dresser next to my bed I pulled it out and poured some liquor into my mouth.

"Well I didn't feel love! I never felt love!"

"You did feel love, honey."

"How do you know? You weren't in my life, remember?"

"I know your father loved you, very much. And even though you couldn't see it in my eyes, I loved you too. I still love you."

"But I never knew. What good is it to give love if the person doesn't know?"

Silence.

"You hate me don't you?" She asked.

"Yes."

She looked hurt. "Is this why you treat your children so badly?"

"Huh?"

"I had a conversation with Madjesty one day. And she made me feel like you don't have a good relationship with them. Both of your girls seem troubled, but I'm worried about Madjesty the most." She paused. "Do you hate them, because you felt abandoned?"

"Who said I hated my kids?"

"I can see it in your eyes. The way you look at them."

"What do you want from me?" I asked skipping the subject. "Why are you really here?"

"I'm here because before I die, I need to know that you forgive me. I need to know that you accept my apology. My soul can't rest until I have that from you. And that's why I got on the plane, against my doctor's orders to come back here." She paused. "Do you forgive me?" She held my hand softly. "Do you believe that even now I love you, and that I want only the best for you and my grandkids?"

I knew what she wanted from me, but flash backs of how Shirley made me eat her pussy every other day, and how her son raped me almost every hour of my life kept entering my mind. So I looked at her, long and hard and said, "No. I don't forgive you. And if I had it my way, you'd rot in hell for the rest of your life."

MAD
SOCIAL SHIT

The social worker came by the house personally to pick me up for school this morning and I felt like busting the bitch in her face. She asked for my sister too but Jace took Jayden already and I was happy because I didn't want to see her face. We hadn't said a word to each other after she stood me up and as far as I was concerned it could stay that way.

I didn't have to worry about seeing her at school because for one, I never went and for two I requested awhile back that we have separate classes. I didn't want the distraction and they agreed and split all of our classes down the line.

When I got to class, and walked through the door to first period, everybody was looking at me. I hadn't been to school in weeks so I guess it was a surprise to them. If my social worker didn't threaten to send me away to some foster home, I wouldn't be there right now.

"Glad you could join us, Ms. Phillips." A teacher said to me. She was a sassy black teacher who thought she knew everything. "Even though you're late."

"Madjesty." I said knowing she would never call me by my nickname Mad. "My mother's name is Ms. Phillips."

Everyone in class laughed.

"Don't get smart with me young lady. This is my classroom, not the other way around." She started writing on the blackboard.

The words *young lady* made me want to walk right back out the door. "Look, I'm just in here to do my work. Leave me the fuck alone. Okay?" I took my seat.

"What did you just say?" she said, the chalk in her hand still against the blackboard.

"I said leave me the fuck alone."

"Madjesty Phillips," she turned around, "you leave my class this instant!" she yelled. "I'm not about to take your insubordination or your distraction especially considering you're hardly ever here!"

I walked up to her, spit in her face and said, "Good because I quit!"

"OUT NOW!!!!!!!" She yelled wiping the spit off of her nose.

I laughed all the way out the door. I know she was going to tell the principal but I was never coming back. There wasn't shit school could do for me.

Right before I made it to the school exit I saw Ursula Givens, Glitter's mom coming inside. She smirked at me and walked into my path. I hadn't seen her since the day I fucked her and never got a chance to offer my condolences.

"Mrs. Givens, I'm sorry about your daughter. I cared about her a lot."

She laughed. "You didn't even come to the funeral. How did you care about her?"

"I couldn't see her like that. But I did love her. Still do."

"Oh…is that why you fucked me, stole my money and wrote dyke on my car?" She paused. "And then never called?"

Why would she want me to call? "Mrs. Givens, what are you doing here?"

"I'm here to see what this principal is going to do about you in this school. I think you're a danger to other students."

She must've been crazy. "No need…Mrs. Givens…because I quit today."

She wasn't smiling anymore. "Now if you'll excuse me I gotta catch a cab."

She put her hands on me. "Why don't you come over my house so we can talk about this. My son is gonna be gone all day." She smiled.

"I'm not coming over your house. That was a mistake and ain't happening no more."

She frowned. "Then I'ma go to the police. And tell them I think you were responsible for Glitter's murder."

"Don't do that." I said. "It won't be good for you."

"We'll see about that."

"Okay," I paused. "But remember you were warned."

Motel

After I left school Mrs. Givens was on my mind. I never met anybody like her and I hoped I never would again. Sugar called me to warn me that she was starting more shit and that I needed to be careful, but she was telling me something I already knew.

"I know, Sugar. It's cool though. I ain't running from that bitch. It's whatever at this point."

"I won't let her hurt you. I can't."

"Thanks, but don't worry about it. I'ma be cool." My other line beeped. "Sugar, my girl is on the other line. Let me hit you back."

She slammed the phone in my ear. Why the fuck is everybody tripping today? After getting off the phone with Sugar, Denise said she wanted to see me right away. She sounded out of it and I was afraid it was over between us before it even started.

I gotta say ever since we kicked it, we talked to each other everyday and spent a lot of time together. My crew was starting think I didn't fuck with them anymore but it wasn't even like that. She's my wife and if anything, they would have to learn to respect her and accept her into our crew.

I got a motel room and when Denise got there, she looked so sexy wearing a blue sweater dress with black boots. She had a brown paper bag in her hand and gave it to me.

"What's this?" I said taking it from her hands. I immediately knew what it was.

"Your magic juice." She said kissing me in the mouth. "My little gift to you for all that you do for me."

"You don't have to give me something because of what I do for you." I paused. "What I do for you is out of love."

"And what I do for you is out of love too."

After tonguing her down I opened the bag and saw my Henny. "Thanks, baby."

"Before we go any further I wanted to let you know that I got my period. And we can't fuck tonight."

"You think I care about your period? I don't give a fuck about that shit. If you with me, I'll drink your bath water."

She laughed. "Yeah right…even after I bled all over your dick and grossed you out the other night?"

"I'm still with you right?"

"Yeah."

"Look, I'm a real nigga. The same things other niggas are moved by don't move me. If you my bitch you my bitch and you having blood between your legs won't stop me from hitting that pussy."

That night we lay in the bed and talked about everything that was important to us. For some reason, I think she was holding back on telling me about her family and I was holding back on telling her about mine. It was as if we both wanted to escape the past and focus on our future.

"What's this on your arm?" I asked pointing to a tattoo in Chinese.

"It means heat, fire and desire."

"I love it. It's sexy."

She kissed me and when the right buzz hit I started feeling horny so I took her jeans off, followed by her panties. I could see the white string hanging between her legs from her tampon.

She covered her pussy with her hand and said, "You sure you wanna do this?"

"You got a tampon on." I told her.

"I know."

"You bleeding heavy?"

"Not really."

"Okay I'ma eat that."

"You gonna eat it?" She laughed. "I mean, I knew we were about to fuck but didn't think you would go that far."

"You got a disease I should know about?" I frowned.

"Fuck no."

"Well I guess I'ma lick that."

I spread her legs apart and put my tongue on her clit and flicked my tongue. She was moving crazily pawing at my baseball cap. The more I licked the wetter she became and although I tasted metal, which probably was her blood, it wasn't a lot. I kept my tongue on her clit and out of her hole because I didn't want too much blood in my mouth. She came in five minutes and I eased up and kissed her gently on the lips.

I lay next to her on the bed and wiped my mouth. "Oh my Gawd, I fucks with you so hard!" She said hugging me. "No nigga I been with ever did no shit like that before! Ever!"

"You were with the wrong niggas."

She looked at me in my eyes and I pulled my cap down some more. She said, "I love you."

"Are you serious?"

"Dead serious." She said. "Now can I hear you say you love me back?"

"I love you. I told you that the second day we kicked it."

"I still like to hear it. I wanna make sure you not going nowhere."

She went to sleep in my arms and I just stared at her. The more time I spent with her, the more time I wanted her. After about thirty minutes later she woke up smiling.

"How come you always staring at me, boy?" She asked.

"Because I love you."

"You ain't just saying that shit are you?"

"No. I'm not. You know that shit. Love this strong you can feel."

"Good," she stirred a little, "because I lost my job, and might not be able to stay with the people I live with no more. That's what I wanted to talk to you about. I don't know what I'm gonna do."

"You don't have no friends or family you could stay with?" It was the first time I pried into her family life and I hoped she didn't pry into mine.

"I'm a loaner."

"I stay with my peoples so you can't stay there. It's too crowded." I thought about Bernie's house but after my pops finger fucked her, I wanted to keep them as far away from each other as possible.

"Then I don't know what I'ma do, Wags."

"I'm sorry. I wish you could stay with my peoples but I got too much going on at my crib."

"It's okay. I guess I gotta move out of town."

"What?" I asked. "Why?"

"Because I don't got no family out here, Wags. I'm really by myself."

"When would you have to leave?"

"Like right away." She paused. "Maybe a few days."

"Don't do anything right now. Give me some time. I need longer than a few days though."

"To do what?"

"To do what I got to do." I said seriously. "Okay?"

"But I don't have nowhere to go so I have to leave in a few days. There's nothing to wait for."

I was about to lose her and my heart hurt. Why was this happening? She was the perfect mix of a freak and wifey material that I liked. Maybe if I was honest about who I was she would give me a chance. I mean, she said she loved me, so finding out I was a girl shouldn't change shit. Then I could convince my mother to let her stay with us.

"Denise, how do you feel about women being with other women?"

She frowned. "I don't feel shit about them. Why?"

"I mean, do you think it's wrong?"

"It's fucking disgusting. I had a cousin who got with another girl and I didn't talk to her for years." She paused. "Why, daddy?"

"No reason." I didn't want to lose her so I had to keep the lie alive.

She looked at me and said, "What I'm gonna do about my living arrangements?" She paused. "I really need your help."

"Give me five days. Just five and I promise to make shit good. Okay?"

"You really care about me don't you?"

"Enough to be myself. Something I've never done before." I paused, thinking how close I came to telling her the truth. "And enough to do whatever I have to for you."

She hugged me tightly and cried in my arms. I knew then that no matter what, I had to do what I could to keep her. Even if it meant running over people in the process.

HARMONY
WE'VE GOT BUSH

I was bent over in a bush on the side of my house. I was fucking the young boy I met earlier in the week. Since I didn't have a car but wanted some dick somebody dropped him off whenever I needed him. Just like tonight.

"I don't understand why we can't go inside." He said pumping me harder. "I can fuck you so much better on top of your bed."

"Don't hurt that brain of yours trying to understand. Just keep hitting this pussy."

I couldn't take him in the house because Irma, Ramona and Laura were inside. Plus Jayden was still moping around about something. If we went inside we wouldn't have any privacy and everybody would be in our business. If he agreed to stay stuck up in my room for days at a time like I suggested a few days back, never coming out until the coast was clear, we could've had some fun. But he kept complaining about having to go to school and all that weak shit.

So on the side of my house, in the dark, I was getting my life. He was hitting the pussy hard and I loved every bit of it. Shit was going good until my ass started itching.

"Fuck!" I said scratching my ass like crazy.

"You okay?" He asked holding my hips like handle bars.

"Yeah...something biting me though. Just keep fucking me so I can cum real quick."

He pounded me a few more times when all of a sudden he started scratching too.

"I think something biting us over here. Let's just go in the house."

When the itching became too much to bare, we separated and jumped out of the bushes. Both of our pants were down at our ankles as we scratched our bodies all over. Him on his dick and chest and me on my ass and back. We were making too much noise and before I knew it, the lights in my living came on and Jayden, Ramona and Laura came outside.

"What's going on?" Jayden asked looking at us. "And who is he?"

THE CARTEL PUBLICATIONS

Ramona and Laura hung in the background and looked at me in disgust. I could tell right then, if I didn't know it before, that they didn't like me.

I was pulling up my clothes when sirens approached the house. It was the police.

"Pull your clothes up, boy!" I told him.

He pulled his clothes up and took off running. I was alone and looked stupid. Once the police car parked in front of my house, two black female officers got out and surrounded me.

"Harmony Phillips?" One of the cops said approaching me. "We have a warrant for your arrest."

Thinking they were here because of his underage ass I said, "I didn't know how old that nigga was."

"If you talking about the boy who just ran out of your driveway he looked like he was about seventeen." One of them said.

"Mam, turn around." The other officer added. Once I turned around she searched my body and placed handcuffs on me.

"But what did I do?"

"Like I said, we have a warrant for your arrest."

"But why?" Jayden cried approaching them. "Can you tell us that?"

"Mam, step back before we take you with us." The other officer said.

"Jayden, let the police do their job." Ramona said. "Your mother must've done something bad enough to be taken away."

"Can you please tell me what I did?"

One of the officers said, "Apparently more than we thought. Out here fucking kids and shit. Now stop wasting our time."

Once I was in the back of the police car I said, "Can somebody please tell me what I'm being arrested for? Damn!"

My mind briefly went back to the last moment the cops were here, when they were taking my father away from me. It was a nightmare that I relived regularly in my dreams.

"You're under arrest because you missed a court date."

"A court date?"

"Yes. In Texas."

"I didn't have court…"

My voice trailed off before I could even complete my sentence. I remembered. The trial date was because of the fight I had with Diamond in the courthouse the day I beat the case for breaking into her house.

Right after the fight I ran into Angie and she told me about my house at Concord Manor. So I left town, and forgot all about that shit. Now I was going to jail for this bullshit! Damn!

-252-

Texas

My body was covered in chigger bites that I got from the bush. It'll be a long time before I fuck outside again.

I was able to post bond once I got to Texas thanks to Jayden. I was also given another court date a few days from now. She asked Jace to send me some money to get a room until my court date since I couldn't leave the state. I picked the money up from Western Union. I would have to stay here for a couple of nights and to be honest it was fine with me. There was somebody I wanted to see and if my fuck game was as good as I thought, he'd be wanting to see me too.

The moment I walked outside the courthouse I saw Dooway, leaning against his blue Benz smiling at me. He was just as fine as I remembered even with him sporting blue jeans, a plain white t-shirt and a jacket. When I called his cell I couldn't believe the number was the same. It felt even better to know he was happy to hear from me and wanted to see me too.

"You coming with me?" He asked opening the passenger side door.

"You know it."

I walked up to him and kissed him on the lips. He pulled me into him and I could feel his dick growing in his jeans.

"Get in, babes. We got plenty of time for all that later." He looked around. "But I don't want my wife rolling up on us."

When I got into his car I couldn't wait to reenact old memories. It had been a long time since I fucked him and I hoped he thought of me as much as I thought of him. We hit a bob, talked about my life and how things were going for him. When we finally pulled up in front of my hotel I was horny and ready to end the night right.

"You coming up right?"

He gave me a sly smile. "You already know what it is. But you want something to drink first? I know you always fuck better with something up in you."

"You know me too well." I laughed. "It's called dick."

He laughed. "You go inside and I'm gonna get us some food and liquor. I'll be back in about fifteen minutes."

"Alright. I'll call you with my room number."

I went into the hotel thinking about all the fun we would have. There was something about sex with him that felt like home. It just felt right.

When I got in my room, I was mad that they only had one washcloth and a hand towel so I called housekeeping to bring me up some more. But after waiting a while for her to show, I decided to wash my ass using the edge of the hand towel. All of my clothes were back home and I didn't have anything to wear after getting clean. So I wrapped my body in one of the extra sheets I found in the closet.

An hour later, a knock sounded on the door and I opened it wide. It was Dooway giving me the *'I'ma fuck the dog shit out of you'* look.

"What took you so long?" I asked.

He walked in and closed the door behind him. "I had some running around to do and I think Diamond knew I was hooking up with you. So I had to throw her off of our trail."

"She always trying to come in between us."

"Stop playing, girl." He laughed. "You know that's my wife."

"But I was fucking you before her. I would've left your father if you asked me to. I'm serious. I miss you so much." He wrapped his arms around my waist and kissed me on the lips.

"You ain't miss me that much did you?" He asked.

"What you think?"

He handed me the bag of liquor and he didn't have any food with him. But who wanted to eat? I barely ate at home and knew I lost about thirty pounds since the last time I saw him. So I drank most of the liquor and allowed him to take the sheet off of my naked body. Looking at me he removed the bottle from my hand and said, "I see you're still sexy as shit." He poured some down his throat. "Even though you lost all that weight."

"I try to stay sexy no matter what size I am."

"You ain't gotta try, baby. You just are."

"Thanks." I said as my pussy got wetter. "Now what you gonna do about it?"

"Get on the bed." He instructed.

Doing as I was told, I climbed on the bed and opened my legs. He crawled on top of me and entered my pussy. Kissing me deeply in the mouth, he pounded in and out of me, which drove me crazy. Sex with us was always on point. We always connected and always vibed.

"Damn, this pussy still like that." He said moving faster.

"And this dick got even better." I said. "But slow down, baby. I don't want you to cum quick. Let's make it last."

He fucked me harder and harder until he took his dick out and nutted all on my face and titties. Then he smiled, took a finger and placed some nut in my mouth. He did it over and over until I licked it all off. Guess I got my meal after all.

"Why you cum so early!" I said hitting him in the arm. "Now you gotta take care of me."

He smiled slyly and rolled on his back. "I did take care of you. I bought you that bottle of liquor."

"Naw...you need to get that thing up again and fuck me right, Doo-way." I said. "Either that or eat my pussy."

"Now I know damn well you know I'm not putting my face nowhere near that twat."

Silence.

"Fuck that's supposed to mean?" I paused. "'Cause I ain't come all the way out here to be getting no half ass dick job."

"You ain't come all the way out here for no *dick* period. You came out here because you had a court date. For fighting my wife."

"Come on, Dooway. I want some dick bad, baby. And I want it done right. I mean, I took care of you."

"Is that so?"

"Yeah that's so." I said slapping and massaging his limp dick hoping it would come back to life.

"Why did you call me?" He asked.

"Because I wanted to see you." I kissed him.

"And where your kids?"

"At home. With their fathers." I paused. "Jayden with Jace and Mad-jesty with Kali."

Then all of a sudden he looked like a different person. "Harmony, I know you had something to do with my father being killed. Had he not met you, that nigga would've never murdered him coming to look for you." He rolled on top of me.

"What are you talking about?"

"They found a nigga named Jace's number in my father's pocket the night he died." He started pressing his body weight on me making it hard for me to breathe. "And I told you that you needed to get your kids out of the house but I never thought he'd kill him. But he did didn't he?"

My eyes widened. "Dooway, what you doing? You tripping hard now."

I tried to move from up under him but his weight penned me down.

"Now that you're here. It couldn't be more perfect."

"What are you about to do?"

The moment I asked him that he wrapped his hands around my throat and started squeezing. I clawed at his hands begging him to stop. He wouldn't. He stole any sound from my vocal cords and I knew that I was a goner. It was obvious that he knew Jace was responsible for Ramsey's death and now he blamed me. He maintained the pressure on my neck and there was no letting up. I could feel myself blacking out when all of a sudden there was a knock at the door.

"Housekeeping." The woman yelled.

He released the hold on my neck and put a finger against his lips. I coughed several times.

"Shhhhh." He looked at me sternly. "If you make a sound I'll kill you."

This nigga was crazy. He was going to kill me anyway. That was the plan all along. Right? So what would I have to lose by staying quiet?

"Housekeeping." She knocked again.

When we didn't answer using her key she entered the room with the clean linen I requested earlier. The moment her eyes found mine I yelled, "Help! He's trying to kill me!"

Dooway jumped off of me, pulled up his pants and ran to the door. Once he was gone she dropped the linen on the floor and rushed over to help me on the bed.

"Are you okay?" She asked bending over me.

"Yes." I said covering my body with the sheet before rubbing my neck. "Thank you for coming when you did."

"Shall I call the police?"

"No." I said putting my hand out.

"Are you sure?" She said touching my throat. "Your neck is very red."

"I'm positive." I said hitting her hand.

When I did that she said, "Oh. I get it. You're a hooker."

"Bitch, get out of my room!" When she didn't move I said. "Now!"

When she was gone I was happy I was still alive. It was getting to a point where I couldn't count the amount of times someone tried to kill me. Sooner or later I knew someone or something would get away with it. I doubted very seriously that I had many lives left.

• •

Concord Manor

When I jumped out the cab and made it to Concord Manor I knew something was up. After beating the case in court against Diamond, I was hoping things would start looking up for me. But something told me before I even walked into my house that things wouldn't be the same.

When I opened the door, the house was cluttered and there were boxes everywhere. Going up the stairway, I looked in Jayden and Madjesty's rooms and neither of them were there. Figures. Outside of clothes on the beds, things looked pretty normal. When I finally made it to my room, the door was open and it smelled like a perfume I didn't own. Something was out of place. All of my stuff was off the dresser and packed in boxes next to the window. When I walked up to the closet my clothes were replaced with clothes I didn't recognize.

"What the fuck?!" I said out loud, sliding the hangers to the side.

"Yeah. What the fuck." My sister Ramona said entering my room folding her arms.

I turned around to see her standing in the doorway. She took a few steps closer to me.

"Whose shit is this in my closet?" I asked.

"Mine."

I stepped closer. "Why did you move my shit out of my closet?!"

She smiled. "Because I'm taking over this room that's why."

"Over my dead body!"

"If that's how you want it."

"What the fuck as gotten into you? You don't come into a person's house and fuck with their shit."

"You have been nothing but rude to my mother and my sister since we got here. And I'm tired of you. It's time to bust you down a notch and I can't wait to do it."

"And how do you intend on doing that?"

"By taking this house."

Silence.

"I like to see you try. Your mother turned this house over to me a long time ago."

I reached for my cordless phone before realizing it wasn't in my room. So I moved to Jayden's room and sure enough the phone was there. She was right behind me.

"Who are you calling?"

"The police!" I said preparing to dial the number. "I want you and your sister out of here."

"Put down the phone, Harmony. Don't make shit worse than it has to be."

"What are you talking about?"

"You were caught fucking a kid in front of your house and they caught up with him. I'm sure once you go to court for that," she said taking an envelope out of her back pocket from the courthouse and handing it to me, "that you'll have to register as a sex offender."

"That don't got shit to do with you trying to kick me out of my own house."

"It will have a lot to do with it. Because it'll mean you can't stay here. If things go as planned." She laughed. "You won't be able to be around your own daughters."

I examined the courthouse paper and realized it was authentic. After all, I'd seen enough of them to know.

"Bitch, I don't give a fuck about this. I'll kick both of them kids out before I move out of my own house." I laughed. "They can stay with their fathers." I paused throwing the envelope on Jayden's bed. "Anyway, your mother transferred this house to me. She'll vouch for me. She said it."

"No she won't." She laughed.

"And why is that?"

"Because mother is dead."

SUGAR
ATTACK

The living room was full of weed smoke in Ursula's apartment. Sugar and Glitter grew up together so Ursula considered her to be family and didn't mind when she requested to come over and talk, even though she buried her daughter.

They were sitting on the sofa blowing smoke into the air talking about the good times when Glitter was alive. "You know Glitter loved you a lot don't you, Sugar?" Ursula said. "She always told me that."

"I know that's why I wanted to come over. To see how you were doing."

"I'm fine. Just working on getting that bitch arrested." She looked at Sugar. "Why do you kids hang out with that girl? She's bad news."

"Mad, is really nice, Miss Ursula." She paused. "You should give her a chance."

"Don't tell me she got you believing her act too."

"No...I just don't think you should tell the police she was involved in Glitter's murder because she wasn't. I was there and she was almost killed too."

Ursula finally understood what was happening. She wasn't there to talk about Glitter. "I didn't tell you anything about the police."

"I know. I heard about it though."

Silence.

"Sugar, take your last pull off my weed and get the fuck out my house."

"Why?"

"Because I know what you're up to."

"Please...Miss Ursula. You'll get Mad in trouble and..."

"Get out!" She yelled pointing at the door. "Now!"

Sugar felt defeated and stood up. She planned to show Mad that she was tough enough to be her girl by getting her to drop the issue. Now she failed.

"Can I use your bathroom first?"

"Go ahead. Then I want you out of here." She said leaning back on the couch.

Sugar went to the bathroom and paced the floor. She made a fool of herself and now Mad would hear about it. If it got out, she definitely wouldn't have a chance with her.

Sneaking out of the bathroom she went into her son's room. She knew he wasn't home because he got in trouble for holding weed while on probation that belonged to Ursula. So he was back in the juvenile detention center again. Searching the room she was looking for something to use as a weapon when she happened upon a silver metal bat under his bed. Ursula had to die and she knew she'd score big with Mad after this. It was her only hope. So she took the bat from up under the bed and walked into the living room.

Ursula didn't see her at first because she was still high. So Sugar called her name. "Miss Ursula." She was shaking so hard the bat almost hit the floor.

Ursula raised her head and laughed. "Girl, you must have a death wish." She stood up and moved toward Sugar. "Go 'head, bitch. If you gonna hit me, hit me."

Sugar backed up and said, "Don't come closer! I'ma use it for real!"

Ursula snatched the bat out her hands and pushed her to the floor. Then she stole her in the face and grabbed her by the hair as she moved toward the door as if she was a Glad bag full of trash.

"Get off of me!" She yelled. "You're hurting my head." Her red glasses fell off and Ursula purposely smashed them under her bare foot.

When her foot bled, Ursula stole her in the face again. She couldn't believe this bitch had a nerve to come into her house and assault her with a weapon. She wanted to throw her down the stairs but when she opened the door, Kali was standing before her. He didn't bother to hide his face. When she stood up and faced him, he took the hatchet off his back and slit her neck. Then he walked up to her to finish her off by stabbing her again. Blood was everywhere. Ursula's body hit the floor and he chopped at her again. He wanted no mistakes and when he saw her eyes roll back, he knew she was dead.

He moved to kill Sugar. "Please don't! I didn't like her either."

Kali remained silent as he tried to catch Sugar as she ran around the living room. She'd seen his face and now she would have to die.

"Please! I was here to do the same thing! That's why she was throwing me out! Don't kill me!" She never saw him before so she didn't know the man before her was Mad's father, coming to her rescue. So Kali wasn't trying to hear any of it. He was on a mission to kill the people who could implicate his daughter in Glitter's murder and that included this girl. When Mad called him and told him what happened at school, he *knew exactly what to do. He went by the motto that dead men tell no tales.*

Kali gripped a handful of Sugar's hair and was about to slice her when she said, "I was doing it for my friend Mad!" She cried. "I was doing it for Mad."

Kali let her go and looked into her eyes. "How do you know Mad?"

"She's a friend of mine." Her sobs were lighter. He was listening. "And this bitch was about to lie on her. I came to help."

Kali placed his hatchet back into the leather strap on his back. "Leave this type of shit to the professionals. Now get your young ass out of here before I change my mind."

She jumped up and wiped her face. "Thank you!"

She was almost at the door until he said, "And if you mention this to anybody, even my daughter, you'll wish I killed you tonight because later will be worse.

JACE
CREEPERS

Jace's car crept slowly up the street which he knew Madjesty hung out on in DC. Antony killed the headlights so she wouldn't see them coming.

She was sitting on a brick wall in front of a DC project with Mad Max. She told them just minutes earlier to prevent Denise from being homeless, that she was thinking about running away to Texas to be with her. They were doing everything they could to talk her out of it, including showing her what she would be missing out on if she left. They were drinking, smoking and listening to music and because of it, their guards were down and they didn't see Jace coming.

"Which one is she?" Antony asked bringing the car to an even slower crawl.

"The one with the purple cap on." Jace said from the passenger seat.

Antony parked the car. "She really does look like a boy."

"Just bring her here."

When Antony stepped out of the car and moved toward the kids, at first not one of them saw him coming. But when they saw his Jason Vorhees's walk and stone face expression, they knew either he was police or meant to do them harm. They all took off running except Madjesty. She would've gotten away with her friends had she been willing to leave the Hennessy bottle which was sitting on the wall behind her.

"Get the fuck off of me!" She yelled swinging wild arms at Antony as he held on to her tightly.

"Stop fighting, kid. You're coming with me whether you want to or not."

"Get the fuck off of me!" She yelled.

He had a grip on her that couldn't be unlocked unless he desired. Mad continued to flail wild arms as he opened the car and threw her in the back seat before climbing in the drivers seat himself. Mad tried to open the door but it wouldn't budge. When she calmed down a little, Jace looked Madjesty over and immediately felt sympathy for her. Even though she was feisty, her eyes were still that of a child and he wished shit didn't have to be this way. But it did.

"WHAT THE FUCK YOU WANT WITH ME?!" She screamed.

"I need you to lower your voice."

"I WANT TO GET OUT OF HERE!"

"Madjesty, I'm not going to ask you again." He paused. *"Lower your fucking voice."* He paused. *"Don't worry I'm not going to hurt you. But somebody I care about is missing and I need to know if you've seen her."*

He handed her the picture. She looked at it, shook her head and handed it back to him. But he saw 'that something' in her eyes that told him otherwise.

"I don't know what you talking about." She said.

"The woman in the picture is my fiancée and her name is Antoinette."

"And I don't know who you're talking about because I've never seen that woman before in my life. Now can I please leave?" She asked moving for the door handle that was rigged and wouldn't open.

"So you're saying you haven't seen your father around her at all?"

"No!"

Silence.

"I don't believe you."

"Well there ain't shit I can do about that now is there?" She started laughing.

"What's so funny?"

"You were responsible for killing my girl and my uncle Vaughn. Both of them died in front of me! Now you asking me about some bougie ass bitch in a picture? Man fuck that bitch."

"Who said she was bougie?"

Silence.

"You've seen her haven't you? I know you have."

"Like I said, I ain't seen that bitch."

"Did you know that the woman Kali lives with is your grandmother?" He paused. *"I think her name is Bernie."*

Silence.

"You didn't know did you?" Jace said.

"I don't believe you."

"Well it's true." He continued. *"Kali lost contact with his mother. She pretty much abandoned him because she was always so high when he was a kid. I'm not sure when he found her or how, but he did and now he's fucking her."*

"It's not true."

"I'm telling you it's true."

Silence.

"I...I...don't..."

"I know it's fucked up. But I got to keep shit real with you. Stay away from him, or you're going to get hurt. This is my final warning and I'm giving it to you personally because you're my daughter's sister, and she asked me to."

"I don't have nothing to do with any of this shit. You need to talk to my father." She paused. "Now can I go?"

"Yeah. Go 'head."

Antony unlocked the door from the front and when she got out of the car Jace watched her walk away. She wasn't letting him in on anything she knew about Kali. And although it slowed progress, Jace respected her gangster.

"Why you let her leave, boss? She knew something."

"Because Paco is tailing, Kali. She's going to tell him about this meeting and if they have Antoinette, they're going to go wherever she is. We just have to wait."

"That's why you're the boss. You always know what to do."

KALI
SWEET ANN

The basement at Bernie's was fly and cozy thanks to Kali. It looked like an apartment and he retreated there whenever things got tough. It was the home he always wanted when he use to stay with his mother as a kid and he finally had it

Antoinette was sitting on the sofa with a glass of vodka in her hands. The condensation from the ice dripped on her fingers as she held it tightly. Putting it up to her lips she swallowed and said, "Kali, this is dumb. What are you doing? You know as well as I do that once Jace finds out I'm missing, he's going to come looking for you." Antoinette continued. "Please...let's just drop this and let me go."

Kali stood over top of her. "I'm not dropping shit. He owes. And until he pays, you're staying right here with me." He paused. "I mean look at you. I don't have you tied up, gagged or bound. You're my hostage but you must admit the living conditions are fantastic."

"But I want to go home." She whined.

"And you will. But don't act like an angel, Ann. It's me, you're talking to." He laughed. "You helped those people get poisoned at Jace's party. You allowed the wrong caterers into the mansion and Massive told me." He paused. "You even arranged to have the innocent caterers killed in the abandoned apartment in DC the same night so that Massive's men could steal their uniforms. Remember? Nobody but me knows the relationship you had with Massive, Ann. But we're partners. Always have been and always will be."

Antoinette put her face in her hands. "I was young and angry. He'd just chosen that bitch Harmony over me." She explained. "She was even wearing my dress the night of the party and everything. But I loved Jace and would have never done something like that if I wasn't angry."

"Ann, cut the bullshit!" He yelled startling her. "You helped Massive get those caterers in way before you found out about that dress. Way before it. You did it for the money. It's cool." Kali continued. "But don't fucking lie."

Ann cried hearing the facts of her deceit out loud. "Please stop! I don't want to hear this anymore."

"Shit was already in motion to kill that nigga but you fell in love. I understand. I loved the nigga too." He paused. "But Jace owes the wrong person now. Listen, all we're waiting on is for Jace to give me my money from the hit I did for him on Massive and you're free to go."

"Kali, when Jace pays you," she paused wiping her tears, "are you really, honestly, gonna let me go?"

He sat next to her on the sofa. "I promise." Then he moved in to kiss her. She willingly kissed him back. "We've been fucking for fourteen years, Ann. And had you went along with the plan when I first suggested it some months back, I wouldn't have had to send my daughter in to get you. You could've been a willing accomplice. But you got scared and I had to steal you in that pretty face of yours."

"You played on my weakness." She kissed him again and wrapped her arms around his neck. "By having that girl fake a seizure. I didn't even know she was a girl."

"That was all my kid's plan not mine." He kissed her again. "But it worked."

JAYDEN
I RUN THIS MOTHAFUCKA

Jayden was on her way to school against her will. That damn Mrs. Sheers! She thought to herself. Why can't she just leave me the fuck alone? She chose to be elsewhere yet the social worker made several pop up visits at school to see if the girls were present.

Mrs. Sheers discovered quickly that although Jayden was making efforts, Madjesty had spit in the teacher's face. And since she didn't go home she declared her a runaway. Mrs. Sheers filed the necessary paperwork to find Madjesty as soon as possible.

Jayden was fucked up with her sister and ignored her calls. Madjesty called Jayden's cell several times that morning, but she didn't answer. When Jayden heard a message Mad left, she wasn't surprised to hear that Jace kidnapped her although briefly, to advise her to once again stay away from Kali. Truthfully she wanted out of their beef altogether because she knew Mad would never listen.

Making money was still on Jayden's mind along with getting through to the girls of Thirteen Flavors. After talking to Jace, she realized she had to throw major game to get the girls to follow her lead.

Once in the school building, Jayden rested against the lockers while waiting on the bell to ring. Foxie, Gucci, Na Na, Queen and to her surprise, Passion walked up to her. She hadn't seen Passion since she walked out of the school arm and arm with Shaggy.

"What's up, Jayden? You ain't been accepting our calls since that shit happened with that dude." Gucci said. "You got our money like you promised?"

After the dude ganked them for their cash, Jayden was held up in her room thinking and crying. It wasn't until she realized that by being weak, she allowed Gucci to win, that she decided to stop feeling sorry for herself and do something about it. So things were going to change starting today.

"I got the money I owe ya'll." She dug in her purse and handed them all their cash. With wide eyes they counted the dough in front of her. Everyone except, Passion of course since she didn't do any work to deserve to be paid. "It's all there."

"Thanks," Gucci smiled slyly. "Now we're talking."

"We not talking about shit, Gucci. Because that's gonna be the last money you ever get from me. You cut." The smile was wiped clean off of Gucci's face. "And so are you, Passion."

"Wait, how you gonna cut us out of the group?" Gucci asked.

"Let me remind you, the number to the business rings to my phone and when my clients want pussy they call me. Plus I know you tried to start your own shit, Gucci. I heard about it." She laughed. "One of my clients said you even reached out to him but he didn't trust you. Notice the word trust."

"I don't know what you talking about."

"This business is built on trust and these men need to feel that if they gonna fuck with us, otherwise they run the risk of getting locked up for fucking young bitches. You thought you were letting him see that you could provide a cheaper price when all you did was show him the snake you are."

Gucci wasn't as confident as she was when she first approached her. "Look, I made a mistake by coming at you like that. But I'm done being childish."

"Good for you." Jayden paused. "But I don't want nothing else to do with you."

Then she looked at Foxie. "I need you to handle Passion's clients. I hired Xion for security and he's going to go with us on the jobs we do. He has a gun and doesn't mind busting if he has to. I talked to him already."

"I can't believe this shit. You're talking in front of me like I'm not even here." Passion said.

"So can you work Passion's clients, Foxie?" Jayden said continuing to ignore her. "Or are you working with Gucci's crew?"

Foxie looked at her friends and said, "Sorry, ya'll but I need the money."

"What about you two?"

"I'm with you." Na Na said.

"Me too." Added Queen.

"There are no more revolving doors. This is my last time asking where your loyalty lies."

The girls remained silent but their eyes told her they knew she meant business. Because although she had a strange, obsessive, connection with Passion, the rest of them were replaceable.

Gucci couldn't believe her ears. Jayden hadn't been in school a full year and already she managed to pin them against one another.

"Jayden, I had shit going on with me." Passion interrupted. *"And I know I'm wrong as shit for letting these niggas get in my head. All they do is hurt my feelings and I'm sick of that. But I'm not gonna be that way no more. You gotta put me back on. I'm ready to work."*

"What, you not listening?" Jayden responded. *"You cut. I'm done with you and I'm dead serious."*

"Bitch, you can't cut us out of shit." Gucci said stepping up to her. *"We own this business just like you do."*

Jayden playing the defensive pushed her out of her face and she slammed into Toni. Jayden's arched enemy.

"How come every time I see you, you in my fucking space?" Toni asked as she and her friends stepped to Jayden.

"Then maybe your world is smaller than you thought! While my world is continually growing around me." Jayden said.

"Bitch, fuck that country shit you spitting. Stay the fuck out of my way."

"Step the fuck off, Toni! We discussing some serious shit over here." Passion said. *"You five seconds from getting kicked out of school anyway. Your mouth too fucking fast."*

"Bitch, how you gonna talk about somebody's mouth? When everybody in school know what you do with yours."

"Yeah, but at least I'm gettin' paid for it."

They were just about to have a fight when they saw the school's security guards. The girls went their separate ways to avoid getting suspended and Passion followed Jayden.

"Why are you following me?" Jayden said looking behind her to be sure the guards weren't coming. *"Your first class is the other way."*

"Jayden, can I talk to you alone?"

"No." Jayden said walking faster. *"So if you thought helping me back there would make me put you back on you got another thing coming."*

"But I need the money. Please."

Jayden stopped in her tracks and looked into her eyes. *"You don't act like it."*

"Well I do."

"Why should I trust you?"

"Because we're friends."

"We not friends anymore, Passion. You were right about that shit. I'm about my mothafuckin money and I'm tired of chasing you around."

"Please, Jayden."

Jayden looked her over harder. For the first time, she saw her. She was strung out. She was on drugs and in Jayden's opinion that was dis-

gusting. This was why she could never hold a promise or keep a job. Her mind wasn't her own.

"What you using, Passion?"

"Huh?"

"I said what you on?"

"I do a little heroin from time to time. But it's nothing serious."

Jayden was mad at first but then she thought about it. This addiction was exactly what she needed. She would supply her habit and keep her in line. And when she was washed up, she'd get another bitch.

"If you fuck up this time that's it, Passion. I'm serious."

Passion smiled and wrapped her arms around Jayden. "I'll show you better than I can tell you. I really am ready to work."

"What about Shaggy?"

"If you want me to leave him alone it's done. He don't spend money on girls no way." She paused.

Jayden smirked. "He spent it on me."

Feeling a little embarrassed she said, "Well, it don't matter no more. As long as we're back together I'm cool."

"Just remember, you better not fuck up this time. Because the only way I'll take you back after that will be on your knees."

HARMONY
SIBLING RIVALRY

Ever since I came home to find my shit taken out of my room, me and my sisters had been at each other's throats. It was like that movie, *War of the Roses* in this fucking house. Doors were off the hinges, holes were in walls and there was constant yelling at all hours of the night.

The police came several times to break shit up and although I told them the house belonged to me, they said because Ramona and Laura were here for over thirty days, based on Maryland law, they were now tenants. To get them out I had to go to the courthouse and have them evicted but my paperwork needed to be in order first. And because the transfer of this house to my name was in process, I didn't have papers to prove shit.

I managed to get my room back when Ramona and Laura left one day to go to the grocers but being able to keep it meant I could hardly leave. And if I did, to get something like food, I'd have to do it when they weren't home like now. That's where Wokie's young ass came in. He'd done everything I asked him for from bringing me food, to helping me get Ramona's things out of my room. He turned out to be a good little errand boy after all.

When my phone rang I answered and was irritated immediately "Ms. Phillips?"

"Yes, Detective."

"Do you have any information for me yet? We still are trying to solve your case you know?"

I thought about turning Madjesty over since she dropped out of school which resulted in my check getting cut in half, but I was hopeful that she'd come back.

"No. I don't have any information for you."

"Well I'll be over there tomorrow to check on you."

"Don't waste your time. I don't know shit because I ain't see shit."

CLICK.

I was about to go make a sandwich when I heard a door close. When I stepped into the hallway, I saw Jace coming out of Madjesty's room. He was frowning and looked angry. "What were you doing in there?"

"Looking for Jayden?"

"You in the wrong room aren't you?"

"I guess." His frown softened a little.

"I told you when you first came over that Jayden wasn't home. She's at the house she rents from that little boy. Why aren't you over there?"

"It's fine. I'll catch up with her later I want to talk to you anyway."

I walked back into my room and he followed me. "About what?"

"First off, what's up with all these boxes and shit? This house use to be so neat and now it's all over the place."

"Irma died and my sisters are trying to take it from me. But I'm having none of it." I flopped on the bed. "If they want to take this house, it'll be over my cold bones."

"You don't even need all of this house. Let them have it."

"You sound like a fool."

"Life can never be normal for you can it? You always gotta keep shit going."

"So much shit has happened in my life, Jace that I'm starting to believe this is normal. Some people have no drama in their lives and I have an abundance of it. That's what makes me interesting."

He shook his head. "I think you right." He paused. "Anyway, I talked to Madjesty. She tell you?"

"No. She doesn't talk to me about much of anything. Plus I think she ran away. I can't control her." I paused looking him over. After all these years, he was still so fucking sexy. I just wished he liked to fuck dirty like Kali. We could've had so much more fun together. "Anyway aren't you asking about the wrong daughter? Jayden is your concern, not Madjesty."

"There's something going on. Ann is missing and I know Kali is involved. Especially now." He said fiddling with something in his pocket.

"You should've killed him when you had the chance."

"I could've, but then your daughter would've been hit too."

"And?"

"How can you be so cold?"

"I don't know that answer anymore." I paused. "Anyway, you know if Ann's missing Kali has her." I continued drinking out of my vodka bottle. "But knowing her, she probably went with him on her own. I don't trust her."

"Stop talking stupid."

"Okay." I said. "Your funeral."

"You all in my shit when you need to be worried about your daughters."

"Just relax, Jace. Shit gonna be okay with both my girls." I paused. "After all, look at how their mother turned out." I laughed.

"You joking right?"

"I'm dead serious." I smiled.

"You know what, you still remind me of the girl I loved when we were kids." He paused. "Sometimes anyway."

"That means you still got a crush on me." I batted my lashes.

"I know if I find out you did Jayden fucked up as a kid I'ma bust your head open."

"Leave it alone already. The girl's breathing. Just admit that you still love me." I said. "We could start all over. You could help me get my face fixed so I can look pretty again for you and I could get clean."

"You serious? About getting cleaned?"

"Yes. I really am." This was the first time I admitted that I wanted to be clean. So it shocked me too when I said it.

"I can put you in a rehabilitation place, only if you're serious. But I could never be with you again."

"Then it won't be worth it."

"You've always done that shit. Gave me ultimatums."

"But you never take any of them." I drank some more vodka. "You don't realize that if you stayed by my side, none of this shit would've ever happened to me. And I wouldn't be the woman that I am now. Sometimes all you need is a good man to hold you down. I never had that."

"You know what," he turned for the door. "I'm out of here. I'm trying to have a conversation with you and you not taking shit seriously."

"Wait!" I yelled. "I'm sorry."

"You being a burnt out alcoholic don't have shit to do with me."

"Tell me how you really feel." I laughed.

"I'm serious, Harmony."

He stopped at the door and I could feel him. He really does blame himself for what happened to me. "It's not your fault, Jace. I was fucked up long before you ever got to me. Shirley and my uncle saw to that."

He put his hands in his pockets but didn't turn around. "What do you want from me, Harmony? Seriously?"

"Let's fuck for old time sake."

He turned around and laughed. "What makes you think I want anything to do with you? Or that pussy?"

"Because I bet money that any bitch you're dealing with, can't fuck you like I do."

"You don't know what you're talking about."

"I do." I stood up and walked over to him. Then I closed the door behind him and locked it. "You still love me. After all these years. Like I still love you."

He tried to step around me. "Move." He was weak.

I dropped to my knees. Unzipped his pants and pulled out his already stiff dick. "Hey there, baby." I said kissing the helmet softly. "I haven't seen you in a while."

Jace's head flew back as I took him into my mouth. Holding his balls softly, I worked the shaft of his dick like only I could. My tongue ran over every inch of his dick and he couldn't hold back from moaning. Leaning up against the door He savored every moment of my head game. I spit on his dick over and over to get it gooey wet. My spit ran down his legs as I suctioned his dick with my mouth.

"Fuck!" He said out loud. "This shit feels so good! I shouldn't be fucking with you though. I know it."

My pussy was getting wet and there was no way on earth that I was letting this hard dick go to waste. So I took off my pants and pulled him to the bed.

"I can't fuck you, Harmony." He was saying one thing but his dick was standing at attention.

"You can let me suck your dick but you can't fuck me?" I laughed. "Yeah right. Get over here nigga."

Before he knew it he was grabbing my waist and banging my pussy raw from the back. The way I liked it. I kept throwing my hips into him as he fucked me harder and harder. I had to admit; his fuck game had come up something spectacular since I last had the pleasure.

"I miss this dick so much," I embellished.

"Damn, you still feel good." He said.

We fucked long and hard for fifteen minutes before we fell out on the bed. He lay next to me like old times although he didn't hold me. "I miss you, Jay."

"You just saying that shit."

"I really do." I said. I could feel he wanted something from me. Could it be that he really did still love me after all this time?

"What you want, Harmony?" He said lying on his back. "Cut the shit. Whenever you fuck me like that you want something."

"I need your help with my sisters. They trying to take my house from me, and if they do, I won't have any place to live and your daughter will be out on the streets."

He laughed. "I don't give a fuck what happens to you, my daughter will never be out on no mothafuckin' streets."

"Well do it for me."

He stood up, got dressed and walked to the door. "Your pussy still good, I'll give you that, but after seeing how you treated those kids and how fucked up they are in the head, there ain't shit you can do for me. I ain't got nothing for you, man."

He walked out but I knew I just needed a little more time and then I'd have him right where I wanted him. In my bed and under my spell.

MAD
SCRIPT FLIPPED

I was looking at three bitches pop their pussies on the floor in Wokie's apartment in DC. He was having another one of his fly by night parties and his house was jammed packed with family and friends. The best part was most of us was under the age of 21.

As always his parents were in Vegas and left the spot to him. I was on my second bottle of Hennessey and my mind was all over the place as I watched the strippers dance. Although they were hot, I couldn't really see what people got out of watching dancers. It just wasn't my thing but I was bored so its whatever.

Jace was on my mind heavy since he took me against my will that night. Especially after he told me that my father was possibly fucking his own mother. I couldn't believe it was true and couldn't get a hold of Kali to ask him. I was missing my pops a lot and hoped he didn't write me off or that Jace got to him.

"You heard about Glitter's mom?" Wokie asked.

"Naw." My heartbeat sped up. This was the news I was waiting on.

"She dead. Somebody slumped her at her crib."

I smiled. "That's fucked up."

"Why you smiling then?"

I wiped the smile away. "No reason. So many people died that I don't even care no more."

"I feel you." He paused. "Damn, look at that bitch right there," Wokie sat next to me on the couch. "She fine as shit."

"Not as fine as my girl." I said thinking of Denise.

I hadn't talked to Denise in days and every time I thought about it, my stomach flipped. Where was she and why was she ignoring my calls? I couldn't even check up on her because I didn't know where she was staying. So I kept calling, hoping eventually she'd answer the phone and that she didn't leave town. Today alone I called over fifty times. Maybe she thought I was obsessed and dumped me. Or maybe she found out I was born a chick and couldn't deal. This shit was driving me crazy.

"She might not be as fine as your girl, but she finer than mine." Wokie said putting his hand on my shoulder eyeing the pink of the girl's pussy as she spread her ass cheeks apart. I threw her a single dollar bill but she wasn't getting shit else.

I looked at him and said, "Nigga, you don't have no girl!"

"I know! So she finer than my bitch."

We both laughed. The girls were sexy but I was the type of nigga who liked a chick I could grow old with. Somebody to love me and somebody I could be with no matter what. Not a slut showing her pussy to a room full of niggas.

"Wokie, what happened that night on the metro? When we crashed that truck out VA?"

"Oh snap! We never did tell you."

"Naw."

"We got fucked up as usual and all four of us was in the drunk zone. And you started talking about trust, and that you needed to feel like we'd do anything for you. So you made us step to this man on the train and demand he give us his wallet." He laughed. "This nigga looked at us like we was crazy until I stole him in the face and Kid and Krazy started kicking him and shit."

"Are you serious?"

"All the way live!" He laughed. "He kept talking about how stupid kids act on the train and how he gonna kill the next dumb kid who steps up to him and all that kind of shit." He laughed. "But get this, the nigga was saying it from the floor."

"Nobody helped him out?"

"Fuck no! They ain't do shit but watch."

"Damn."

"He was talking out the side of his neck but he gave us his wallet."

"What happened then?"

"We got off the train and took the money out. He had about two hundred dollars in cash. But what really fucked us up was that he had the key to his Range Rover tucked in one of the pockets. We had his ID so we knew where he lived. We caught a cab to his crib and stole his truck." He paused. "Man we had so much fucking fun that night. After that we went to the movies and got kicked out because you was arguing with this dude who kept telling you to shut the fuck up. We was all about to bank his ass but the cops showed up. So, we just left, jumped back in our ride and got something to eat. But we was drinking non-stop, man. That was the most fun I ever had in my life until your ass went to sleep behind the wheel and almost killed us."

I shook my head. "Damn. And I don't remember none of it."

"It's cool." Wokie said patting me on my back. "If you don't go to Texas, there will be plenty more fun where that came from."

When Wokie got up to put some money in the girl's g-string, Sugar sat next to me. It was kind of chilly outside but she was dressed like one of the dancers. Sugar was still coming at me full speed. It was making shit uncomfortable because our crew wasn't about that type of shit.

"When you gonna give me a chance?" She asked. "I mean, if you were mine, you wouldn't have to pretend that you a boy. You wouldn't have to pretend to be anybody you don't want to be."

"What you talking about?" I frowned. "I'm not pretending to be shit."

She frowned. "You know I didn't mean it like that. I'm not saying you fake or nothing. I just see how bad shit be with these girls out here. Give me a chance is all I'm saying...to see if I can be the one."

"You're not my fucking type, Sugar! I fucks with you but that's about it. We could never be more than friends."

"That hurts."

"I know. And I'm sorry I shot you down like that but I gotta keep shit real. Had I not been going through so much it might not have come out like that. But you caught me at a bad time because I got a lot on my mind."

When I said that she sat on the top of the couch behind me. The wall was directly behind her back so she rested against it as her fishnet covered legs hung on the right and the left of me. The red-strapped shoes she wore brushed my arms and the strippers frowned thinking she was trying to make some cash. I can't say that I blamed them. After all she was dressed, in this little itty-bitty black dress. This had been the warmest October ever but at night shit still got cold.

"Dirty bitches." Sugar said watching them crawl to another victim. "They not making no money no way."

She took my jacket off and the only thing I had under it was a black wife beater and my chains. I pulled my cap over my eyes. I didn't bind my breasts because I didn't care about shit at the moment...plus I hadn't been to my house because Mrs. Sheers was after me.

Sugar tried to take my hat off but I stopped her and said, "You know I never take my cap off."

"Why? You so pretty!"

"Sugar, please!" I felt like pushing her away. "This the type of shit I'm talking about. You don't understand me because you only hear yourself. I don't want to be told I'm pretty. You got it?"

"Sorry."

After pissing me off, she started massaging my shoulders and it felt good to fall under a woman's touch. I know how it felt to want somebody who didn't want you back and I tried to remember that every time she came at me sideways. Still, at the end of the day she simply wasn't my type.

"Give me a chance, Mad." she said massaging my shoulders harder, "I'm telling you I can make you feel so good if you let me."

I rolled my eyes. She wasn't listening. "Sugar, you my homie."

"I don't want to be your homie! I want to be your girl!"

I was just about to respond when my phone rang. It was my sister. "Hello."

"Mad, you can't come home for awhile. Stay away as long as you can."

"Jayden, what the fuck you want with me? We haven't even been talking, and now you call me talking about don't come home."

I hung up on her without waiting on a response. I called her a lot lately and all my calls were ignored. Now she hit me up with some bullshit. We hadn't talked since we were supposed to spend time together some days back.

"Is everything cool?" Sugar asked.

"Naw...my sister tripping." I said as I swigged my Henny. "She talking crazy."

When she called back, I started to ignore her but decided to unleash on her ass. Who the fuck did her and Jace think they were? I'm sick of people trying to control my life. "What, Jayden?"

"He found some ring in your room when he was over here yesterday." She said quickly. "He said he's going to have another conversation with you. And that you might not like what he got to say this time."

My heart dropped. "What...what ring?" I asked as Sugar's touch grew annoying.

"He said it's the ring of his missing fiancé. And I'm not sure, Mad, but I think he might hurt you this time...maybe even kill you." She paused. "Do you know what he's talking about? Did Kali do something to his friend? And did you have her ring?"

"I gotta go. Bye."

When I hung up on her the room started to spin. I never once thought he would hurt me because he went out of his way to protect me. And I never thought he'd go into my room either.

Needing another buzz, when I went to swig some more of my liquor it was gone. So me and Mad Max caught a cab to the liquor store leaving the party going without us. Although Wokie was with us too, his cousins were at his crib and would make sure shit didn't get too far out of hand.

Walking into the liquor store, Sugar and Wokie got into a fight about America's Next Top Model. We loved picking the most ridiculous fights so we'd have something to joke about later. Sugar said the winner should be one person and Wokie sounding gay said it should've been another model. The rest of us were stealing all kinds of liquor courtesy of the diversion they were causing in the front of the store. When we finally made it to the door something went wrong. The storeowner just finished up with a customer and saw Krazy stash a bottle of beer in his jacket. We tried to tell him to be more careful but he was drunk and not thinking straight.

"STOP!!" He yelled going under the counter to grab something. "THIEF!"

The next thing we knew this nigga started busting his gun at us. Shit wasn't funny no more. Bottles crashed and shit splashed everywhere. My heart was racing and I felt I was definitely going to die tonight. Luckily we all made it out of the store but ran as fast as we could to get away from him. We didn't know if he was going to call the cops or keep busting until he hit one of us.

When we were sure he was nowhere near us, we fell out on the ground to catch our breath.

"I still got the beer, mothafucka!" Krazy laughed from the ground. "After all that shit he ain't touch us!"

"Man, I though I was going to shit on myself." Kid said.

"Ya'll wild as shit!" I added holding my stomach from all the laughing.

"Hold up!" Kid said standing up laughing harder. "Were ya'll really in there fighting about America's Next Top Model?"

"That shit was Sugar's idea." Wokie laughed. "I know we looked so fuckin' stupid."

"Let's keep walking," We all stood up. "We don't want this fool rolling up on us in a car."

"Let me piss first." Wokie said.

"Yeah...I got to go too." Krazy added.

Both of them pissed in the bushes and we waited hoping this fool wouldn't come around the corner. I'm not going to lie, I had to go too but couldn't bring myself to bend over and pee in front of them. My shit would have to wait. After they finished, we walked down the street drinking and talking.

"You ain't serious about leaving are you?" Kid asked. "

"After all that fun we had back there." Krazy added.

"Right, 'cause ain't shit for you in Texas no more." Kid replied.

"I don't know." I paused, "But my social worker might try to put me in one of them foster care joints if I don't go to school. Maybe I'll just keep running away in Maryland." I paused. "For real I don't know what I'm gonna do."

"Yeah...runaway until you eighteen." Wokie said. "You know you could always stay at my crib. My peoples fuck wit' you."

"For real?"

"Dead ass serious! Don't go to Texas unless you know for sure she the one man."

"Right! And we ain't even met this bitch yet!" Sugar added.

"Easy," Krazy said to Sugar. "Why you getting hype?"

Sugar rolled her eyes.

"Let me see first," I said thinking about Denise. "Because it was supposed to be me and her but now I don't know what she gonna do."

"Fuck that, bitch!" Sugar said.

"I can't believe you really got it in for, Mad." Krazy said.

"Yeah, this nigga gets all the bitches." Kid added. "Including the ones he don't want."

"So you could never see yourself being with me?" Sugar said in a sad tone.

We all did the Mad Max drop and as always somebody went too far and fell on the ground. It was Wokie.

"Sugar, you my peoples, but I can't get down with you like that. I told you already. I'm sorry."

Wokie stood up and brushed himself off. "Look, I don't want you to leave," Wokie said. "You my nigga."

"Me either." Krazy said.

"Yeah, man, don't go." Kid laughed.

"And you already know how I feel." Sugar added.

"Let me think." I said looking at all of them. "For real that's all I can say right now."

Everybody was quiet after that as we walked down the street at night, drinking and thinking. Since they were starting to get me down, I figured it was time to bounce.

"Look, I'm bout to go to my pop's crib. I got to put him down on some shit. I'll catch a cab and get up with ya'll later."

"Aight, then we all gonna share a cab." Sugar said. "And ya'll niggas bet not fake!"

We gave each other dap and set out to catch separate cabs home. And since I'd given away most of my money to Denise I was broke and just like my friends would have to jump out and run without paying. As always I got away without a problem and carefully walked up to Bernie's house.

When I knocked on the door, Bernie opened it. Kali was sitting on the sofa with one hand in his pants and the other hand wrapped around a beer. I looked at them for a moment, trying to see the family resemblance. The harder I looked the more it became clear, this was his mother.

Bernie sat back down and I stood in front of them both. Her gold wig rested on the glass table. "Is this my grandmother?"

Kali looked at me strangely before smiling. "Who got to you? Jace?"

"You not answering the question, pops?"

"Boy, what you talking crazy like that for in my house?" Bernie said. She lit a cigarette and inhaled smoke. "If you can't handle your liquor don't drink. Cause I ain't got no kids alive."

"I keep telling you this is a girl, not a boy, Bernie." Kali said with an attitude. "I'm not gonna tell you again."

"Whatever it is, it's lost its mind if it thinks I'm its grandmother!"

I knew then that either Jace was right about her not knowing, or she was a pretty good liar. "Pops, is this my grandmother?"

He looked at Bernie and then at me and said, "Yes."

Bernie looked like she was about to pass out. "But...that's...that's impossible."

Kali reached into his pocket and pulled out a picture. Now I see why she was never allowed to go into his pockets. He handed it to her and put his hand back in his pants as he sipped beer. None of this seemed to phase him and I hoped eventually I could be the same way. Where I didn't give a fuck about anything or anybody. It seemed freeing to me.

"What is this?" She said, the picture shaking in her hand. "How did you get a picture of me when I was younger?"

"You don't even remember it do you?" He asked. "You don't remember your brother taking this picture of you? Of us?"

"No." She said, tears rolling down her face. "I...I don't remember, but it looks like me."

"It was taken in DC, a few days before you left me in the house by myself to die. With dogs." Then he lifted his shirt to show her the dog bites. I looked too, unable to take my eyes off of the whole scene. "You didn't care whether I lived or died and I guess you must've forgotten all about me."

"I remember I had dogs." She smiled. "Pretty dogs."

When she said that Kali shot her an evil look. "You remember the dogs, but not the son you gave birth to?"

Bernie was holding her head. "So...so you're my son? They told me my kid was dead. They said...they said he died." She dropped the cigarette on the floor and I put it in the ashtray.

"Well they lied." He laughed. "Grand pops and Grandma wanted to keep you away from me. They told you I was dead and told me you were dead. But I never believed them. Ever."

"But…but…"

"You can't remember." He said completing her sentence. "I know. You said that shit already. But the truth is you stayed high, Bernie. Or shall I say, Bernice. As a matter of fact, I can't remember you ever being sober. If you weren't smoking crack, you were doing heroin or drinking. But you were never a fucking mother. Not to me anyway."

"But…but we had sex." She sobbed. "We did things together that…you and me. Oh my God! You and me."

"I know. And you loved it!"

"GET OUT!!!!!" She screamed pointing to the door. "GET OUT OF MY FUCKING HOUSE!"

Kali glared at her. "You better lower your fucking voice.

"I DON'T GIVE A FUCK!!! LEAVE NOW!!!!"

When she screamed again Kali hit her in the throat with the side of his hand silencing her instantly. Then he stood up, grabbed his jacket, his keys, and his hatchet.

"Come on, kid. I'm done with this bitch."

My eyes widened as Bernie held her throat and dropped down on the couch in pain. We were in Bernie's car for twenty minutes until we made it to an apartment in Southeast DC. He held keys so I guess it was his new spot. When he opened the door I was amazed to see a very fly one-bedroom apartment.

"Who lives here?"

"I do." He said.

"By yourself."

"Yeah."

"Can I ask you something?"

"I already know."

"Know what?"

"That you want to ask me about Bernie." He paused. "Look, there are a lot of things you don't know about me. That bitch back there ruined my life and made me the monster I am today. If I had a better mother, I wouldn't be so fucked up in the head. But she was my mother, so I used her for all she was good for. A good nut."

I didn't like his method of getting back at her, by fucking her, but since Harmony was my mother I knew where he was coming from.

"I got it…" I said sitting on the sofa in the apartment. "But before I forget, Jace found the ring. The one I took from that lady."

Thinking he would be upset, I was surprised when he said, "Good."

"You not upset?"

"Naw. The nigga was gonna find out sooner or later I was involved. But if he wants his bitch back, he gotta pay me double what he owes. I'm putting a call in to his people tonight."

"Where is she?"

"In a place I can get to her when I need her." He winked. "She put Bernie's wig on and walked out the house pretending she was her. Jace's people were out there and everything."

"So she ain't dead?"

"No. I gotta keep her alive." He went into the fridge and grabbed two beers. He threw me one and drank from the other. I had my Hennessey in my pocket but wanted something cold so I took a few sips. "I gotta keep her alive for now anyway."

"Oh...well he's after me now." I told him.

"You're scared?"

"Fuck no!" I lied.

"Good because you ain't got shit to worry about as long as I'm your father. And I took care of that bitch too so she won't be calling no police. I'll leave it at that." He stood up, went to the linen closet and handed me blankets and a pillow. I was surprised at how neat everything was. "You sleep on the couch."

"You not worried that Jace's people might follow you?" I asked.

"Naw...I got to Paco. The nigga he had following me and he's going to help me out with a few things or else."

"Paco? Jace's man?"

"Yes. He has something to lose and I made a visit to his girl and his son the other day. He's going to throw him off my tracks as long as he can. Jace don't have people around him he can trust. They break easily." He yawned. "I guess everybody can be touched if you know where to touch them." He put his hand on my shoulder. "Now get some sleep."

As I looked around I found it hard to believe he lived here by himself. "So nobody lives here with you for real?"

"Why? Just because I'm a fucked up nigga my crib gotta be fucked up too?"

Silence

He laughed. "There's a lot about your father you don't know but gonna find out." He moved toward the bedroom door. "I'll talk to you tomorrow." He continued before dipping into his room, closing the door behind him.

• •

The Next Morning

The next morning something didn't feel right. My head was banging and I was all over the place. I reached for my phone and noticed that only one battery bar was left. I had to get to my charger before my phone went completely dead and I missed Denise's call. When I looked at the screen I saw I five missed calls all from Sugar but none from my girl. What did she want that she had to call me so many times?

Dialing her number I waited for her to answer. But the moment she said hello, I knew something was up. She sounded like she'd been crying and her voice was real hoarse.

"What's wrong?" I asked sensing fear.

"You gotta come to Wokie's house! You gotta come now. We all over here waiting on you."

"Why?! What's up?"

"You shouldn't be by yourself, Mad. Please come over."

"STOP FUCKING AROUND! DID SOMETHING HAPPEN TO MY SISTER?!" I screamed.

"No."

"Then what is it?"

"We jumped out the cab last night. But we had some African dude this time, Mad. And it wasn't the same. Shit went wrong." She paused. "The cab driver's name was Thabo or something, I think."

The color felt like it drained from my skin. "Thabo?" I remembered him. He was the driver that chased me awhile back and left his cab in the middle of the street. "What…what happen?"

"Me, Krazy and Kid got away but he caught up with Wokie."

"And what happened?"

"He…he killed him."

The room spun around even though I was sitting down. "What you talking about?"

"He's gone!" She cried. "Wokie's dead!"

JAYDEN

BOTTOM BITCH BLUES

When Jayden walked through the school's doors everybody was crying in the hallways. Her neck swiveled from left to right as she tried to find out what was going on. Since she was still kind of new, she wanted to ask one of her classmates but she didn't have many friends. Judging how people were sobbing uncontrollably, she knew someone died but her only question was who.

Finally seconds after closing her locker, Foxie walks up to her from behind and said, "I'm sorry, girl! Are you okay?"

"Why wouldn't I be?" She frowned, standing by her locker, her purse draped over her shoulder.

"You don't know do you?"

"Know what?" Jayden asked searching her eyes for answers. "What happened?"

"Girl the school is going crazy today. Two people were murdered last night. We ain't never have no shit like this happen before."

"What...what...what you mean am I okay?" She stuttered.

"I figured you two were close. I'm sorry."

After her words exited her lips, the first person Jayden thought about was Madjesty. And when the thought entered her mind, her legs failed her and she lost balance.

Foxie, Na Na, and even Gucci helped her up before she hit the floor. They came at the right time. Although Gucci and Jayden were beefing, Gucci put the pettiness aside for the day's sake.

Jayden thought about how she'd stood her sister up and how Madjesty only wanted to hang out with her, to spend time with her, only for Jayden to always be busy. Money was Jayden's motive and now she never got the chance to tell her twin how much she loved her.

"I'm sorry," Na Na said. "I knew you would take it hard but I didn't think it would be like this. I should've waited until you were in class. At least you'd be sitting down."

"Why didn't you think I'd take this hard?!" Jayden screamed in her face. Tears poured out of her eyes. "My fucking sister is dead."

She thought about Jace and how he told her straight up what he would do. And now he'd made good on his promise and her only sister was gone.

"Your sister?" Foxie said inquisitively looking at the other girls. "No," she said shaking her head realizing her mistake by not providing more information, "that's not who died."

"Then who was it?"

"This kid name Wokie who we really don't know like that. And Xion." She said. "He was murdered along with his aunt at the house you lived in." Foxie continued. "We thought you knew because you live there."

"Xion?" She said looking at the floor. Relieved it wasn't her sister but upset that his life had been taken she exhaled. Too much was going on. Too much was happening and her mind was in overdrive. "I...I stayed in Concord Manor last night. I didn't go to that house."

Katherine Sheer's antics had saved yet another life. Because if she didn't demand that Harmony be a more effective mother, Jayden would not have been home last night and could quite possibly be dead right along with Xion and Nadine.

"Good thing you did stay home. It could've been you too, girl." Queen said.

"Where is Passion?" Jayden asked looking at all of them. "Did she make it to her job last night? I set up a client for her."

They all looked at each other. "After hearing Xion was killed, she said she's dropping out of school. She said she doesn't feel safe and that she's out of the group again. I think she's serious this time."

The rage Jayden felt couldn't be explained. What the fuck is wrong with this bitch? She thought. Why couldn't she make up her fucking mind?! Why couldn't she do as she was told? Suddenly Xion's death seemed to be the least of her worries. This time shit was different. She would find Passion right away. But first she'd have to visit an old friend.

• •

Shaggy's House

"What are you doing here?" Shaggy asked as he opened the door to a small hideout apartment he rented in DC. He was drunk early in the morning and he seemed all over the place. "How did you know about this spot?"

"I asked my father." She said looking around. She closed the door behind her. Bottles of liquor were everywhere and the place looked like a dump. "And why you drunk in this mothafucka so early? Feeling guilty about what you did to your own friend last night? Oh, I'm sorry, your old friend."

Hearing her accusations, he ran up to her and was about to hit her in the face. "Nigga, put your mothafuckin' hand down. Or have you forgotten who the fuck my father is?"

He dropped his hand. "You don't know what you talking about." He threw his drunken body into the sofa. "I just heard about that shit too. It wasn't me."

"Yes it was." She walked up to him and knelt down between his legs. "Why did you do it?" She smiled seductively. "Tell me. It's okay."

"I don't know what you mean."

Jayden unzippened his pants and pulled out his dick. "Sure you do," she said kissing it softly on all sides. "Now all you gotta do is tell me why." She winked. "I finally get you, Shaggy, and I'm not going to lie, this last move kind of turned me on. But now you gotta keep it real with me. Did you do this because of me?"

"You really wanna know?" He asked as she put his dick in her mouth. She could taste his salty piss but that wouldn't stop her work. Like her mother said when she taught her how to properly suck a dick using a carrot, some dicks don't come washed. Besides, she was on a mission. To get some answers and to get some help.

"Yes." She mouthed. "I wanna know. And I want you to tell me."

Enjoying her seduction he threw his head back and said, "I saw him taking Passion to Nadine's house. They looked like they were in a rush though because from the window I could see Xion running around looking for something. I think it was his gun." Jayden knew what he was doing and Shaggy was right. Since he was playing bodyguard for Thirteen Flavors, he needed his weapon and accidently left it over his aunt's house when he was kicking it with Jayden one night. "Anyway, I knocked on the door, and said I had to talk to him. The moment Passion saw my gun, she bolted out the back door. But I caught up with Xion and killed him in the living room." He laughed. "The shit was so quick I doubt he knew what happened. But then...then his aunt came home. I never saw her home that early before in the evening. She came home and saw me standing over her nephew's body. So I had to kill her. No witnesses you know?" He continued moaning and pawning the back of her head. He was silent for a few more seconds before he came in Jayden's mouth. She swallowed. He smiled. "And when I get my hands on Passion, I'ma kill her too. I can't leave her alive. She may tell."

Jayden wiped her mouth, "No you won't kill her."

"Hold up." He said closing his pants. "Did you just swallow?"

She smiled. "What you think?"

"Damn! I ain't think you was that nasty."

"Damn, nothing." She paused. "My mother always told me when you swallow, you could ask for whatever you want."

"And what you asking for?" He said slyly.

"I'm asking you to find Passion and bring her to me." She paused. "I'll convince her to keep her mouth closed. Trust me. She strung out now and all she cares about is heroin. But I need her, Shaggy. She makes me a lot of money and I need her alive."

"What's in it for me? If I do let this bitch live?"

"What do you want?"

"I want two things."

"First things first, nigga."

He laughed. "Go back to the door, get on your hands and knees and crawl over to me."

Without question, she switched her sexy ass to the door, dropped to her knees and crawled all the way to him. With her hands on his knees she said, "Now what?"

"I want that virgin pussy of yours I been hearing about. Don't get me wrong, that mouth was on point, but I want a little more. Something no nigga has ever had." He smiled slyly. "I want you to be my personal whore. Only giving your body to me and doing whatever I ask."

"Hold up...you want me to be your girl or your whore?"

"Both. I want you to be all mine."

"I don't think you know what being with me means."

"I can handle it. I took care of you for awhile remember?"

"I do. But that wasn't the real me. We're talking about a total different relationship now. We're talking about a total different person. A total different experience. You may not like what you see if I give you my heart, Shaggy. You may not be able to handle it."

"I'm ready." He paused. "That's why I killed that nigga. I made you and cleaned you up when you didn't have shit. And for this dude, who was supposed to be my friend to come snatch you away wasn't gonna fly with me."

"You know my daddy told me to stay away from you. And I'm daddy's little girl."

Shaggy smiled. "That's because I did a few favors for your pops. He'll get over it though; after he sees how good I'm gonna treat you."

Jayden thought about his request for a while and decided she wanted Passion so bad that she'd do whatever. "You got it. First bring her to me." She paused. "And, Shaggy."

"Yeah?"

"Whatever nigga she fucking with this time, leave his ass dead."

SHAGGY
MASKS

Shaggy followed Passion's cousin's car, which she'd stolen again, as she drove to a motel in Washington D.C. He carried a gun, rope and duct tape, all of which he planned to use that night. When she parked, he parked also, three spaces away from her. Once she got out, and looked both ways, he waited to catch her slipping before running up on her. Rushing behind her as she stood at the door, he held a gun firmly to her waist.

"Open the fucking door." He said in her ear. He looked behind him and no one was in sight. "Before I kill you."

"Please don't hurt me! I won't tell nobody nothing, Shaggy. I promise. I'm leaving town and everything," she cried. "As far as I'm concerned Xion and his aunt had it coming. The police won't be able to ask me shit."

"Open the door." He said slowly.

"I'll do whatever you want, just don't hurt me." She continued.

"I got a lot I want from you." He said. "For starters open this door and don't make me ask you again."

Once the door was open he pushed her inside and saw someone sitting on the edge of the bed watching TV. It was slightly dark inside the room so his eyes had to adjust.

"Sit over there next to your nigga." He said.

"What's going on?" The person said. "Who is he, baby?"

Shaggy hearing his voice walked up to them and said, "Hold up, this the nigga you fucking with?" He cut the lamp on.

Passion nodded. "Yes."

"This the one you say you love? The one who recently had your mind fucked up and made you cut me off?"

"Yes. This him but I promised Jay I'd leave you alone, too."

"I know you!" Passion's nigga said to Shaggy. "You...you killed my girlfriend, Glitter!"

Shaggy squinted and said, "Oh snap! I know you too. I was gonna kill you that night, with your girl, but my mans didn't want no parts of *it." He laughed. "It's a small fucking world." He looked at Passion and said, "Wow, Passion, I can't believe you fucking a bitch! For real?"*

"What are you talking about?" Passion said looking at her boyfriend sideways. "I'm not dealing with no bitch."

He lowered his eyes and said, "Hold up, you don't know?" He said moving his gun between them both. "You really don't know this a girl. She go to school with you and everything."

"You go to Friendly?" Passion asked.

"Yeah. You too?" Madjesty responded.

Everything happened in a matter of a few months. And with Madjesty never going to school, and never meeting any of Jayden's friends, the girls never crossed paths.

"I can't believe this shit!" Shaggy joked.

The look in Madjesty's eyes pled with him to leave the matter alone. Pled with him to keep her secret. She'd rather die than to see her secret revealed to Denise, who she now knew as Passion. When it was all said and done she'd rather die than be ousted as a girl.

"This is not a girl." Passion frowned. "This is my boyfriend. I've had sex with him and everything. I seen his dick."

He laughed. "Did you really see this nigga's dick?"

"Yes."

"Well he must got both!" He couldn't get over the situation and decided to have a little fun before fulfilling Jayden's wishes. "You trying to tell me, that this bitch fucked you before?" he chuckled. "With a dick?"

"Yes. More than once."

"This is Jayden's sister. I think her name is Madjesty or some shit like that." Then he looked at Mad. "What's your name?"

"Wags!" Denise interrupted.

He shook his head and pointed the gun at Passion. "Shut the fuck up!" He looked at Madjesty. "What's your name?"

"Mad."

He laughed so hard he temporarily lowered his weapon. "See."

"I'm confused." Passion said. "I...I don't understand."

"Stand up." Shaggy said deciding to get the fun started. "I'ma show you what's up right now."

"What are you doing?" Madjesty asked.

"Stand the fuck up!" She stood. "Good. Now take off your shirt."

She removed one. "Please don't do this." She pleaded.

"Damn, how many of them mothafuckas you wearing? Take the other one off too."

"No." Madjesty said shaking her head. "I can't do this. I can't do this in front of her."

*Suddenly nothing was funny anymore. "You think I'm fucking play-
ing with you? You think it's a fucking game?" He paused. "TAKE YOUR
FUCKING SHIRT OFF NOW! ALL OF 'EM!" he screamed.*

*Against her will, she took off all of her shirts and stood before them
with a bounded chest. The Ace Bandages wrapped so tightly around her
breasts, that it eliminated all form.*

"Take that shit off too. Whatever the fuck that is."

*Madjesty looked at Passion who was crying so hard her face was
completely wet. Seeing the disappointment on Passion's face caused
Mad's heart to ache all kind of ways. She lied and manipulated someone
who she grew to love, and now she would be ousted as fake, a phony, and
even worse in her opinion...a girl.*

*Not being able to deal with the humiliation, she dropped to her knees
and said, "Kill me! Please! I asked you before to kill me but I'm begging
you to do it now."*

*Shaggy remembering she wanted to die the day he killed Glitter,
wouldn't fulfill her request tonight either. He wouldn't be satisfied until
he stripped her of her clothes and dignity. Truth was he didn't like the
idea of Passion dumping him for a broad, and he hated that Madjesty
was trying to be one of them. A man. A dude.*

*Shaggy had a lot of shit going on at home which caused him to hate
so hard. For instance his mother was dying of complications associated
with Syphilis and his father fucked every girlfriend he'd ever had. He
hated his life and he hated the people in it.*

*"No. I'm not gonna kill you. I want you to take off the fucking ban-
dage. Now." She wouldn't move. She'd given up and he knew it because
he saw it in her eyes. He couldn't threaten someone who was ready to
die. Thinking on his feet he thought of plan B. "Take it off or I'll kill
her." He walked up to Passion and pressed the barrel to her head. Then
he cocked his weapon. "I'll blow her fucking brains out; I'm not fucking
with you."*

"No!" Passion cried. "Don't kill me, Shaggy!"

"Please...," Madjesty said with outreached hands. "Don't hurt her."

*"Well stand the fuck up and take off the bandages. And while you're
at it, your other clothes too!"*

*Not wanting her lover to die and attempting to spare her life she
stood up and unwrapped the bandages until she revealed a fully developed set of 32 A cup breast. Passion couldn't believe it as her boyfriend
transformed into a girl right before her eyes.*

"The pants, too. Take them off."

*Slowly Madjesty removed her pants, her body jerking as the tears
came down harder. When her boxers dropped to the floor, a brown rub-*

ber dick, matching her skin tone, which was connected to a black leather strap hung between her legs.

Shaggy walked up to her and snatched the strap and the dick off revealing a hairy mound. "This is what you fucked?" He said walking up to Passion with the rubber dick in his hand. "This is what you thought was real?" Passion was beside herself with embarrassment. "Open your mouth."

"What?" Passion replied.

"I said open your mouth." He repeated.

"SHAGGY, PLEASE STOP!!!!!" Passion screamed.

"Bitch, shut the fuck up," he paused. "I just want you to taste the difference between rubber and a real dick. This is for future references only of course." He laughed.

Passion opened her jaws and he shoved it in her mouth. The rubbery scent made her feel foolish. How could she think that was real? When he finished with the rubber dick he dropped it to the floor. Then he unzippened his pants and forced his soft dick into her mouth, all while the gun remained pointed at her head.

When he was done proving a point, he pulled his penis out. Still limp he said, "Taste the difference?"

"Yes." Passion cried. Looking at Madjesty she said, "So s...so when we were making love." Passion continued, her face red, "that day. With the blood. You...you had your...you had your period didn't you?"

"Please, baby. I'm so sorry." Madjesty cried. "I wanted to tell you but you said you didn't like girls. And I didn't want to lose you. I didn't want you to leave me."

"ANSWER THE FUCKING QUESTION!" She pointed at her, crying harder than ever. "Stop playing games with me and answer the question." She looked at her with pleading eyes. "Please. You owe me that."

"Yes." Her head dropped in shame.

Not being able to hold her day's food, Passion threw up in the trashcan next to the bed. It took two minutes to regain control of her bodily functions.

Madjesty stood in the middle of the floor covering her breasts with one hand and her hairy vagina with the other.

Thinking the shit was beyond funny Shaggy said, "Something still ain't right." He looked her over. Suddenly as if he had an idea he said, "I know...take off the cap."

"Please...I've done everything you've asked me. I can't..."

Her speech was halted by a crashing blow to the face.

Slowly he said, "Take off...the fucking hat."

Reluctantly, she did and an extremely attractive female appeared before his eyes. So attractive that where his dick was soft when it was in Passion's mouth a minute ago, it was now rock hard. Madjesty Phillips' body was flawless. From the curves of her hips to the fullness of her breasts, she was perfect in his eyes.

He had to have her because unlike Passion and a lot of other bitches at school, he would bet the house that no nigga fucked her before. His mind went into overdrive at how he'd be able to fuck two sisters. He was beside himself with excitement.

"Sit down." He told her. "On the bed."

Once Madjesty sat down he tied Passion on a chair in the room and duct taped her mouth shut. When he was sure she couldn't move, or speak, he ordered Madjesty to lie down on the bed.

She didn't move. She knew what he wanted.

"How do you pronounce your name again?" He asked walking up to her.

"Madjesty." She said in a low voice, her tone feminine because she was scared. Since he stripped her of her self-respect, she felt helpless.

"Madjesty, huh? I like that name."

"Thank you." She said lightly. "I did what you wanted me to do. Can you...can you please let us go? If not me...can you let her go? I don't want her to see me like this anymore."

"Naw, baby." He said walking up to her. "I ain't letting nobody go right now. I want you to lay on the bed with your legs open."

Madjesty looked up at his face and saw his lust. "Wh...why?"

In a low hush voice he said, "Don't make me ask you again." He said pointing at Passion with his gun. She flinched. "Because the next thing you'll hear will be the sound of my gun and the splatter of her brains against these walls." He whispered. "I'll make it so she'll have to have a closed casket funeral. I promise." He paused. "Now you say you love her. So prove it. Lay down. Legs open."

Madjesty lay on the bed and he crawled on top of her. Admiring her small breast he ran his tongue around the nipple and it felt like bugs were crawling all over her body. Just his touch. Just his feel. Made her want to die. Taking his pants down he allowed his dick to roam free.

"Please don't. Don't do this." Madjesty cried. "Don't do this to me."

"Hmmmmm," he kissed her neck. "I think you gonna like it." He smelled the masculine cologne she wore on her skin and was slightly turned off until he pawned her breasts with his free hand. The gun remained firmly in the other as he suckled her breasts.

"OH MY GOD!" she trembled. "DON'T DO THIS TO ME! PLLLLLEEEEASSE!"

As his tongue ran over her nipple life was taken out of her body. His touch, his caress exemplified everything she hated about her body and she cursed God for making her what her mind said she wasn't.

"I'm a boy! Please stop!" she cried. "Please!"

Thinking she was losing her mind he looked at her and said, *"Shawty, if you are a nigga, I'm officially gay."*

As if he didn't humiliate her enough, he entered her. The tightness of her pussy aroused him so much, that he knew he couldn't get more than ten or fifteen pumps tops, before it would all be over and he wanted the moment to last. So he looked at her pretty face and stopped moving. A face that although wet with tears, was beautiful.

"Why you wanna be a boy? When you so fucking sexy?"

When she didn't answer he used his dick as a weapon and said, *"Don't make me put this in your ass. Now answer the fucking question."*

"This all I know." She cried. "All I know…"

Not knowing what she meant or even caring, he raped her over and over again. He'd bust one time and rested. Raped her again fifteen minutes later and took a longer break. The entire ordeal lasted for over an hour. Madjesty checked out after the first two times and she no longer cared.

Her mind went to happier times. Like the day she first met Wagner, and how much love he poured on her. She thought about Jayden, and how they would play the roach game at home when they were alone. She even thought about Tisa before her mind moved quickly to Glitter. She wanted those thoughts to keep her company because she knew after this, life for her was officially over. If not by him by her own hands.

When she glanced over and saw the disgust on Passion's face, she knew Passion would rather die than to be with her again if they made it out of this alive. This gave her nothing else to live for. The smell of metal was heavy in the room as she bled from her virginity being stripped away by a complete lunatic.

When he was done, he rose up, got dressed and untied Passion. He let the duct tape remain over her mouth so he could get her out of the room without her saying a word.

When Passion was no longer bound he said, *"Stand up."* Passion did. Then he looked over at Madjesty who was in a fetal position balled up on the bed. Naked. *"You got some good ass pussy."* He said. *"Too bad I'm got orders to kill you."*

With that he shot her and walked out of the room with Passion.

Leaving Madjesty for dead.

SHAGGY
WHORE

Shaggy drove in silence. There was nothing left to be said because there was nothing that could be undone. Still, Passion's heart broke for Madjesty despite her dishonesty. To watch her be brutally raped and shot was too much for even the greatest sinner. So what she'd lied and manipulated her, she still cared about Madjesty. And then to learn that she was Jayden's sister was an even tougher blow. She couldn't imagine how this would go over once she spoke to Jayden. Passion was judgmental, and as the night grew old, she was starting to believe that her attitude inspired Shaggy to push the envelope and go even further.

Besides, who was she to point fingers? She was dishonest when she'd given her birth name to Madjesty instead of Passion, the name she was known by. Simply because she was running from her past. Then there was her growing heroin addiction, which caused her to lie to Madjesty about the use of her money. She was wrong in all senses of the word. She was just as guilty.

Shaggy saw the spit in her eyes so he snatched the tape off her lips. "Speak on it."

"You didn't have to kill him." Passion said looking at him, before looking back out the window. "You raped him and then you killed him. Why?"

"After all that shit, you still think that bitch was a dude?" He asked maneuvering down the street. "Is that what you gonna tell people? That I raped another nigga?"

"I meant her."

Shaggy growing angry at her disposition, stole her in the face. Her head crashed against the window and blood poured from her mouth.

"What are you?" He asked, wild eyes alternating from the road back to her face. When she didn't respond he got louder. "What the fuck are you?"

Holding her face she said, "What do you mean?"

He stole her again. "I said what the fuck are you?"

"I don't know what you want me to say?" She sobbed.

"A whore. You're a fucking whore." He paused. "Now say it!"

"I'm a whore." She cried. "I'm sorry."

"I know you sorry. And because you a whore, sometimes you need to be put in your place. Don't you agree?"

"Yes." She cried.

"And all whores whether they know it or not need to be told what to do. Correct?"

"Yes."

"Good. Now strip off all of your clothes."

Already knowing he hated to repeat himself, she removed her clothes as quickly as possible. When she was done he pulled up to a convenience store that was full of people and ordered her out.

"Get out." He paused. "You need to air out a little."

"No! Please don't do this!"

"You really gonna make me say it twice?"

He looked at her and she opened the car door. He should not have needed to say that much. She witnessed Madjesty's rape and murder and knew what kind of man she was dealing with...an uncompromising one.

When she got out of the car and everyone saw her naked body people were shocked. Some thought she was high but most thought she was crazy. Camera phones flashed as they watched the sexy naked girl expose her nude body to the world.

"Walk down the street." He yelled from a rolled down window.

Barefoot and naked, she walked slowly down the street as he drove next to her. It was impossible for her to be more humiliated and she suddenly had a taste, albeit small, of how Madjesty must've felt moments earlier. To have your self-respect stripped from you and not be able to defend yourself was the lowest offense known to man. Now she felt even worse for how she reacted back at the room. Who was she to point the finger when she herself was not perfect?

After laughing hysterically Shaggy said, "Get in the car." She did quickly and covered her breasts with her hands.

Once inside he said, "Now...what are you?"

"A whore?"

"Good and this is what I'm telling you to do." He paused. "When we tell the story, about what happened back in the room, it will go like this. I came to the hotel to get you, that bitch fought me and I killed her. We will not mention a rape, or anything else am I understood? Especially to Jayden."

She wiped some tears off of her face and said, "Yes. You're understood."

"Good, because if you don't do what I say, what I will do to you will be far worse than anything you've ever experienced. I guarantee it."

She nodded.

"Now look in the glove compartment," he paused. "I put something in there for your troubles."

Passion opened the compartment and removed a small bag of heroin. "Thank you!" She smiled, wiping the snot and tears from her face. She didn't even put on her clothes first before she started cooking it.

He laughed and said to himself, "What a difference a little dope makes."

JACE
DRUNKEN HOT GIRLS

Jace sat in Harmony's room and watched her consume glass after glass of vodka. They were on the bed and music played softly in the background. She was so happy that he agreed to spend more time with her, that it never dawned on her that he could have ulterior motives. At first he was hiding the gun under his shirt, but after a certain point in the evening he knew the barrel could be at her head and she wouldn't notice. She was washed up. Spent...mentally and spiritually dead.

"Why you not drinking?" Harmony asked, approaching her limit at the speed of light.

"I want you to drink. And I want to talk."

When she swallowed what was left in her cup he poured her another. "Harmony, what happened the night of my party? The night you ran out of my life."

She swallowed the cup of liquor. "I...I...don't know..."

Suddenly she'd fallen asleep and he slapped her in the face. This drunk fest wasn't about drinking until you dropped. This was about an old debt that he wanted to settle. It pissed him off that Kali had Antoinette and that his daughter, Kali's spawn, assisted somehow. He wanted revenge and he wanted somebody to pay before he could get his hands on him.

With wide eyes she asked, "Why'd you do that?"

"Because I want to talk to you." He smiled. "Now tell me, what happened the night of my party? The day you walked out of my life. Did you tell Massive where I was? Is that how he found me? And did you steal my money?"

Harmony's head rolled around like a bobble head toy and it angered him. He'd given her too much to drink and now she couldn't talk. At the present moment she couldn't speak the truth or lie for that matter. Alcohol called her to the place of, 'I Could Care Fucking Less', and she loved every minute of it. It was her all time favorite place to go.

"I...Jace...I...love you."

"I know you do." He said no longer smiling. Why fake anymore? The bitch was drunk out of her mind and he would mean mug her until she answered his question. *"But you gotta tell me about that night."*

"I...I got Grand." She said feeling heavy. *"Remember Grand?"* She smiled, her eyes rolling to the back of her head.

"Yeah. He was my peoples." He paused. *"A good man."*

"He...got that man. In prison. The one....Jace...you got some more liquor?"

"Not until you tell me what I need to know." He looked at her with piercing eyes. *"Did you have something to do with Massive poisoning all those people at my party?"*

"Yes." She said, head rolling around again. *"I...I was mad at you."*

"Did you take my money?"

"I took some."

Jace stared at her. Watching her eyes close again, he slapped her harder in the face and put his hand around her throat. The gun was on her forehead and he was about to pull the trigger. The only thing was he had such a grip on her neck, that one couldn't be sure which would kill her first. The choke or the bullet. However at the moment, both would do him just fine. He wanted her dead.

Gone.

Vanished.

Fuck this bitch for stealing his heart after all these years, and even at her worse, never letting go. The world would be better off without her and he knew it.

When the life was leaving her body, she slowly opened her eyes, and put her hand gently over his. A hand that at the moment was taking her life.

"It's okay." She smiled. *"You can do it. I love you."*

A vein popped in the middle of his forehead as he watched her shut her eyes again. He hated her. No he loved her. No he hated her! No he loved her! He was confused and because of it, he let go.

He couldn't do it.

He couldn't do it!

He stood up, wiped the sweat off of his head and walked out of her bedroom. Harmony would never remember the night she walked away with her life. And Jace would never say a word.

MADJESTY

SLICE

When I woke up, the first thing I saw was an open door with people walking past it and I didn't know where I was. That is until I heard, '*Paging doctor Vandal, Paging Doctor Vandal*' on the intercom. Maybe I went into the *drunk zone* and was brought to a hospital to recover. Maybe everything that happened over the past few days, including losing my friend Wokie and getting raped was all a bad dream.

And then scenes flashed in my mind. Of him on top of me. Of him touching me. Did I actually get raped? Did someone actually remind me of the thing I hated most in the world, that I was a boy, stuck in a girl's body?

"I killed his father. And I'm still looking for the boy." I heard someone say.

When I turned my head to the right I saw my father sitting in a chair. He looked angry and I didn't know if he was mad at me or somebody else.

"Huh?" I said in a low voice. My throat felt dry.

"I killed the boy's father. Paco." He stood up and approached the bed. Then he placed my hat on my head. I smiled. "And I put the word out so they'll bring his son to me next."

Did he know what happened? If so, how? "You know? About the…"

"Yes." He said touching my leg. He loved me. In his own way he loved me and I could feel it. I never felt love from someone with my bloodline that strong until now. "I know what happened, Mad and you don't have to say it."

"But how?"

"The woman, who called the police, when she heard the gun go off, said she heard the name Shaggy being called several times. That's Paco's son, so I took care of Paco. He's dead. And I'm taking care of Shaggy when I find him."

Good! I wanted him gone! Tears rolled down my face and with his callous hand he wiped them away. "What I tell you about that? You stronger than that shit." His voice got lower. "I remember crying when I

-302-

was a kid, and nobody came. Tears are useless. Just reminders that you better watch your back because you're on your own out here."

"I'm sorry."

"Apologies are unnecessary evils too."

Saying nothing more he put a scalpel in my hand and walked toward the door. "What's this for?"

With his back faced me he said, "When you were in and out of consciousness, you said you hated your breasts. If you really want 'em gone, cut 'em off here. They can save your life, and take them away at the same time. But you're going to have to do it yourself. It's up to you." He walked out the door and out of sight.

I tried to hold back my tears but I couldn't. I don't know if I was crying because finally somebody offered me the solution to something that was plaguing me all my life, my breasts, or if it was the fact that he cared so much to defend me. I knew then that I didn't care how crazy people thought my father was, he was my father and I was going to stay in his life no matter what. That is, if I lived.

Looking at the scalpel in my hand, I moved it from side to side. The ceiling light hit it and it blinged. I could see my reflection. A reflection that I hated and a reflection that must've been pretty enough to make a man want me in that way. To make a man kiss me. There was no way in this world I could keep my breasts after what he did to me. I just couldn't. So in my bed I sliced deeply into the left breast first.

"Ahhhhhhhhhh!" I screamed out in pain before cutting the right. "Ahhhhhhhhhhhh!" Blood poured onto the white floor making it the color red.

The pain was excruciating. Worse than I imagined and I immediately felt I made a mistake. That is until I thought about never having breast again. That thought was the last thing I remembered before hospital officials rushed into my room, only to find my breasts hanging loosely from my body.

After that…shit faded to black.

KALI

SEVERITY

Kali was in Atlanta in a hotel watching Antoinette eat fries from the two-piece whiting meal she ordered at a carryout spot. Jace would never allow her to eat that way. He liked his women lean and mean but Kali didn't give a fuck.

"Which one is his number?" Kali asked holding her cell phone.

"All of 'em in there." She chewed the fish with her mouth open. "His father's number, Kreshon...all of 'em."

"I need the home number." He paused, pushing different buttons.

She took the phone from his hand and found it. "It's the first one."

The phone rang twice before Jace answered and she sat back down.

"Hello." Jace said.

"What's good, man?"

"Kali?"

"What you think?"

"Where's Ann?"

"Listen, she's gonna be good. I changed shit up a little but you gotta pay me first."

"I know...you asking for a million now. You doubled the payment." He paused. "I got your money though, just tell me where she at."

"Naw...I changed shit up even more."

"What you mean?"

"I just want you to pay me the five hundred G's."

"So you don't want the extra five? Why?"

"I want Shaggy. Where he at?"

Jace laughed. "So you did have something to do with Paco being murdered?"

"Jace, I told you when you ganked me for my cash at the deli that you made a mistake." He paused. "But you're only realizing that mistake now." He paused. "Paco wasn't no good, dude. He sold you out. Now me and your girl out of the state. I was the best man on your team and you lost me. Simply because I bark when I bite.

"What you talking about?"

"I was able to pay Paco to get off my trail when you were on to me about kidnapping Ann." Kali laughed. *"I bet you didn't know that shit."*

"So why you kill him? If you had business with him?"

"Because his son raped my daughter...and I was trying to get at Shaggy and he wouldn't hand him over. I guess he did have some loyalty, at least to his family." He paused. *"Bring him to me, along with the five, and all debts will be paid in full."*

Jace laughed. *"You think you running shit don't you?"*

"Actually I do."

"And why is that?"

"Because you move by your heart and I move by my heart."

"That shit don't make sense."

"That's why you'll always come out on the bottom." Kali said. He kissed Ann softly on the lips and she quietly begged him to get off the phone. She wanted to fuck, not be bothered with Jace anymore. She was done with him and on to the next one.

"Explain." Jace said.

"You care too much. You cared about Harmony when you shouldn't have. You cared about me when you should've put a bullet in my head and you cared about my daughter, Mad." He laughed. *"Now I got her heart too. Heart where I don't give a fuck about what I gotta do, or who I gotta kill. If I stand by it, I stand by it even if it means my death. That means anybody in the way gets dealt with."* He paused. *"If I was in your shoes, I would've murdered Harmony, Madjesty and my entire crew. But you couldn't. You not built for this shit. You never were. You needed a nigga like me, who was bred for this game but you weren't loyal. You wrote me off over a bitch."*

"You really feel that way don't you?"

"Come on, Jace. Since when do I say shit I don't mean?" He paused. *"I need my money. Don't fuck with me. Give me my dough, with Shaggy and you get your bitch. I'll call you later with the details."*

When he hung up, Ann was nervous. It sounded as if he'd kill anybody, even if it meant her. *"So you'd kill me too?"* She asked when he sat on the bed next to her.

He kissed her softly on the lips. *What the fuck you think? He thought.*

MADJESTY
HALF CRAZY
MONTHS LATER

Some of us were black and a few owned corporations. Others were white and went to college. And then there were people who'd been in here since they were kids and now they were senior citizens. Through it all there was one thing we all had in common. We were all considered crazy.

I couldn't believe all of these doctors were right. If you saw some of these people you'd think the same thing. For instance if you had a chance to talk to Sally Porter, a white girl who went to Yale, you wouldn't believe she'd bitten three of her own fingers off her hand. And then there was Dynamite, a short black girl from South Africa, who could pick any lock you placed in front of her, that they claimed had multiple personality disorder. Then there was me...a girl from Texas, who sliced off her own breasts and in its place, had a mutilated chest which I loved. They said I had Gender Identity Disorder. I guess I'm crazy too.

Being in this mental institution proved one thing, that there were so many different people in this world, and that we all had a story. Still I was tired. Tired of getting the calls that everyone else was having fun out in the world. And tired of getting the calls that my own sister betrayed me. I was alone. Cut off by my own twin. A person who shared the same womb as me. And a person who more than anything knew what I'd gone through with Harmony as a mother.

"Madjesty, you have your call for the day." The doctor said holding the cream phone in his hand.

"Who is it?" I asked with hopeful eyes.

"Your mother."

I reluctantly took the phone because at least she called regularly. "Hey, ma."

"How are you?"

"I'm cool."

"They not over medicating you are they? Because them white peoples love to overmedicate folks."

"Ma, I don't know. You been down here how many times?" I paused. "You tell me."

"At least five times and I still don't trust them."

As my mother ranted on the phone I watched Dynamite picking the lock to the door, which held our medications. After all this time the employees still didn't understand that she couldn't be trusted around locks.

"You there, Mad?" Harmony asked.

"Yes, ma."

"So how are you?"

"I'm fine. I just miss, Jayden."

She sighed. "Madjesty, I told you she's gone on with her life."

"Well did you tell her I asked about her?" I said. "And that I want to see her?"

"For the hundredth time...yes! Pretty soon you gonna realize you just have me. Ain't I good enough?"

I ended the call five minutes later without her question being answered. She knew she wasn't good enough but she kept asking the same thing and each time my answer was no. Where was Jayden? And my father? And why didn't they want to see me?

"Madjesty...look." Dynamite said pointing to a roll away cabinet full of drugs. The door was wide open. They were supposed to take the cabinet out of the rec room after administering our medications but for whatever reason they didn't. "I popped that shit!"

Dynamite laughed at her handiwork and I smiled. If I ever got out of here, I had plans to take her with me. But as it stood the doctors wouldn't give me a release because I refused to see myself as anything other than a boy.

"*SHE MIGHT BE DOWN HERE!*" I heard a familiar voice yell in the hallway outside.

"*BITCH, SHUT UP! YOU ALWAYS TALKING SHIT WHEN YOU BE WRONG!*" My heart raced as I picked up on another voice

"*FUCK YOU!*" Sugar said. "*BET I'M RIGHT!*

When I saw their faces appear through the glass window in the door I couldn't believe it. Was I having a bad moment? Was my recovery failing?

"MADJESTY, DID YOU REALLY CUT YOUR TITTIES OFF?!" Kid asked.

I laughed.

"FUCK ALL THAT!" Krazy said. "YOU COMING WITH US OR WHAT?!"

Standing at the door, was Mad Max. And because we'd been cut short, the only members left were Sugar, Kid and Krazy. It broke my heart that Glitter and Wokie could never come back. I thought about them every day.

I grabbed my shit and said, "I'm rolling with ya'll!" Looking at Dynamite I said, "And she coming too!"

••

In The Car

Kid drove down the road silent at first. I already slid in the street clothes they brought me and I couldn't believe how flat my chest was under my t-shirts. No longer would I have to bind myself. The hospital gave me a fucked up cosmetic surgery to save my life and now I was breast-less and happy as shit.

"Ya'll got my joint?" I asked.

"Yep. It's in that bag." Krazy replied. "Your father gave us your phone, too. All your stuff in there."

"You talk to my pops?"

"Yeah...he said he'll reach out when he can."

I smiled.

"You got fat as shit!" Sugar said out of nowhere. "It looks good on you though."

"Thanks. I think."

"So who is this chick again?" Kid asked looking at Dynamite

"Why? Who you?" Dynamite said.

"Her name is Dynamite." I told them. "And trust me when I say she'll come in handy one day."

Dynamite looked at them before focusing on the door. "Hey, Mad...You think I can pick this lock?"

"You talking about the door? From the inside?" I said.

"Yeah!"

"It opens by itself. You ain't gotta pick it."

"Oh..." She said softly.

My friends shook their heads.

"So you really gotta go back there?" Krazy asked. "To Concord Manor?"

"I just have to see about something." I paused looking out the window. It felt good to be free. "I won't be too long."

"But we busted you out because you need to stay away from there." Sugar said. "Not got back. If you do, your mother might tell them peoples on you. And they'll come get you."

"I'm never going back permenatenly. Just let me see what's up. I have a few unanswered questions and I'll get back up with ya'll."

"What we gonna do with her?" Sugar said frowning at Dynamite. "This your new girl or something?"

I shook my head. "No."

"So what's up?"

"Just keep her with ya'll." I paused. "Until you hear from me."

"You don't want us to wait when we drop you off?" Kid asked.

"No…But I got my phone. I'ma hit you when I'm ready."

As we drove closer to my house I thought about something that bothered me. I missed Glitter's funeral and always felt like shit about it. I didn't plan on missing another friend's funeral but it was out of my hands.

Wanting to know but not really I asked, "So how was it?"

"Wokie's funeral?" Sugar said.

"Yeah."

"We were in the drunk zone. If we remember we'll let you know."

JAYDEN
TWIN TRAITOR

Jayden was in her room in Concord Manor, pacing the floor. She and Shaggy were an item ever since he came through for her by finding Passion, but lately she couldn't get a hold of him on the phone. It had been two hours since she last spoke to him and it was driving her crazy. She needed to speak to him every hour and if she couldn't she felt something was wrong with the relationship. Calling his phone again she was happy when he finally answered.

"Shaggy, why you ain't answer the fucking phone? Don't fuck with me!"

"Baby, I had something to do. I told you that."

"Are you sure?"

"Yes! What you think was happening?"

"Did I do something wrong, Shaggy? Say something wrong? Or anything like that?"

"No!" He sighed. "Why you always think you said something wrong because you don't talk to me every hour? You know niggas after me and shit."

"I know, and I want to help you."

"But you can't."

"I can. But you gotta trust me." Jayden cried. "I don't want you to leave me. I want us to be together forever. Even if I gotta kill us to make that happen."

Silence.

"I won't leave you, Jayden. But you gotta give me my space, baby."

"Space?" She frowned. "Since when do you need space?"

"Jayden, I been meaning to talk to you about this. I mean, you starting to crowd me, and I'm gonna need you to back off a little."

"So you saying it's over?"

"No! I'm not saying that! I'm just saying I need a little time. Please."

After he said that he hung up in her face. She called him back immediately and said, "I'm gonna come over your house after my company leaves. You better be there when I knock on that door."

"Don't threaten me." He said.

"NO! You don't threaten me. You belong to me, Shaggy. That was our agreement."

"We haven't even fucked yet!"

"That's not my fault. You afraid to be around me. And when we do see each other it's rushed."

"Jayden..."

"Jayden, shit!" She yelled. *"Now you said you wanted to be with me, and I agreed. But now that you got my heart, nigga, you better act right."* She told him. *"Like I said, I'ma be there when my company leaves. Don't go nowhere."*

Shaggy had her fucked up if he thought he could just play with her heart. That wasn't happening. He couldn't believe the change in Jayden. She was obsessive, crazy and jealous. He never thought she could turn so quickly and now that she had, he wished they could go back. He didn't understand that she purposely shielded her heart for fear it would be broken. She suffered much heartbreak in her day and the feeling of loss was hard for her to handle. So now that she opened up to him, in her mind it was for keeps and it couldn't possibly be any other way. Unless she killed him.

When she hung up on him, she waited for Madjesty to call back. After a month finally they would see each other again.

Shit got crazy over the month that she hadn't spoken to Madjesty. For starters, their aunts and mother were fighting over who owned the house. They had a future court date about whom the house belonged to. To make matters worse, Harmony had to register as a sex offender and wasn't allowed near small children because of that boy she fucked in the bushes.

Then there was Passion. Although things were better in Jayden's mind between them, Passion was scared out of her mind by Jayden's erratic behavior. She told anyone who she could trust that Jayden was crazy. But there was nothing she could do. Jayden's obsession with her couldn't be fully explained but it was definitely strong.

About an hour later, Madjesty arrived and the only person home was Jayden. The moment Jayden opened the door, she wrapped her arms around Madjesty but the feeling of love wasn't returned. Something in Madjesty's eyes said she'd turned for the worse but Jayden couldn't be sure.

"Still mad at me?" Jayden asked separating herself from her twin before closing the door.

"Naw. Been through a lot." She said walking around her. *"I see ya'll really fucked up this house. Where's all the furniture?"*

"Aunt Ramona and Aunt Laura sold it. It's a long story." She paused. "Well come up to my room. So we can talk."

Madjesty followed Jayden up the staircase and into her room. "Where is Harmony? I got to see her before I leave."

"Why?"

"Don't worry about all that," Madjesty smiled. "Just know that before I leave, I got to see her. Cool?"

"Cool." She said sitting on her bed. "Sit down next to me."

"Naw. I'll stand." Madjesty said.

"So what you been up to?"

"You mean besides losing one of my best friends, getting raped, shot and being committed in a crazy house for a month?"

"What?" her eyes widened.

"Yeah. Life for me was fucked up!"

"I'm so sorry, twin." She stood up to hug her and again Madjesty backed away. "Why didn't you call me, Mad? I told ma, over and over I wanted to talk to you. I knew she knew where you were, but she was keeping that info top secret."

"She never told you I wanted to talk to you?" Madjesty asked.

"Never."

Mad didn't believe her. "Where is your father? You guys still close?"

"We're close but a lot of shit been happening between your father and mines so I've been seeing him less these days. I've been busy anyway. So it's not too bad."

"Shit going on with our fathers like what?"

"I don't really want to talk about it." Jayden said.

"See...that's why we'll never be like we use to be. Ever."

"Don't say that." Jayden said wrapping her arm around Madjesty's shoulder. When she shot her an evil look she removed it immediately. "We...we gonna be close like we use to. We just have to work on it."

"You mean how we were working on it before I left?" She said in a condescending tone. "Because if I can recall, whenever I reached out to you, you never had the time. And then when you made the time you would take it back by standing me up."

"That was then! I think we can be better now. I think we can be like the kids we were in Texas."

"Never." Madjesty said playing with the perfumes on her dresser. "Things will never be the same."

"Okay...you want me to open up?" Jayden said. "And keep it real with you?"

"I want it if you want it. But I'm not pressing you no more."

"I want it. And if we gonna be close, we have to stay out of our fa-thers' businesses. Their beef has torn us apart."

"I don't have a problem with staying out of their business."

"Okay...tell me where you been?"

"Before I do that, answer my initial question." Madjesty said hold-ing her ground. *"What kind of beef do our fathers have?"*

"Okay...I'm gonna trust you first." She paused. *"My father is after yours because he thinks he kidnapped his friend. Antoinette."*

"Tell me something I don't know already."

"Okay...well your father has admitted to having her but now he's changing the game. He's saying if my father doesn't pay him five hun-dred thousand and hand over Shaggy, Paco's son, then he's going to kill her."

"So why doesn't he do it?"

"He's torn. Because Shaggy is my boyfriend and I love him. I don't want to lose him and don't even understand why Kali wants him." Jay-den said with wild eyes. *"You see?"*

"You know Shaggy like that?" Mad asked. *"I mean, I know you knew him but when shit get there?"*

"Why?" She paused looking at Madjesty sideways. *"I just said he's my boyfriend. Do you know him too?"*

"Yes."

"How?"

"Well, let's just say that he raped me. He raped me and sucked on my chest in front of my girlfriend before he took her away. And when he was done, he shot me in my arm, and left me for dead." Madjesty laugh-ed insanely.

"You were the boy/girl they were talking about?"

"I guess." She paused. *"I don't know what story you were told. But then...check it...I get to the hospital, and I cut my breasts off."* She lifted her shirt to show her mutilated chest. Jayden was scared. *"And they thought I was crazy so they committed me. Can you believe it? They thought I was crazy because I didn't want any part of my body that he touched. They couldn't understand that so they said I'm crazy!"* She laughed harder. *"Well maybe I am!"*

"I...I don't understand. You...you were Passion's boyfriend?"

"Yes."

"They said they killed some dude/girl but...but I didn't know it was you." She paused. *"Had I known it was you I would've never told Shaggy to kill you."*

THE CARTEL PUBLICATIONS

"Hold up." she paused. "You gave the order for him to kill whoever she was with didn't you?" Madjesty paused. "Because that's what he said."

"Yes. But I didn't know it was you." She paused. "I would've never given the order for some shit like that! Ever. Think, Mad, how would I know you were posing as a boy? And how would I know you were with Passion? I never saw you guys together at school."

"That's because I never went to school and neither did she."

"More shit happened then I know about in that motel room." Jayden paused. "So let me go make us something to drink so we can talk about all this shit and get it out in the open." Jayden said. "Sit down, sis." She did. "You still drink Henny?"

"That's all I'll ever drink."

Jayden smiled and said, "I'll be right back."

As she went downstairs to get the drink, Madjesty looked around her room. She saw pictures of her and Shaggy everywhere now that she paid closer attention. When she first entered the room, Jayden was the apple of her eye, but with her gone she saw things for what they really were. Not trusting her sister anymore, she picked up the phone and pressed mute.

"Hi, Kreshon. When you talk to my father can you tell him to call me back? She's here but I'm not sure how long I can keep her!" Madjesty's heart broke as she listened to her sister's deception. "I'm sure Kali will give Antoinette back now if my father kidnaps Mad. Then maybe Kali will leave my boyfriend alone too."

"Okay, Jayden. I'll tell him." He said. "Just keep her there."

Madjesty heard enough betrayal and hung up the phone. She realized that Jayden knew about the rape and chose Shaggy anyway. When Jayden came back upstairs, she handed her the Henny and she drank some. It felt good. She didn't have a drink in months. "Thanks, sis."

"No problem." Jayden smiled. "I love you so much, Mad. I'm so glad you're here."

"I love you too." Madjesty said stepping closer to her. When she was close enough to touch her, she crashed the glass against her face and knocked her to the floor. "Oh, I'm sorry." Madjesty laughed. "Did I just cut your pretty little face?" Blood was everywhere. "The funny thing is, you really look like mama now."

"Why did you do that?" She asked from the floor.

Madjesty dropped to the floor. "So what's the plan? To get back at my father, you decided to sell your own sister instead? You love him that much more than me?"

"I don't want Kali to kill Shaggy. And if Jace has you, he won't do it." She cried. *"I love him and you know Jace would never hurt you."*

"Now he's Jace, huh? Not daddy?" Madjesty's stomach turned listening to her lies. *"So you would trade me for Shaggy?"*

"I really am sorry, Mad. Don't hurt me anymore."

Madjesty dropped down to the floor and got on top of her sister. *"You know, Harmony told me not to trust you. But I didn't believe her. Matter of fact, I don't believe shit that bitch says. But what do you know, for the first time in her life she was right."*

Putting her weight on top of her sister she lifted her dress and pulled down her own jeans. Then she rammed the dildoe she wore inside of Jayden over and over.

"How does it feel, sis? How does it feel to be violated, huh?"

"Stop!!!" Jayden begged moving wildly. *"Please stop, Madjesty!"* She cried. *"It hurts."*

"Does it? Because that's how it felt to me. When your boyfriend took what he wanted. He didn't give a fuck." She continued pounding in and out of her. *"I bet you were saving this pussy for him wasn't you? He wanted to be the first to hit this, huh?"* She laughed. *"Well guess what; tell him an eye for an eye!"* When Madjesty started feeling like she was going to cum, she raped her harder until she reached an orgasm. Then she kissed her passionately in the mouth before knocking her out. *"Sneaky, bitch!"*

With Jayden out cold on the floor, she ransacked her room. She found a gun she was sure Jace gave her for protection, along with four thousand dollars in cash. She took the money and the weapon and tried to get into Harmony's room so she could approach her but it was locked. Twenty minutes later Harmony came through the front door only to see Madjesty waiting in the foyer.

"Madjesty," she said stunned. She looked at her stomach. *"You're...you're home."*

"Yes, mama. I am."

"What are you doing here?"

"I live here."

"I know but you...you not supposed to be here though."

"I escaped, mama. I have nothing to live for but I don't plan on spending any more of my days there."

"So now you mad at me? Again?" She smiled. *"Even though I'm the one who visited you once or twice a week?"* When she said that Madjesty raised the weapon and aimed. *"Baby, please put the gun down. I thought we had a connection."*

"Why didn't you tell Jayden where I was?"

"I did tell her! She didn't want to come! I promise you."

"I don't believe you."

"Well it's true." She looked into Madjesty's eyes. *"But I was right wasn't I? She shouldn't be trusted."* Harmony probed. *"She stabbed you in the back just as I predicted."*

Having quarterbacked the end of their sisterhood made Harmony smile.

Just when she said that Madjesty's phone rang. It was a new number. *"Hello."*

"Baby...it's me. Passion."

Silence.

"Passion?" Madjesty repeated her heart thumping wildly in her chest. Was this a set up?

"I mean, it's me. Denise. How are you, baby? I...I really miss you."

Although she made the name clarification she knew who she was the moment she heard her voice. *"I'm fine. I...I'm just surprised you called."*

"Baby, I heard you're home. But you gotta get out of the house because Shaggy is coming to kidnap you. He has Jace and Kreshon with him. You gotta get out of town or something."

"Where am I going to go?"

"Anywhere! Just get out of the house. Please!"

"Okay...I'll do it. I miss you so much, Denise. I'm sorry about the lies. I really am." She said looking at Harmony who was afraid to move for fear of being shot.

"I miss you too." She paused. *"You got a plan?"*

"Yeah. I think I know where I'm going."

"Can I go with you?"

The feeling Madjesty felt at that moment couldn't be explained. At first she thought there was no chance they could ever be, and now she learned she was wrong.

"Yes, baby. You can."

"Where you want me to meet you?"

Madjesty backed away and whispered quietly into the phone. *"The New Carrolton metro station. I'm catching an AMTRAK train from there and then we can get on a plane to another state."* She said, not wanting to say which state with Harmony in the room. She didn't trust her even if she was about to kill her.

"You got somebody to get the tickets for us? Since we under age?"

"I got a fake ID. We'll be fine. Don't worry about your clothes either. Just bring one bag and come on. I'll buy you all new stuff when we get there. I promise."

"Okay...I'm coming now. I love you."

"I love you too."

After Madjesty ended the call she pulled the trigger to fire at Harmony. But the gun didn't go off. Reaching in her pocket she grabbed her knife and charged after Harmony. Leaving town or not, she couldn't rest until she knew her mother was dead. She was just about to lunge the knife into her flesh when Ramona and Laura entered the house and grabbed her wrist.

"Stop, Madjesty! Don't do this to yourself." Ramona said.

"This bitch has ruined my life!"

"I know. And she'll get what she deserves, baby." She said. "I promise. But don't end your life like this. She's not worth it." Laura added.

"Plus you're pregnant." Ramona said.

"What?" Madjesty said dropping the knife. "What you talking about?"

"You're not pregnant?" Laura asked.

Madjesty rubbed her stomach. "Fuck no!"

"I thought you were."

She thought her aunts were delusional. She couldn't be pregnant because boys can't get pregnant. Not wanting to miss Passion she got up and looked down at Harmony whose eyes were wide with fright.

"The next time I see you, nobody will be able to stop me. You better off killing yourself."

With that Madjesty escaped Harmony's tyranny for good.

HARMONY
MORE DRAMA

After that bitch tried to kill me yet again, I grabbed me something to drink. I was through with her for good! I didn't bother thanking Ramona and Laura for saving me; because I knew when we went to court they would add this incident to the reasons why I didn't need this house or need to be around my children.

But I had a plan too and it involved Detective Tassel. I planned to tell him that they were the ones who tried to kill me. And since they were trying to take the house, I'm sure there was a way I could prove it. So I wasn't as dumb as they thought I was and it was just a matter of time.

When they went to their rooms I decided to go outside to get some air. The moment I opened the door, I saw someone I hadn't seen in a long time. Ebony. And who did she have with her? Half dead ass Trip who was wearing a pair of dark glasses and walking with a cane. Trip looked as if she would blow over any minute. While Ebony looked like she had work done on her nose and that they'd taken too much off the tip.

"Hi, Harmony." Ebony smirked. "You remember Trip right? Shaggy's mother?"

"What are ya'll doing here?"

"We came to see you."

"How did you know where I lived?"

"I ran into Mrs. Duncan." She smiled. "She came to my wedding and I couldn't believe my ears when she said you said hello. You gave her your address when she was taking you home and she gladly gave it to me."

"So now we're here." Trip said.

"Well I'm busy."

"Nonsense...we have a lot to talk about." Ebony said pushing past me as Trip followed.

And without my invitation, she and Trip walked into my house. It would go down in history as one of the longest nights of my life.

MAD
A Ticket Out Of Here

I was standing on the platform waiting on Denise to come down the escalators at any moment. I left her ticket at the Ticket Counter and was excited about seeing her face again. It had been so long and I never thought this moment would come.

I don't know what made her change her mind, about being with me, the real me, but it makes me think that Glitter had something to do with it. Maybe she's my angel and she finally started putting in work in my honor. Glitter was the one person, no matter what, who loved me for me and I never thought I'd ever find that again. I just wanted everything to go smoothly, with no signs that things would go bad.

Suddenly my sister's betrayal didn't bother me anymore. In my mind, it is what it is. Maybe it was the fact that my mother had been filling my head daily with thoughts that my sister didn't love me. Or maybe I was just tired of chasing her. Whatever it was, I knew our relationship wouldn't be the same especially after I raped her on her bedroom floor.

And what did my aunts mean by saying I was pregnant? That shit was funny and I thought about it all the way in the cab ride over here.

"Hey! You like my plane?" A little boy asked. He pretended as if the plane was taking flight a few feet from the ground.

Feeling in a good mood, I looked down at him and said, "Yeah...it's pretty cool."

"My daddy bought it for me." He said pointing at a couple a few feet away from me who were kissing. When the man finally came up for air, he saw the boy near me.

I waved at the man who said, "Antwan, get over here."

The moment I heard his name I immediately disliked the kid. I know it wasn't his fault that he had the same name of the person who bullied me when I was younger, but I hated him for it all the same.

"I'm just talking to the boy, daddy." he said. "I'm not being bad."

"I'm sorry he bothered you." The father said. "He loves talking to strangers."

"Not a problem." I responded tugging at my cap over my eyes.

Walking a few feet away, I hoped the name Antwan wasn't some omen. Would she change her mind? Would she not love me like she promised?

Checking the time on the clock on the wall, I noticed she still wasn't here and time was flying by. If she didn't make it in the next twenty minutes we'd miss the train. I bought us two tickets to New York, so that we could have some fun there before boarding a plane to Texas. I called Rocket and told her when I got to Texas, that I needed her to meet me us at the airport and she was excited about our arrival. Things were really looking up.

"Where are you, Denise?" I said to myself, as the station filled with more people. "Don't do this to me. Please. Don't let me down."

"Hey...watch this," Antwan said flying the plane next to my leg again. I frowned at him this time wishing he'd get his bad luck ass away from me. "See I can fly high."

"That's good...but why don't you go back over to your father."

"They kissing." He pointed at the lovesick couple. "See."

My stomach flipped because I wished I could do the same thing. I wanted to hold my girl and tell her I loved her. I wanted the opportunity to take care of her, no matter what I had to do. I wanted the family I always dreamed about. I wanted her.

"Go over there anyway, Okay? I really want to be alone."

"Okay." He moped walking back to his father.

The moment he said that, my phone rang. It was the same number Denise called me from earlier. "Hello?"

"Wags," Denise said. "I...I'm not going to be able to come. You need to go ahead without me."

I sat on the bench a few feet from where I stood and held the phone closer to my ear. "What? I mean...what happened?"

"I realized I can't be with a girl." She cried. "I thought I could, Wags, but I realized the person I thought you were, you aren't. I thought you were my boyfriend, the one who wanted me to have his kids, but you can never give that to me."

"But I can! I promise. There are ways we can make this happen."

"You can't!" She yelled. "And that picture of you standing in front of me, naked, with the same parts on your body I got on mine keeps running through my mind. Your breasts, your hips...I just...I just can't do it!"

Silence.

"Please don't do this. I'm gonna die without you, Denise. Do you hear what I'm saying? I'm gonna die?"

"Don't say that. You'll be fine. You have to be."

"Why did you come back into my life?" I sobbed. "I was finally realizing it was over between us! So why didn't you just leave me alone?"

"I don't know. But I'm sorry I reentered your life too. But this is it for real, Wags. Goodbye."

Sitting on the bench everything looked blurry. It took me a moment to realize I was crying. I hadn't cried since my father gave me the scalpel back at the hospital. He made me realize that when you cried, nobody really gave a fuck. Sure they'd hold you, caress you and even tell you things would be okay. But nobody really cared once they left your presence.

The entire time I was in that mental institution I never once, not once cried. Yet here I was, doing it again and I hated myself for it. I realized my life is a joke and unless I felt like dying, I'd have to live with my life as it is.

Dying.

Dying.

Dying.

Unless I felt like *dying*, I'd have to live my life as it is. Standing up and looking at the clock I realized I had two minutes before the train came. Now the station was crowded and people were standing everywhere waiting to board. I knew what I had to do. I finally understood that my life was not meant to live out fully.

In one minute I decided to leap for the tracks.

Thirty seconds.

Twenty seconds.

Fifteen seconds.

The moment I moved to hop on the tracks the man whose son I spoke to grabbed me. "WHAT ARE YOU DOING?!" He yelled, holding me as my body dangled. I was neither on the platform or tracks. Just suspended in mid air.

"LET ME GO! LET ME DIE!"

Another man saw him and helped, even though I was swinging wildly to get away from them both. "LET ME GO! PLEASE! STOP!"

They couldn't get a hold of me. If they let me go, I would jump. If they pulled me up and I continued to fight they would fall with me. So they just held on to me trying not to let me hit the tracks.

"YOU'RE GOING TO GET US KILLED!" The man who joined us said. "COME BACK ON THE PLATFORM."

"I WANT TO DIE!" I cried. "PLEASE LET ME DIE!"

When things couldn't get any worse, a third man joined to help but they still couldn't get a good hold of me. I fought so wildly that nobody could get a solid grip.

"Let's pull her up with all our strength on the count of three."

When I heard this I swung even wilder and the three men who were trying to save my life tumbled onto the tracks. And out of nowhere a forth man pulled me up to safety. The three of them tried to climb back up but it was too late. The train was coming at lightening speed. Stunned, they gave up the fight and looked at the train that was about to end their lives.

I heard a loud screeching noise and could tell the train conductor was trying to hit the brakes to prevent from hitting the men. But it was too late. Before my eyes all three men were killed instantly. People were screaming and yelling at the sight and mothers covered their children's eyes.

"OH MY GOD! HELP MY HUSBAND!" A lady screamed. "

The men were smashed under the train, which still hadn't completely stopped. Everyone looked at me. Like I was crazy. Like I'd caused all of this.

My life was spared, and their lives were taken.

And all I could do was think about was how lucky the three of them were.

PRESENT DAY
GREEN DOOR - ADULT MENTAL HEALTH CARE CLINIC
NORTHWEST, WASHINGTON DC

"So that's how all those people died." Christina Zahm said. "In a train crash as they were trying to save your daughter's life."

"Yes. Three men died on the tracks and two people died inside the train as it tried to stop. But when she went back into that institution, she started telling them how she grew up in a bad home and suddenly the news wasn't about the five men who died. It was all about me.

"Can you understand how everything connects?" She paused. "I mean, can you see that?"

"Yes. I do."

Christina was shocked. This was the first time Harmony bothered to show any responsibility for her actions and she was hopeful that they were making progress.

"Was Madjesty pregnant?"

"That's another long story."

"What about Jace? And Kali?" Christina paused. "What happened to them?"

Things between them two got out of control, but that was before he got sick."

"Who?"

"Jace?"

"I don't understand."

"I unknowingly contracted HIV and gave it to him." She paused. "To this day it's one of my biggest regrets."

Christina was silent and gave her a few moments. Besides, even she needed some time to digest the news. "You mentioned that the electrician installed cameras in your daughters' rooms earlier in your story."

"He did."

"How did that end up?"

"Because of the tapes, I got locked up for a brief time."

"Who found it and what was on it?"

"I sold it to a pornography company. I'll leave it at that for now." Harmony paused. "I really am tired."

"Okay, let's resume on Monday." Christina paused. "When you come back we'll discuss everything, starting with Jayden."

"Okay."

"Before we leave, how did Jayden react after her own sister raped her?"

"She…she wasn't the same." Harmony swallowed. "Jayden, if you can believe it or not, ended up being worse than Madjesty ever was."

CARTEL PUBLICATIONS

PRESENTS

The Cartel Collection
Established in January 2008
We're growing stronger by the month!!!
www.thecartelpublications.com

Cartel Publications Order Form
Inmates ONLY get novels for $10.00 per book!

Titles		*Fee*
Shyt List	_____	$15.00
Shyt List 2	_____	$15.00
Pitbulls In A Skirt	_____	$15.00
Pitbulls In A Skirt 2	_____	$15.00
Pitbulls In A Skirt 3	_____	$15.00
Victoria's Secret	_____	$15.00
Poison	_____	$15.00
Poison 2	_____	$15.00
Hell Razor Honeys	_____	$15.00
Hell Razor Honeys 2	_____	$15.00
A Hustler's Son 2	_____	$15.00
Black And Ugly As Ever	_____	$15.00
Year of The Crack Mom	_____	$15.00
The Face That Launched a Thousand Bullets	_____	$15.00
The Unusual Suspects	_____	$15.00
Miss Wayne & The Queens of DC	_____	$15.00
Year of The Crack Mom	_____	$15.00
Familia Divided	_____	$15.00
Shyt List III	_____	$15.00
Raunchy	_____	$15.00
Raunchy 2	_____	$15.00
Reversed	_____	$15.00

Please add $4.00 per book for shipping and handling.
The Cartel Publications * P.O. Box 486 * Owings Mills * MD * 21117

Name: _____

Address: _____

City/State: _____

Contact # & Email: _____

Please allow 5-7 business days for delivery. The Cartel is not
responsible for prison orders rejected.

CPSIA information can be obtained
at www.ICGtesting.com
Printed in the USA
LVHW111346231119
638277LV00001B/105/P

9 780984 303069